Beating About
The Bush

Linda Taylor

ARROW

Published by Arrow Books in 2000

1 3 5 7 9 10 8 6 4 2

Copyright © Linda Taylor 2000

Linda Taylor has asserted her right under the Copyright, Designs
and Patents Act, 1988 to be identified as the author of this work

First published in the United Kingdom in 2000 by William Heinemann
The Random House Group Limited
20 Vauxhall Bridge Road, London, SW1V 2SA

Random House Australia (Pty) Limited
20 Alfred Street, Milsons Point, Sydney,
New South Wales 2061, Australia

Random House New Zealand Limited
18 Poland Road, Glenfield
Auckland 10, New Zealand

Random House (Pty) Limited
Endulini, 5a Jubilee Road, Parktown 2193, South Africa

The Random House Group Limited Reg. No. 954009

www.randomhouse.co.uk

A CIP catalogue record for this book
is available from the British Library

Papers used by Random House are natural,
recyclable products made from wood grown in
sustainable forests. The manufacturing processes conform to
the environmental regulations of the country of origin

ISBN 0 09 940615 2

Typeset in Palatino by SX Composing DTP, Rayleigh, Essex
Printed and bound in Germany by Elsnerdruck, Berlin

For Geof

'*Everything should be made as simple as possible – but not simpler*'

Albert Einstein

Acknowledgements

With thanks to Alan Brown and all the students I met at Horton-cum-Studley for inspiring me with their warmth and enthusiasm, and especially to John for the white-knuckle rides. To all at the Darley Anderson Agency and at Heinemann for working so hard. My very special thanks to Elizabeth Wright for her support, to Lynne Drew for making it all seem so easy and to Thomas Wilson for his cheerful efforts behind the scenes; also to Kate Elton, Kate MacWhannell, Ron Beard, Mike Broderick and Mark McCallum for all they've done. And with my love and thanks to my family and all my friends. You've been fantastic.

Beating About The Bush

Linda Taylor worked for the Civil Service in London and Angola, and as a vice-consul in Sri Lanka before teaching in Japan. On her return, she read English at Oxford. When her first novel, *Reading Between The Lines*, was published in 1998 it immediately became a *Sunday Times* top ten bestseller; her second novel, *Going Against The Grain*, was published in 1999 to great acclaim. She lives in Oxford.

Praise for Linda Taylor's previous novels:

'Funny, original and thought-provoking' Katie Fforde

'Thoroughly enjoyable . . . a real page-turner, a book that leaves you wanting more' *U Magazine*

'Take the phone off the hook and pull up your favourite chair . . . Unputdownable' Christina Jones

Also by Linda Taylor

Reading Between The Lines
Going Against The Grain

Chapter One

It was an Indian summer. The trees framing the college lawn had a mottling of orange but the sun shone with clear, unobstructed force throughout the day, from a fresh yellow in the morning to a gold evening glow.

Throwing her weight behind the lifting iron while casting one eye across the lawn at Matt, Ella could feel perspiration gathering on her forehead. Her scalp was damp and warm, and she straightened stiffly, allowing the handle of the iron to lean against her leg. She found a screwed-up elastic band in the pocket of her jeans and fastened her hair in a knot. The thick brown tendrils that escaped tickled the side of her face. She brushed them away, wiped her forehead with the back of her hand and stopped to gather her breath again. Her superfluous jumper was slung round her waist, leaving her dark, bare arms to absorb the sun's rays. When she was younger her mother had sent her everywhere with an extra woolly 'just in case'. It was probably why she'd spent most of her life looking like a cricket umpire.

Today was as hot a September day as she could remember. It was also her birthday. She squinted up at the tiny shreds of cloud wafting over the blue dome of the sky.

Twenty-nine Septembers. She wasn't sure for the moment if she was smug or horrified.

Pierre stopped on his knees, a length of string in one hand, and peered up at her.

'You would like us to swap now?'

She gazed down at him. He was only about twenty-one. Even his hair looked more energetic than hers. The thought gingered her up. She shook her head.

'No, I'm fine. I'm getting years of accumulated toxins out of my system. You measure, I'll dig.'

He nodded with a slight smile and turned his attention back to tracing a lattice of exact proportions on the turf she was to dig. In the classroom, before they'd all come outside to turn their practical skills to turf lifting on the practice lawn, Matt had sketched a huge square on the blackboard and hatched it with aplomb. He'd given them dimensions which she'd absorbed mentally, noticing Pierre to the side of her earnestly replicating the diagram on to his practical sheet with a sharpened pencil, a ruler and a set square. Ella's vision of horticulture was closer to mud-wrestling than geometry, but she supposed it took all sorts. Whilst most of the class arrived clad in old jeans and T-shirts, slinging plastic bags crammed with steel-capped boots and overalls on to the floor beside their seats, Pierre tiptoed in delicately, straightening his lapels, wiping his feet compulsively on the oversized doormat the rest of them ignored before grinning at them all in apparent delight to be there and settling down to arrange the gleaming contents of his pencil case on the table in front of him.

Ella allowed herself another short break from

hacking at the turf and gazed around her. Pierre was probably the youngest of a motley crew. He'd followed his English girlfriend over from France, and had managed to land himself part-time work in the gardens of Le Manoir aux Quat' Saisons, not too far away from the college. He was applying himself to the horticultural course with the vigour of an eleven-year-old in his first week of senior school. Unlike John, for example, who'd been unemployed for over five years and had been stuck on the course by an optimistic benefits officer. Or Nev, already working part-time for the council in the Parks department and getting day-release to improve his skills. Or Valerie, in her fifties at least, who seemed to have every material thing a woman could want and was doing the course so that she could manage the substantial acreage of her own back garden. And there were Kathy and Emma, both in their twenties, who'd known each other before they started and always teamed up together. There were others she hadn't got to know very well yet, all in all about fifteen of them. And there was Matt, their course tutor.

She watched Matt from a distance. He was observing John as he shouldered the lifting iron with immense strength, flipping an exact square of turf on to the wheelbarrow beside him, never stopping for breath in his running commentary on what he thought, what he thought the others thought, and why this was a waste of time considering he could be at home getting stoned. Matt was standing next to him, his hands casually resting on his hips, agreeing or disagreeing where he could get a word in. He didn't have any of John's volatile energy. Matt's energy was more subterranean, as if any spikes or prickles had been rubbed away by all the physical effort of his work, like a pebble with a mysterious inner force, smoothed down by the elements.

She allowed herself a small sigh. Matt was a perfect shape from the back, and no disappointment from the front either. She heard him laugh with good humour in response to John's retort of, 'You're only saying that because I'm black.' It had the others looking up too.

Ella met eyes with Kathy, who shrugged and got back to her last square of turf in businesslike fashion. It pulled Ella's thoughts back to her lattice of lawn. She'd caught up with Pierre now, and while he was untwisting the thin string to make sure it was absolutely straight, they'd still got only half the turf lifted on their patch. Ella watched him for a moment, his tongue protruding from the corner of his mouth in total concentration. It was unfair to keep trying to hurry him, although as they'd found themselves regularly paired up due to sitting next to each other in the class, the differences in their approaches to their work were becoming more apparent, and the urge to shout 'for God's sake, get on with it!' was becoming more pronounced.

'Er, why don't I go and empty the wheelbarrow, Pierre? That way you'll have marked a few more squares by the time I get back, won't you?'

He smiled at her happily. It was impossible to get annoyed with him. Even though Matt was now crossing the lawn with even strides, imparting comments to the groups he passed, and heading down to their efforts. She didn't want him to think she was totally incompetent. Even though her attempts to slide the lifting iron under the grass had resulted in the sharp end getting stuck in the earth each time. It looked like a team of moles had been doing head-stands in the mud.

Matt arrived at their wheelbarrow as Ella skipped towards it. He picked up a square of turf, turned it over and pulled a face at the hillock of earth attached to the back of it.

'Ah. You need to slide it, you see.'

'Yes, you showed us,' she agreed breathlessly.

'Let me do another one for you.'

His eyes rested on hers for a split second. She felt the gravitational pull again, the one she felt every time he looked at her. It was as if she was being sucked towards him. She swayed but stopped herself before she folded at the knees and fell into his arms. Instead she stood back with a serious expression and watched the muscles on his back ripple underneath his thin T-shirt as he sliced effortlessly through the earth and flipped a square of turf past her nose towards the wheelbarrow. It landed perfectly on top of the mound she'd already created. She could bet he was a whiz at tossing pancakes.

'I see.' She nodded at him, trying to look intelli-gent. He straightened for a moment, leant on the lifting iron, and studied her. He had a way of watch-ing her without expression. A burst of heat spread up from her stomach and she self-consciously picked at her damp vest top.

'No regrets so far, then?' He gave her a lopsided smile.

'Oh, no. Not at all. I just have to build up a few

5

muscles, that's all. Sitting at a desk selling shares wasn't exactly good for my biceps.'

'No, I guess not.'

He tried to look understanding, but she guessed that the concept of spending all day every day – and most evenings too – locked in an airless trading room was as alien to him as forgetting to water the plants.

'And I need to get fitter. I used to burn up a lot of adrenaline, but it's not the same as having physical stamina.' She fiddled with her belt thoughtfully. 'And I'm not as young as I used to be. I think you get a bit lazy as you get older.'

'You're not exactly middle-aged though, are you?' he twinkled at her, his blue eyes catching the sun. He really meant it, and a quiver of pleasure tiptoed over her skin.

'I'm twenty-nine.'

'Twenty-eight, I thought?'

'It's my birthday today.' She lowered her voice so as not to proclaim the fact to the whole group. This was something that had crept up on her in her late twenties, the need to state her age to innocent people and watch for their reaction. It was a bid for reassurance. For the first time she was starting to have sympathy with old ladies who proclaimed, 'I'm eighty-five!' at you and waited with suppressed aggression for your response. You needed somebody to say, 'Oh, that's good.'

'Today?' Matt's tawny eyebrows lifted in surprise. 'Celebrating later, then?'

'Well, um,' she played with her buckle until she realised she had unhooked her belt. She did it up again quickly while keeping her eyes on Matt. Her subconscious was getting the better of her. She'd be rolling up her top and flashing her bra at him next. But then, she guessed her attraction to him must be fairly evident. He didn't seem to mind it. In fact, she felt increasingly that he liked it. He was good with the group and spent time with all of them individually, but he always stopped to talk to her about things other than seedlings and ideal potting compost. And now she wondered why she hadn't told him about her birthday drink before. There was always a chance that he would wriggle out of any other commitment and show up. She cleared her throat so as to sound utterly casual.

'A couple of us are going down to the Plough for a drink. Just the two girls I share my cottage with and possibly one or two others. I'm not sure how many of us there might be. It's not exactly a great event.'

She managed to shut her mouth before she added, 'and it'll probably be incredibly dull'.

'Well. Sounds like the ideal tonic.' He smiled broadly and she sat back on the wheelbarrow trying not to look hopeful.

'It is your birsday?'

Damn. She'd forgotten Pierre was there, on his knees with his string and his geometry kit. Glancing down she saw that he hadn't managed to mark any further squares, but the string was beautifully unknotted.

'It's no great shakes, Pierre. I'm not thirty yet.'

'Ah, but we will join you for a drink to celebrate.'

'Lovely,' she beamed down at him.

'And you will come, Matt?' Pierre enthused up at their instructor. 'And your wife will come out and

7

meet us too? I would like to meet this famous person. They are so close, the Nature and the Art, don't you think?'

Ella let out a long breath, her eyes drawn to the glinting gold band on Matt's tanned finger. She knew he was hitched, of course. She also knew his wife was a local artist of some repute. But that was his business. Whether he remembered his married status when he twinkled at her was not really her problem. However, it would not make for a euphoric birthday celebration to have Matt's wife dumped opposite her at a table in their local pub and to have to make complimentary comments about her artistic vision all evening. To make matters worse, there was actually one of her watercolours in the lobby of the pub. It smacked you in the face as you walked in. She'd admitted to herself that it was good, but she wasn't going to go any further than that. Now whenever she went to the pub she sidled in with her eyes down to avoid appreciating it. Matt laughed again, handing the lifting iron back to Ella and glancing at his watch.

'Time for lunch. You lot have a good time later, won't you?'

'Looks like heroin. Where did you get it?' Miranda called from the kitchen.

Ella heard the opening and closing of the fridge door, and the unplugging of a half-empty bottle of wine. Miranda reappeared to lean casually against the door frame. Even with a plastic bag over her head and purple dribbles of Magenta Midnight sliding down her forehead she still looked like something

Michelangelo had knocked up out of marble in his spare time. Ella tried not to be churlish. She'd chosen Miranda as a lodger. If she looked bewitching in whatever she grabbed hold of, be it a silk blouse or a kebab wrapper, it had to be endured. She glanced from Miranda back to the partially opened foil packet which Faith had dumped on the coffee table as she'd come in from work, and frowned again.

'I found it.' Faith swivelled round in the armchair to stare at Miranda over the wings. Her glasses flashed in the overhead light. Miranda's face tightened. Looking from one to the other, Ella had a bizarre notion to yell to Faith, 'Stay perfectly still! Her vision is based on movement!' but she kept quiet. She couldn't organise everything and everyone around her. There were times when she had to let nature take its course, and Miranda's evident urge to poke Faith in the eye whenever she spoke was one thing she couldn't control.

'I took the lid off one of the bins to stick a Crunchie wrapper inside,' Faith explained, 'and there it was. This foil packet. Just sitting there.'

And, Ella reminded herself as Faith scratched a mole on her upper lip with her little finger, she'd chosen Faith as a lodger too. Faith was local, she was reliable, she was living away from home for the first time, and she was uncomplicated. And next to her Ella felt incredibly glamorous, but she was still only half-admitting the latter reason to herself. She tried to formulate a sentence, but Miranda was off again.

'Which bin?' Miranda raised a purple eyebrow.

'Does it matter?'

'Possibly.'

9

'The green one.'

'Did you look in the other one?'

'Yep. There was only the bin bag we dumped in there this morning.'

'Hmmn.' Miranda took a sip of wine and gazed distantly across the room. Ella scratched her head and waited. Miranda was about to explain everything. She usually did. 'Hmmn.'

She sniffed, prodded at the plastic bag on her head, and drifted back across the sitting room to the latched door that led out to the small hall and the stairs.

'Better get this stuff off before I turn into Mrs Slocombe. Aren't you two going to get ready? You've got a lot of work to do by the looks of it.'

Teasingly said, with a mock-disdainful glance at Faith's raincoat and the dried smears of mud on the shins of Ella's jeans which ran right down to her thick socks. Mud had a mind of its own. It worked its way into clothes, nails and hair. She ruffled her fringe and a cloud of dried particles sprang out.

'The bathwater's hot, Ella. Why don't you dive in now? We'll have to leave in about half an hour.'

'Miranda!' Ella tried to pull herself up out of the soft sofa. It wasn't easy. That sofa had a habit of swallowing people whole. Miranda was already halfway into the hall. She poked her head back around the door.

'Damn, you've got purple on the gloss.' Faith leapt up, produced a stringy tissue from her pocket, and began to wipe the edge of the door. 'I'm sorry, Ella. You spent hours painting that.'

'Don't worry, Faith.' Ella smiled nonetheless. At

least Faith noticed these things. Miranda tutted at Faith's dabbing efforts impatiently. 'Before you dive off, Miranda, just a small question. We've got a class A drug sitting on our coffee table. What the hell are we going to do with it?'

Miranda frowned at Ella as if the question was unexpected. She considered her for a moment with her head on one side.

'Put it back,' she said without a quiver of emotion.

'What?' Faith stepped back, purple tissue in hand, her mouth extending from a circle into an oval.

'You heard. Now shall I run that bath for you, Ella? Or are you going to turn up looking like Rab C. Nesbitt? That's not going to increase your pulling power, is it?'

Ella stood up, wobbling as the sofa released her.

'I'm not in the mood to pull anyone. I'm twenty-nine today and the only present I've had so far is a packet of narcotics.'

'Er, yes, but you never know, do you? Be prepared, that's my motto. Speaking of which, do you need any condoms?'

Ella's head spun, visions of drug smugglers combining with visions of her evening ahead. Condoms were, of course, useful for all sorts of reasons other than the obvious one. Or at least, she'd heard that they were.

'I've got some anyway just in case you get lucky. Now I'm going to run your bath for you, and you're going to get in it. As it is I'm going to have to go on ahead and warn the others you're running late. And seriously, Ella,' Miranda put on a serious expression under her plastic bag. 'It is *your* birthday, and everybody's making a big effort for you. It might be nice to dress up a bit.'

'Look, I didn't ask for a do. I'd have been happy for us to crack open a bottle of fizzy and watch *Frasier*.'

'Don't start that again.' Miranda held up the hand which was clutching the glass. 'Be grateful. I would if I were you. Nobody bothered to do anything for my twenty-ninth. I was crewing on a flight to Dublin while a paralytic MP twanged my knicker elastic. We're doing our best, so the least you can do is enjoy it.'

'I was looking forward to it, but then Faith came in and presented me with a lorryload of heroin. It was a slight distraction from filing my nails.'

Miranda shot a glance at Ella's nails. Ella looked down at them. No, she hadn't really been filing her nails, and it showed. They were still encrusted with mud. She'd have to soak them in the bath, and hope it all came out. She curled her fingers into her palms.

'How do you *know* it's heroin anyway?' Faith asked Miranda breathlessly.

Miranda gave a huge eye-roll, wandered back into the room, stuck her finger into the powder, sucked the end and closed her eyes for a moment. Faith gave Ella a horrified look.

'Yep, heroin.'

'But how do you *know*?' Faith insisted, her forehead crumpling.

Miranda tutted even more loudly. 'I went to Benenden. Put it back where you found it.' This time Miranda was intent upon departure. Faith followed her out to the hall and called up the winding staircase after her.

'What, just like that?'

'Just like that.' Ella heard her voice becoming fainter as she trailed back to her bedroom.

'But – why?' Faith yelled. There was a pause before Miranda answered.

'Because,' she began elaborately. Ella could tell from the volume of her voice that she was leaning over the banisters. She had a horrendous vision of purple drips cascading through the air and hitting the pale cream wool of the new hall carpet. 'If you don't put it back, whoever put it there will wonder where it is, won't they?'

'Ye-es?' Faith computed this audibly.

'And if they think you've got it, they'll probably want to get it back from you, won't they?'

Faith was silent.

'And if you want that to happen, then your imagination's a lot more barren than I gave you credit for. Put it back, and don't tell anybody else that you found it there. It'll probably be gone by the next time you look.'

'Of course,' Faith's voice cleared. 'The bin men will take it.'

'No, Faith. The dealer who's been told to pick it up from the green dustbin outside this cottage will take it. Comprende? Now are you going to do something with your hair tonight, or not? You look like Olive from *On the Buses*.'

Ella heard Miranda retreat to the bathroom and kick the door shut. She could see Faith through the open door, standing in the hall, staring up at the space Miranda had been filling only moments before. Both of them were too stunned to move, let alone sneak back outside and insert God knew how many thousands of pounds' worth of hard drugs into their own dustbin.

Faith returned to the room, white-faced, and stared at Ella. She quietly closed the door behind her.

'I don't think we should put it back there,' she said in a whisper. Ella's heart began to thud. Miranda's carelessly slung scenario was just starting to take hold in her brain.

'I don't know what else we're supposed to do,' she whispered back.

'I just can't cope with this. Not on top of everything else,' Faith shook her head. 'I can't bear to think about some dangerous criminal rooting around outside in our dustbin. And our bedrooms are at the front, Ella. We won't be able to sleep at all. We'll be terrified.'

'On top of what else?' Ella frowned at her.

'Oh, you know. New vet's arrived.'

'What's he like?' Ella allowed herself a wriggle of anticipation. Faith scratched her nose again.

'Dickhead.'

'Damn. Fat and ugly?'

Faith didn't answer. Ella wondered uncomfortably whether she needed to explain that she was referring to the vet, not Faith herself. She watched her expression carefully, but Faith had turned morbid eyes back to the foil packet.

'We can't put it back, Ella. And we can't tell the police. We'll get involved, and that'll be even worse. Drug dealers do horrific things to grasses.'

Ella swallowed. Faith might be basing her deductions on what she'd seen on the telly, but they sounded a little too plausible. She thought about it as rationally as she could for somebody who was also pondering the consequences of nearly being thirty.

'Oh God.' Faith began to tremble. 'What if they've decided this is their handover spot? What if they're always going to be out there, hiding drugs all over the place? In the bins? The front garden? The back garden? Inside the house?'

'They won't,' Ella assured her, disguising a small gulp.

'What if the police find out anyway? They'll think it's us.' Faith looked as if she wanted to cry.

Ella propelled her over to the sofa and pushed her down into it. Faith's legs shot up as the cushions engulfed her. One of her flat-but-practical shoes fell off. Ella dropped to her knees and put it back on for her. Somebody had to take control. They couldn't just allow their dustbin to be used like this. What if it did become a regular occurrence? They'd have to get the drugs away, right away from their home.

'Listen, Faith,' Ella offered a cleaner tissue from the pocket of her jeans as Faith's nose was now running. She took it and wiped her eyes with it. 'You have the bath first while I drive out somewhere and dump this. When I get back we'll go to the pub together. How does that sound?'

Faith nodded jerkily.

'So there's no need to worry. We'll deal with it. But we'll have to keep quiet about it. This is just between you and me. Okay?'

Faith nodded again. She looked up. Ella studied her eyes through the lenses of her glasses. Not for the first time, she noticed what a beautiful shade of green they were. It was just that her glasses were the wrong shape for her face and made her look like Elton John. But where Miranda mercilessly pointed such things out, Ella refrained. Somehow she had to keep the dynamic of the house friendly.

'I'm dreading tonight,' Faith said in a dull voice, licking her lips and apparently realising with a flush that her nose was running. She stuck a tissue over her face quickly. 'I'm no good at parties.'

Ella patted Faith's knee reassuringly.

'I'd rather it was just a few beers and a game of pool. But Miranda wants an excuse to get a crowd together, so we've got to go along with it, haven't we?'

'Have we?'

'Yes,' Ella said a little more firmly. She was relying on Faith to come to the pub with them. Miranda was gregarious. So much so when she was on form that she made Ella feel like Marcel Marceau. And Faith was good company in a group once she warmed up. It was only the thought of it that threw her into panic.

'She's a bit bossy, isn't she?' Faith lowered her voice again, a gleam of conspiracy in her eyes. Oh no, Ella thought quickly. They shared the cottage, all three of them. Forming allies was just not possible.

'Bossy, but great fun. And just think how dull it'd be without her. There'd be me rambling on about trees, and you and your sorry animal stories. We'd bore each other to death. We need Miranda to add a bit of glamour to our lives. Look at it that way.'

Faith nodded and looked down. Ella glanced warily at the half-opened foil packet on the coffee table.

'Right then.'

Decisively, she bent over it and rewrapped the foil carefully around the contents.

'Where are you going to take it?' Faith stared at her with round eyes.

'What you don't know can't be wrung from you under torture.' Ella gave her a broad wink. Faith's eyes blackened with alarm, and Ella continued rapidly, 'don't give it another thought. It's dealt with.'

Faith stood up unsteadily.

'If you're sure . . .'

'Course I'm sure. Go on. Bugger off.'

'But—'

'Bugger off, Faith!' Ella yelled, abandoning self-restraint. It was unexpectedly satisfying.

It had been the logical solution, to take lodgers. Not that anything that had led to Ella buying a tatty cottage in a sprawling village – which was more of an extension of the town than anything you'd see on a postcard – on the outskirts of Oxford had struck anybody else as logical. But to her it had made perfect sense.

For nearly a decade she had clawed, manoeuvred, bellowed and scowled her way up the corporate ladder in international banking. She'd had a good degree behind her, a fantastic start with a major bank, and nothing to hold her back. She'd been as tough as she needed to be. She'd been warned that it was a sexist world, and she hadn't been disappointed. But she'd twirled her pen, hammered her keyboard and learned to juggle a dozen telephones along with the best of them. Then, at twenty-eight, she'd found herself with more money than she knew what to do with and a bad case of nervous exhaustion. It was all around her. Young guys turning greyer by the day with dark-ringed eyes, increasingly volatile tempera-ments and hands that shook as they raised the first pint of the evening. She had a salary she'd never have dreamed she might command, and no time to spend it. She could afford exotic holidays which she couldn't get the time off to enjoy. She had a BMW convertible which she never had time to drive, and a designer flat in Docklands with a leather sofa that she never had time to sit on. And as her bank balance expanded and her world became dominated by artifice, she began to crave the natural world until it became an obsession.

Quite suddenly there came a moment when she yelled, 'Enough!' into the air, and walked out, a salmon and cream cheese wholegrain bap untouched on her desk, a roomful of amazed faces watching her stride to the door, which she slammed. But once that was done, she knew that the despair had been building for several years.

She sold the flat, the car and all the executive toys she could feasibly offload and found herself a course in a horticultural college in Oxfordshire. It wasn't quite haphazard. She'd been brought up locally, nearer to Reading than Oxford, but the area still felt like home. She put down a deposit on a run-down terraced cottage three miles from the college and had since then set about smartening it up.

She'd moved there herself in July and advertised in the local press for two female sharers to help cover the mortgage. She'd interviewed a selection of candidates, and decided to share with women who were utterly different from herself – and from each other. That way she knew they wouldn't encroach on each other's territory. She made it quite clear that the reasonable rent meant an obligation to help out with home improvements too. Miranda and Faith had joined her and now it was September. So far, there had been no serious arguments, traumas or mercy killings. Her course was fantastic, her course tutor was even more fantastic, and she was happily in control. It was all going according to plan, class A drugs excepted. But they were only a temporary blip.

'C'mon, you sod!' Ella ground the gears of the Fiat and urged the car up the hill. A second-hand rust bucket was a necessary economy, but it worked. That was all that mattered.

The lanes were beautiful this evening. There had been a light sprinkling of rain and the air sweated with the sweet smell of damp grass. The peachy sunset had darkened into a flicker of violet streaking the sky ahead of her as she reached the brow of her favourite hill. She pulled over into a lay-by where she often stopped and gazed peacefully at the mossy valley ahead. It looked soft and comforting in the dying light, only the streetlamps of the next village spiking the dusk. She levered open the car door and got out, pushing her face into the cool air.

She loved this place. Whenever she came here and gazed over the landscape she wanted to award herself a trophy for making a brilliant decision. The rush she got from being out in the open beat the thrill of any financial deal she'd ever closed. She was deep in the countryside in glorious autumn, with mud in her nails and the wind in her face, and it felt fantastic. There wasn't a better time and place to cope with a birthday. Here she had space. She was alone with the fields, a handful of grumpy cows and her thoughts.

'Evenin'.'

She leapt around as a lone dog-walker trundled past pulling up his collar. He headed off down the slope of the lane towards the next village. He wasn't to know that she had a bagful of heroin in her glove compartment.

'Yes, lovely evening, isn't it?'

Her voice followed him down the hill but he was going at full pelt, the dog's legs spinning like Catherine wheels. He vanished into the gloom.

She squinted at her wristwatch – a chunky Argos digital which she'd substituted for the dainty Cartier she'd used to wear to work in the City. It was probably prime dog-walking time. It would be better to dump the drugs and get away quickly before anyone else crept up on her. And Miranda would be drumming her finely shaped nails on the bar with impatience by now. She'd have to get a move on.

She crawled into the car and removed the Sainsbury's bag from the glove compartment. She chewed on her lip and stood in the lane wondering what to do next. Alongside the passing place was a five-bar gate leading to a dome-shaped field. It was bordered with a thick hedgerow tangled with briars and dark berries. The undergrowth was thick enough.

'Right.'

She hopped over the gate, swinging her legs and

landing agilely in the field. She crept down the line of the hedge until she found a dense patch of bracken. Working quickly, she cleared a hole, pushed the packet inside, and pulled bramble and dead grass over the evidence. Then she stood up and brushed her hands on her jeans.

'Done. End of story.'

She heard the whine of a car engine approaching and instinctively dropped back down to the grass. The car appeared to slow, but it was a narrow part of the road. She breathed softly and peered through a gap in the hedge. No, it had swept on past. She got to her feet again and raced back along the edge of the field.

She flipped back over the gate, a bubble of laughter caught in her throat. Adrenaline shivered across her stomach as she dived back into the car, slammed the door and started the engine. She let out a sharp breath. Now she was getting in the mood for a birthday party. Who cared if she was almost thirty? So, she'd probably have a hard job talking herself into a Club 18–30 holiday from now on, but that was something of a blessing. Life was striking her as sweeter by the moment. In high spirits, she crunched the gears and steamed off into the lane. Her smile spread to a wide grin.

After all, the Plough was a curious place. You never quite knew who was going to turn up.

Chapter Two

The sound of 'Roll over Beethoven' thumping from the jukebox confirmed one thing to Ella as she sidled past the watercolour in the lobby with her eyes on the ground, and pushed her way into the public bar. Faith was in the pub, somewhere.

The cottage had been empty when she'd got back. Her first thought had been that Miranda had dragged Faith kicking and screaming to the Plough regardless of whether her hair was still in curlers and she was still in her bra and knickers. Miranda hated going out alone although she very much liked to divest herself of female company once she'd arrived. Ella had already spent several evenings studying the beer mats scattered on her table with acute fascination while Miranda flitted off in pursuit of testosterone. Her second thought had been that Faith was hiding to avoid going out, but a quick search of her bedroom had clarified that she wasn't under the bed. Her third thought was that the drug dealers had arrived, found Faith alone in the cottage, abducted her, and were now forcing her to watch recordings of *Pet Rescue* in order to find out where the drugs were. But on balance, she'd stuck with her first thought.

Ella had thrown herself into a shallow bath and made herself up. She was quite pleased with the result. She'd fluffed up her dark brown hair, ringed her dark eyes with black eyeliner, thrown on a black dress from her wine bar days. She looked slinky without heading towards Gothic, which was good. She'd added a pair of scarlet button earrings as a contrast, grabbed her coat and headed off up the lane.

Kevin and Andrea were behind the bar. Andrea was a student who looked like a supermodel. Kevin was a barman who looked like a jockey. He always seemed to be serving whenever Ella went in, and he was always in love. At the moment, he was in love with Andrea. Derek, the landlord, who wore a permanent expression suggesting he could smell something nasty, was making a guest appearance. There was a cacophony of conversation and laughter just managing to make itself heard above ELO throbbing from the speakers. And Ella knew only one person who consistently put ELO on the jukebox – that was Faith. She edged her way towards the bar. Better to grab a drink first, then find out who Miranda had bullied into turning up for her birthday.

'Hi, sweet pea!' Kevin bobbed down the bar towards her, balancing four full pints against his chest. 'I hear you're the birthday girl.'

Ella groaned as Kevin deftly delivered the drinks and turned to her with enthusiasm.

'Don't remind me.'

'The big Three-O's creeping up on you,' he taunted with a wink. Two men in their twenties turned to give her an all-over appraisal.

'Thanks so much, Kevin. Shall we just hire a banner and stick it over the door?'

'No need. Miranda's got publicity sorted.'

Ella held on to the edge of the bar. Kevin laughed at her expression.

'I thought you'd be happy. Women peak at thirty and you've got another year to go. I read that somewhere.'

Ella grimaced as the two men beside her gave her an even more attentive appraisal.

'Mid-thirties, I'd read. And in any case, it doesn't stop every man in the universe lusting after eighteen-year-olds, does it?' She gave him a meaningful look as Andrea swept past like the figurehead on a speeding warship and Kevin's eyes swivelled.

'Nah, that's crap,' one of the men to her left ventured with a flirtatious glint. 'I like a nice older woman myself.'

'Oh, a *nice* one?' Ella gave him a short smile. 'Counts me out then.'

'What are you having? First one's on me.' Kevin twinkled at her. 'Something suitably strong.'

She nodded. She was in the mood for something strong now. The flirtatious man next to her rolled up the sleeve of his T-shirt to display his muscles and muttered something about being suitably strong. She ignored him.

'Make it a large vodka and tonic. And don't spare the lemons.'

'Sure thing.'

'Well, if women peak in their mid-thirties,' the man with the biceps next to her continued with vigour as Kevin shot off to get her order, 'it gives you another six years of practice, doesn't it?'

She turned to look at him properly. He wasn't bad looking.

24

'And?'

'If you're looking for someone to practise with . . .' He delivered an earthy laugh.

'Well,' she tutted. 'If you've got a younger brother, you could put a word in for me. Men reach their peak at eighteen. I read that somewhere too.'

'Eh? I didn't peak at eighteen!'

'You did,' she advised him. 'Though you might have missed it.'

She smothered a giggle and turned back to Kevin as her drink arrived. There were urgent mutterings to her left.

'That's not right, is it, Dave? Have you ever heard that?'

'Nah, must be bollocks.'

'Thanks for the drink, Kevin. See you later.'

He vanished in Andrea's slipstream to the other end of the bar. Ella turned to survey the cavernous room, wondering where Miranda and Faith might have pitched themselves. She pushed her way through the drinkers and headed for the far corner, leaving the two men urgently exchanging theories at the bar. She spotted Miranda's glossy curls in mid-toss. The Magenta Midnight had added rich red highlights to her neck-length auburn hair. She looked as sleek as a horse chestnut. She stood up and beckoned wildly as she saw Ella approach.

'There you are! Where the hell have you been? Faith said you'd forgotten something at college and had to go back.'

Ella reached the table and glanced around with a hesitant smile.

'Yep, sorry about that. Hi, everyone.'

'What on earth did you forget that was so important?'

'Eh? Oh, you know. Some cuttings.'

'Cuttings?'

'Yep, they just needed a bit more . . . Baby Bio.'

'You went all the way back to feed the plants?'

Ella glared at her. She didn't appreciate Miranda making her look neurotic.

'I just wanted to be sure that my cuttings were going to make it through the night.'

She replaced the glare with a smile as she looked at the faces around the table. Faith was there, wedged between the table and the jukebox. She looked as if she'd been eating blackberries, and Ella guessed that Miranda had forced her to borrow her lipstick. Beside her was a woman with a wide mouth and a perky nose. Her straw-blonde hair was cut into a practical wedge around the chin. Faith seemed to be leaning away from her, but it could have been an attempt to squash her ear against the jukebox to get the full ELO experience. There were two men Ella didn't know, both throwing feverish glances at Miranda, and, to her delight, three fellow students from her course had bothered to come, Valerie, John and Pierre. She gave them a big wave and settled at the table.

'Thanks for suggesting this, Miranda.'

'We're not all here yet,' Miranda said vacantly, peering over Ella's head into the throng. 'Few more to come.'

''Appy Birsday,' Pierre leant over the table and handed her a gold paper envelope. She flushed with pleasure as several more envelopes appeared.

'And drink that,' Miranda instructed, nudging a tumbler under her nose. 'We bought it for you. You've got some catching up to do.'

Ella took a large gulp, and alternated with sips from her own glass as everyone settled into conversation again. The blonde woman with the perky nose stuck her hand across the table at her.

'We haven't met, have we? I'm Suzanne. I'm one of the vets at the surgery.'

Ella raised her eyebrows but stopped herself from saying, 'Ah, so *you're* Suzanne!' She shot a covert glance at Faith as she took the politely offered hand. Faith was looking away. In the last month or so Ella had heard a lot about Faith's colleagues. The practice was run by an older vet who seemed to be generally worshipped. As far as Ella could work out, Suzanne was next in the pecking order, but from Faith's comments she had expected her to be much older, much fiercer, and much more butch. Suzanne looked far too delicate to heave cows around by their hooves, but the firm handshake that followed had Ella wincing. She wriggled the circulation back into her fingers as they were released.

'Nice to meet you,' she gasped. 'I share the cottage with Faith.'

'Yes, I know,' Suzanne said with a blank face. Ella waited for her to elaborate with some sort of jocular comment but she didn't.

'So, um, I hear the new vet's arrived?' Ella ventured.

'Hmmn. Giles.' Suzanne's eyes seemed to brighten. Ella shuffled forwards on the bench.

'Sounds . . .' Ella encouraged, eyebrows raised. She

wasn't put off by Suzanne's stern manner. Her own past life had been blighted by a lack of female friends, and it was one reason she'd been so keen to share the cottage with women now. Perhaps Suzanne was in need of some girl-talk? She persevered.

'Faith said he was a . . .' She hesitated over the word 'dickhead'. In fact, that was all Faith had said. She ransacked her brain.

'He's drop-dead gorgeous, if that's what you were wondering.' Suzanne's lips twitched. Ella elaborately pushed one eyebrow higher than the other.

'And . . . ?'

'Single.'

Both Ella's eyebrows now met at her hairline.

'And . . . ?'

'And he's a dickhead,' Faith finished as Suzanne opened her mouth. She stood up abruptly. 'Another drink anyone?'

She stalked away without waiting for an answer. Ella tutted after her.

'Obviously hasn't won Faith's heart, anyway. Did he spurn her or something?'

Suzanne watched Faith's retreating form thoughtfully.

'She'll be fine,' she said with unexpected sensitivity. 'He's a bit tactless, that's all. You get that sometimes with the more academic ones. Faith gets too emotionally attached. She falls in love with all the waifs and strays. I'm surprised she hasn't persuaded you to take any of them in yet. When she lived with her parents she seemed to take one home a week.'

'Did she really?'

'I think that's what finally persuaded her mother to

kick her out. They needed her bedroom for the goats.'

Ella took another swig of vodka and considered. They hadn't shared for very long, but she supposed Faith might have wanted to ask if they could have an animal there. She couldn't really see a problem with it. As long as it was a small one. And as long as it was only one. And as long as it didn't suddenly die just when they'd all grown to love it. And it struck her too that Faith was probably missing her animals, and that it might put a spring into her step. She certainly hadn't seemed particularly happy in the time Ella had known her.

'I'll tell her she can think about adopting something.'

'Good move,' Suzanne nodded. 'Oh. There's Giles now.'

Ella swallowed her mouthful of vodka with an audible gulp. Giles? Giles the drop-dead gorgeous vet? Was also coming to join her birthday drinks? Things were looking up. She straightened her shoulders, stuck out her chest, brushed a hand through her thick hair and casually turned round to stare.

He wasn't disappointing. He had golden hair, golden skin, and as he got closer clutching his pint, she could see an amazing pair of dark brown eyes. As soon as he glanced at her she'd be ready with sultriness, but when he looked up from the throng to find their table he met eyes with Suzanne and instantly broke into a warm smile.

A *warm* smile, not a friendly one, or even a pointlessly flirty one, but a really warm one, as if he'd come all the way from wherever it was just to see her.

Ella fiddled with her glass and withheld a pout as Suzanne returned the smile with equal warmth.

So that was it then. He'd only just arrived in the village, the vet's surgery was the only place that had had the privilege of laying eyes on him so far, and Suzanne had already bagged him. And she couldn't be described as glamorous by any stretch of the imagination. It was obviously an attraction based entirely on her personality. What a cow.

'Oooh, who's this?' Miranda whispered urgently into Ella's ear.

'It's the dickhead,' she whispered out of the corner of her mouth before Giles arrived within earshot, set down his pint, pushed a hand through his hair, and devoured the occupants of the table with his eyes. Ella glanced sideways at Miranda. Up until that point she'd been flicking her curls from side to side opposite the only two eligible guys there, seemingly having some difficulty deciding which of them was the cutest. Now she'd curled her body into an impossible 'S' shape over the table and was running her fingers up and down her long glass as she peered at Giles from under her lashes. Even Valerie, whom Ella had been surprised to see in a young and noisy pub like the Plough, was leaning forward for a better look.

Suzanne introduced him around the table, Ella managing to find out in the process that the two men opposite Miranda were called Oliver and Mike, and he shuffled to one side and then the other looking for somewhere to sit down.

'I'll just perch next to you, shall I, Suzie?'

This time Ella and Miranda's eyes met. Ella looked

away quickly, hiding a smile. Suzie, eh? That really was quick work. He hadn't been in the location long enough to unpack his socks from his suitcase, but Suzanne had shot straight in there. Probably over the tweezers and swabs. With a wrinkle-faced pug called Napoleon conked out, half stitched up on the table.

'We'll have to shuffle up,' Suzanne suggested, peering down the bench. There was a general effort from Oliver, Mike and Valerie, who was stuck on the end, to make more room. Valerie teetered at the end of the bench and was caught by John sticking out a hand. She giggled. Faith reappeared at the table and looked down at Giles. He was in her place.

'Oh, right,' she said ungraciously.

'Oh hi, Faith,' Giles stood up again quickly. 'Can I get you a drink?'

'I'm not thirsty,' she replied, stony-faced.

'If I promise not to tell any more jokes about three-legged cats, will you sit next to me?' He grinned at her, his luminous eyes teasing her into humour. All heads turned back to Faith for her reaction. She stood firm, boring him out with a hostile glare. Was she human? Why wasn't she on his lap by now?

'Actually,' she said, knocking back the short she'd bought herself in one go and setting the glass on the table. 'I've got to go now. Thanks for the offer.'

'Faith?' Ella reached for her elbow. 'Sit here, next to me?'

'Faith!' Miranda all but bellowed from Ella's side, making her jump. 'You can't go yet. You just can't.'

'Why not?'

'Because!' Miranda seemed to be giving Faith a message with her eyes. Faith sniffed.

'Look,' Ella said, standing up. 'I've got to go to the bar anyway. Come with me and help me carry some drinks.'

Without waiting for a reply, Ella grabbed Faith's elbow and pushed her ahead of her into the standing groups of drinkers. When they were well away from the table, she stopped and squeezed her arm.

'Listen, I'm going to buy you another drink. I want to see you smile tonight.'

As Ella watched Faith's quiet green eyes welling up, she felt her heart soften yet again. She'd known when she'd interviewed Faith for the house-share that she'd lived with her parents until that point, and she was twenty-six now. It was late to start out on her own. Not that she'd gone far from home – her parents were on the other side of the village. But Ella detected a childlike aura around Faith. She had a feeling that she found the world difficult to deal with. At times it made her want to push her face into a wall, at other times it made her feel absurdly protective. Tonight she just wanted to see her enjoy herself.

'I hate busy pubs,' Faith said, pulling a face as she was jostled to one side. 'I prefer the Rose and Crown. Nobody ever goes there.'

'All right, next time we'll go there, but for tonight we're stuck here, aren't we? So are you going to make the most of it? It's Friday night, woman!'

'That business earlier shook me up.' Faith's eyes widened. She pressed her mouth to Ella's ear. 'Did you get rid of it?'

Ella laughed.

'Is that all that's bothering you?'

'And Giles,' Faith added, as if she didn't want the

list to be curtailed just yet. Ella nodded. There was something else in Faith's eyes, as if she was sulking. Well, it was no wonder. A fabulous guy had turned up to work in the surgery, under her nose, every day, and he would probably never look twice at her. Suzanne, on the other hand, seemed to have been waiting to club him over the head and drag him off. She bit her lip and thought hard.

'I was talking to Suzanne,' she said, starting to propel Faith towards the bar. For the moment she seemed to have forgotten that she was leaving in a huff.

'Oh yes?' Faith pursed her lips.

'Yes,' Ella persisted, noting the frosty reaction and making her final deduction. Faith was jealous of Suzanne. It was as simple as that. 'About animals.'

They reached the bar. Ella nodded affirmatively at Faith who looked none the wiser.

'You know, ill ones.'

'Yes?' Faith seemed to be hunting the meaning of the information. Ella took a breath and started again.

'I wondered if you wanted to bring one home.'

Faith scratched her chin. 'What, any one I like?'

'Well, no cows or chickens, but something fluffy would be nice. I reckon we can just about manage that in the cottage. We could be foster parents for a bit, for some of those kittens you're always on about while they're waiting for proper homes.'

'Kittens? We haven't got any kittens at the moment.'

'Well, anything.' Ella put an elbow on the bar and rummaged for her purse as Kevin danced past, waving. 'A hamster or something.'

33

'People don't abandon hamsters. You don't find them in sacks on the hard shoulder. Not like dogs or cats.'

Ella gave her an arch look, wondering if she was being treated to sarcasm, but Faith seemed perfectly serious.

'Well, whatever. I don't know. What have you got?'

Faith thought hard while Ella attracted Kevin's attention again and gave him her order, indicating that he should make Faith's gin and orange a large one. She turned back brightly.

'Decided yet?'

'I don't suppose you'd want a terrapin?'

'Is it fluffy?'

'You don't know much about animals, do you?' Faith said with an air of superiority. Ella decided to concentrate on Kevin instead as her drinks gradually arrived.

'You put those blokes' noses right out of joint,' he said grinning. 'They've gone to conduct a survey of the pub now. The consensus seems to be twenty-five so far.'

'Twenty-five what?' Ella was getting more confused by the minute.

'The age at which men are most sexually active,' Kevin explained patiently, taking the money she offered.

'Oh, I see. When were you most sexually active, Kevin?'

'February the fourteenth, nineteen eighty-five.'

'You don't like snakes, do you?' Faith said.

'Who? Me?' Kevin paused as he was about to dive back to the till.

'No,' Faith tutted. 'I was asking Ella.'

'Course!' Kevin slapped his head, gave Ella another wink and disappeared.

'There's an elderly python that needs a home. We can't keep it at the surgery.'

Ella tried to concentrate on what Faith was saying without smiling. She guessed a python at the surgery, however elderly, might account for the lack of hamsters and kittens.

'No. Snakes are right out. Here, take these.' She handed her two pints of bitter.

'Well in that case—' Faith stopped in mid-sentence. Her face froze.

'C'mon, carry these and I'll do the rest.'

But Faith's eyes were levelled somewhere over Ella's shoulder. Her mouth had dropped open and her eyes were fixed with horror.

'Faith? What the hell's the matter?'

'Oh my God,' Faith muttered under her breath.

Ella swung round to stare behind her.

'What is it?'

'It's the Old Bill.'

'The what?' Ella mouthed, scanning the heads of the drinkers avidly, looking back to Faith, and trying again to follow her line of vision. Then she spotted it. The policeman's helmet, visible beyond the crowd. It seemed to be working its way towards the corner where they were all sitting.

'Oh, that's it then. We're in big trouble now,' Faith whimpered.

Ella took a second to compute the situation. There was a policeman in the pub. He had certainly headed over to the corner, and standing on tiptoe she could see that he appeared to be talking to Miranda. It was impossible to read what anybody might be saying, but all at the table had stopped talking and were concentrating on him. She felt a thud of anguish, but straightened herself and turned to Faith.

'Now listen, we've done nothing wrong. We're going to go back to the table with the drinks as if nothing's happened.'

'We're accomplices,' Faith said faintly. 'We've concealed evidence.'

'Yes, but nobody knows that apart from you and me,' Ella said, holding Faith's wavering gaze firmly. 'And we didn't know what we were doing so it doesn't count.'

'Ignorance of the law is no defence,' Faith's voice was almost inaudible. Ella wondered just how many episodes of *The Bill* she'd sat through in her parents' house. Her face was now completely white apart from her blackberry-coloured lips.

'Come on,' Ella instructed. She gathered the rest of the drinks and led the way back through the mass of bodies towards their table. As she approached she swallowed and took a steadying breath. She arrived with a manic smile.

'Here we are! Drinks all round!'

'Ella?' Miranda cleared her throat. Her face was a mask of serenity. All around the table sat agog.

'Yes?' she sang back, as if the officer standing at her left elbow had completely escaped her notice. Miranda nodded up at him.

'There's somebody here who wants to talk to you.'

'Oh, really?' Ella sparkled, her pulse now crashing in her ears. 'Did I forget to buy him a drink or something?' She giggled and took a quick fortifying gulp of her fresh vodka. 'Don't tell me, he wants to ask me if it's really true that men are most sexually active at eighteen? It was only an opinion, you know. I don't think it's illegal to have an opinion.'

Her comments were met with some fairly confused faces. Ella crossed her arms defensively and turned to face him at last.

'Yes, what is it?' she shot into the young face. Incredibly young, in fact, probably no more than twenty-one. It threw her off her stride a little.

'Ella Norton?' he asked, reaching into his pocket for a notebook. Ella squinted down at his uniform. Something wasn't quite right. It was very tight across his chest, he didn't have any numbers on his shoulders, and he seemed to be missing a radio. And the buttons didn't quite look like buttons. It was as if they were just decorative and the uniform was being held on with – there was a ripping sound.

Velcro.

She sank on to the bench, her knees finally giving way.

'You are charged with being twenty-nine today,' he smouldered at her, pulling at his jacket until he had loosened it completely and flinging it to one side to reveal a rippling chest.

'Oh my God!' Ella sank her face into her hands. 'You haven't done this to me!'

She peeped through her fingers. He had produced a bottle of baby oil from somewhere and was handing it to her while caressing his smooth chest with his other hand. The suggestion seemed to be that she should do likewise. Her hand was grabbed and a pool of cold oil squirted into her palm. A crowd had gathered around them to cheer. As the officer whipped off his trousers to reveal a black plastic posing pouch, there was a collective 'oooh!'.

'I'll kill you when we get home, Miranda!' Ella hissed sideways.

'Happy birthday!' Miranda mouthed back.

She couldn't disappoint the crowd. Even Valerie was practically standing on the bench at the back of the table for a good look. Tentatively, she put a hand out to the pectorals which were being pointed at her, and rubbed. It felt surprisingly good. She cast a sideways look at Giles the vet. Would he be hairy, she wondered? Smooth? A small sprinkling perhaps? She turned back to her birthday present in high spirits, and froze in horror. The black plastic posing pouch was flying through the air. They watched as it arched over the table and landed in Valerie's drink. Valerie held it up in fascination.

'Oh, I say. Thank you very much.'

'Now look here,' Ella began, finding herself, seated as she was, talking directly to the stripper's vital organ. He began to flip it around in time to the music. She stuck out a hand to stop him, leaning back as far as she could, and shrieked as her fingers were placed on an area of soft, warm flesh.

'Ella?' A voice assailed her from a distance. She jerked her hand away, realising with a shock that she had grabbed the stripper's member, but not before Matt had pushed his way forward with an uncertain smile and got a good view of Ella yanking a naked man towards her by his willy. The stripper let out a yelp.

'Oh God, Matt! I didn't think you'd come!' She stared at him in anguish. This wasn't the scene she'd prepared for him if he did show up. She was supposed to be reclining in a sensual manner over the table, talking about sophisticated things with her friends. He was supposed to be impressed. Her whole body tensed. The stripper let out another throaty whimper.

'You can let go now!' He rolled bloodshot eyes at her.

'Oh, I'm so sorry!' She unclenched her fingers quickly and he staggered back into Derek the landlord, who was clutching a tea towel and striding towards them with a purple face.

'Not in my bloody pub! Get off me, you nonce!' Finding himself with a young man's buttocks pressed up against his apron, Derek gave him a hearty shove. He teetered forwards and was caught deftly by Miranda, who promptly placed him on her lap.

'No need to get narky, Derek. It's only a bit of fun for Ella's birthday.'

'Well not here,' he snapped. 'Tell him to get his clothes on and get out of here.'

'All right, all right. Cool it.' The naked officer stood up and gathered his clothes together with a semblance of dignity. 'Anybody seen my pants?'

Ella darted a glance at Valerie, who looked away insouciantly.

'My pants, anyone? They're expensive to replace, you know.' He shook his head and tutted while he strapped his uniform back on without his posing pouch. 'This always happens. I get through two pairs a week, you know.'

'Oh, you poor thing.' Miranda stood up and patted his head. 'Come on, I'll see you to the door.'

Ella steadied herself with more vodka as Miranda helped the stripper into the last items of his outfit, balanced his helmet on his head for him, and led him away. It hadn't exactly been a resounding success as far as birthday presents go, but it was the thought that counted. She rubbed at her cheeks to try to bring the colour back, forgetting that her hand was covered in baby oil, and turned to Matt with a welcoming smile and a shiny face.

'So, Matt! You came here just for me. I'm deeply honoured!'

Instinctively she shuffled up on the bench to make room for him next to her. He sat down, and turned to her, his face only inches from hers, and looked at her with his glittering blue eyes.

'Well, my wife's away this weekend,' he said, just loud enough for her to hear.

'She is?' she breathed, her throat constricted.

'Yes,' he murmured. 'And seeing as she is, I wondered if I could make love to you.'

Chapter Three

Ella had wanted Matt from the first time she clapped
eyes on him. She'd driven up from London in the
early summer to talk to him about the course. She
was still in slick, city mode then, and had only
realised how inappropriate a power suit with a short
skirt and high-heeled shoes was for the interview as
she'd turned into the entrance of the college, driven
up a concrete drive spattered with cow dung and
mud and surrounded by fields, and found a place to
park next to what looked like a barn. She'd picked
her way towards the office building – a small
bungalow in the midst of tractors, diesel mowers,
and teenagers in holed jumpers and wellies – and
stopped at the entrance to shake the clods of mud
from the points of her heels. There had been several
office staff mingling inside, but her attention had
immediately been grabbed by a man clutching some
papers under his arm, giving the photocopier a hefty
kick with a pair of sturdy DMs, and laughing loudly.

He had an aura about him. Of energy, fresh air,
good humour, and sensuality. She'd watched him
from the doorway, hoping nobody would spot she
was there so that she could have a moment to absorb
everything about him. He was probably in his late
thirties, was incredibly tall, about six foot three or
four, and solid all the way up. It had been a warm

day, and he'd been dressed in a plain white T-shirt – a well worn one, not one with designer creases – and a snug pair of faded blue Levis. His hair was dishevelled and mid-brown, his skin tanned from the elements, and she'd been leaning at an odd angle to try to get a glimpse of his eyes when he'd looked up and stared directly at her. She'd swallowed back a smile of appreciation. Blue eyes, bright and full of life. He'd looked her up and down, taking in the suit, the fine tights, the Italian handbag, and raised a humorous eyebrow at her.

'You've just *got* to be Ella. Either that or you've come from the BBC to offer me my own programme at bloody long last.'

'I'm Ella,' she'd confirmed.

She'd tiptoed towards him, shaken his hand, and they'd smiled at each other. And as their skin had touched, her pheromones had been captured in a jam jar, hermetically sealed, and handed to him to have with his toast for breakfast.

She'd wanted to do the course anyway, had loved the drive through the country lanes to find the college, had been fascinated by the chaotic scramble of equipment, students and farm animals surrounding her, but if she'd needed one final, decisive nudge to knock over the teetering pile of wooden blocks that was her old life, Matt had provided it. From that moment on, she was going to talk her way on to this course if it took bribery, corruption or murder. And as they'd sat in his cramped office, piled high with files, strewn with gardening tools and overlaid with rainproof clothing, she'd found he didn't need much persuading. He seemed amused by her, interested in her reasons for changing direction, and stimulated by the thought of having her on board. She'd danced away in a cloud of euphoria and driven back down the M40 at ninety miles an hour with a CD blasting. It was fate. Everything inside her shouted that it was right.

It was only once she'd started the course that she'd found out that he was married.

'Ella, you're not doing what I think you're doing, are you?' Faith caught hold of Ella's arm in the kitchen as she yanked the cork from another bottle of wine.

Matt was reclining in the living room, Miranda had brought Oliver *and* Mike home from the pub, her indecision apparently dogging her up to the last minute, and Faith had been lurking around, trying to find somewhere to sit, punching the beanbag and generally looking uncomfortable since they'd all crashed in. Suzanne and Giles had both disappeared sometime around last orders – much to Miranda's disquiet – and the others had wafted off into cars or walked home. So they had stumbled back as a group, dodging the late-night drivers, and fallen into the cottage. Now Ella was starting to wonder how she could discreetly whisk Matt off upstairs to her room while the others sat and stared. At the moment there was a lively buzz of conversation above the music, but they couldn't sit up and drink all night while they waited for everyone to drop around them. Or perhaps they'd just have to.

'What d'you mean, Faith?'

'I mean,' Faith stuck her face up to Ella's ear. 'You're not going to bonk him, are you?'

'Who?' Ella quizzed, burying a tipsy laugh.

'Your bedroom's next to mine. And anyway, you said before, he's married, isn't he?'

Ella pulled a mug from the draining board and splashed some wine into it. They all had glasses in the other room, but talking to Faith was bringing on the need for fortification. She offered the mug to Faith, who shook her head with a frown, and took a long sip herself.

'It's my birthday. I can do what I want, can't I?'

'I thought he had a wife,' Faith grimaced. 'What with your taste for married men and that revolting bare man in the pub, I feel really sick.'

'Faith!' Ella gave her an old-fashioned look, ignored the dig about married men, and leaned against the sink to stop herself teetering. 'Bare men aren't revolting. What are you on about?'

'It was the way he wiggled it.'

Ella stopped herself from laughing. Faith looked genuinely put out. Ella sipped from her mug and tried to focus her mind. Faith had very pretty eyes, even Miranda had commented on that. But she buried herself in layers of clothing and as far as Ella could see she had never made an effort to attract anyone. It was highly likely that she hadn't had much experience of men, bare or otherwise. She put out a finger and flicked the ends of Faith's brown hair. Faith looked startled.

'What are you doing?'

'You need a make-over.' Ella wagged a finger. 'Why don't you let me and Miranda do you over?'

Faith looked even more startled.

'With a make-up bag,' Ella explained. 'Just to see if

44

you like it. I mean, Miranda's a top class air hostess. She knows all about being glam, doesn't she? And she can cut hair too. She said so. We could make you so gorgeous that any man would fall over with delight at the thought of you.' Ella leaned forward with a secretive smile. 'Even Giles.'

'Euw, God no.' Faith grabbed a mug, took the bottle from Ella and slopped herself out some wine. 'I can't stand him. He fancies himself so much.'

'Well,' Ella thought about it. 'What sort of man do you go for, then? I mean, what's your usual type? How about Oliver or Mike in there? Miranda can't have both of them. Well, she can, but even I'd draw the line at that. It's only a small cottage, and the walls might be solid but they're not completely sound-proof. But they're both quite cute, aren't they?' Ella urged, adding with slight confusion, 'whoever they are.'

'I know who they are. I went to school with them.'

'You did?'

'Yep. That's why they're ignoring me. They know exactly who I am. The one whose dad had the veggie van. They used to say I smelt like a turnip.'

'Oh, that's mean.' Ella took another sip of wine. From the next room she could hear Miranda and Matt bantering. That was all very friendly, but she didn't want to be out of sight for too long. She didn't know Miranda well enough to be sure that she knew when a man was out of bounds. 'Look, there must be some sort of guy that turns you on. Someone on the telly, perhaps?'

Faith gathered her jacket around her body. It was closer to an anorak really, and Ella had noticed that while everyone else had come in and flung their coats in a heap in the hall, Faith's had stayed on. It was as if it gave her another layer of protection. But protection against what, Ella wasn't sure.

'I've never . . .' Faith flushed. She fiddled with her glasses and took another sip of wine from her mug. 'I've never. You know.'

'You mean, you're . . .' Ella opened her eyes wide with encouragement.

'I've never had . . .'

'You can say it. You're a virgin.'

'. . . a boyfriend,' Faith finished.

'What the hell are you two doing, whispering out here? We're all dying of thirst and you just don't care.' Miranda had yanked open the kitchen door and stuck her head inside. She looked from Faith to Ella and back again. 'Did I hear you right?'

'Sshhh!' Ella pressed her finger to her lips.

'Blimey. A virgin at twenty-six?'

Ella frowned at Miranda severely. Her curls were lopsided and her eyes were unfocused. And she evidently didn't realise she was shouting.

'Good God. I was in triple figures by twenty-six,' Miranda went on. Ella wasn't sure if it was exaggeration. It was quite possible. Even though Miranda had been married for, what was it she'd said, four years? Ella had a feeling she hadn't been entirely single-minded throughout the experience.

'Look, just take the bottle and fill everyone up.' Ella pushed the bottle of white into Miranda's hand but she was still staring at Faith as if she'd just walked down the steps of a UFO.

'But how do you *manage* it? I couldn't. I'd go blind.'

46

Faith looked down at her mug, her skin puce.

'Go on, Miranda, piss off,' Ella directed. 'I'll be through in a sec. I just want to have a quiet chat with Faith first.'

'No, I'm fine.' Faith shook back her hair, nudged her glasses up to the bridge of her nose, and put her head in the air. 'You two don't have to keep treating me like a child. I can take care of myself.'

'Yes, I know you can, it's just—'

'Don't patronise me!' Faith slammed the mug down on the draining board and Ella jumped. Miranda jumped too, knocked her head on the side of the door, and uttered an expletive.

'Blimey, calm down, will you?' She rubbed her head.

'I'm perfectly calm. And if I'd known that this household was going to turn into – into a den of iniquity, then I'd have thought twice about moving in with you.'

Ella and Miranda stared at her blankly.

'There's no need to look so innocent.' Faith raised her voice and heaved a breath. 'Seducing married men, three in a bed, and I can smell marijuana, so don't play dumb.'

Ella inhaled deeply.

'Crikey, she's right. I'd rather they didn't, Miranda. Can you say something?'

'It was me who skinned up.' Miranda stood up assertively, rubbed at her head again, and took a step inside the kitchen. 'Now look here, Faith. We're adults here. This isn't the flipping school common room. I've been around, I've been all over the bloody world, and there's no way that I'm going to be

47

lectured on how to behave by an overgrown sixth former.'

'Steady on, Miranda,' Ella said softly. Part of her wanted to snap and say the same thing, apart from the having been all over the world bit, and she'd been a little concerned that Faith might cramp their style a bit. But there was no need to hurt Faith's feelings. Her cheeks were quivering emotionally, and Miranda was very drunk. Tomorrow they'd all wake up and have to live together. There had to be a way of establishing ground rules pleasantly.

'Well, bollocks!' Miranda exclaimed. Ella could now hear a daunted hush from the living room. Three men sipping their wine (and apparently passing round a joint), probably exchanging exasperated glances while the three women had a bust-up in the kitchen. It wasn't the image she wanted Matt to receive of her household and the way she did things.

'Balls to you too!' Faith grabbed the lapels of her thick jacket and brought them together huffily. 'You flit around as if everyone fancies you, picking up men like a tarty adolescent, and you're thirty-five. You're not a teenager, but you think you are.'

'I'm not thirty-five!' Miranda yelled.

'Yes you are!' Faith screeched. 'You must be, because you said you got married when you were twenty-nine, you were married for four years and you've been divorced for two years. I added it up.' Faith stuck her chin out aggressively. 'It's just maths!'

'You cow,' Miranda seethed.

'Look, come on.' Ella put out her hands. 'Insults won't get us anywhere.'

'Well, if you can't stand the heat,' Miranda stuck her hands on her hips and glowered at Faith, 'go back to your parents. Sit and watch soap operas with greasy hair night after night if that's what you want. Let Ella and me get on with our lives in peace.'

'I'm not going anywhere.' Faith pulled herself up to her full five foot six. 'I've got a legal contract and I'm staying. And Ella and I are perfectly happy when you're not around. Why don't *you* move out!'

'RIGHT!' Ella thumped her fist on the draining board. Two cereal bowls slid off and rolled across the floor. 'Nobody is going ANYWHERE! It's my house and I say that we all stay here. No arguments.'

There was a pause. Miranda took a swig of wine directly from the bottle and concentrated on Ella's face. Faith bit her lip and peered at her too. Ella breathed out slowly.

'Now listen to me, you two. I took you both on to share this house with me because I knew it would work.'

She stopped for a moment of consideration. The two women glared back at her.

'I knew it wasn't going to be easy because we're all different. But that's why I was sure we'd jog along. You can't have three women with similar personalities in a house together. It's brilliant for a couple of months and then it goes pear-shaped. I know people who've done it. So whatever happens, we're going to make this a happy house. That's the way I planned things. Okay?'

Faith looked at Miranda from under her eyelashes. Miranda took another swig from the bottle. She sniffed loudly.

'Okay. It doesn't suit me to move out at the moment.'

'Good. Faith?'

Faith chewed on her cheek and appeared to give the matter a great deal of thought.

'Come on, Faith. Tomorrow, when we're all sober again, we'll sort this out. We'll do something fun together. That shower screen needs a hook putting into it. If we put our heads together I'm sure we can manage it.'

'You need the right drill,' Faith mumbled.

'There, you see!' Ella flung out a hand triumphantly. 'We can't do without you, Faith. We need you to tell us about the right drill.'

Faith shuffled her weight to her other foot.

'You're indispensable,' Ella exaggerated. 'Please stay, and please let's make it work.'

Faith pouted, looked down and nodded.

'All right. If you haven't changed your mind about me bringing an animal home.'

Miranda stuck her tongue in her cheek and raised her eyebrows at Ella.

'She means a real one,' Ella pointed out patiently. 'You know, animal coloured and everything.'

'I'm allergic,' Miranda stated bluntly. Faith's face dropped. 'But just to cats.'

'Well, there you are then. No cats.'

There was a pause. Faith relaxed her hold on her anorak and seemed more peaceful. Miranda rubbed at her head vacantly.

'So can I get back to our guests now we've decided all that?'

'God, yes!' Ella started.

Miranda rolled her eyes and disappeared back into the living room with the wine bottle. Ella touched Faith's arm gently.

'You look tired. And no, before you say anything, I'm not trying to get rid of you. Join us if you want, but it's fine if you go up to bed. You can do whatever you want. It's your home too.'

Faith gazed back weakly. Ella noticed that she really did look pale.

'If – if I go up now, you lot aren't going to have a good laugh at my expense, are you?'

Ella frowned.

'Of course not.'

'Okay. I might just go up and listen to some music before I go to bed.'

'You do that. Tomorrow will be a lovely day, and we'll wonder why we fell out at all. You'll see.'

It was difficult to seduce to the throb of Aretha Franklin with ELO belting out over their heads. Miranda twitched several times as if she was going to leap upstairs and take a hammer to Faith's CD player, but Ella restrained her with warning glances. As they struggled to appreciate the sultriness of 'Do Right Woman, Do Right Man' to the backing of 'Don't Bring me Down', Miranda lunged at the stereo and stabbed at the button.

'This time, she wins,' she muttered, flopping back on to the sofa where Mike had strategically laid an arm in anticipation of her return. She closed her eyes and curled herself into his shoulder in drunk but deliberate fashion. Oliver stood up, swayed, and headed for the door.

'See you around then.'

Ella waved at him faintly from her beanbag. She heard the door bang as he let himself out. One down, two to go. She cast a covert glance at Matt from under her lashes. He was looking utterly relaxed in the armchair, his long legs stretched out over the rug. He caught her eye and winked at her.

'Well,' he stood up slowly and drained his wine glass. 'I really should be heading off now.'

'Hmmmn.' Miranda raised an indifferent hand from the sofa without opening her eyes. Mike was intent on ruffling her hair with his nose and didn't reply. Ella struggled to her feet disconsolately.

'Well, I'll, um, see you out then.'

She unlatched the door to the hall and wandered out. Matt followed and closed the door quietly behind him. ELO was still crashing down on them from above. Ella glanced up the stairs. There was no other sound of life coming from Faith's room, and usually the thumps of footsteps – especially Faith's – were very audible from below. Ella had a feeling she'd fallen asleep with the CD on. She just hoped she hadn't put it on loop. Matt touched her shoulder.

'How are you going to get home? You left your car at the pub, didn't you?' Matt's eyes consumed her. She tried to puzzle it out. 'I'll have to ring you a taxi, won't I?'

'I'm not going anywhere,' he whispered into her ear, his fingers caressing her shoulder and inching up to her neck. His breath was warm on her skin. Her knees wobbled.

'You're not?'

'How else were we going to get out of that bloody

room without actually saying, "We're going upstairs to make love now?" It's not really anyone else's business, is it?'

'Oh,' she breathed at him, her heart skipping. 'In which case . . .'

'You'd better take me upstairs to your room, hadn't you?'

The third time that the introduction to 'Horace Wimp' pounded through Ella's bedroom wall, Matt sat back on his haunches and shook his head wearily.

'I'm sorry, Ella. I just can't concentrate with that racket going on.'

'It's all right.'

She allowed him to shift his weight to the sheet next to her, and pulled up the duvet to cover them both. It wasn't how she'd pictured it. It was gone four in the morning, and she was doing her best to stay optimistic. Initially it had been quite good fun to try to make love with music shaking the walls around them. It stopped them being inhibited in the small house knowing that Faith was to one side of them and Miranda just across the landing. The fact that Miranda hadn't stuck her head round the door by now resting a bloodied axe on her shoulder, saying, 'It's okay, Faith won't trouble us any more,' meant that she was obviously far too drunk, or distracted, or both, to care about ELO. But now Ella was tired, and all she wanted to do was cuddle up to Matt and fall asleep with him. They hadn't even had a chance to talk properly, certainly not intimately, about what it all meant.

She slid her legs out of bed, shuffled across the soft

carpet to the door and unhooked her short towelling dressing gown. She put it on, glancing at Matt. He had propped himself up on his elbow and was smiling at her.

'That's very sexy, you know. You're all legs in that. Have you been on a sunbed?'

'What, me?' She let out a short laugh. 'I'm naturally this colour.'

'Lucky you. Don't be long, will you?'

She gave him a warm smile in return. Perhaps all was not lost. He was still awake, and there would be the morning too.

She crept out of the room and closed the door behind her. Two steps along the landing and she was outside Faith's door. She knocked loudly as Horace was building up the courage to ask the girl if maybe they could marry. She hesitated. The word 'marry' bothered her briefly, but she was tired, and she'd had too much to drink. And she hadn't yet had satisfying sex with the man she'd been fantasising about for months now. She thumped again on the wood with less patience. When no reply was forthcoming, she pushed open the door and walked into Faith's bedroom.

Faith's bedside light was still on. A small, pink lamp with a frayed lace edging that she'd brought with her from home. Ella guessed that it was one she'd had since she was quite young. Faith was in bed, humped up, her knees tucked up to her chest, and she was sound asleep. A closer inspection revealed that she had earplugs wedged into both of her ears. She was snoring contentedly.

Ella tutted, her impatience flashing. She crossed

the room to the CD player and poked the 'off' button. The music stopped abruptly, leaving a thick silence in the room. Ella's ears began to buzz. She stalked back to Faith, wanting to shake her, to pull out her earplugs and berate her for being selfish, but she stopped at her bedside and looked down at her instead. Her fringe was damp and lying in strands across her forehead, her cheeks were hatched with red, as if she'd been touched by a strong sun. Without her glasses on, her lashes appeared longer and finer. They were spiked. It looked as if she had been crying. Ella hovered over her a moment longer, her brow furrowed as she teased her addled brain into thought. Then she gently switched off the light and crept back out of the room.

Matt was snoring loudly when she returned to her own room. She stopped at the door to unwind her dressing gown and hang it up again, this time unappreciated by him. She let out a low, silent breath. Was it always like this when you built somebody up in your imagination? This strange sense of anticlimax she felt? Perhaps Matt could never have lived up to her expectations. His body was powerful, lean, toned, shaped just as she had pictured it. There was nothing that had disappointed her there, and their mutual disrobing had been erotic and full of promise. But once they had got down to the serious business of making love, she had almost felt as if he was painting by numbers. Or that he was applying his acquired skills to the case in hand. It hadn't felt unique, and that was what bothered her.

She tiptoed over to the bed and crawled in beside him. He shuffled up as if on automatic pilot and immediately began to snore again. She clicked the switch of her bedside lamp and lay in the darkness, straining her ears for sounds of the night to comfort her. It was so quiet on this side of the village. Not even the distant sounds of trains that she'd become accustomed to in London. Normally she relished it, but tonight it made her feel tense. Sure that she wouldn't sleep at all, she found herself drifting away with exhaustion.

It seemed only minutes later when a violent hammering came from across the room, and her door was flung wide on its hinges.

She pulled herself up in bed in shock clutching the duvet, and blinking into the harsh light of day. It was obviously late morning. There was no sign of Matt, his clothes had gone, and Faith was standing in the doorway with a face like death.

'Jesus! God, what is it?'

'They're here,' Faith stated abruptly. She looked as if she was about to be sick. Ella swung her legs out of the bed and swallowed.

'What? What's going on? Who's here?'

'The police,' Faith stated. 'They're downstairs and they want to talk to you.'

56

Chapter Four

'Don't panic,' was the first thing Ella could think to say. She dragged her fingers over her face to massage some life back into her skin. Bit by bit, the realisation that Matt had gone but the police had arrived was starting to sink in.

'Right then.' She strode over to the door. Faith blinked at her naked form. Faith always wore pyjamas to bed, and discovering that not every other woman did might be part of her education. She seemed glued to the spot, her eyes wide and nervous. Ella grabbed her towelling bathrobe and slung it on, pulling the belt tight, her brain moving quickly.

'First, you stay up here. No need for you to get involved at all. Second, what do you mean by "they"? How many of the buggers are there?'

Faith gulped in a breath, spluttered, and stumbled over to Ella's bed where she sank down shakily.

'There's two.'

'Two,' Ella repeated, grabbing a hairbrush and wrestling with her tangled chestnut knots. 'Better than three, worse than one. Okay. And what did they say?'

Faith swallowed loudly. It was clear that she was in the middle of a major panic, but the police would have to be dealt with. Faith would have to be hidden. That was all there was to it.

'They – they said, who owns this house,' Faith managed.

'Right.' Ella threw down her brush and ruffled her hair with her fingertips. It was no good trying to sleek it down. She looked like an explosion in a wig factory. 'And what else did they say?'

'They said could they come in please.'

'Okay, and as they're downstairs, you presumably said yes. Then what?'

'I pointed them towards the living room and came up to get you.'

'Right.' Ella swallowed a little noisily herself. She couldn't have Faith seeing that she was alarmed too. That would throw her into hysterics. She took a long, slow breath. 'Right,' she said serenely. 'That's fine. And Miranda's still in bed, I take it?'

'I don't know. I'd only just come out the bathroom and got dressed when I heard the door.'

'Okay. And – er – you didn't see Matt, I suppose?'

'Matt?' Faith looked blank. 'Why would I see Matt?'

'Don't worry about it.' Ella smiled brightly. 'So there are two policemen downstairs, Miranda's in bed, and they want to see me. That's fine. I know where I stand now. So you just get back to your room and do something in there for as long as possible and I'll come and get you when they've gone. Okay?'

Faith's bottom lip was hanging open as she drank in Ella's instructions.

'What should I do?'

Ella stopped looking for an elastic band for her hair.

'What do you mean?'

'I mean, what should I do that's normal? What would I normally do in my bedroom on a Saturday?'

Ella gazed at her while she tried to assemble the questions.

'Read a book or something.'

'I haven't got any books.'

'It doesn't matter what you do, Faith, just do it quietly.'

'Can I borrow a book? Then I could lie on the bed reading it. Just in case they do a house search.'

'They're not going to—' Ella stopped. The police were in the living room. And there was an ashtray down there with a roach in it from the joint that Miranda had rolled up last night. There had only been one, but the evidence was down there, somewhere.

'Oh shit.'

'Ella?' Faith stood up as Ella raced to her bedroom door.

'No time.'

'Can I borrow this book then?'

Ella glanced over her shoulder. Faith had picked up *Men are from Mars, Women are from Venus*. Ella gave her a pained look.

'If you really want to.'

Faith trotted out of Ella's room with the book in her hands and vanished into her bedroom. The latch clicked decisively behind her. Ella glanced down the stairs. She couldn't leap down them in one go. Now she had to catch her breath, be calm, and deal with the police naturally. After all, she had no involvement with drugs. She never had. Even when some of the guys at the bank were snorting cocaine to keep them buzzing, she wouldn't have any truck with it. She was innocent.

'I am innocent,' she whispered to herself under her breath as she descended the stairs, yanking the belt of her dressing gown tightly around her waist. 'Ella Norton is innocent.'

She reached the living room door, took one last breath, and entered the room. She closed the door behind her.

Two men were standing silently at the far end of the room. With the sun blasting through the window she could only see their silhouettes. She opened her mouth to speak, but spotted something out of place from the corner of her eye. There was somebody on the sofa.

It was Miranda, on her back in the peacock blue kimono she wore around the house in the morning, her feet draped over the arm of the sofa. She was moaning softly under her breath and she had two pieces of cucumber placed over her eyes.

'Zat you, Faith?'

She evidently couldn't see a thing, and from the way she stretched her arms over her head languidly, Ella had a creeping feeling that she'd been snoozing. She wriggled her shoulders and the kimono slipped down to reveal half of a creamy breast.

'Miranda!' Ella hissed at her. 'Get up.'

'Oh, Ella, it's you. I can't move. I don't think I'm ever going to be able to close my legs again. You'll have to bury me in a Y-shaped coffin.'

Ella thought she heard a muffled snort from one of the silhouettes at the back of the room but neither of the men spoke.

'Miranda,' Ella stated more firmly, walking over to the sofa and delicately pulling the kimono back into place. 'Take your cucumbers off.'

'I can't. My head hurts. That boy Mike has got a dick like a Canadian redwood. I know how a shish kebab feels now.'

'Stop saying things like that. There are two policemen in the room!' Ella said through gritted teeth.

Miranda gurgled a laugh.

'Tell them to come back when I've healed up.'

'Miranda, I'm serious!' Ella lunged for her cucumbers and ripped them off. Miranda blinked up at her blearily.

'What's up with you? Didn't Matt produce a result?'

'Sit up, look around, and bloody shut up, will you?'

Miranda sniffed, wriggled up on the sofa, scowled at Ella, and gazed around the room. She put a hand up to shield her eyes as she stared towards the window.

'Good grief, you're right. I do apologise, I must have been asleep when you arrived. Would you like some coffee? I put a pot on a couple of hours ago, but it might be a bit stewed by now.'

'Coffee would be lovely, thank you.'

Miranda dragged herself to her feet looking ravishing. She pushed a hand through her curls, gave a sheepish smile, readjusted her kimono and wandered towards the kitchen door.

'And do make yourselves comfortable, please. Ella? Would you offer these gentlemen a seat?'

Ella gaped at Miranda as she slid away into the

kitchen and closed the door quietly behind her. She thought she heard a stifled expletive from behind the door, but was distracted by the two men walking out of the light and into the middle of the room.

'Can we just sit anywhere?'

It was a uniformed police constable that spoke. Ella realised now that the other man, the taller and more swarthy of the two, wasn't in uniform. He was casually dressed in jeans and a shirt and tie, a jacket slung over his arm. She gathered herself quickly, envious of Miranda's quicksilver ability to adapt to any situation that was thrown at her, and now conscious of the scantiness of her robe. With the evidence that they'd seen in that room, they probably thought they'd stumbled across a knocking shop.

'Yes, please. Armchair, sofa, beanbags. The choice is yours.'

The constable headed for the sofa and sank into it, his legs swinging into the air as it attempted to swallow him.

'Oh, don't worry. It does that,' Ella assured him quickly. The other man seemed happy to stand. He was watching Ella a little too closely for her liking. And she realised now that it was the police constable that was doing all the talking. So far the other man hadn't said a word.

'You are the owner of the house?' the policeman asked, flipping out a notebook. Ella swallowed, her limbs freezing into position. Why was he taking notes? Shouldn't he have warned her that anything she said might be used in evidence?

'I am. Ella Norton.'

'Right. And you share the house?'

'Yes. With Miranda and Faith.'

'Miranda and Faith,' the constable repeated thoughtfully. 'That's Miranda in the kitchen, is it? She doesn't look like a Faith, somehow.'

He gave her a slight smile. Ella took heart from it. Would he be giving her slight smiles if he was about to whip out a pair of handcuffs and lead her away?

'Yes. And Faith's upstairs.'

'Upstairs,' he repeated, nodding. He fell silent. Ella watched him as he gazed around the room, taking in the empty wine glasses, several empty wine bottles. And the ashtray with the roach in it. On the coffee table next to the armchair. Her heart began to thud uncomfortably. Whatever time Miranda had floated downstairs, she'd made no attempt to clear up, and certainly hadn't emptied the ashtray. She'd have to keep him talking to distract him.

'Faith's reading,' she added brightly, stepping forward and allowing her robe to part right up to her thighs. The constable glanced back at her and seemed duly distracted.

'Reading,' he repeated idly.

'*Men are from Mars, Women are from Venus*.'

'I see.'

'It's what she's reading. Not my opinion on our origins.' She laughed lightly. 'It's a book.'

'Yes.'

'It's, er. About relationships. How to overcome differences, to heal resentments and rebuild marriages.'

Was she going too far? The man in plain clothes had put his head on one side and was regarding her thoughtfully. She stared straight back at him defensively. He had dark eyes, so dark that they were like black holes, swallowing up the light. They made her feel uncomfortable, and she looked back to the constable quickly. His younger, freckled face and light eyes were less threatening.

'You should read it,' she added pointlessly. 'If you're in a relationship. Or even if you're not. It'll help you when you have the next one. Women are like waves, you see.'

'Well, thank you for your advice. I'll bear it in mind.' The constable nodded at her pleasantly enough. She just needed to distract them for long enough to get rid of the ashtray and all would be well. Probably.

'Didn't help me much, but it will do one day. I reckon,' she affirmed.

There was a short silence. This was no good. Silences led to people gazing round rooms.

'Perhaps I'll just get rid of this mess,' Ella said, lurching towards the empty glasses and starting to gather them. 'If you don't mind.'

'Miss Norton.' It was the plain clothed man who spoke. She stood up with an armful of glasses and looked at him unhappily.

'Yes?'

'Aren't you curious to know why we're here?'

It was the simplest, most obvious question. She stood dumbstruck and stared at his face. She took in every detail of his features. He was very dark skinned as well as dark eyed, with a strong jaw and black eyebrows. His nose was slightly hooked, but not fine. He looked like a lion that had been punched in the face. Jesus, she berated herself. She'd watched *Columbo*. Hadn't she flung herself around the room

64

with frustration that the criminals always gave themselves away right from the start by not showing any curiosity about the crime? And why? Because they already *knew* all about it. Even Faith would have got that bit right.

'Yes, I am. Of course I am.' She gave an embarrassed laugh. 'You'll have to forgive me. It was my birthday yesterday and we had a bit of a celebration. It was a very late night. More of a late morning, in fact. I'm afraid I'm not quite myself yet.'

'Pig of a hangover?' the constable quizzed sympathetically.

'Very much so,' she emphasised to him.

'Give her a break, Jaz,' the constable said in a low voice. 'Let's get some coffee down our necks first, shall we?'

The taller man neither assented nor dissented, but he relaxed his shoulders a little and allowed Ella to pass with her armful of glasses and wrestle with the kitchen door. Miranda was arriving with a tray of coffee as she opened it.

'Ah, there you are. I'm just clearing up,' Ella said meaningfully, catching Miranda's eye in the doorway. 'All the rubbish from last night. Glasses, *ashtrays*, bottles, you name it. It looks like a bomb site.'

Miranda stared back.

'Okay, do what you want. I need to drink coffee.'

Ella dumped the glasses and returned to find Miranda handing her a mug with milk and sugar already added. 'And sit down, you're making me dizzy,' Miranda said with a hint of grumpiness. 'We can clear up later. I'm sure these guys haven't got all day to sit and watch us doing the housework.'

Ella took the mug, noticing with dismay that the man who'd been called 'Jaz' was now seated comfortably in the armchair and was resting his own mug on the coffee table, right next to the ashtray. She pecked at her coffee.

'Sit down!' Miranda instructed, falling on to the sofa next to the constable, who reddened slightly and brushed an imaginary bit of fluff from his trousers. Ella sank into a beanbag on her knees.

'Okay, I'm comfortable.'

'Tell me, Miss Norton,' the constable began.

'Call me Ella.'

'Ella. How long have you lived here?'

'Only a couple of months.'

'I see.' He stopped to take a note. Ella stared fixedly at Miranda, who finally glanced over. She allowed her gaze to wander to the ashtray and back again. Miranda frowned. Ella gave her a severe stare in return and glanced at the ashtray again. This time when she looked back at Miranda she saw that her face had visibly paled. They stared at each other with wide eyes, then Miranda uncurled her feet from under her kimono and rose as elegantly as possible from the sofa.

'Excuse me, gents, I can't stand the smell of stale smoke. It's making me feel queasy. I'll just get rid of this.'

She glided over to the coffee table and leaned down casually to pick it up. She clamped her hand over the ashtray, her thumb reaching into it and covering the offending roll of cardboard. Then she sailed off into the kitchen. Ella heard the lid of the plastic bin swing open and shut. She returned empty handed with a wide smile.

'That's better. Now where were we?'

'The thing is,' the constable continued, his concentration swinging between Ella's expanse of thigh and the flash of Miranda's cleavage as she repositioned herself on the sofa, 'how well have you got to know your neighbours?'

Ella glanced at Miranda, who had acquired a poker-face. She seemed to be leaving Ella to do the explaining.

'Not well, to be honest. We're mostly out all day and we haven't been here long. We've met Doris next door, but she doesn't say much.'

'She may well be dead,' Miranda said factually. 'She looked pretty much on her last legs when I saw her a week ago. Is that why you're here? We haven't smelt anything funny.'

There was a silence.

'And we wouldn't have heard anything,' Miranda added. 'Not with ELO at full volume all the time.'

'ELO?' The constable seemed nonplussed.

'Faith,' Miranda and Ella said at the same time.

As if on cue, there was a resounding thump from upstairs. They all raised their eyes to the ceiling.

'That's her,' Miranda explained. 'She's overweight.'

'She's the one who's reading,' the constable nodded, piecing it together.

'Christ, no. She never reads. Doesn't own a book. Does nothing but watch soaps.'

'She's reading,' Ella stated, boring Miranda out with a hard look. 'I lent her John Gray. She's reading it right now.'

Miranda raised her fine eyebrows ironically.

'That'll be handy for her.'

'She got relationship problems, has she?' the constable asked with a hint of compassion. 'Can make you overeat, you know. My girlfriend eats nothing but Bounties when she's depressed. I find the wrappers everywhere. But she moves on to Kit-Kats when it's her time of the month.'

'Faith eats Crunchies,' Miranda informed the constable, appearing to warm to the subject. 'And as far as I can work out, she eats them all year round.'

'Andy,' the soft voice coming from the armchair caused them all to sit up straight. 'Let's get on with it.'

'Right. Well, as I said, it's about your neighbours and what they do.'

The plain-clothed man stood up suddenly as if he'd been watching a learner struggle for long enough and was about to demonstrate how it was done.

'Let's start again. This is police constable Andy Havers, I'm DI Jasbinder Singh. Your neighbours to one side are dealing in drugs. Soft stuff, but also heroin, and that's why we're here. We'd like to use your house for surveillance purposes. You've got ideal views from the front of the property which will give us the angles we need to collect evidence of who is coming and going from the house. It will be done discreetly and with as little disruption to your everyday lives as possible. We can't catch big time dealers like these without evidence, and to get evidence we need to catch them in action. Having said that, some people find the prospect of involvement in matters like this daunting. The choice is yours. You can think about it and let us know. It'll probably involve setting up surveillance cameras in one of your front rooms upstairs, and it will require the occasional presence of a member of CID.' He stopped, looked straight at Ella, and added, 'Me.'

Ella was breathing so silently that she couldn't hear herself. He had commanded the complete attention of every one of them, including the constable, and all without raising his voice. He slipped his thumbs into the belt around his jeans and regarded Ella for a moment longer.

'It's your house.'

'Yes,' she whispered.

'Bugger me, Doris is a dealer!' Miranda whistled.

'The house we're interested in is number eleven,' the detective inserted factually. 'Two doors down on the other side. These houses look over fields so we can't set up opposite. The immediate neighbours are worried about their proximity, so you are our only other chance.'

Ella nodded and swallowed.

'We always bring a uniformed officer on an initial visit so that the public can be assured that it's a legit police matter.'

'I'm assured,' she said faintly. Thank God. It was somebody else they were after.

'From now on, the only comings and goings from this house would be by plain clothes. Any equipment brought in would look innocuous. As if you had workmen in, perhaps. Nobody would know.'

'But you both steamed up today in a squad car. Don't you think that looks a bit suspect?' Miranda had obviously gathered her wits.

'We didn't come in a squad car, and we happen to know that the occupants of the property in question are away today. There is no way that you can be implicated by our coming here.'

'So far so good then,' Miranda quipped. 'Ella?'

'Um.' Ella pulled her dressing gown around her thighs, trying to think. Cameras? Upstairs? And this creepy man with the unearthly black eyes sneaking around their cottage whenever he felt like it? The words 'no thanks' were on the tip of her tongue. She tried to think of something to say that was citizenly but not cowardly.

'Couldn't you use Doris's house?'

'I guess you'll want to check out the rooms upstairs?' Miranda interrupted smoothly. 'If you are going to put cameras up there, it'd be nice for us to know how much they're going to get in the way.'

'I was coming to that,' the DI told her. 'A quick look now would be useful. That way I can act on it when I get back to the station.'

'Wh—' Ella began.

'I'll show you up, then.' Miranda got to her feet slowly and pulled at her kimono. 'Which room are you interested in? There are two that look over the front.'

'I think it's best to get up there and make our decision based on the best view.'

'Fine,' Miranda smiled. 'Follow me.'

Miranda led the two officers from the room, leaving Ella on her knees on the beanbag. She tried again, a little more loudly in their direction.

'Wh—'

She got up, shaking the circulation back into her legs, and followed them up the stairs. They were already assembled on the landing.

'Now hang on.'

'And this is Faith's room,' Miranda declared. 'Good view of the road from here.'

She pushed open the door without knocking. Faith was on her hands and knees on the floor with her ear pressed firmly down to the floorboards. Her face was screwed up in concentration.

'Faith?' Miranda said lightly.

She opened both her eyes and jumped up.

'It wasn't – I didn't – Ella?'

Ella pushed her way in front of the group and pulled Faith's door shut. It slammed in front of their noses.

'My room,' she stated. 'In here. Best view. Follow me.'

'What was she doing?' the constable whispered to Miranda as they followed Ella into her bedroom.

'Yoga,' Miranda said wisely.

'Ah.'

'So here,' Ella threw out her arm to show off her room, 'is where you can set up. That way we can leave Faith in peace. I've got a big bay window. I guess you'll be able to see the front path of number eleven from there.'

It was then that she noticed the black suspender belt and stockings strewn over the headboard, the ruffled sheets and the half-used bottle of massage oil with the top sitting beside it. She shot to the window and flung wide the curtains, yanking at the window latch to get it open and release the room from the suffocating aroma of Acacia Fire. She heard the constable clear his throat overtly as if he was trying not to laugh, and when she had the courage, she looked back over her shoulder to see what DI Jasbinder Singh made of the scene. Were Asian women encouraged to live sexually free lives? She could guess that he might disapprove. And he was CID, to make it all worse. They weren't exactly famous for being woolly liberals.

His face showed no interest. His expression was as stony as it had been since he'd arrived, as if he hadn't noticed the components of the do-it-yourself seduction kit littered around them. He joined her at the window and looked down at the small front garden, the gardens that were visible to either side, the muddy fields opposite, and the stretch of road where Ella and Miranda parked their cars. He gazed along the lane to the neighbouring paths, craning his head. Then he stood back again, chewing his lip thoughtfully.

'Jaz?' the constable queried tentatively.

'I'll set up in here,' he said. He turned to Ella and stared at her. She squirmed under his scrutiny, wanting him to look at something else. Even the massage oil. His tireless assessment was making her skin crawl.

It was just what she didn't need. A hard-nosed, macho know-it-all with a downer on sexual liberation flitting in and out of her bedroom whenever the fancy took him. He probably believed that adulterers deserved the death penalty. That'd do wonders for her flourishing relationship with Matt. And above all, she'd only recently managed to get away from male chauvinist pigs when she'd left the trading rooms of the City banks behind her. All that effort to escape only to have one turn up at her house and set up camp in her bedroom. And now that Miranda had acquiesced to the whole idea there was bugger all she could do to stop him.

'Is that all right with you?' he asked, his eyes questioning her.

'Of course,' she replied sweetly. 'Why on earth wouldn't it be?'

Chapter Five

'Jesus, God, blimey, balls, Miranda!' Ella stalked around the living room, not caring now if her dressing gown was flapping and her hair looked like a mushroom cloud. 'I mean, bloody hell!'

Miranda had resumed her position on the sofa. She appeared to have thought better of replacing the cucumbers. But she had her eyes closed, which Ella was finding infuriating. Faith was hovering in the doorway to the kitchen, neither in the living room nor out of it. She was there but not there. For the moment, Ella ignored her.

'For Christ's sake, Miranda, explain yourself. Why did you get us into this?'

Miranda let out a tired groan.

'Calm down, will you? I'm hungover and I haven't slept. I can't deal with this right now.'

'I really don't care. You set me up. What else could I say to them? I had to say yes, and it was all your fault.'

'No it wasn't,' Miranda said languidly. 'It's your house, it was your decision.'

'No, Miranda. It wasn't like that. You left me with no choice.'

'You've always got a choice.' Miranda stretched her toes and relaxed again. 'Why is it nobody can ever face that? You have a choice, you make a decision, you blame someone else. Rule of life.'

Ella stopped to tug at her towelling belt.

'That's just sophistry and you know it.'

'You'd better explain that word to Faith. I know she's lurking out there, and she'll lose the thread if you don't.'

Ella shot Faith a look. Her eyelashes fluttered behind her glasses. She stepped back into the kitchen and pulled the door closed behind her.

'Oh no you don't.' Ella hopped over to the door and opened it again. Faith looked alarmed. 'You come in here and sit down. This concerns you too.'

She stood firm with an implacable expression while Faith crept into the living room and wandered along the wall to the window. She nodded at Ella as if to confirm that she had reached her final destination.

'Right.' Ella brought her hands together decisively.

She'd run team meetings. This was no different. The way forward could only start with honest expressions of feeling. Once they'd all been honest, they could move on to a constructive strategy that they were all happy with.

'This affects all of us. Thanks to you, Miranda, we're now going to have the Keystone Cops swarming over this cottage day and night.' Ella strode back across the carpet again, wishing that Miranda would open her eyes so that she could at least observe the physical display of dissent taking place in front of her. 'And I don't like it.'

'Hardly the Keystone Cops.' Miranda let out a long sigh. 'That guy knew what he was doing. I'm sure he'll be discreet.'

'That's not the point,' Ella insisted. 'We should have had an opportunity to discuss it first. As a house. As a team. That way, we could have come to a mutual decision.'

'Fine.' Miranda sounded bored. 'Let's all hand round the salt pot and only talk when it's our turn, shall we? We're grown-ups, Ella. If we've got something to say, we'll say it.'

'But I couldn't say it!' Ella stopped, her fingers tightening. 'I would have had to say it to that creepy bloke, and he'd have thought I was hiding something, or that I was churlish, or miserable, or involved, or something. So I had to say yes.'

Miranda sniffed. Ella continued.

'So all I want to say, very calmly but honestly at this point, is that we should all state our feelings and get it out in the open.'

'My feelings obviously aren't as complicated as yours, Ella.' Miranda opened one eye. Ella did a quick stalk backwards and forwards to make the most of her attention. In the past she'd been attributed with 'presence' at meetings. People had always listened to her. Miranda should be doing the same. Miranda shuffled into a more comfortable position on the sofa. 'I'm easy.'

Faith guffawed. Ella frowned.

'It's my bedroom that they're using. I'm going to be the one with speed cameras all over the place.' Ella took a short breath. 'I should have had the final say.'

'You did have the final say,' Miranda said in a tired voice. 'Look, I've been involved with police matters before. It happened when I worked for Saudi Airlines, and more so since I've been doing private flights. A lot of them are sensitive. It's no big deal.'

'Yes, but.' Ella stopped. She had the feeling that she was losing the battle. She gave up and sank into the armchair with her back to the window. 'All right. I had the final say. I just want to point out that if anything like this happens in the future, we should have a period of discussion before we commit ourselves.'

'Message received and understood.' Miranda gave Ella a sleepy smile. 'Anything else we need to bring up right now that we're in a house meeting? Leaving the cap off the toothpaste? The smell of oxtail soup in the kitchen when a certain person doesn't wash up the saucepan after eating? The Crunchie wrappers breeding in the bathroom pedal bin?'

Ella let her head roll back and stared up at the ceiling. She felt a tingle of tension and sat still while the feeling passed. Coming back to Oxfordshire and throwing plants around wasn't about tension. Banking was about tension. This was supposed to be about enjoyment.

'I just wanted us to establish open channels of communication,' she said, wincing as her phraseology rung bells of familiarity. 'But that's all I've got to say. I think we can cope with this new development. We just need to pull together.'

'Righto,' Miranda said, and closed her eyes again.

'And perhaps the CID guy won't be so scary once we get to know him.'

Miranda opened both eyes and gave Ella a straight stare.

'I thought you liked him. My instincts are shit hot, you know. I should run a dating agency. I'd make millions.'

'I don't like him at all.' Ella was horrified. There was nothing fake about her protest. He represented everything she'd shunned.

'Okay, I was wrong,' Miranda conceded.

'And,' Ella persevered, 'seeing as we're all up and about now . . .' She eyed Miranda's slumped form, 'I suggest we do something. What about getting that hook up?'

There was a pause. Miranda looked vacant. Ella heard Faith move behind her. She'd forgotten that she was there, hovering by the curtains.

'We need the right drill,' Faith said. 'I'll ask Mum to drop it round.'

Faith wasn't exactly tall for a woman, but as her parents stood on the doorstep in their waterproofs wearing identical crash helmets, Ella realised that Faith was a giant compared to them. Neither of them could have been above five feet tall. They had arrived on a scooter and they wore matching protective clothing, his green waterproofs a marked contrast to hers in yellow. The legs were turned up and crumpled at the ankle, revealing rubber boots. Their outfits had caused Ella a slight frown of confusion when she'd opened the door in bare feet and khaki shorts with a loose white shirt rolled up to the elbows. It didn't look like rain. The sun was beating down outside and the sky appeared cloudless. Faith's mother handed her a plain cardboard box with 'drill' written in marker pen on the outside.

'She rang and said you needed this.'

'Oh, lovely.' Ella took it gratefully and opened the door wide. 'And you must come in for a cup of tea.'

Faith's father's eyes smiled at her from inside his crash helmet as he took a bold step forward, but the material of his jacket was grabbed and he was yanked backwards before his booted foot could reach the ground.

'That's very kind of you,' Faith's mother said, ' but we'll be on our way now.'

There was a slight pause. Ella looked from one to the other of them. They both looked back at her.

'She's—' Faith's mother began and stopped. She shuffled her rubber boots. 'She's all right, is she?'

'Of course,' Ella beamed. 'She's fine. I'll just get her for you and you'll see for yourselves.'

'No need for that. We'll be on our way now.'

Ella nodded. Nobody moved.

'Look, why don't I call her? She's upstairs looking at the shower screen with Miranda.'

'Looking at the shower screen?' Faith's mother seemed satisfied. 'Well, that's good. We won't disturb her.'

'Oh, okay. Up to you.' Ella smiled again.

'Yes, she knows her DIY.'

'I'd rather hoped she would.' Ella pulled a face. 'I'm full of ideas but not as practical as I'd like to think I am. Faith seems . . .' Ella stopped as she tried to find the right word.

'She's practical,' her mother said factually. 'There's nothing she can't do for herself. It's the way we brought her up. She used to drive the van for us, before she got her job at the surgery, that is. I do it now. And she's strong too, isn't she, Clive?'

Faith's father nodded, his eyes still smiling.

'Well,' Ella put her hands together in a gesture of

contentment. 'I'm really grateful for that. I think between us we can have this cottage looking pretty in no time.'

'That's right,' Faith's mother continued evenly. 'A woman needs to know things. It's an uncertain world.'

'Yes,' Ella found herself agreeing. 'And perhaps you'd both like to come round for supper one evening? You'd be more than welcome.'

'We'll see,' Faith's mother returned non-committally.

She watched them as they turned away, headed off down the garden path and climbed back on to the scooter. It was Faith's mother who was at the controls, her father settling behind her on the seat. She watched a moment longer, the box containing the drill clasped in her hands, then closed the front door.

'Drill's here!' she yelled, and mounted the stairs two at a time.

She found Miranda sitting on the toilet seat yawning as she tried to light a cigarette while Faith was tapping the shower screen with her fingernails. Ella squashed herself into the bathroom with them.

'Why do we need to do this, again?' Miranda asked vacantly. 'It seems like a lot of faff.'

'So that we can hang something on the hook,' Ella explained cheerfully. 'It's so tiny in here, and with all our stuff it's getting really cluttered. I want to hang a wash bag here.'

'Okay,' Miranda conceded, looking bored. She glanced at the box Ella was holding. 'Is that thing going to make a noise?'

'Drills do,' Faith said without looking round.

Miranda pulled a spoilt face at Faith's back and looked at Ella appealingly.

'Then do you really need me in here as well? There's hardly enough space for us to all stand up, let alone all put a hook in. Can't I just applaud your efforts from my bedroom?'

Ella drew in a patient breath.

'The idea,' she said brightly, 'is that we all do something together. It's part of the bonding experience.'

'You've done too many seminars,' Miranda quipped. She stood up, taking her cigarette and the ashtray with her, and sidled past Ella.

'You're not really going to miss out on the fun, are you?' Ella asked her back as she disappeared.

'Everything always looks better as you leave it behind,' Miranda stated, glancing over her shoulder at Faith who was examining the shower screen at close quarters. 'Yes, definitely. Now I can go and sit in my room and wish I was in here with you.'

Faith looked up at Ella as they heard Miranda's bedroom door swing shut.

'What did you say this was made of again?'

'Perspex. That's what I ordered.'

'Have you still got the label?'

'Hell, no. I peeled it off after the guy had fixed it up.'

Faith stood up straight and regarded Ella with puzzlement.

'You got a guy to fix this up?'

'Yes,' Ella said confidently.

'What, and you paid him to do it?'

'Yes.' Ella felt her face reddening. 'But anyhow, that's done now. Let's just make a hole and put the hook in. I didn't expect it to be a major exercise.'

'Okay.'

Ella watched as Faith took the box that her parents had brought, removed the electric drill, and fumbled around in the bottom for something else. She retrieved a pair of plastic goggles and fastened them around her head over her glasses, the elastic strap pushing her hair up into a bouffant. She looked like John McEnroe. They had already marked a dot where Ella wanted the hook to go. Faith pushed the plug into the hall socket, held the drill purposefully and switched it on. It whined deafeningly. Faith turned and mouthed something to Ella which she didn't catch. She nodded emphatically in response anyway.

This wasn't going to plan at all. Miranda had slunk away, the whole thing was more complicated than she wanted, and the object of the exercise had been to bring them closer together. Best now to get this over with as quickly as possible and think of something else they could work on. She had a vision of them all happily piling into the car and heading off to the stores on the ring road in search of shelving. Then they could put that up together. That would be more edifying than a bathroom hook. And Miranda would have to be interested because she'd said herself that she wanted some shelves in her bedroom. She inched closer to Faith's efforts. Now she was pointing the drill at the shower screen. She watched a little enviously as Faith's steady hand pressed the point against the Perspex and pushed gently.

There was a resounding bang. It sounded like a bomb going off. It was so sudden that Ella jumped physically into the air and screamed. Faith leapt back and fell against the toilet. A thousand fragments of glass shot through the air. The sound of the drill stopped immediately.

There was silence, only broken by Miranda's door being ripped open and her raised voice as she threw open the bathroom door and stared inside with a white face.

'What the fuck – Jesus! Ella, you're covered in blood!'

'I should have trusted my instincts.'

'Stop mumbling, will you?' Miranda snapped at Faith from the plastic seat beside her in the casualty section of the John Radcliffe hospital. 'I think we've established that Ella was wrong and you were right, even if you didn't quite manage to say so when it mattered. Happy now?'

'I knew it.' Faith looked down at her hands. There were several small red incisions where the glass had entered. 'I meant to say.'

'Well, Ella's going to have more scars than you. Does that make it quits?'

Faith fell silent.

Ella blew upwards, fanning her fringe and cooling her hot face.

'It was the manufacturer's fault. I asked them for a Perspex one. I was sure that was what they'd delivered.'

'It was fortified glass,' Faith whispered. 'I knew by the sound when I tapped it. I should have said.'

'Well, yes, if you'd said none of us would be here now. We'd be down the flipping pub, wouldn't we?' Miranda threw her weight back on her chair. 'But you didn't say, so here we are.'

Faith sniffed. Ella poked her cheek tentatively. It was very sore, but at least it was only one side and at least, miraculously, the stray fragments of shattered glass had missed her eyes. The surge of blood had come from several cuts on her lower arm where her shirtsleeves had been rolled up. She glanced down the row of seats at Faith, who was now studying her trainers as if they were fascinating. She had tiny dots of red on her face, but only beyond the area of her goggles. She looked as if she'd been sunbathing in very big sunglasses.

'I'm sorry, Faith,' Ella said firmly. 'It was my fault.'

Faith's shoulders dropped.

'No, it was all my fault. I should have said.'

Miranda shot to her feet and paced across the tiled floor. Around them, patients waiting philosophically for attention looked up.

'How many times do you want to say "I should have said"? Shall we just get it over with now? Say it fifteen times in a row, and get it out of your system.' Miranda's voice was stretched with impatience. 'If I hear it once more, I'm going to scream.'

Faith looked up slowly, wincing as she pulled her hands on to her knees.

'Scream then,' she said quietly. 'It'll make you look like a loony, but it won't scare me.'

'Come on, you two,' Ella interjected, her finger placed over the biggest cut on her arm to stop it leaking. 'This doesn't achieve anything.'

'No,' Faith said, her eyes still on Miranda. 'But she uses her temper as a threat. And I'm not threatened by it. As long as she knows that, she might stop doing it.'

Ella blinked at Faith. Miranda twirled round to turn her back on Faith as if to block out her comment. She stalked across the corridor and pretended to read a poster stuck to the wall. It read, 'Do you know anybody who hasn't got a spleen?' Ella blinked at Faith again, not quite sure what to think. A nurse rustled towards them with an inappropriately cheery smile and addressed them in a perky Irish accent.

'How are we? Ready to have this dealt with now?'

'Yes.' Faith stood up.

Ella hesitated. She wanted to say no and go home again, taking all her bits of glass with her, but she stood up and followed Faith, her stomach melting like a jelly in a warm room. She tried to make a noise as positive as Faith's but it came out as a croak.

'You won't need me,' Miranda said, finding her seat possessively. 'I'll wait here.'

Ella and Faith sat side by side as the nurse worked away at them in turn. A few minor injections of local anaesthetic in the places where the glass had entered most deeply, but otherwise they might as well have sat at home with eyebrow tweezers and pulled the specks of glass out themselves. It took an hour to clean them both up, daub them both with antiseptic and dot them with plasters. Ella escaped with only two plasters on her face, one above her eyebrow and one on her cheek. Faith emerged with five plasters around her face, one fastened squarely under her nose. It looked like a small pink moustache.

'There,' the nurse finished, tossing the tweezers into a kidney dish and patting down Ella's last plaster. 'And in future, get the experts to do it. Exploding shower screen, dear me!' She pealed off into laughter. 'That's the best I've had in here all week. On your way, now!'

Faith said nothing. The nurse was called away, leaving them to roll down their sleeves and make a move in their own time. Ella fastened her shirt at the cuffs.

'Faith? Do I look as stupid as you?'

Faith assessed her face calmly.

'Yes.'

'Right. A night in then.'

'Ella? About the surveillance guy?'

Ella stood up stiffly.

'Yes?' The thought of it made her breath tighten. Both the arrival of the police and the exploding shower screen had been situations that she hadn't been able to control. It brought on a feeling of bewilderment that she wasn't accustomed to.

'Did I mess it up when those guys came round?'

'Not at all.'

She tried to pull a comical face at her. Faith pulled down the sleeves of her loose jumper and stood up.

'It's funny,' she said. 'I was so terrified when they came round earlier, but now you've explained it, I feel left out. They could have used my room.'

'Don't be daft.' Ella took her arm. Faith stiffened. Gracefully, Ella released it again as they left the curtained cubicle and walked back through Casualty to find Miranda.

Miranda was flicking through a copy of *Good*

Housekeeping, her face a picture of disgust. She stood up with relief as she saw them approach and threw the magazine on the seat of the chair behind her.

'There you are. I thought you'd both been admitted for the night and forgotten to tell me. These bloody places—' She stopped as they both reached her and surveyed both of their faces in turn. 'Christ, Faith. You look like Hitler.'

'And you look like Barbara Cartland,' Faith retorted. 'At least my moustache's only temporary.'

'You could write scripts for Hale and Pace,' Miranda returned flatly. 'And I wouldn't be so certain that your moustache's only a temporary feature. Get yourself a magnifying mirror.'

Ella stood at a loss for words. As she did exercises with her mouth trying to think of something constructive to say, Miranda produced her car keys and jangled them.

'Home?'

'Too bloody right,' Faith said.

'Right then,' Ella contributed, trying to keep up with them both as they strode ahead of her towards the exit.

Chapter Six

There was still no message from Matt. Ella couldn't quite understand it. She ran his words through her head over and over again. He'd said that his wife was away for the *weekend*, not just for Friday night. The whole weekend. Which should mean that he could use the phone. He had her number on the class list, and she knew he took his paperwork home with him – she'd seen him packing it away into a battered leather case in the evening.

It was possible he was worried about her number showing up on an itemised bill. That would be understandable. In which case, he could have nipped out to a phone box or rung her from a pub.

One thing she was quite sure about – she was not going to become Matt's mistress. When she was younger, more naive, and more gullible it was possible for her to be hoodwinked into becoming a regular mistress. That was something she could pass off as the inexperience of youth. But she wasn't going that far again. There was strong physical attraction between herself and Matt, and they obviously found each other intriguing. Whether it was a relationship with the potential to blossom, and whether or not his marriage was in such trouble that he was ready to move on, was something she couldn't know until they'd had a chance to talk about it properly. And if only he'd get in touch and give her the opportunity to explain things from her own point of view, she wouldn't be feeling quite so much like a hopeful teenager.

She'd always been rational about relationships. Nobody had broken her heart, and she wasn't aware that she'd broken anyone else's either. Her mother had often said, 'One day, my girl, you'll fall headlong. And that'll be it. You'll join the human race.' But she would expect her mother to say that. Her mother understood love and devotion, but she'd never understood independence.

It wasn't that Ella herself was cold. She'd had boyfriends, and she'd been upset and disappointed when relationships hadn't worked out – but she'd never been desperate or devastated by a rejection. She had an ability to reason herself out of trauma, a cool head she'd always assumed she'd inherited from her father. Or perhaps that he'd installed inside her. With no son to mould in his image, he'd turned to Ella for company, and as she grew up, conversation and stimulation. He'd been a financial consultant – a highly successful one – until his retirement, and he'd welcomed Ella into his study from her earliest years to show her his work, to explain what he was doing. She remembered being invited into his room to share time with him when it was out of bounds to her mother. He'd taken her small hand and led her into his world. She'd felt chosen. When she was very little and desperate for his attention, she'd felt that somehow she'd got one over on her mother – she must have been more interesting to him. She was sought out when her mother wasn't.

As she'd got older, she'd just accepted it, as her mother had. There hadn't been any bad feeling about it.

Her father had a view on marriage which he'd shared with her. 'Love comes and goes, but team-work stays. It's more important to work together than to play together.' Maybe she wouldn't have used those words herself, but she had no reason to believe him drastically wrong.

So, with Matt, she was acting on physical attraction and their shared interest in things horticultural. They'd be a good team. She wasn't naive enough to believe that men only had affairs when their marriages were dead in the water – but with Matt it wasn't just about having a fun time on the side.

No, she would not be his mistress. She'd make all that clear as soon as she had a chance to talk to him privately. And seeing as they'd been intimate on Friday night, and seeing as he wasn't a gauche adolescent, she was sure he would find a way to contact her over the weekend, just to address the situation in an adult manner.

By Sunday he still hadn't called.

'I'm meeting a friend in Oxford this afternoon,' Miranda announced, wafting past the television, and stopping next to the sofa to give Faith a black look. 'Why do you need to watch the *EastEnders* omnibus, for flip's sake? You watched every single episode in the week.'

Faith looked up from her spaghetti rings on toast and adjusted her glasses.

'Actually you had a phone call on Tuesday night, if

you remember. You talked all the way through the last fifteen minutes.'

Miranda shook her head and strolled on to the kitchen.

'Well, I guess if you had any friends, you might get phone calls too. Can't expect you to understand.'

Ella looked up from *The Tree and Shrub Expert*. She was trying to identify some conifers from a photocopied sheet Matt had given them. Badly drawn – but that would be his impatience with tiny detail. It had been making her smile. But she noticed Faith's cheeks were flushed with annoyance again and the plaster under her nose was twitching. Miranda was slamming things around in the kitchen.

'Going out?' She decided to opt for a pleasant tone. 'Don't you want to come to B&Q with us?'

Miranda stuck her head back round the door.

'You two are going to B&Q? Looking like that?'

Ella patted the plaster on her forehead.

'It's not that bad, is it?'

Miranda raised an eyebrow and said nothing. She swung her handbag on to her shoulder, car keys in hand. Ella leant over the side of the armchair.

'So who you meeting in town?'

'An old friend.'

'Not Mike then?'

'I'm meeting an old friend,' Miranda said starkly, in a tone of voice that suggested that there would be no debate.

'Oh, right. Sure. Have a great time.' Ella gave her a casual wave and turned her attention back to her book. After she'd heard the front door slam she let her book fall on to her lap and gazed at Albert Square instead.

'A friend?' She heard the clink of Faith's fork landing heavily on her plate and glanced over. Faith gathered herself together and stood up.

'I can't eat any more of this.'

'Can't say I blame you. We should have clubbed together and done a roast or something. Maybe next week?'

Faith wandered out to the kitchen. Ella sat quietly whilst she heard the crashing of crockery in the washing up bowl. She scratched at her plaster thoughtfully.

Why was everybody in such a bad mood? Miranda had a date whenever she wanted one. She'd said before that since her divorce she only saw men as snacks, so she had no reason to be unhappy. Faith didn't have a date, but she didn't want one anyway so it didn't matter. Ella was the one who should be being churlish. She was the one who didn't know where she stood. She was the one with the reason to be complicated.

'Actually,' Faith interrupted her thoughts as she shuffled back through the living room in her slippers. 'I think I'll go and read in my room.'

Ella sat up straight, disconcerted.

'I thought we were going to B&Q?'

'Maybe next week? I'm not in the mood any more.'

Ella opened her mouth to protest but Faith headed for the latch on the door, flicked it, sidled out into the hall, and the door closed behind her. Ella heard her heavy footsteps on the stairs.

'Oh, fine!' Ella tossed her book on to the floor.

'What's the point of sharing a house if you all fuck off?' She pulled a grotesque face at the door and added, 'I said, fuck off!' for good measure.

She slumped back into her chair and stared mutinously at the television. Phil Mitchell said, 'got it sorted', but still she couldn't raise a smile. She swivelled her eyes to the telephone, polished and silent on a small table near the kitchen door. Her eyes bored into it, sending Matt an urgent psychic message, and she gave it several seconds for him to respond. Nothing. She let out a long breath. She mustn't slump, whatever she did. That wasn't allowed.

'No problem,' she urged herself, getting up from the armchair and kicking her book across the carpet. 'I'll just paint the frame on the mirror then. And I'll do it on my own.'

She paused as she was about to stride out through the kitchen to the garden shed and retrieve the heavy, second-hand mirror she'd found for the hall. She glanced up at the ceiling and frowned. Faith in her bedroom, reading? Really?

Faith pulled her bedroom door closed behind her. As soon as she did, the relief flooded through her. Sanctuary. She wandered across the rug to her small stereo, picked up a CD, slipped it into the tray and pressed Play. She fiddled with the volume control. At first she set it to play very loudly, then she inched it down gently until it hummed as background sound. There was no reason to remind Ella that she existed. Most of the time, Ella remembered. And she'd heard the back door go which suggested Ella had gone out to play in the garden shed again, so her point would be lost anyway. If Miranda had been in the house it would be a different matter.

The knot tightened in her stomach again when she thought of Miranda. Beautiful, serene, confident. At ease with herself and at ease with the world. A woman who had always known exactly who she was, and had the arrogance to think she could sum everyone else up after a split second of assessment. The thought that she was putting herself about with the likes of Mike and Oliver was revolting. She had no idea what they were really like. Especially Mike.

She gazed around her bedroom. It was the smallest of the bedrooms, but she'd had first choice of the two that were still free when Ella had chosen her to share the house. She preferred a small room. It made her feel bigger.

She'd had very little stuff to bring with her. She couldn't understand why Miranda had arrived with a carful of bags and boxes. Faith had her bedside lamp, the rug with the dolphin on it her uncle had made for her when she was a child, some blankets and her bedspread from her old bed. She'd brought her bedside table too. It was one her mother had knocked together for her from a wardrobe that she'd dismantled once. She hadn't wanted to intrude her personality on Ella's house, that would have been presumptuous, but the bedside table didn't take up much space. There was room for her radio alarm on the top, and now the book Ella had lent her was placed there too.

Ella hadn't minded at all about her bringing her compact stereo to put in the bedroom either. She'd stood it on the chest of drawers Ella had provided. Her parents had never minded it, although she'd never, ever turned the volume up at home. Her father had chuckled when she'd bought it, two years ago, and they'd sat round on a Saturday night at the kitchen table and all read the instructions through together before trying to set it up. They'd let her father attempt to attach the wires to the right holes at first, but just as he'd been announcing that it was broken and that she'd have to return it and get another, her mother had stepped in and pushed the leads into the correct sockets. He'd smiled amiably and tutted.

She sat on the edge of the bed and gazed over at the window, homesickness gnawing at her. It was Sunday afternoon. After *EastEnders*, her parents would be making the most of the afternoon, out in the small field they owned, digging and sorting for the van. She loved the field. She'd spent her weekend afternoons out there since she was a toddler. At first, just playing. Making castles out of the mud with empty seed trays, chasing white butterflies, and crawling between the bean poles to stick her head out from the leaves suddenly to make her father laugh. Later, when she was at school, she'd look forward to the weekends in the field. It was a place where they couldn't get her. Even when her mother urged her to do something with her friends, she'd shake her head and say that she was happier watching them both, helping with the work, enjoying the oasis of calm before the beginning of the next school week.

She had brought friends home once or twice. Some of them knew that the veggie van sold confectionery too. There was always a small stock of boxes in the outhouse full of chocolate and crisps. Friends who came home always asked to see the outhouse, and she always showed them. Then they would ask her if they could have a Twix, or a packet of crisps, and she'd say no initially, because she knew her mother would say no, and otherwise it was theft. But they'd talk her into it, and she'd hand over something, knowing that otherwise they'd leave. Then they'd want to see the kittens, or the puppies, or whatever attraction it was the house provided. She'd show them, they'd ignore her while they played with the animals, then they'd stand up, full of crisps, chocolate and satisfaction that they'd seen the pets, and say that they had to go.

Then they'd tell the others that her house smelt of cat wee, that her parents were dwarves with ugly faces, and that Faith was even more boring at home than she was at school. Not a game in the house, and nothing but the telly to keep them all from descending into total madness. And they all smelt of veg too. There wasn't even an upstairs bathroom, so it was no wonder they never washed. And Faith was getting fatter and fatter, almost visibly by the day. It was no wonder she smelt like a turnip. She was turning into one. It was so, so funny.

Faith threw herself back on her bedspread and curled up, pulling her knees up to her chin and wrapping her arms securely around her legs. ELO washed over her. She closed her eyes and listened, allowing the music to carry her away to a world where everybody was interesting. It was her first happy memory, 'Mr Blue Sky'. Her parents had bought her a tiny radio for her birthday one year. She must have been about six or seven. It was such a responsibility, to own a radio. And she'd put it on radio two, which was what her mother listened to when she drove the van. That afternoon, as she'd fiddled with the tiny, serrated tuning wheel, she'd heard 'Mr Blue Sky' for the very first time. It had filled her with joy. It was a happy song. It made her feel happy too.

She'd discovered another thing that made her happy as she'd got older and as one by one the others at school stopped talking to her. The beautiful people were good at English, and History, and Art. She didn't know why, but they were. They could say what they meant, put it into words that she hadn't thought of. But they could never do science. To Faith, science was obvious. It became the one arena of her life, apart from the field, where the mist fell away and the world was revealed in a clear light, where colours were bright and distinguished.

She never answered questions in class. It only made the others snort with laughter. But she always knew the answer and sat patiently with it in her head until somebody else said it, or until the teacher gave up and explained it on the blackboard. Once, in Chemistry, she'd made a big mistake. She was fifteen. She'd sat the end of year exam and she'd worked her way through the question paper, her brain racing, her pen speeding as she wrote the answers down. When the papers had been marked and handed back, the rumour had got out that she'd got over ninety per cent. That afternoon, on the way home from school, she'd been followed. They'd punished her for it.

From that point on, she made sure she never distinguished herself at anything again. It was only when she was sitting her 'A' levels, when she knew she was leaving the school after the last exam and would never have to sit in a class with them again, when she knew that she wanted to work with animals and that good 'A' level results were important to being allowed to do so, that she answered the questions to the best of her ability. The results had been sent to the school. Unlike the others, she didn't rip open the envelope in the corridor, shout, laugh or cry about it with the crowd, or join them down the pub for the end of year celebrations. She slid away in silence, took her envelope home, went into her bedroom with it, sat down on the dolphin rug, and opened it carefully. At first she couldn't understand the bold print on the thin sliver of paper. She had to look at it for a long time to work it out. But it wasn't a mistake. She'd got three straight As.

She told her parents she'd passed and done well, but she didn't tell them about the grades. They would only feel guilty and miserable if they thought she wanted to leave them behind to go to university or some such thing that the others were doing. And she couldn't. The thought of it made her breathless with panic. They'd followed her home from school, not just once, but particularly on that awful occasion. What would it be like if they could get into her room and find her when she was alone? What would they do to her? What would they call her, there? Turnip, or something worse? And anyway, she knew where she was happy. At home, in the field, or with animals. They noticed her, and they responded to her. They didn't look at her and see a fat, ugly thing. She drove the van until the job came up that she wanted, in the surgery in the High Street, near home. She fretted and cried at night until she got the letter saying that they were delighted to offer her the job. Then she cried even harder, on her own, in her room. It was the first time she'd been chosen above anybody else.

Until Ella had chosen her. Faith blinked across the room at the wall where the clusters of pink flowers on the wallpaper were fading. Ella had said they'd give all the rooms a lick of paint in time. She wasn't sure she wanted that. She quite liked the flowers. Perhaps she'd talk to Ella about it.

It had been her mother's idea that she move into a house where she could share with other women. It wasn't that she really wanted to move herself, but her mother was usually right when she had ideas, and she said that at twenty-six, Faith should really think about being around people nearer her age. She so rarely went out. Occasionally with her colleagues from the surgery, but nobody bothered to ring her especially.

She'd come to the cottage to be interviewed by Ella, and had seen a strong-featured, striking woman with long tanned legs and humour in her eyes. She looked Italian. Nothing like any of the women Faith had met before. She was worldly and self-assured. Faith had assumed she'd be a businesswoman of some sort. She looked like one, even though on that day she'd been in shorts with a silky cardigan thrown over the top. Faith was surprised to hear about her horticulture course, and her reasons for wanting to do it. She'd told her about the field and the veggie van, and Ella had seemed to be interested, although she hadn't asked her much about it since. But Ella wasn't going to have a field and a veggie van. She'd probably set up some huge nursery somewhere, if she stuck to it, and make lots of money. Maybe she'd design fountains, or garden statues or something. Or landscape rich people's lawns. She could see her doing that, but not digging up vegetables. After the interview, Faith had thanked Ella for her time, knowing that it was ludicrous to think that Ella would want her in her house. She was stunned when she'd offered her a room there and then.

She reached out and picked up the book that Ella had lent her. Idly, she flicked it open and began to read a passage somewhere in the middle. She settled into the bed comfortably, her head on the pillow, and leafed through some more pages, picking out the headers and the short paragraphs below. A slight frown furrowed her brow. What men want? Do this, but don't do that? But Ella knew exactly who she was and what she wanted. Why on earth had she gone out and spent money on this book?

Browns was vibrating with gentle chatter and the click of cutlery on crockery. A diffusion of light filtered down from the glass of the roof, filling the vaulted dining room with thick shafts of sunlight as if it was a spacious aquarium. The restaurant was full considering the university term hadn't started, packed with families, groups of friends, tourists, and lovers. The smell of steak and Guinness pie teased

Miranda's nostrils as she pushed her way in and stopped at the neat box of the reception desk to speak to a striking girl in a white shirt and short black skirt who had dutifully shot towards her.

'I'm expected. A table in the name of Anderson?'

'Let's just have a look.' A clear, white smile as the waitress ran her pen down a list. 'Yes, your friend's already here. I'll show you to the table.'

'Thank you.'

Miranda followed the elegant, swaying young figure, aware that between the two of them they were attracting appreciative looks from men who happened to glance up from their family groups, cutlery grasped. She shook back her hair and straightened her shoulders. Bloody Faith and her bloody maths. So, she might be thirty-five, but her looks were as vibrant as they ever were. Her age was just a number. It certainly hadn't stopped her being a regular choice for the private, exclusive flights she now crewed for. The money was superb. Enough for her to be very picky about the work she decided to do. The work was sporadic, but that was all part of freelancing. What she was offered was exciting. She'd crewed for U2 in the summer, and another job had just come up going to the Middle East, one where the staff were required to have top level security screening. That wasn't a problem. She'd played the game strategically and used her brain. She was as likely to be on the shortlist for high-profile politicians as major celebrities. The Middle East job would be the highest paid of her assignments to date, but it would overlap with a job which would take her to the States, and she would need to go back to the States again soon. She was mulling it over.

But Oxford was a pleasant base. The cottage was cosy. It was perfect for access to Heathrow and London if she needed to be there, and at least she wasn't alone. God, how she hated being alone. She'd had enough of suburban hotel living in her days as a stewardess for the novelty to have died a death, and her last base, a fashionable flat in Kensington, had been lonely in the gaps between the parties. She could afford something better than a room in Ella's cottage, but it suited her. She'd wanted to get right out of London, right away from the sprawl and into a rural environment. It was the closest thing to a home she'd known in a long time, and that was good enough for now. In between assignments, she was picking up temping work in the town which kept her busy. It was an experiment in many ways, but it was different, and she'd needed a change from the way she'd done things before. Ella was fine, if a bit of a control freak. Faith was just a freak. But they both amused her in different ways.

The waitress stopped at a small, round table for two set against the wall at the back of the room. He was already seated, smoking a cigarette, his black hair combed back, a pair of mirror shades reflecting the bustle of the room.

'Can I take your coat?' She was treated to another broad smile from the waitress. She felt a spike of envy. She'd been gorgeous and smiling herself at twenty-odd years old. She was still told she was gorgeous, but what had happened to the smiling part? How long since she'd smiled because of a happy feeling that came from deep down inside?

'Thank you.'

She divested herself of her thigh-length brown leather jacket, unwound the loose chiffon of her gold scarf, and handed them to the waitress, who disappeared. She paused to consider her companion, took an undetectable lungful of breath, and pulled out her chair.

'Hello, Patrick,' she addressed him, sitting down and drawing in her chair. She produced a smile, something she was so used to doing that it no longer bore any relation to feeling like smiling. Her face felt tight. She hesitated over her next question but voiced it smoothly. 'How's Lance?'

'Hello, Miranda.' His lips remained straight. 'Lance is concerned. I think you'd better explain what's going on.'

Chapter Seven

'Jesus, what the hell is that!'

Ella careered into Miranda's back as she stopped abruptly in the hall. A piece of toast and marmalade shot off her plate and skidded along the cream carpet.

'Oh, now look! You can't just stop in here. There isn't room. And I'm going to be late at this rate. I haven't even done my face.'

'What's that!' Miranda pointed at the full-length mirror which for the moment Ella had leaned against the hall wall, hoping that at some point Faith would see it and offer to get the right sort of drill from home to fix it up. And this time, she'd leave Faith to deal with it from start to finish. She'd painted the ornate frame yesterday afternoon, propped it against the shed to dry out, and found it was dry by the time she went to bed. So she'd brought it in and put it on the floor near to where she hoped it would end up. Miranda obviously hadn't spotted it when she'd come in, very late, the night before.

Ella picked up her toast and groaned at the sight of blobs of wool on her marmalade. At least there wasn't so much marmalade on the wool, but she was starting to realise what a stupid colour cream was for a hall carpet.

'I just thought it would be nice to have a mirror

down here, so that we can check we're gorgeous before we rush out in the morning.'

'Well, nice idea I suppose, as long as Faith's reflection doesn't crack it.' Miranda pulled on a long linen jacket from the hooks where all their coats were bulging. They really needed some more hooks too. It looked as if a pregnant woman was hiding behind the coats. Miranda pinched the ends of her hair, looking over her shoulder at herself in the mirror. 'You could paint the frame. Then it'd look quite nice.'

Ella stood up, toast in hand, and stared at Miranda's reflection.

'I have painted it.'

'Oh, I see.' Miranda was reaching in her handbag for her car keys. 'Sorry, didn't mean to be rude. That's the undercoat, then.'

'No!' Ella pulled her shirt more firmly about her body with her free hand and tried not to get aggravated. It was bad enough having to contemplate facing Matt again and trying to find a moment to speak to him on his own. That was about as much as she could cope with first thing on a Monday morning. 'That's the finished product.'

'Oh.'

Miranda stopped to assess the mirror again. She looked at Ella expressionlessly as she moved towards the front door.

'It's fashionable!' Ella asserted, anguish rising in her stomach. 'Haven't you watched any of those programmes where they transform furniture? You paint it, then you take a cloth and dab away at it until it's got that – that natural look.'

'So you paint it and wipe it all off again so it just

looks like an undercoat. And in mint green too. Nice.'
Miranda's clear eyes sparkled. 'Look, ignore me. I'm
going to be late if I'm not careful. Byeeee!'

She slipped out of the front door and crashed it
closed behind her. Ella stared at the door disconsolately.

'You weren't even here to offer advice, you
miserable old bag.'

'Morning.' Faith's soft voice greeted her as she
plodded down the stairs with wet hair, heaving the
enormous bag she took to work over her shoulder.

'What's wrong with that?' Ella pointed at the
mirror. Faith stood away from the mirror so that she
couldn't see herself and studied the frame.

'Is that what you were doing yesterday?'

'Yes.' Ella bit her lips together. 'What—' She
swallowed. 'What do you think? I mean, what do you
really think?'

Faith glanced at Ella uncertainly, nudged her
glasses up her nose, winced as she caught a fingernail
on the plaster under her nostrils, and considered the
frame again carefully.

'I quite like the way you can still see the gold paint
through the green.'

'You do?'

'Yes. Sort of. Sorry, I've got to start walking now,
Ella. Can I talk to you about it properly this evening?'

Ella took a savage bite of her toast and earned
herself a mouthful of carpet fluff. She quickly spat it
out again on to her plate.

'Sorry. It's just I have to be on time because Janet's
always late and somebody has to be there to take the
early calls. I'll have to run as it is.'

'Oh, sure. Off you go.'

Ella opened the front door for her and waved her through. Faith slipped past, fastening the buttons on her raincoat.

'Sorry.'

'Bugger off.'

'Okay.'

Ella stood, plate in one hand, the other hand on the latch of the door, and wondered if her frame would look better in natural light. There was no window in the front door, and it was a bit stark under the hundred watt bulb of the hall light. She pulled the front door wide open and shifted the mirror along a bit to examine it. Her mouth drooped.

Last night it had looked like a success. She'd done exactly what she'd seen them all do on the telly and she'd felt a buzz of satisfaction that she'd emulated it. Today it looked as if she'd handed a pot of green poster paint to a gang of three-year-olds and let them loose on her frame.

'Bollocks!' she ejected as forcefully as possible. And she was running late, and although she'd got her jeans and shirt on already, she'd have to rush her face. Today, of all days, when she wanted to look stunning in a healthy and natural sort of way for Matt. 'Oh, bollocks again. Big, hairy, bulgy, fat BOLLOCKS!'

But there was no time to stand and swear. She turned to the front door to close it and did a double-take.

The man from CID was standing on her doorstep. Literally just standing there, quietly, looking at her over the threshold. She felt her face paling. For a moment she couldn't move or speak. She clutched her plate with the furry toast on it with an iron grip.

'Good morning,' he said.

'Morning,' she echoed.

There was another short silence. He put his head on one side to examine her.

'I'm sorry I didn't ring. I was hoping to catch you before you went off to work.'

She nodded. He must have heard her saying 'bollocks'.

'I hate Mondays,' she said by way of explanation.

'Me too,' he said.

It was the most human thing she'd heard him say so far. Almost friendly. But his eyes weren't friendly. They were still black and obscure. She'd reserve her judgement on how friendly he was.

'Can I come in?'

'Oh, yes. Sorry.' She stood aside to let him walk into the hall, sidling around the huge bulge of their coats and ending up buried in Faith's anorak as she twisted around to let him past and shut the door behind him. She heard a loud clonk and a cry of pain.

'What was that?' She pushed the anorak out of her eyes and stood up straight. He was clutching his shin through his black denims and wincing at her.

'I caught my leg on that bloody mirror.'

'Oh, I'm sorry. It's just there temporarily.'

He nodded tensely, glancing at it again with dislike.

'When you've finished painting it you'd better hang it up, otherwise someone's going to do themselves a serious injury.'

She stared at him feeling a new, strange urge to do

him some serious injury. Pushing her furry marmalade toast into his face would have been satisfying. But then she'd be up on an assault charge trying to explain that it was because he'd turned up, insulted her mirror, and made sure by his timely arrival that she would have no time to do anything with her face other than a squirt of moisturiser and a quick flick with the mascara. What a bastard he really was.

'So what is it you want? I'm in a hurry.'

He looked at her with surprise this time. Well, perhaps she'd been a wimp when he'd come round on Saturday, but she could do bossy too, and she could do it bloody well. She'd known for a fact that several of the guys on the trading floor had actively avoided her because they were frightened of her. She arched an eyebrow at him impatiently. Something flickered across his black eyes. She hoped it wasn't amusement.

'I've come round to set up. We need access to the house and at the moment we can only do that when you're actually in.'

'Obviously,' she said.

'Although it would be very helpful if you'd let us have a spare key so that we can come and go when we need to.'

'What?' Ella slammed her plate of toast down on the stairs and stuck her hands on her hips. She glared at him indignantly. 'You want a key to my house? Jesus, no way! I'd never know from one minute to the next if you were going to stroll in when I was in the bath, or in the kitchen in my underwear, or having friends round, or – do I need to go on?'

'No.'

'Good.'

'So the other alternative is that you're here when we're here. Or I should say, when I'm here. There'll be a couple of us setting up today, but after that I'll be on my own.'

'I can't do that. Obviously. I've got a life.'

'I didn't suggest you hadn't.'

'I can't just take time off from my course when I feel like it. I'm studying for a professional qualification. Course work and practical assessment are crucial to it. I can't just nip off halfway through a session saying that the cops are coming round.'

'I wasn't suggesting you do that either. And for your own safety, you'd be better not to tell anyone that the cops are coming round.'

'I wouldn't really say that.' She stood up tall to him. He seemed to be getting taller and taller with every sensible statement he made. 'But I can't babysit for you when you need to be here. You'll just have to do it on your own.'

She'd tried to sound as acidic as possible. He looked back at her blankly, pausing only to rub at his shin again.

'How do you suggest we get in, then? Chimney? Through a back window? Blow a hole in the wall?'

'That's really your problem, isn't it?'

She glanced at her watch in agitation. Twenty to nine. No time now for moisturiser even. And she'd have to put her mascara on while she was driving. She clenched her teeth. He was still studying her with something akin to patience. She didn't think that was what detectives, or whatever he was, were famous for. Didn't they run around with their ties over their shoulders shouting, 'Freeze!' at the end of every sentence? She ran his words through her head again.

'Well, if you are going to blow a hole in the wall, do it quietly or Doris next door will die of a heart attack. She nearly has a stroke every time I say hello to her when I'm hanging the washing out.'

He took a deep breath and exhaled slowly.

'Look, Miss Norton—'

'Ella.' She wasn't going to be prim with him. Let him fear her for her personality, not her choice of title.

'Ella. You've agreed to let us use the house, for which we're very grateful. Getting cooperation from the public is intensely difficult. You wouldn't believe how often we can't prosecute through lack of evidence.'

'I didn't think it usually stopped you.' The words were out. She shut her mouth again quickly. He was obviously not amused.

'I'm not here on a PR mission. We've got a serious job to do. If you've changed your mind about helping us, just say so now, please. That way we can stop wasting each other's time.'

She scratched at her forehead while she thought about it. Her plaster caught her fingertips. She pulled her hand away quickly. She'd got used to it being there – and the smaller one on the side of her cheek too. He hadn't commented on them. But then, he wouldn't. He was very focused on his job. Perhaps that's why he riled her. It was almost as if she was irrelevant to him, just a faceless figure in the way of his work. She wondered if he was married. She couldn't imagine him climbing into bed in his pyjamas and giving someone a goodnight cuddle. He'd have a bachelor pad, probably. Full of black and chrome. With a lamp shaped like a corkscrew in the corner. With a big spike on top. She flashed a glance at his hand in search of a wedding ring. No evidence of that, but men often didn't wear them. Especially not the macho sort. Very few of the married guys she'd known in banking bothered with rings. They said it cramped their style.

'What we could do, for example,' he continued calmly, 'is come in now and let ourselves out when we're finished. And in future I can let you know when I need access and only come when it suits you. In the morning before you go to work, or later in the evening. We can forget about a key. I understand your concern.'

She suddenly felt churlish and unreasonable. It wasn't very public spirited of her to throw him out and refuse to cooperate because she hadn't had time to do two coats of mascara. She took a long breath and let her shoulders drop. She pushed her hair out of her eyes and tried to look more pleasant.

'Look, DI Jasmin-bin. Mr Singh. I'm sorry, I can't remember your name.'

'Jaz will do.'

'Thank you. Jaz. I apologise for being snotty. I'm late for my class, I haven't identified my conifers and I think my phone's on the blink. My shower screen exploded this weekend and I spent three hours painting a mirror which now looks like something from *Vision On*. I've now got three seconds to transform myself from Marc Bolan into Sophia Loren. Your timing wasn't brilliant.'

'Sorry,' he said. He almost looked rueful. His eyelashes looked longer and blacker when his expression softened. He must have been a beautiful child. She surprised herself with the thought. But she could picture him with soft, silky, jet black hair and luminous dark eyes, running round a garden somewhere with a water pistol. She frowned at him, as if the vision that had flitted through her head were entirely his fault.

'I've got to go. Let yourself out when you're done,' she said curtly.

'Fine. I'll collect what we need from the car now and bring in my colleague. And thank you, Ella. You've no idea how important this sort of attitude is to us.'

'No problem.' Ella turned and vaulted up the stairs, putting her bare foot on her toast and marmalade.

'Oh for God's sake!' she hissed under her breath. She turned round with a red face to see what he'd made of that display, but he'd already gone.

Ella cast a covert look at the cottage two doors down as she drove past, then looked back at the road. It wasn't a house she'd particularly noticed before. It was boring and ramshackle, like most of them in the row, and indistinguishable from a normal house. It wouldn't do to start taking a special interest in the comings and goings of number eleven, but curiosity needled at her. Somewhere beyond the initial alarm that the arrival of a brace of policemen had brought on was a tiny thrill that she was involved in something important. She'd never been judgemental about drugs, or given it a great deal of thought, but was sure now that number eleven must be crammed full of hard-nosed, Pete Postlethwaite lookalikes hiding behind the closed curtains. She wasn't sure if that was how it worked, but deep down her sense of moral duty stirred. As long as they didn't know who Jaz was, or think it strange that a hunky Asian guy had taken it upon himself to pay frequent visits to their cottage, everything would be fine.

'Hunky.'

She drew her brows together as she gained speed on a straight bit of lane and stabbed at the radio for a snatch of the news. Well, he was hunky. That thought had slipped out. Would he be offended if he knew she thought of him as a 'hunky Asian guy'? That wasn't something she'd given much thought either. But it was hardly likely to crop up in their conversations, if they ever had any. 'How should I think of you, DI Jaz Singh?' No, it was ludicrous. What would he say? 'Think of me just as a git who's invading your space.' That would be accurate enough. As long as he didn't fiddle with anything. Or move anything around. She knew where everything was, and it always jarred when somebody else took it upon themselves to reorganise her. But he'd sense that. He'd seen the menacing look in her eyes.

She swung into the entrance to the college, pulling off at the muddy car park by the paddock where a couple of horses were chewing quietly to themselves and gazing at each other soulfully. Wasn't it tough for black and Asian officers? She'd read enough about it to think it was. She urged the car into a space and looked at her watch again.

'Oh, bugger.'

She grabbed her bag from the back seat, leapt out and slammed the car door, stopping to twist the keys in the lock.

'Hi, Ella!' It was John hailing her from across the car park. He trotted towards her in his clumpy boots, a wallet folder under his arm, tossing a cigarette to one side. 'Get your conifers done?'

'No, I ran out of time. Did most of them. What about you?'

'I was hoping I could sit next to you and cheat.'

'Somehow I think Pierre will be thrown completely if he has to change seats with anyone now. He seems to like routines.' She gave him a warm smile as they turned and trotted towards the hut where the classes were held. 'Thanks for turning up for the drinks on Friday.'

'Hey, no problem. It was cool.'

'Look, John, can I ask you a strange question?'

He laughed into the air as they jogged along.

'The answer's yes.'

'Yes?'

'You can have my body.'

She giggled at him. The sun appeared from a stretch of cloud and warmed them. She took a deep breath of farmyard air. It was great to be here, doing this on a Monday morning, whatever sort of reception Matt gave her. They slowed as they reached the concrete steps leading up to the hut.

'What's the question, then?' John asked, grinning at her.

'Well, actually, I wondered where you were born.'

He gave her a strange look, then he threw his head

back and laughed again. She wasn't sure there was so much humour there this time.

'Bloody hell, nothing strange about that question. I get asked it every five minutes.'

'Oh no, I didn't mean that. I'm so sorry. It's about something else. I—' She felt herself going red. 'Look, I really am sorry, John. It's just I've got this – this friend. He's Asian. I mean, he's obviously British, but must have had family from Asia. At some point. And I was just wondering some things that I hadn't really wondered before.'

It was getting worse. She was rambling and making a twit of herself, and John, who she liked, and who liked her, was giving her a very odd look. The last thing she wanted to do was offend him. She wished she could take her clumsy question back now.

'Look, Ella, if you want to discuss race relations, I really need to do it with a fag in my hand.'

'Okay.'

'Let's get inside.'

'Yes. Sorry.'

He pulled open the door and stepped back to allow her to enter the lobby first. She hesitated on the step.

'Look, I shouldn't have put it like that. There was no way it was going to come out right.'

'Stop treading on eggshells, you stupid woman. I was born in Clapham but I support the West Indies at cricket. Is that the sort of thing you mean?'

She cleared her throat, her cheeks hot.

'Sort of.' She stepped into the lobby and plucked at her shirt, ready to walk into the classroom. 'I – would you ever have thought of joining the police?'

She glanced back at John's face. His mouth was open, his eyes like golf balls, and she seemed to have stunned him into silence. She reached for the door handle, trying to compose herself. She could already hear Matt's voice resonating in the classroom. She heaved a sharp breath.

'Forget I asked that,' she mumbled, and pushed her way through the door.

Matt stopped in his monologue, his hand stretched out towards the blackboard, and waited for Ella and John as they stumbled to their seats.

'It's her fault,' John began instantly. 'We would have got here seven seconds earlier, but she suddenly turned into David bloody Dimbleby outside. And I haven't learnt the conifers. Sorry.'

'There's a surprise,' Matt quipped with good humour. 'Sadly, neither of you've missed the test. You need to get here much later to manage that.'

'I'll remember next time.'

Ella settled into her seat, returned Pierre's delighted grin with the warmest smile she could muster and took the spare test sheet which he'd saved for her.

'Thanks,' she whispered, slipping off her cardigan and hanging it over the back of her seat. She pulled a pen from her handbag, fiddled around as much as she could to avoid looking up, and ultimately gained enough composure to raise her eyes and see if Matt was going to acknowledge her. He glanced around the room as he began to explain the morning's routine, just as he would do usually, with a twinkle in his eye, plenty of humorous rejoinders, especially directed at John who sat right at the front and always had a challenging comment ready. It was definitely business as usual. Ella kept her eyes firmly on Matt. And then, just as she felt nothing in the world had changed between them, he winked at her.

A flood of warmth filled her body and she smiled stupidly back at him. Obviously there was a reason he hadn't phoned. His wife had probably come back early. Or his mother might have been ill. Perhaps he'd had a call from a friend in trouble, and had to ditch everything to offer support. Anything could have happened. She shouldn't be assuming the worst of him. Later they'd talk, and she'd feel much happier about the whole thing. And soon they'd get together again, and this time it would be somewhere far more romantic than the bedroom of her poky shared house. A country hotel, perhaps. Or a weekend in Paris. She'd be able to show him exactly how she was usually, when she was in charge of things. A sophisticated woman with a stunningly successful CV, who could get out there and seduce a man into a gibbering wreck whenever the mood took her. She shook back her hair with a glow of confidence. The class fell quiet as they each began to concentrate on the conifer test.

'Ella?' Pierre hailed her urgently.

'What is it?' She smiled at him graciously.

'What did you do to your face? You have plasters all over it, no?'

She gripped her pen hard and had the presence of mind to maintain her smile. John's voice boomed over the class.

'Cut yourself shaving, did you, duck?'

So perhaps she didn't look cool just at that moment. But she could act cool, and she would make sure that Matt would find out about that before too long.

Chapter Eight

Ella didn't have a chance to talk to Matt until the afternoon. The class were touring a nursery in the grounds of a manor house several miles from the college, now open to the public but quiet in the autumn. The curator of the nursery, Gordon, had taken them around the greenhouses while he launched into a comprehensive explanation of the range and number of plants the nursery produced, methods of propagation and growing on, and saleable plants in the area. Gordon had all the animation of rolled tarmac. John had been surreptitiously trying to roll a joint at the back; Pierre's eyes had glazed over as he cleaned his nails with a biro top; even Valerie was picking shoots from a tray of cuttings while staring through the condensation on the glass surrounding them. Probably planning the entrée for her next dinner party. But Ella was transfixed by the detail. Of all the aspects of horticulture that the course was covering, she thought that this might be her future direction.

The issue of what she was going to do with her qualifications once she'd got them was something she hadn't stopped to consider too carefully when hurling herself into the course. She was fighting her natural urge to have a plan for every step she took. Her whole life up to this point had been precisely plotted, initially by her father, and later by Ella herself. But for once, she wanted to feel the freedom of making her mind up as she went along.

She could freelance in landscaping, but couldn't quite visualise herself as Charlie Dimmock. She was quite fond of her bra, and she didn't want to spend every day flinging boulders around. Not that she couldn't do it – with the aid of nightly weight training down at the gym and seven boiled eggs a day – or hire the labour to do it, but it all seemed a bit haphazard. She could go into amenity horticulture and find herself a niche with the council, but she instinctively shied away from another big organisation. Banking seemed to have cured her of that. And she couldn't quite see herself trundling around the parks on a tractor, or playing chicken with the rush hour traffic in an attempt to stuff the roundabouts full of marigolds.

But there was something about the nursery that grabbed her. The statistical challenge of it tickled at her senses. Investing in rows of tiny seedlings, some of which were destined to conk out, leaving the muscly ones to survive, was as logical a venture to her as any financial risk she'd taken. And the geometrical pattern of the stock laid out in the greenhouses was as satisfying as any spreadsheet. There was a precision to the lattice of thin shoots in their trays that pleased her.

She caught Matt's elbow as the class trooped outside to appreciate the benefits of a good mulch. She was still hoping a good mulch was on the cards with Matt. She loitered as the others disappeared ahead of them and Matt slowed too.

'Hi. Have a good weekend?'

She gave him a broad smile while her heart ticked slowly awaiting the crumpling of his face. He would tell her, of course, that it had been a dire weekend because he hadn't spent it with her. She gazed calmly into his blue eyes, momentarily clouded with thought.

'It was fine. Much as ever. Hmmn.' He nodded at her with a slight smile, as if to say that he wouldn't be drawn further.

'Fine,' she said limply, smiling again. It wasn't fine at all. He should say more things. 'So . . .' She touched her fingertips together lightly and raised her eyebrows at him.

'So.' He laughed. 'How do you like the tour? I thought you really lit up in there. All those questions. Gordon's not used to that. Most of the students do their best to demonstrate how boring it is.'

'Oh, but I wasn't bored at all.'

'That's because you're doing this course because you want to. Not because someone else put you on it.'

'Well no, you wouldn't expect that at my age. I think my father might offer to put me on a husband-finding course, but that'd be about it.'

'Hmmn.' He looked at her thoughtfully again. 'But you found a husband without the need for a course, didn't you?'

It was one of those rhetorical questions that there was no answer to. She found herself feeling she should apologise, but that was confusing because he'd asked to spend the night with her. She knitted her brows together, listening to Gordon droning behind a tall hedge which separated them from the group, and feeling the breeze spring up and prick at her bare arms. Matt noticed the strength of the wind and gazed at the border shrubs, rustling in the sudden blast.

'I think the Indian summer may be coming to an end.'

'It hasn't really even started yet, has it?' she found herself protesting, rubbing at her arms. He wasn't talking about the weather. She blinked up at the sky anyway. Clouds were accumulating, edged with light grey and straying towards the sun.

'I think we were lucky to have a taste of it at all.' His jaw was set, making his face look unusually solemn. She hadn't seen this expression on him. He was supposed to be Mr it's-all-great-fun features. Not Mr it's-all-over features. But as she studied the unsmiling line of his mouth, his eyes, the straightness of his eyebrows, the flatness of his cheeks, she knew what was coming.

'Ella—'

'Oh, don't, Matt. Spare me this.'

'No, please. I want to explain.'

She'd started to move away, but his hand reached out and brushed against her arm. She felt a prickle of desire through her skin. But it was no good lusting after him if he was backing away. And they'd have to get back to the others soon. At some point the rest of the class would miss them.

'What is it?' she said ungraciously, fighting back the stirring attraction within her and fixing her face into a strained expression, somewhere between polite interest and disappointment. She probably looked as if she was constipated.

'I – it's the first time I've ever been unfaithful. I know you probably don't believe me, but it was very significant for me.'

She nodded, biting the insides of her cheeks. It wasn't that she could say that she was emotionally involved and justify the gloominess swooping down on her, but somehow she'd allowed herself a smidgen of hope that this one might come to something. The fact that he was married had been a distraction. She hadn't been close enough to him, to the details of his life, to feel anything more than that.

'I – I need to think about what it means. If Lorna knew about this, one-night stand as it was, I think she'd leave me.'

Ella stood perfectly still, turning over his words. Now she wanted to be on the other side of the hedge with the class, taking notes, listening to boring Gordon and planning her life. Not being waylaid by Matt's emotional dilemma. It passed her off as a one-night stand, and it had been many years since she'd been only that to anybody. And she couldn't be expected to sympathise with poor old Lorna, surely? Was that what he wanted? An open display of sisterly loyalty to make him feel loved all round? 'Matt, you're a babe magnet, but Lorna must have you, obviously, because she was there first, and although I want you madly, I'll give you up to save your marriage?' No, surely not. His marriage had nothing to do with her. He was a grown-up. His decisions were his own business. She felt her stomach churn with unhappiness.

'Look, Matt, I need to get back to the group. I'm missing the talk.'

'Sure.' He nodded, still fixing his eyes on the shrubs. 'It's just, I wondered if I should tell Lorna. Or not. You're a woman. You've been in relationships. I – I'm not sure what to do. I'm not sure if it would be better if she knew, you see. It's just – is honesty the best policy? As far as women go?' He cleared his throat uncertainly while Ella stared at him in amazement. Was this the same Matt? Confused? Stricken with guilt? Asking her what to do? He was the tutor, the big man, the boss, the one with all the answers. She opened her mouth, shut it again, and opened it once more.

'You don't seriously think you should tell your wife you spent the night in another woman's bed, do you?' She fixed him with disbelieving eyes. He stuck his thumbs into the pockets of his jeans.

'Should I, do you think?'

Her brain revolved with the possibilities she could answer him with. But she had been here before. The very fact that she had been in this situation before, and not just once, and still couldn't focus on what it might be telling her about herself was something she wasn't ready to face. But there was one element that was different about this situation. Matt's reaction. He seemed to have really taken their encounter to heart, as if it had huge significance in his private life. She wasn't ready to face that either. She decided to answer him simply.

'No,' she said.

'So I shouldn't – I thought if maybe . . .?'

'No, you shouldn't. I've got to join the others now.'

*

Ella crashed into her bedroom when she got home, kicking the door open, slamming it shut behind her, throwing her bag towards the bed, not caring about the huge thump as it hit the floor, turned to her CD player and stabbed the button. She twisted the volume and let Billy Idol blast out. She slumped on to the chair at her dressing table and stuck her head in her hands.

'Fuck,' she issued. 'Fuck, fuck, fuck, fuck.'

She took a deep breath and put her head in her hands again, ripping away the scrunchie holding her hair up, and twisting round to fling it at the bed.

Her eyes met those of the detective. She stared at him blankly, trying to remember his name. Zap. Zing. Jiz. Jaz, that was it. He was standing by the curtains, his fingers fiddling with a delicate camera on high legs positioned at an angle a yard from the window, his eyes wide open and on her. 'White Wedding' clanged from the speakers.

She stood up, stabbed the CD controls to silence Billy Idol, and turned back to him, her eyes flashing.

'Just what the bloody hell are you doing in my bedroom?'

He didn't move from his position, his shoulders bent over the camera, his face upturned to meet her glare.

'This is where we agreed to put the surveillance camera.'

'Yes, I know that,' she snapped at him. 'I meant, what are you doing in my bedroom *now*?'

'I'm making sure the equipment's functioning, and otherwise doing my job.'

She inhaled again, so noisily that he must have

heard it, and raked her fingers through her hair. It sprang out in all directions again.

'This isn't on. You can't just lurk around up here whenever you feel like it. I've just come in, I've had a crap day, and I want to – I want to swear.'

'I noticed.'

That was it. No apology. Not even a sorry expression. She wanted to fasten her scrunchie around his neck and pull on it until he went blue.

'Why are you still here, anyway? Don't you work nine to five? It's gone half past, the others will be in soon, and you'll be in the way. It's one thing having you here when we're not at home. That's fair enough. But you can't just creep about when we're in. We've got things to do.'

'I understand.' He stood up straight, his face still controlled. His eyes were not quite so controlled. She thought she saw a spark of irritation in the black depths, but irate as she was, it was comforting. A good row was just what she needed to get the adrenaline out of her system. She stalked forwards a couple of paces until they were either side of her bed, staring at each other.

'I was just about to take all my clothes off and go and have a shower. That's what I normally do when I get home,' she seethed. He raised an eyebrow.

'That's funny. So do I.' It was sarcasm. He said it in a tone of voice that suggested that they had something unique in common.

'I mean that I could have done that without realising that you were lurking over there by the window, then I'd have turned round, and you'd have been in a tricky position.' She felt her nostrils flaring.

She tried to control them. Her mother had told her she looked like a cross between Colonel Gaddafi and a racehorse when she lost her temper. It was in one of their less convivial moments.

'I don't want to make you uncomfortable or intrude on your private space any more than necessary, Ella,' he said. She felt slightly appeased. He was on a back foot now. 'But,' he added, 'being a bloke I would have been fascinated to see you take all your clothes off and head for the shower.'

Her jaw dropped. Indignation bolted through her.

'Right. That's it. You're fired.'

He stared back at her for a moment, then he let out a short laugh. It became a cough instead. He shook his head.

'I'm sorry, it's not funny.'

'Too right it's not bloody funny. I want you to get out.'

She pointed to the door with her arm outstretched, pulling a severe expression. He scratched at his head and tutted to himself as if he was thinking.

'Now!' she barked. 'What's the matter with you? Haven't you got a wife to go home to?'

'Not yet. I will have very shortly.'

That was it. Her temper fired out of control.

'Right. That's just utterly typical. You want an eyeful of me in my underwear, and meanwhile some poor cow's sitting up the road in Oxford waiting for you. I thought you were professional, but I couldn't expect much more from somebody in the police, I suppose. I know all about macho environments, believe me. I used to work as a trader in a bank. There's nothing you could surprise me with.' She shook her head emphatically. 'I'd be the next canteen joke. Well, I'm so sorry to deprive you of your material, but it looks as if you'll have to put the camera in Doris's house after all and just take the risk of her sudden death.'

'Luton, actually.'

She paused as she was about to jab her pointed finger at the door once more to make it very clear where she wanted him to go.

'What?'

'Luton. That's where my fiancée is. Not in Oxford. Although at the moment she's in Madras.'

She maintained her outstretched arm, even though he still hadn't moved.

'As in India?'

'As in India, rather than as in chicken, yes.'

She screwed her face up at him. This had been a nightmare of a day.

'Why are you telling me that?'

'Because your assumption was incorrect. I don't have a poor cow waiting for me in Oxford. I have a poor cow waiting for me in Luton. I thought I'd set the record straight.'

'Right.' Her arm dropped to her side. She could still feel her chest heaving from the shock of finding him in her bedroom. She was tired, sweaty and frustrated from her day, and she'd been tantalising herself with the thought of a long, hot bath full of scented bubbles before Faith and Miranda got in and while she had a moment's peace. But her anger was subsiding a little.

'Why do you call her a poor cow if she's your fiancée?'

He dropped to his haunches to pack some technical bits and pieces into a holdall. She peered over the bed to watch him. It was obviously true that he hadn't finished his work by the time she arrived, put Billy Idol on full blast, and swore loudly.

'Your choice of epithet, not mine,' he said calmly, the metal bits and pieces clinking as he tossed them into his bag.

'And is she a poor cow?' Ella sank on to the edge of her bed, still watching him. Now he wasn't looking at her, but was concentrating on the job in hand. He had some sort of notepad, and he flicked through it as if she wasn't there, flipped it shut and threw that in the bag too. He stood up and pulled the bag on to his shoulder.

'I'm sorry I startled you today, and I'm sorry if I made a tasteless remark about you heading off for the shower. I need to come back tomorrow to check the set-up. Tell me when's a good time for you, and I'll try to make sure I'm not here when you come home.'

'Oh.' So he wasn't going to be drawn on his fiancée, and when he walked around her and to the door, which she'd been graphically indicating he should go through at great speed only a few moments ago, she felt disgruntled that he hadn't satisfied her curiosity. 'Aren't you – I mean – don't you have to be here most of the time, then?'

'Not at all.' He stopped at the door. She stood up too, feeling at a disadvantage.

'But . . . I wondered—' She noticed again the long eyelashes. He was staring straight at her again. No evidence of like, dislike, or interest. He seemed utterly dispassionate. She faltered, forgetting for a moment what her question was. He put his hand on the door handle.

'So? You were going to ask something?'

'Just that – I wondered what made you want to join the police.'

If he was thrown by her question, he didn't show it. She was starting to realise that he wasn't big on body language to give away his feelings. Or even facial language. Or even language. She suddenly wanted to laugh at him, standing there, so totally under control, when she was in a shirt and jeans, smeared with mud, her hair shot to pieces around her head, and a couple of plasters attached to her face. God, what must he think of the human tractor he was looking at?

'Why do you ask me that?' He seemed analytical, rather than deeply interested.

'Well, you know.' She found herself twisting her fingers into her Levi leather belt. 'I'm curious about people and their career choices. Having ditched mine to go for something else. I always knew what I wanted to do, you see. Since I was a child. And then suddenly I knew it was all wrong for me.' She stayed calm even though he didn't offer any feedback. 'I never felt this strong urge to contribute to society before. I was out for myself, if I'm realistic about it. But now I get such a warm feeling about being out there, touching the earth, smelling the air, fingering the leaves. Now I feel I'm a part of a bigger experience. It's like,' she sought for the right words. 'It's as if now I can see it all in terms of molecules. We're all made of molecules, and the plants too. And it makes you feel as if you're a little pot of molecules in the big laboratory of life. It's comforting. It makes you feel cosmic. Even death isn't frightening any more, because you know you'll just change from one pattern of molecules into another one.'

He was expressionless. But he was listening. She carried on.

'And for the first time, I don't feel as if I'm being so selfish. So I think I can understand a sense of duty. A sense of wanting to contribute something. Even if it's only giving people something that makes them happy, like a bedding plant or something, rather than screwing them to make a massive profit for the company you work for. I only really went into banking because my father wanted it so much. There wasn't an option. Parental pressure's an amazing thing. You don't even realise it's happening because you're living the life they wanted you to lead before you stop and think about it. And by then it takes double the courage to get out, because you've led them on to believe that you wanted it for yourself too. My father still can't cope with what I'm doing. He was in finance. He took it as a personal insult when I backed out.'

She jammed the verbal brakes on. She'd been gazing around as she spoke, then dropped her eyes back on him, and he looked totally bemused. There was a silence. She pulled her fingers away from her belt and more assertively rested them on her hips. He twisted the door handle.

'What was the question again?' he asked.

'I—' She flicked her hair back casually. 'I wondered why you joined the police. That's all. It seems an unusual choice.'

'An unusual choice for . . . ?' he prompted her.

'For . . .' He let her struggle with the silence for a while.

'For an Asian lad?'

'No, not that. I was just thinking about me, and careers, and things.' She took a step towards the door, ready to show him out.

'I didn't join the police out of a sense of gratitude to the British.' He paused, and she flinched, knowing that it was halfway to what she'd been thinking. Wasn't that what her parents had always said? That the Asian community were a good bunch because they 'put something back'? What did her parents know? All of their friends were rich, white and middle-aged. Her father's opinions were always stolen from the *Telegraph* leader articles, but it had taken her a while to realise that. They could know nothing of the thoughts of a young man like Jaz. And neither could she.

She looked at Jaz again. His expression had lost its sarcasm and was genuine. 'I joined the police because I saw *Shane* when I was a kid.'

'The film?'

'The film. I wanted to be a Wild West hero. The police was the next best thing.'

Ella nodded. His words catapulted a track from Faith's ELO album into her mind. There was something about riding off into the sunset with a Western girl. Well, he was going to ride off with an Eastern girl, but other than that, she could see where he was coming from.

He'd opened the door and was heading down the stairs. Ella followed him, feeling it was ungainly not to show him out. They reached the door.

'If I get here tomorrow at half past eight, can you let me in before you go off to your course?'

'Look, why don't you have a spare set of keys. It's daft for you not to be able to come and go if you need to.' She dived off into the kitchen, found one of the spare sets she had secreted in a drawer and brought it back to him. 'If we're going to cooperate, I guess we might as well do it properly.'

He took the set of keys and closed his fingers around them.

'Thank you, Ella. That makes life a lot easier.'

'That's fine.'

She let him out with a bright wave and retreated again, closing the door before he'd made it to his car. Then she bounded up the stairs and pushed her way back into her bedroom. The evening sun was casting a yellow light across the room. The fragile camera was on its stalks, gazing out of the window at an angle, and there was no other sign he'd been there. She threw herself on the bed, let her legs flop on the duvet and gazed up at the ceiling. She ran their conversation through her head again. Why had she felt the need to gush at him like that? Why would he care what her motivation was, or what her father had felt was right for her? What on earth had just happened to her?

She closed her eyes. It had just been a dizzy moment, brought about by the shock of finding him there. And it had been a strange day from start to finish. And the last thing she wanted to think about was men. Especially married ones. Or engaged ones who had fiancées in Luton currently visiting Madras and who wanted to watch drug dealers from her window. It made her think about things she hadn't planned to think about. It would actually be nice if life would just be a little less complicated.

If only Matt wasn't so darned attractive, life being less complicated could be achieved with merely a burst of willpower. Ella gazed at him soulfully from her desk in the classroom, fiddling agitatedly with a biro top. Why did he have to be one of those men for whom jeans seemed to have been invented? He had a perfect bum and strong thighs shaped by the denim. And now Ella knew that he was just as delicious with his jeans on her bedroom floor. He seemed distracted as he rubbed a diagram of a dissected plant from the blackboard with the sleeve of his jumper. He blinked at the smears of pink and green chalk on the wool as if he was confused as to how they got there, then looked up at the class brightly.

'Well, never mind. We don't need the blackboard for this. We need to do some health and safety. I've got handouts for you.'

'Oh God, blimey, not that boring old bollocks,' John objected, throwing his head into his hands dramatically.

'Yes, this boring old bollocks.' Matt shuffled around in his briefcase and produced a folder.

Pierre leant sideways to Ella, sniggering with his hand over his mouth.

'I sink I learn more colloquial English here zan anywhere else. I like that. God, blimey, what boring old bollocks.'

'Just don't repeat it to the customers of Le Manoir,'

135

she whispered back. 'I don't think Raymond would appreciate it when he's serving up one of his specialities.'

Pierre tapped his nose in complicity and grinned.

'You won't think it's boring when you're in charge of your own establishment one day,' Matt advised John, pulling out a sheaf of papers and giving them to him to hand around the class. 'If you have staff working for you, you're answerable under the law. Anything from a wet floor to not instructing them to wear the proper protective clothing for the job could land you in deep trouble.'

'Can't see myself ever running an establishment. Unless it's a brothel,' John mused, handing back the papers to Valerie, who took them with a vacant expression.

'In which case, health and safety would still apply,' Matt retorted, returning to his desk to sit on the corner and swing a leg casually in the air. 'In any case, it's part of the course and I have to be satisfied that you've all understood it.'

'All right then,' John conceded, straightening his handout on his desk in front of him, letting out a pained groan, and bracing himself to read it. Matt smirked down at him as he became silent, absorbing what was in front of him.

Ella watched Matt. The handouts were making their way around the class. He still wouldn't make eye contact with her. It had been like that all day. He'd been bright and breezy, if a little jittery, but apart from general sweeping glances around the class earlier when they were out at the potting sheds, and this afternoon while they were busy with classwork, he hadn't acknowledged her existence. At least before he'd voiced his guilt about spending the night with her he'd twinkled at her, even given her a wink. But it was as if now he'd put his anxious feelings into words they had become more real. Pierre handed her a sheet and she took it and placed it on her desk.

She let out a noiseless sigh, resting her chin in her hand and watching Matt rub away at the chalk on his sleeve with a slight frown over his normally untroubled eyes. The class settled into silent reading of the health and safety sheets. She chewed at her cheek thoughtfully.

Was this really it, then? She'd anticipated perhaps a burst of remorse, a few words demonstrating that he'd felt like a bit of a cad once Lorna had returned from her weekend away. But she hadn't thought it would be permanent. He'd told her it was the first time he had ever been unfaithful. Could it be that he was telling her an earnest confidence? Could it be that the guilt he felt was not just a surface reaction to seeing his wife's face again, but a real guilt, one that indicated that spending the night with her was something that he actually should not have done?

Quite suddenly, he looked up to find her watching him. Their eyes met. She sat up, pulling her hand away from her face. For a while they were both expressionless. Then, gently, she smiled at him.

He blinked at her, then looked away.

'Let me introduce you to Simon,' Faith announced.

Ella paused in her assessment of the three-inch hole she had made in the living room wall in her attempt to tap in a nail with a hammer. Miranda put her head around the kitchen door with a straining spoon in hand. She was already tossing her hair over her shoulders. But then, Simon was a man's name, so she would be tossing her hair just in case. They both stared as Faith indicated a bundle in a blanket under her arm. Sticking out of the blanket was a wet black nose.

'Simon?' Ella said faintly.

Faith pushed back the blanket and a pair of round brown eyes were revealed. A low, throaty whimper emanated from the wrapping. 'It wasn't easy getting him home, so I decided to wrap him up and carry him. It's raining, you know.'

Ella left the window. Her curtain ties, which were meant to be easy to hook up, could wait for later. The three-inch hole in the wall wasn't so important now either. There was a damp, whimpering thing wriggling under Faith's arm. And Ella realised that this thing was not just on a flying visit.

'Faith, is this the thing I said you could have?'

'Simon's not a thing, are you, darling?' Faith put her nose to the wet black protuberance and snuffled at it. 'You're a poor little lost soul, and we're going to love you, aren't we?'

Simon whimpered in return. Ella felt a strong tug inside her stomach and steeled herself against it.

'It's a dog, isn't it?' she queried pointlessly.

Faith glanced up and squinted through her rain-spattered glasses.

'Well, it's not a terrapin. The hairy face should tell you that much.'

Ella bit her lip. Faith's sarcasm skills seemed to be

increasing daily. She crept up to the wet nose and looked into the startled eyes of the animal.

'Hello, you,' she said softly. Then she looked up at Faith with more authority. 'Faith, it's a small dog. Not a grown-up one. It's going to be leaping about all over the place and weeing everywhere. It's not something we can cope with. He's lovely, but I'm going to have to say no. I'm sorry.'

Faith dropped her chin, gazed down at Simon, then raised her eyes to Ella in peaceful appeal.

'Okay,' she whispered. 'You explain that to Simon. But tell him gently. He's got a broken leg, you see, because his last owner got bored with him as soon as he wasn't a puppy any more and threw him out of a bedroom window. I don't want him thinking nobody wants him.'

'Oh Jesus!' Miranda clunked her head against the doorframe in resignation.

'Oh, Faith!' Ella agonised. 'Why did you have to tell me that?'

'Because it's true.' Faith looked insouciant. 'Think of it as a bonus. He can't leap about because he's got one leg in a splint. So he's not going to do as much damage as a dog of his age normally would because he can only stumble around. Which makes him a bargain. Especially,' Faith added throatily, 'as he's free. He's a mongrel, and nobody wants a mongrel.'

'Oh, please!' Miranda's straining spoon hung limply by her side.

'God, Faith, you should freelance for charities. I'd give you my life savings,' Ella huffed, putting out a tentative finger to the black nose. A pale pink tongue appeared and licked her fingertip.

This was not at all how she'd envisaged things, what with one thing and another. She felt the dog's whiskers bristle on her fingers. Simon tried to get his teeth around her hand playfully. A gangly paw extended from the blanket and patted her arm. She looked into his eyes. His eyebrows seemed to shoot up pleadingly. She wriggled her hand, and he kept a firm but gentle grip with his teeth.

'So,' Faith said. 'I'll take him down to the animal sanctuary tomorrow then. It'll be a bit lonely in one of those wire cages, but they usually keep them for a few months before they put them down.'

'We'll keep him,' Ella shouted.

'Only on one condition,' Miranda said, unfixing herself from the doorway and standing up straight. 'He sleeps on *my* bed.'

'No, it's okay,' Ella asserted. 'He can sleep with me. I was the one who said Faith could bring an animal home. It's only fair.'

'No, Ella,' Miranda's lips twitched. She approached Simon and stuck a finger out to rub the top of his nose. He gave a low groan of appreciation. 'See? He likes me best. He can crash out with me. No problem.'

'He'll have less disturbance in my bedroom,' Ella said, giving Miranda a meaningful look. Miranda raised her eyebrows in return.

'Not if last weekend is anything to go by, sweetie. And we can't inflict non-stop ELO on such an impressionable little soul, so Faith's room's out. It has to be my bedroom.' Miranda stuck out the straining spoon as Ella was about to counter her. 'And no arguments. It's settled.'

'You two!' Faith shook her head at them. 'You're so

140

selfish. He's got a broken leg. How on earth do you think he'd make it up the stairs?'

She unwrapped the blanket and carefully placed Simon on the carpet. Once he was revealed, Ella's heart curled up with pity. One of his front paws was bandaged tightly like a pole. He hobbled up to Ella and panted up at her. She sank to her knees and allowed him to flop over her lap. He just wanted to get on with life, and the splint was in the way, but he was living for the moment. She couldn't help admiring him. She rubbed at his head, then impulsively dropped down to kiss him. He yelped back at her with pleasure before lolloping away to investigate Miranda, who had also dropped to the floor regardless of her finely meshed tights.

Ella looked up at Faith, still in her raincoat and folding up the damp blanket. She felt an urge to embrace her.

'Yep, he's peeing on the carpet,' Miranda proclaimed. 'I have the feeling this is going to be an interesting experience.'

'We need to give him a bed down here,' Faith nudged at her glasses. 'And to show him early on what the rules are. I'll walk him morning and night so that he gets used to his toilet routine. And I can pop home in my break to check on him too.'

Ella nodded. On this occasion she was out of her depth. Whatever she and Miranda knew about anything else, Faith was the expert on animals.

'And it's best if you two don't go soft and let him upstairs if he whines. We can fuss him down here, but he'll get used to being downstairs if we train him.' Ella and Miranda let out a simultaneous 'ooh' of protest, but Faith shook her head. 'Trust me. It's the best way. And—' She peered over Ella's shoulder. Ella blinked at her.

'What is it?'

'The wall. What have you done to it?'

Ella glanced backwards at the crater left by her effort with the nail and hammer.

'I wanted to put some ties up. For the curtains. So that I could drape them.' She could hear her voice fading under Faith's analytical stare. 'So that they'd look pretty.'

'That's a hard wall. You need a drill and a rawl plug, or the right sort of nail.'

Ella nodded again from her knees. The right sort of nail. The right sort of drill. The right sort of bed for Simon. Faith knew about the right sort of everything. It was a bummer she couldn't give advice on the right sort of bloke too.

'Faith, will you marry me?'

'Don't be stupid.' Faith delved into her enormous bag and retrieved a tin of dog food. 'Now I'm going to feed Simon, then you two can devise a bed for him. Okay?'

'Okay,' Miranda and Ella said, both turning their eyes longingly on the overgrown puppy as he rolled over in Miranda's lap and stuck his legs in the air.

'Men,' Faith tutted, and walked past Miranda towards the kitchen.

The phone began to ring. Ella stared at the intrusion resentfully, but then it struck her that it could be Matt. Miranda was busy rubbing Simon's stomach.

'I'll get it.'

She crawled to the phone as Simon rolled off

Miranda's lap in raptures and did an unintentional cartwheel. Ella snorted into the phone.

'Miranda?' a male voice with a smooth American accent queried.

'Er—' Simon threw himself excitedly at Ella's face and bit her nose. She splurted with laughter as she rolled backwards.

'It's Lance here. Is this a bad time to call?' Ella lay back on the carpet, realising she was in Simon's wet patch, and peered over at Miranda who was cooing at the dog in an attempt to get him back on her lap. Lance? Miranda's ex-husband Lance? How many American Lances were there in the world? It had to be the same one.

'She's just here,' she said and held the receiver out to Miranda, covering it with her hand.

'Oh, thanks,' Miranda whispered back, taking the phone and clearing her throat. She got to her feet and turned her back on Ella while Simon did a flying leap and landed heavily on Ella's chest.

'Come on, you,' Ella whisked him up into her arms. 'Out to the kitchen. It's dinner time.'

She left the living room, pulling the door gently closed behind her.

Chapter Nine

Faith was taking an appointment over the phone on a quiet afternoon when Giles wandered into the reception looking around vaguely. The crisp cellophane enfolding a bunch of roses rustled under his arm. She glanced at him, noted the flowers, and looked back quickly at her appointments book.

It was a couple of weeks since Simon had been introduced to the household, and so far it was going very well. Things had been ticking over nicely at work too, until Michael had landed her in it that morning.

She used to love the afternoons. She'd worked regularly with Suzanne down in the operating rooms in the basement, and Suzanne always took the time and effort to explain exactly what she was doing. It wouldn't take much for any of the vets to talk through their procedure while they were working, but only Suzanne really bothered. The older ones, though polite, seemed to assume the veterinary nurses were more interested in clearing up and getting out than studying the operations closely, and only debated the technicalities with each other. Suzanne and Faith worked fantastically well as a team, and Faith was starting to gain confidence in voicing her observations aloud. More than once Suzanne had peered at her over her green mask with an expression of surprise. That look gave Faith a bigger buzz than anything else. Suzanne respected her intelligence.

But now it was decided that she should work mostly with Giles. Michael, the senior partner at the practice, had suggested it at an early morning meeting and Faith admired him too much to let him see how put out she was. He'd also twinkled at her, as if she'd do handstands of pleasure at the idea of being Giles's little helper. It had been flattering in a way. He'd been implying that as the longest serving assistant at the surgery she'd be an invaluable help to Giles while he found his feet. So her bottom lip had slipped only a little while she'd nodded in agreement. Only Suzanne had noticed her expression, and had stopped by in reception later to squeeze her arm and offer a whispered reassurance before she'd gone out on a call.

Faith deliberately took her time extracting details over the phone while Giles stopped to examine the news board with great interest. After a few moments, his turned back began to grate on her. They were alone in reception, with only faint barks and whimpers drifting up the stairs from the animals waiting for surgery that afternoon, or convalescing. She jammed her hand over the receiver and glowered at the tufts of blond hair touching his collar.

'She's gone out.'

He turned round and blinked his luminous brown eyes at her.

'I beg your pardon?'

'Suzanne.' She nodded at the flowers. 'She's out on a call.'

She returned to the phone, assured her caller that an evening appointment would be an appropriate occasion to give Odysseus a worming pill, and hung up. Giles was still staring at her. She got back to her paperwork, shuffling a handful of loose forms and taking them over to the steel filing cabinets, yanking the drawer open so that it rolled out noisily and hit her in the stomach.

'Actually, I wondered if you and I could have a chat.'

She stiffened, laying out the forms on the top of the cabinet and ruffling her fingers through the filing cards.

'What about?'

'Well, I brought you these for starters.'

She turned round slowly. Giles was extending the bunch of roses towards her. He was smiling.

'What for?'

'I seem to have offended you. I'm not sure how, but we haven't got off to a very good start, have we?'

She hesitated, resting one hand on her hip, suddenly feeling uncomfortable about what to do with the other one. She scratched her ear with it, and as he was still extending the flowers and she couldn't move, she fiddled with her ear lobe instead.

'There's no need for flowers,' she heard herself snapping. She felt her face grow hot. What did you do when somebody gave you flowers? She had no idea. But she'd always imagined that if it ever happened, it would be romantic. And this wasn't romantic, it was a way of getting her to cooperate. It was like a bribe, so that she'd forget all the tasteless jokes he bandied around with the other nurses, who all hooted and shook their hair at him. If he'd offered roses to Janet or Debbie, they'd have giggled at him and stuck their breasts out so that he could get a better look. She hunched her shoulders, holding her chest in defiantly.

'Why don't you take them anyway,' he suggested, waving them at her. 'I've got nobody else to give them to, have I?' He grinned charmingly. Her heart hardened.

'How about Mrs Khan? You could give them to her as compensation for failing to save her collie. She'll be in at about half past five.'

She heard his sharp intake of breath.

'Nobody would have put money on him making it through the op. Christ, Faith, the tumour was like a tennis ball. She should have brought him in ages ago, when it was only the size of a cricket ball perhaps.' He shook his head. 'It wasn't my fault. I've talked to Michael about it too. These things happen. You know that.'

'You shot through that operation like a dose of the squits.' She was startled by her own language. And more than a little alarmed that she was being overtly insolent to a superior, but she couldn't stop herself. 'Suzanne would have taken much longer over it.'

He let the roses hang by his side.

'And what would it have achieved, if I'd patched the poor creature up just so that he could come back in a few weeks with liver failure? He was old. He was dying.'

'You would have given Mrs Khan time to say goodbye to him. As it is, she's got to come and pick up a dead dog.'

147

He blinked at her again and she swung back to her filing quickly, fanning the papers with trembling hands and blindly jamming them in the cabinet.

'It was kinder this way, Faith,' he said, dropping his voice. 'If Mrs Khan had been given the choice, she might have opted to take him home and let him fade away there. He would have been in agony. It would have been selfish.'

'Except,' Faith almost yelled with her back to him, 'that Mrs Khan would never have done that. When Harvey had to be put down two years ago she went in with him for the injection. She said then that if anything happened to any of the others, she wanted to be with them.'

He let his breath go heavily.

'How was I to know that?' She didn't answer. 'And in any case, this animal was suffering. It was kinder to let him go under anaesthetic. I'm sure she'll understand that.'

Faith slammed the drawer shut and marched back to the reception desk, throwing herself into her chair. What annoyed her above all was that she knew Giles was probably right. It was the arrogant way he made assumptions that riled her. And she wasn't going to be working during the evening surgery herself, which meant that the way the news was broken to Mrs Khan was out of her hands. She knew how important moments like that were. If it was handled as if it was just another event in the day, it could be something that stayed with the owner for the rest of her life.

'I didn't rush the op, Faith.' Giles leant on the counter, putting the roses down. 'We were phenomenally busy yesterday afternoon, but it made no difference to the collie.'

'Okay.' She wrestled with the appointments book, grabbing a handful of receipts to check.

'Faith? You and I are going to have to work together. You've got to stop resenting me just for being here.'

Her cheeks glowed.

'Okay,' she said lightly, as if her mind was on something far more important.

'Suzanne said you're bloody bright. She told me you're the best nurse she's ever worked with.' Faith's stomach churned.

'Suzanne notices all sorts of things,' she responded ungraciously, laying her hands down on the desk in defeat. Her nerves were jangling like cow bells. If only he'd take his flowers and bugger off.

'So I was the one who asked Michael if I could work with you, to start with at least. Both he and Suzanne thought it was the best thing for me. I'm hoping to learn a lot about the way things are done here. And I'd appreciate your input.'

She looked up at him and jammed her glasses up her nose abruptly.

'That's fine by me,' she lied.

'So . . .' He captured her eyes. 'I'm asking you to give me a chance.' He nudged the roses towards her, leaning on to his elbows to peep over the counter at her. She nibbled her lower lip. Any moment the phone would ring and save her from this embarrassment.

'No bad jokes, I promise,' he added.

Debbie came crashing in, whistling. Faith was sure

she'd only started to whistle when she saw Giles was in reception. She didn't normally whistle, and she wasn't very good at it.

'Hiya!' she breezed, flicking her blonde ponytail around like a whip. 'Ooh, roses. How romantic. They for me, then?' She laughed raucously, slapping Giles heartily on the back. He lurched forward, recovered himself and offered a gentle, non-committal laugh in return.

Faith grimaced overtly, caught Giles's eye, and saw that he was grimacing too. She sucked in her cheeks to stop herself smiling. She'd assumed that he found the indiscriminate adoration of women flattering. She'd assumed he must have an ego the size of Uganda by now. But he seemed quite uncomfortable.

'Just divest myself of this coat and I'll be back. Busy, Faith? Any major disasters?'

'The usual,' Faith muttered. Debbie didn't normally throw a string of inane rhetorical questions at her. Or at least, if they were inane, she usually had the decency not to shout them across the surgery. She was obviously doing everything she could to impress Giles. It was painful. Why did so many women have no sense of dignity? It was like Miranda, slobbering all over Mike and Oliver. They were ten years her junior. She should have realised they'd see her as an easy conquest, have a good joke about it with the gang they hung out with, and move on to someone else. She'd never been like that herself. She never would, even if it meant staying celibate until the end of her life. She'd vowed it to herself years ago, and she repeated the vow every time she watched another woman lose her marbles and start gibbering.

As Debbie disappeared, Giles raised his eyebrows and opened his mouth to speak.

'I'm back,' Debbie yelled breathlessly. 'Flipping weather. Was it like this last year? Tons of sun followed by shitloads of rain? I can't remember. Mind you, I was preoccupied then. Wasn't I, Faith?'

'Were you?' Faith grabbed the receipts again and looked down. She wasn't going to be dragged into a double act for Giles's benefit. She knew Debbie was talking about a man she'd met in Ibiza late last summer, whom she'd seen for a few months when she got back to England. She'd given them all intimate details of every sexual encounter, until Faith felt she could have contributed an appendix to the *Kama Sutra*.

'Well, I've got to get downstairs,' Giles said, glancing at his watch. 'See you down there, Faith. We've got an interesting fracture first. About ten minutes?'

'Fine.'

He swept away, smiling politely at Debbie, who nearly knocked herself out as she sprung jokily out of his way and collided with a plastic chair. She looked back to Faith wide-eyed with envy.

'You doing ops with Giles this afternoon?'

'Yes.' Faith put her brain into gear as she ran her pen over the appointments, made the necessary notes, and flipped the book shut. Debbie was still staring.

'Lucky cow. How did you wangle that?'

'I didn't. Michael asked me.'

'Phew-ee. I'd give anything to be shut in an operating room with *him*.'

'Be my guest. I'd rather work with Suzanne anyway. You'll have to clear it with Michael though.'

'Don't be daft.' Debbie tossed a hand aside. 'I wouldn't actually ask. Giles would find out. That'd be really uncool.'

Faith raised an eyebrow.

'Crikey, he's forgotten his roses.' Debbie leapt forward and grabbed them. 'Who are they for, d'you reckon? I bet it's Suzanne. Look, there's an envelope. Would it be really nosy to read it?' Faith didn't answer as Debbie was already working the small card out of the envelope. She read aloud. 'For Faith, with affection, Giles.' She let the roses drop on the counter, her jaw dropping. 'What?'

'I'll take those, thank you,' Faith said. Having finished her work at the desk, she stood up, took the roses, and walked away. The phone rang shrilly.

'But, Faith!' Debbie called after her retreating form. 'What happened? How did you do that? What did you say?'

'Phone,' Faith issued, nodding at it as she left the room.

She bounded down the stairs, stopping to inhale a deep breath from the sweetly scented petals. Her spirits lifted, as if a fairy had waved a wand over her head. A smile crept over her lips. Debbie? Two-snogs-per-night-club Debbie? Was jealous of her? Surely not. Her smile widened. Perhaps working with Giles was going to be quite good fun after all.

Ella found a note in the kitchen when she got home. She caressed Simon as he cast himself into the air and headbutted her crotch, landing with impressive

152

balance on his three good legs. He jammed his soft teeth around her hand and wrestled with it.

'Hello, darling!' She dropped to her knees, holding the note up so that she could read it. Simon set about her face with his tongue. She wriggled, laughing at him. 'I'll take you out for a walk next. Just let me read this.'

It was from Jaz. She was surprised he'd left anything written on paper. Wasn't it evidence of his activity there? What if she'd been burgled during the day, and someone had found it? He'd arrived again just as they were all leaving that morning, the fourth time now he'd popped back, and she'd only had time to fling a wave at him as they sailed past each other on the doorstep and he'd quickly got himself inside the house.

Apart from quick chats, she'd managed to talk to him at greater length when she'd found him there one evening when she'd got home a few days ago. She'd made him some coffee and they'd had nearly an hour together before Miranda had floated in from work. What amazed her about him was how calm and relaxed he seemed about everything. And how easy he was to talk to when she wasn't throwing sparks at him. She'd actually been quite miffed when Miranda had trilled in and dumped herself on the sofa with them, but he'd decided to leave at that point, and that had been an end to it. She had learned a little more about him. She'd talked about her family in passing, and he'd made some comments about his. They were factual statements, though. She had the feeling after he'd gone that it had all been polite conversation with perhaps the aim of keeping her mollified, but it had been interesting nonetheless.

She hadn't expected him to be at the house when she got home tonight, but she felt a bit flat finding just a note. It made her feel like the milkman. She read it.

It wasn't about his work there at all. It said, 'Your dog particularly likes my tie. You should call him Jaws.'

She smiled. She supposed dogs could be an occupational hazard for him, especially young ones with a tendency to chew everything in sight, but they were obviously getting along famously. She stuffed the note in the back pocket of her jeans and grabbed Simon with both arms, rubbing his head with her face.

'Time for grub. And I've got a little surprise for you!' He gave her a quizzical look with one ear extended, and she caught herself repeating, 'Yes I have,' several times in a stupid voice.

She retrieved the dog food from her bag and piled it into a bowl. She set it down for him and he did a headstand in it. The noise of him eating still amazed her. They'd have to talk to him about his table manners. She flopped on to the lino next to him and watched him eat with a warm swell of satisfaction. She supposed all over the country there were scores of twenty-nine-year-old women doing this – except with babies. Simon was more fun than a baby. And nobody would leave her a note saying, 'You should call your baby Jaws.' But babies didn't eat quite so noisily. She didn't think they did anyway, never having really met one. Miranda interrupted her stream of consciousness as she flung open the kitchen door.

'Honey, I'm back!' She growled at the dog. 'Oh.' She looked down at Ella flatly. 'I thought I'd be the first home.'

'Shhh!' Ella put her finger to her lips warningly. 'He's eating.'

'I could hear that from the ring road.'

'He's gorgeous, isn't he?' Ella gazed at Simon with gooey eyes. He'd now distributed food way beyond the boundaries imposed by the centre pages of Saturday's *Guardian*. He'd also managed to flip a chunk on to the cupboard door. Ella watched it slide down the gloss, mesmerised.

'I've got him some things.' Miranda sidled into the kitchen with a shopping bag and delved into it.

'Oh, have you? So have I.' Ella stood up and reached into her bag. ' A rope toy.'

'Got one of those.' Miranda produced hers.

'Three squeaky balls.' Ella flung them out of the bag and dumped them on the unit.

'Oh. I've only one squeaky ball. But I've got a rat thing that jingles.'

'A pretend shoe?' Ella waved it. 'Good for teeth, they told me. He'll like that more than a rat thing.'

'Er,' Miranda ferreted around in her carrier bag. 'What about this then?' She produced a rubber bone and gestured with it.

'Not very original.' Ella screwed up her nose. Miranda made a noise of exasperation.

'It doesn't have to be original. It's not Art. It's a dog toy.'

'Okay, but I've got a lead, even nicer than the one Faith nicked from the surgery. Look.' She jingled it at

Miranda. Simon instantly left his polished bowl and hurled himself at Ella's knees. Then he sat back, opened his mouth, and began to howl.

'Blimey,' Ella gazed at him in awe. 'That's a big noise for a small dog. Doris'll definitely keel over now. She'll think we're all werewolves.'

'A signal to walk him, I think.' Miranda checked the kettle for water and flicked the switch, stifling a yawn. 'You don't mind doing it, do you? I'm bushed. I need to flake out on the sofa and make some phone calls.'

'Right.' Ella glanced up at the mention of phone calls. She'd been pondering Miranda's mysterious call from her ex-husband. It wasn't the only mysterious phone call she'd received recently. Her love life was obviously even more intriguing than Ella had given her credit for. She was dying to ask her why Lance had rung, but it would sound as if she was prying. Which she was, of course, she just didn't want it to sound that way.

'I need to flop.' Miranda drifted through to the sitting room. Ella concentrated on fixing the lead to Simon's collar while he decided to chase his tail, his splinted leg clonking on the lino. Then she heard a shriek.

'You okay, Miranda?'

Miranda started to giggle then stopped. Ella stood up and stuck her head round the living room door.

'What—'

Her mouth hung open as she took in the scene. The curtain pole was wedged diagonally across the window. One of the curtains was now scalloped around the hem with a neat row of dog bites. Her favourite scatter cushion had been scattered – in several chunks. The rug was in a rumpled heap and the *Radio Times* looked like origami. Her *Ficus Elastica* appeared to have been watered with a hosepipe that had missed the plant and hit the wall instead. And it looked as if someone had taken a pair of pinking shears to the wires leading to the stereo.

'Whoops,' Miranda said in a hushed voice. She was chewing on her cheeks in an effort not to laugh. Ella ran to the stereo wires. Simon lolloped after her and grabbed an end in his mouth to claim responsibility.

'No, you stupid mutt!' Ella yelled in panic, grabbing it back from him. 'Do you want an afro?'

'Not plugged in,' Miranda confirmed, holding up the loose plug for Ella to see. 'Luckily. Otherwise we'd have a hot dog. And the shock would have sent him flying through the window. That would definitely have surprised Doris when she was hanging out the washing.'

'It's not funny, Miranda.' Ella felt herself flushing with frustration. She'd bought the curtains when she moved in, and she was very proud of her effort to put up the curtain pole. It had been a complicated one, and she hadn't got a man in to do it until the very last minute. She thought of Faith and buried her face in her hands.

'That bloody, bloody woman.'

'Doris? She's all right really. Bit too silent to have round for a dinner party.'

'Faith!' Ella bellowed, sprawling on the floor with her legs apart and leaning back on her elbows in despair. She felt something hard under her back and

157

reached round to pick it up. It was the case to her Aretha Franklin CD, cracked across the front and chewed around the corners. 'Oh no!' She fell back in despair and stared at the ceiling. The trendy uplighter she'd fixed up on a wobbly fitting chose that moment to sway, dislodge itself, and fall off. It landed squarely on her head.

'Bugger it,' she announced in defeat.

Miranda pulled a rueful face.

'You've just got rid of the plasters on your face. You don't want to start wearing lampshades. People will think you're strange.'

They heard the front door slam. It sent Simon into another flurry of hysterical whimpers.

'And he loves her best, however much we try,' Miranda said grittily.

'Well, she did tend him at the surgery. I suppose he's just being polite.'

'Look at it this way.' Miranda surveyed Ella with overt curiosity as she failed to remove the uplighter from her head. 'Now he's got all those toys, what would he want with the house wiring?'

'Or the soft furnishings? Or my CD collection? Or the TV listings? Or my beautiful new curtains?' Ella stared back at Miranda. 'Except we didn't buy him any of those things, we bought him a bloody rubber bone. We should have bought him rubber sodding curtains. It's perfectly clear now.'

They heard Faith lumber through the kitchen. She pushed the adjoining door wide and appeared in the living room clutching the biggest bunch of red roses Ella had seen since one of her ex-boyfriends turned up to announce that he and his wife were patching things up and going on a second honeymoon.

'Faith!' Miranda launched in first. 'This dog, sweet as he is, is a complete liability. Look what he's done to all Ella's lovely things! The least you could have done is brought home an animal that was house trained. You just don't think, do you?'

'Who let him in here?' Faith frowned at the bomb site. 'I came back at lunchtime and walked him, and when I left I put him in the kitchen as usual. I told you, we can't let him have the run of the house until he's a bit older.'

'Well, you obviously left the living room door open,' Miranda insisted.

'No.' Faith shook her head. 'I wouldn't have done that.'

Ella was too busy staring at the roses to be angry just yet.

'Where did you get those?'

'Oh, these?' Faith sniffed and studied them without much interest. 'Giles gave them to me.'

Ella sat bolt upright and took the lampshade off her head. Miranda just gaped.

'Giles the vet?' they both managed at the same time.

'Yeah.' Faith wrinkled her nose at them. 'Got any vases?'

'Now just hang on.' Miranda strode forward purposefully and wrested the flowers from Faith. She examined them closely, as if she expected to find that they were plastic, or the sort of flowers that squirted water into your eye. 'Why?'

'Yes, why? What happened?'

Faith grabbed the roses back and returned to the

kitchen. She began rummaging through the cupboards.

'Spill the beans!' Ella instructed.

'I think he might like me after all.' A flush grew over Faith's chin and spread up her cheeks as she twisted the tap to fill the vase she'd found. 'And, um, I wondered if you two could do something for me.'

Simon had started to yap at the back door and it was very clear he wanted to get out and divest himself of some energy. Perhaps it wasn't Faith's fault that he'd attempted to demolish the house while they'd been away. Perhaps it was normal behaviour for an overgrown three-legged puppy. Ella was prepared to think it was.

'What would you like us to do?' she said.

'Well, you know you said you'd give some advice on things. Just perhaps how to do something with my hair. It gets a bit hot around my neck.'

'You want a make-over!' Ella jumped in eagerly. There were many things she wanted to do to Faith with an eyeliner pencil at that moment, but she thought she could stick to putting it around her eyes.

'Nothing dramatic,' Faith said quickly. 'And maybe I'm just being silly. Perhaps I don't need one after all.'

'Oh you do,' Miranda said emphatically.

'Leave it to us,' Ella assured Faith. 'Once you've walked Simon and I've cooked us all a nice hot supper, Miranda and I can have a stab at you.' Ella shook the image of the eyeliner pencil as a weapon away again. 'I mean, have a go at making you look lovely.'

'I don't want to look lovely, just a bit neater.' Faith

plonked her roses in the vase and handed them to Ella. 'You put them somewhere nice.'

'My bedroom? Only joking.'

'And I'll take Simon out now. It's late for his exercise. One of you two could have done it seeing as I was late.'

Miranda and Ella fiddled about pointlessly in the kitchen while Faith expertly took Simon's lead, called him to her ankles, and marched away with him down the hall to the front door. 'And don't even think about putting that curtain rail back up yourself, Ella. You need the right sort of—'

'Drill,' Ella chanted in a bored voice. 'I know.'

'Ability,' Faith corrected, and let herself out.

Chapter Ten

With the shower attachment in her hand, Miranda felt a deep thrill of power. Just a flick of the hot tap and she could have Faith screaming in agony, a nudge towards cold and she'd be yelping with shock. Ella was perched on the loo seat looking on sympathetically and shooting Miranda warning glances every time she adjusted the water flow. Bent over the bath, Faith was at Miranda's mercy. Miranda had smothered her in shampoo and conditioner, insisting that if she was going to trim her hair she wasn't going to use the glorified washing-up liquid Faith bought for herself. Perched on the side of the bath with a cigarette balanced between her fingers, she angled the shower head towards Faith's neck and let it blast there for a while.

'Finished, then?' Faith queried in a small voice.

'Not yet.' Miranda took a leisurely drag on her cigarette.

'This shampoo smells really lovely. What's it called again?'

Miranda told her, insisting once more that if she'd only use a bit of imagination when she went shopping and not rely on the supermarket Value range for everything from baked beans to newspapers, she might reach out into civilisation.

'I just get what Mum used to get. I never really

thought of doing anything else.'

'Well, you can borrow my shampoo until you have a chance to go shopping and get yourself a decent one.'

'But—'

'No arguments,' Miranda said firmly, leaning over to play with the taps and causing Faith to squeal.

Miranda wasn't sure where this magnanimity was coming from. Faith was mad, she'd determined that by now. And very, very irritating. She didn't usually have any patience with mad or irritating people, tending to believe that it was all their own faults for not correcting their deficiencies. Her careers advisor at school had said, 'Whatever you do, Miranda, don't even consider going into teaching.' And she'd known he was right. It was up to each individual to fight their way through life, and if she could do it, then every other bugger could do it too. But here she was, perched on the bath, washing Faith's hair and sharing her shampoo with her. It gave her a queasy feeling in her stomach.

'Right,' she said sharply, tossing the shower head into the bath so that it landed face up and blasted water into Faith's eyes. She leaned over to turn off the taps while Faith was spluttering. 'Towel, Ella?'

'Towel.' Ella passed it, and Miranda wound it round Faith's head. 'You can get up now.'

They all trooped into Miranda's room. It was chaotic, strewn with bottles, lotions, cotton wool balls, clothes, magazines, and a couple of full ash trays. Miranda liked it that way. If she didn't know where anything was, she could find it just by standing on the bed and looking around. Not like

Ella, whose efficient filing of her shoes in alphabetical order of colour made Miranda cringe. Miranda had gained her fill of order at boarding school. Rules and regulations designed to squash the individuality out of you, no space to expand, always someone else's square foot of territory to consider.

It had been just the same at home. Her mother would empty her bedroom of 'rubbish' each time she went away for a new school term, and when she got back she'd find stories, books, letters, photos, even old toys she'd loved, had been cleared out, leaving a guest room in its place. It was like going to stay in a hotel. When she went to visit her friends in the holidays, she was amazed at the junk that crowded their bedrooms, and the animals that bounded around the house. That was how she imagined home from books, but she'd never experienced it. She became accustomed to keeping anything of value about her person, in a bag she took away to school with her, and never unpacking for fear of her things disappearing. It made a job where constant travelling was required the ideal occupation. No time to settle anywhere, no space to call your own. She carried her anchor with her, unpacked it when she arrived, and packed it up again in good time to leave.

So when for moments in her life, like sharing this house, she had a room of her own, a private space that nobody could sort out on her behalf, her suitcase exploded, her belongings stayed where they landed, and she loved it, accruing as many possessions as possible while it lasted. She used five different brands of perfume for different moods, sometimes just squirting them all into the air to mark her presence.

'Sit here,' she instructed, pulling out a stool for Faith to sit opposite a table cluttered with make-up. Faith sat down and peered at herself in the huge stand-up mirror.

'I can't see much without my glasses. Can I put them on?'

'No,' Miranda and Ella chimed.

Miranda stubbed out her cigarette, eyeing Faith critically. Of course, this didn't have to be a benevolent gesture. Her sense of artistry was tempted by having the opportunity to shape a blank canvas into something pleasing. Or at least, something more pleasing than what was there before. At the moment Faith's face was red, presumably from being upside down for nearly fifteen minutes, her eyes were pink and bleary, and her jowls were set. She didn't look as if she was enjoying it much. And with a pink fluffy towel piled on her head she looked like a strawberry sorbet. But Miranda was inspired by the challenge of the job.

She whipped away the towel and Faith's brown hair stuck up in wet spikes. She fingered the ends and pulled them about.

'What are you going to do?' Faith whispered nervously.

'Hmmn.' Miranda stood back, put her head to one side thoughtfully and glanced at Ella, who had dragged up a chair and was flopped in it with one leg over her knee, all attention. 'What d'you reckon, Ella?'

'Needs some colour,' Ella said. 'Henna would be good.'

Miranda took a long comb and raked her way through the strands, peering at them closely.

'I don't want dyed hair. It looks tarty,' Faith stated.

Miranda yanked on a knot and Faith winced. Miranda had tinted her own hair so many different shades of red since she'd been a teenager she'd forgotten what colour it really was.

'Fine. We'll stick to mud-brown then. What about the shape, Ella?'

'Sort of French?'

'Dawn French?' Faith ejected, startled.

'Just be quiet, you.' Miranda knocked Faith on the skull with the end of the comb. 'We know what's best. Let's have a look at your face.'

Miranda examined her raw material. She leant against the table and looked from a distance, then prodded Faith's cheeks and nose. She was genuinely surprised at what a close look revealed. Faith's face wasn't fat, for a start. She'd always thought it was, but it must have been the combination of hair and Elton John glasses that achieved that effect. Her nose was straight, if a little short, her chin was more firm than it appeared, and she had a full bottom lip that with the right shade of lipstick could look quite appealing. But her eyes were her best feature. A striking green, with large clear irises. And her lashes were naturally dark brown but fair at the ends. A good lick of mascara and they'd look wonderfully long. That was the benefit of not pulling them out with a pad of cotton wool and make-up remover every night. She pulled at the straight strands of wet hair until they reached down to Faith's shoulders.

'Courtney Cox,' she decided.

'Yes.' Ella nodded her agreement. 'And a bit of fringe, just a wispy one.'

'Agreed. Scissors?'

'Now hang on.' Faith tried to get up but Miranda pushed her down again. She landed back in the chair with a thump. 'I just want a trim. And I've never had a fringe. They get in the way. It's just not practical.'

'Being beautiful *isn't* practical,' Miranda said, brandishing the scissors like a Hussar on the attack and lunging in with a firm snip. Three inches of hair fell on to the carpet. Faith let out a loud whimper.

'Trust me,' Miranda urged, shearing away at the hair before Faith could leap up again. 'I'm an air hostess.'

'Well, I reckon we can go for a drink now.' Miranda glanced at her watch. 'What do you say?'

'Great idea.' Ella, who had been supplying them all with coffee for the last two hours, was now in need of a walk in the fresh night air and a nightcap. Miranda had gone a bit overboard with the hairspray at the last minute, and they were all getting high on the fumes. But it had been a surprisingly therapeutic way to spend the evening. She'd thought of Matt from time to time as Miranda worked skilfully away, wondered what he was doing, what he was thinking, whether Lorna was stabbing him to death with a paintbrush or cuddling up with him in front of the television. She'd thought of his eyes, his body, and tingled at the possibility of seeing him intimately again, feeling a niggle of hope that he'd sort it out with Lorna so that they could start again like a normal couple, but she had been constantly pulled from her reveries by Miranda barking, 'comb!' or 'cigarettes!'

And it was surprising too how Faith had seemed to enjoy being pampered once she'd got over the shock of being hacked at with the scissors. Miranda had ignored Faith's recurrent complaint that she didn't want to be turned into a coconut and snipped away until she'd produced a very satisfactory result. Then she'd turned to Faith's make-up, at which point Faith had gone limp and compliant, like a sparrow who knows that its best chance to escape from a cat is to feign death.

Now Miranda was fluffing up her own hair and pulling on a jacket while Faith crouched forward, attempting to see herself in the mirror.

'I really do need to put my glasses on.'

'Oh all right then,' Miranda conceded, passing them to her. 'But only to look. You'll have to take them off for the pub. We'll guide you up the road.'

'Pub?' Faith twisted round, shocked. 'I'm not coming to the pub looking like this!'

Miranda tutted impatiently. 'So what is the point of making you up if you're going to go and sit in your bedroom and listen to ELO? Nobody's going to see you in there, are they?'

'That's the whole point,' Faith asserted. 'I don't want anyone to see me like this. It's just for fun.'

'But Faith,' Ella contributed, gazing warmly at the pretty face. Miranda really had brought out the beauty in her eyes. 'You look stunning. You really do. That hair's a massive improvement. You can see your lovely long neck now. And she's done your eyes up brilliantly. You can't just wipe it all off.'

Faith looked as if she was going to burst into tears.

Her lower lip, lined with Mulberry and painted over with Bramble Frost, wobbled.

'I don't want to go out.'

Miranda heaved an irate sigh.

'Fine. Suit yourself. I'll go with Ella, we'll have a laugh, a couple of drinks and wander home tired and happy, and you go and mope in your room. Coming, Ella?'

Faith's eyes filled with tears. Miranda checked her purse for money, snapped it shut and rammed it in her handbag. She headed for the door. Ella sat quietly for a moment. She tried to fathom why Faith was suddenly so unhappy. They'd tried to help her, and she'd asked for the make-over after all. Miranda had been a bit gung-ho throughout, but she was always like that, and Faith was increasingly giving as good as she got. Ella even got the impression at times that they enjoyed their sparring.

'What's worrying you, Faith?' she coaxed gently.

'I just – I can't go out like this. People will see me. People I know.'

Miranda guffawed and yanked the door handle.

'I'm off. Coming, Ella?'

'In a minute.'

'I'll see you there,' Miranda said, and was gone. Her footsteps cascaded down the stairs and the front door slammed.

Ella sat still for a moment, wondering what to say. Faith was peering at her reflection soulfully and giving the occasional sniff.

'Do you want to borrow some make-up remover?' she asked. Faith nodded.

Ten minutes later, Faith's face was pink and shiny,

only a faint smear around the edges of her eyes where the eyeliner had been. She still looked lovely, in a morose sort of way. Ella handed her the comb.

'There. Now fling that round your hair until you're happy with it. I'm going to bung a jumper and some lipstick on, and we'll walk up to the Plough together.'

'Ella?'

'Yes?' Ella turned as she reached the door.

'Thank you for understanding.'

'I don't think I do understand really. You look much nicer. Miranda's done wonders with your hair. You might just say thank you when you get the chance.'

'I'll buy her a drink at the pub.'

'That'd be a nice gesture.'

Ella rushed round her room, avoiding the spindly camera legs and getting changed away from the gap in the curtains she had to leave in order for the camera to record overnight activity outside. She glanced at it curiously several times as she yanked a tight red jumper over her bra and buttoned on a clean pair of Levis. When would she see Jaz again, then? It seemed very open-ended now. She hadn't even thought to ask how long the surveillance operation would last. It was strange, but however much his presence in the house disturbed her, she did feel safer when he was around. The novelty of the equipment being set up was easy to deal with, but how would she feel if weeks rolled by, and the chances of the gang of Pete Postlethwaites at number eleven catching on to their involvement increased?

She pushed the thought from her mind. Faith

appeared at her door in a floppy tracksuit top and jeans, her glasses back in place.

'Let's go and get hammered,' Ella said.

This time, when she entered the pub lobby Ella loitered to examine Lorna's watercolour in more detail. It was a view of Christchurch Meadow she recognised, and it was unique, with impressionistic splashes of pink and blue which set it apart from the usual postcard reproductions. It was no wonder she managed to sell so many of her paintings. Ella felt a prickle of admiration for her talent. Matt had said she taught too, private classes held around the country for enthusiastic amateurs who could afford the luxury of residential courses in beautiful surroundings. She wondered for a moment what she was like. Anything like herself? Tall, dark and strong featured? Or petite and fair? She hadn't got a clue.

'Come on,' Faith held the door to the public bar open.

It was buzzing for a week night, but the addition of Sky Sports in a spacious bar at the back had ensured a regular flow of drinkers at most times. Kevin was behind the bar. He shot over to them as soon as he saw them.

'It's my favourite gardener and my favourite veterinary nurse!' he greeted them cheerfully.

'Where's Andrea tonight?' Ella peered around the bar but there was no sign of the blonde bombshell.

'Threw us over for the King's Arms. It's nearer her college, so she says, but I think she found her attraction to me too overpowering. So I'm single and dangerous. Watch yourselves, girls.' He gave them both a wink as he pulled himself up to his full five foot four and peeped over the beer pumps. 'Vodka?'

'Yep. And a gin and orange for Faith.' Ella grinned down at him.

Kevin glanced at Faith as he reached up for some glasses, and did a double-take.

'Crikey, you've changed your hair.' He leant forward for a better look as Faith went scarlet. 'You look amazing.'

He disappeared in the direction of the optics. Faith mumbled under her breath, fiddling with her shoulder bag.

'Sarcastic git.'

'No, he meant it.' Ella looked at her in surprise.

'I expect Miranda told him what she'd done. He's just teasing me.'

Ella frowned but looked around for Miranda anyway. She couldn't see her at any of the tables. Kevin returned with their drinks.

'Seen Miranda?'

'In the small bar at the back. Playing darts.'

'You what?' Ella almost choked.

'With a couple of blokes.' Kevin raised his eyebrows meaningfully. 'One of them was in here for your birthday. Blond geezer.'

'Mike,' Faith picked up her drink and took an uncharacteristically large slurp.

'Well, we'll join them then,' Ella said breezily, grabbing Faith by the elbow and steering her towards the back bar. It was like getting a racehorse into a starting cage. Ella stopped at the swing door and turned on Faith.

'What's the matter? I thought you were going to buy Miranda a drink and be friendly?'

'It's Mike. I hate him.' Faith gripped her drink tightly.

'Why?' Faith didn't answer, so Ella pushed open the door and nudged her into the back bar ahead of herself. 'Look, you don't have to talk to him, do you? Let's just relax.'

It wasn't Mike playing darts with Miranda – it was Giles, and with him was an equally broad and dynamic looking man of about the same age. That was great news, and the even greater news was that there was no sign of Suzanne. Ella's spirits shot up. She nudged Faith playfully, and sauntered across to them.

'Hello, you lot. Fancy banging into you here, Giles.'

In a bottle-green cotton shirt and jeans he looked gorgeous. His companion wasn't bad either. Darker, and less likely to be offered an on-the-spot Hollywood contract than Giles, but sturdy with an intelligent face. Giles greeted them enthusiastically, smiling broadly at Faith and winking at her.

'Great hairdo. It really suits you.' Faith muttered a thank you. Ella was relieved to see that she didn't call him a sarcastic git. 'This is Paul. We were at university together. He's come to check out my new set-up.'

'Are you a vet too, then?' Ella uncoiled a hand and extended it to him. She realised as he got close that he was a lot shorter and wider than Giles. He could have played prop forward, and by the looks of his nose, might have done at some point. But single men of the right sort of age and chest dimensions were not that easy to come by locally, and not to be spurned without careful consideration.

'Yep. I work out in the sticks near Hereford.'

'Don't tell me. Lots of cows, not many poodles.'

'That's about right.' He grinned and Ella decided he was very sweet, whilst realising that nobody she thought of as 'sweet' had ever progressed to 'fantastic'. But perhaps her life was complicated enough at the moment.

'Hi, Faith!' Paul leant past Ella and put his hand out. 'Giles has been telling me all about you.'

Faith's eyes gained a sparkle behind her glasses while her cheeks went from pink to maroon. She played with the toggle of her tracksuit hood until it pinged out of her fingers and hit her on the chin.

'Has he?'

'He's lucky to have a colleague like you. Hard to come by, you know.' Paul jammed one hand in the pocket of his jeans, taking a swig of his pint. 'Lucky devil.'

Faith made an odd noise which sounded like a baby choking.

'D'you want to play doubles, then?' Miranda sashayed over, laying a hand on Giles's shoulder. She was clutching a trio of darts in her hand with the ends pointed somewhere in Faith's direction.

'Why not? I'll have to have a practice first though.' Ella took the darts from Miranda and tossed them at the board in turn. The last thing she wanted was to miss the board completely in front of two hunky men and end in a flurry of airy giggles. Her years spent socialising with male colleagues had paid off. She managed a twenty, an eighteen and a five.

'Ooh, can I partner you?' Miranda cooed. 'How about boys against girls?'

'That's an unfair advantage,' Paul said with a slight smile.

'Hardly,' Miranda pouted back. 'Ella might be good, but my misspent youth revolved around restaurants and night clubs. I've got more chance of hitting the chip shop than the board. We'll take you on anyway, and no concessions.'

She retrieved the darts from Ella and cast them elegantly at the board. Two bounced off the wire and the third landed firmly outside the number three. Ella gave an exaggerated groan.

'You two had better play with blindfolds on if Miranda and I are going to stand a chance then.' She raised her eyebrows at Giles.

'No,' Paul said slowly, looking a little confused. 'I meant you have an unfair advantage as there are three of you.'

There was a silence. Ella realised with a thud of humiliation what she'd done and turned round to find Faith. Miranda busily gathered the darts and flung them at the board again.

'What, Faith? She won't want to play.'

Ella noticed Giles was frowning as he sipped from his pint. Her discomfort grew. Asking Faith to play now did not disguise the fact that she and Miranda had ignored her completely. She realised it now, but she hadn't realised it until somebody else had pointed it out, and she felt dreadful. She bit her lip and looked over at Faith, who was leaning against the pool table clutching her gin and orange and fingering the bluntly cut ends of her hair. A large sign on the table read 'This Table is Alarmed'. Next to it, Faith looked as if she was echoing the sentiment. Paul approached her, holding out another set of darts.

'Faith, would you like to play?'

Faith blushed deeply and gurgled again.

'Tell you what, you play with Miranda and I'll sit out,' Ella ventured quickly.

'Oh thanks!' Miranda rolled her eyes. 'They might as well play Simon with four broken paws if they take us two on.'

'I haven't played for a bit—' Faith mumbled.

'There, you see!' Miranda exclaimed.

'—although we had a board in the outhouse.'

'Have a go.' Paul handed Faith the darts with a gentle smile. 'It'll come back to you after a couple of throws.'

Faith swallowed hard, took the darts, put her toe against the line, chewed her lip, squinted and threw each in turn. Miranda blinked at the board.

'Was that a fluke?'

Faith retrieved all three darts from the twenty, where they had landed comfortably.

'I'm warmed up now. Shall we play?'

Ella found a stool and resigned herself to watching. It was a relief that they'd slipped out of that situation with a little dignity. Poor Faith. It was just that it took her so long to relax in a crowd, it was sometimes easy to forget she was there.

Miranda seemed happy once the game kicked off. Giles was being friendly towards her, asking her a lot about herself, Miranda being flippant, as usual, with her replies. More than once Ella caught an expression of fascination on Giles's face. However loyal he felt to Faith as a colleague, she guessed Miranda's charms were just too intriguing to be passed over without proper assessment. Faith seemed to settle in too, and Ella was happy that Paul was making a genuine effort to be friendly to her. Bit by bit her replies to him were becoming less monosyllabic and more elaborate. When the guys won the game and Miranda demanded an immediate rematch, Faith even smiled.

It was only Ella herself who was now stuck on the sidelines, left to ponder on the state of her affairs – or not, given that Matt was being elusive. And as the others fell into a contented foursome, tossing occasional banter in her direction but concentrating on preventing Miranda from causing anybody an injury, Ella allowed herself a moment to wallow in self-pity.

Where was it all going wrong for her? Peering over at Miranda picking one of her darts out of Giles's beer with a laughing apology, and at Faith hitting the numbers like an expert, she felt inadequate. Miranda was too stunning and funny for it ever to matter to a man whether she was good at anything – although she was good at plenty of things. And Faith – well, she was just turning out to be good at bloody everything, Crunchie fetish or no Crunchie fetish. And with a sharp new haircut that changed her appearance dramatically, she had Paul's rapt attention, even if she'd rather bathe in icebergs in the middle of winter than have a man show interest in her.

She glanced at her watch, feeling ignored. An hour until closing time. She felt a growing urge to be at home, tucked up in her duvet, listening to the sounds of the night.

'I've got a headache so I'm slipping off,' she whispered to Faith as the others were on their hands and knees trying to find one of Miranda's stray darts which had ricocheted under a table. 'Mention it to the others if they miss me. See you later.'

Faith nodded, but she seemed more interested in the view of Paul's rear. Ella suppressed a sigh and left the bar.

The car park was well lit, and Ella marched through it, buttoning her jacket, and headed down the wide lane. It was only a ten-minute walk back to the cottage, and the road was dotted with streetlamps right up to their row of houses. Occasionally a car swept past, and she kept to the narrow pavement along the way.

She took a deep breath and gazed up at the clearing sky. It was fairly warm still, the smell of damp grass, earth and a hint of chestnut in the air. Orion's belt was bright tonight, and she could see Mars hovering as a small pink dot. And in the midst of her petulance, she realised that she'd never sat and looked at the stars with a lover. It was something she'd missed out on, and for some reason, this made her want to have a good cry.

She walked on, past the darkened windows of the small newsagent, attempting to reason it through. She'd never stargazed with a lover because, in the last few years, her relationships had been with men who weren't let out at night, and if they were, it was to steal a night away in a hotel room or at her London flat. There hadn't been time to sit and look at the sky. In short, in the last few years, all of her relationships had been with men who happened to be married.

She hadn't sought them out, they had approached her. But nonetheless, instead of telling them to sod off, which she knew some of her friends would have done instantly, she'd played with the idea until, more than once, it had become a reality. And now it was almost as if she had marked out a future for herself. While she had severed herself from the practical constraints of a job and city life she'd grown to dislike and leapt off to the country feeling free, she'd taken her habits with her.

She wasn't free. Not until she allowed herself to wonder why it had happened again. And something was nagging at her which told her that only a trip home to talk to her father was going to help her solve that. She knew it, but she was putting it off.

She turned the corner in the lane, jamming her hands in her pockets and eyeing the welcome sight of light shining through their front door in the distance. A ripple of wind played in her hair, and she shook her head to prevent a shudder. She wanted to speed up now. The breeze was rustling the gold leaves of the sycamores along the path, and in her uneven frame of mind, she almost thought she could hear footsteps creeping about amongst the dry leaves and twigs.

She shot a furtive look into the darkness. The shadows played as the branches of the trees swung backwards and forwards over the streetlamps. She swallowed and stepped into the road, away from the path. Better to be exposed than lurking along a hedgerow, that was only sensible. She thought she heard a twig snap.

She broke into a trot. The cottage was less than a hundred yards away now. A gust of wind threw the trees into a flurry of activity, and her trot became a run. She fumbled for her house keys in her bag. Only a minute now and she'd be putting them in the door, slamming it behind her, and laughing at herself for being an idiot. The road danced up and down before her eyes as she careered towards their front path, not daring even to cast a look at number eleven. Just pretend it's not there, she urged herself.

What happened next was so quick, it was like a dizzying sequence of camera shots. She ran into a solid form impossible to distinguish in the darkness. The wind crashed in her ears. She screamed. A sickening crunch filled her mouth as she was hit around the head with something hard and solid.

Her senses faded and she blacked out.

Chapter Eleven

Ella's first sensation on opening her eyes was that she was cold. The ground was damp under her body, and her cheek was flat against the hard concrete of her front path. The yellow spears of light from the streetlamp rotated backwards and forwards then steadied again. She pulled herself up slowly and a blinding pain shot through her temple. She widened her eyes at the dustbin next to her. It was on its side, the lid a few feet away where it must have rolled. A bin bag had spilled out on to the path. She rubbed at her forehead with a clammy hand and felt a gritty stubble across her skin where she had landed.

'Oh blimey,' she breathed in horror.

She pulled herself up quickly and got to her feet, wobbling towards the front door, and reaching in her bag for her keys. Her pulse quickened. She jammed the wrong key in the lock, darting a look over her shoulder, too hazy to work out whether anybody was still around, and fumbled until she wedged the right key into the door, twisted it, and threw herself inside, slamming the door behind her.

She yanked the chain on the door, flipped the catch on the lock to fix it in place and grabbed a quick lungful of air. Then she staggered into the sitting room, dropped her bag on the floor, and snatched up the phone.

Somewhere slotted into the telephone directory along with the Indian, pizza and Chinese menus they saved was a piece of paper with Jaz's contact details on it. She grappled with it, her fingers trembling, until she'd got it the right way up. Then she stabbed at the buttons, got a wrong number – the answerphone of a beauty parlour which she furiously told to get off the line – and finally got through to a deep voice which simply barked a name at her. It wasn't Jaz's.

'Don't tell me I've got another flipping wrong number. Who the hell are you?' she yelled, her nerves in shreds.

'DC Graveney. Can I help you?'

She closed her eyes in a tidal wave of relief. She'd found them. Now she didn't feel so alone.

'Get me Jaz, please. I need to talk to him right now.'

'Who is this?'

'Ella Norton.'

'And what is it concerning, please?'

'Just get him, will you?' she bellowed. 'Thanks to you lot I've just been mugged outside my own house. I want him to get his butt right here, right now and sort this out.'

And then, she added silently to herself, I'll feel safe. When he gets here.

'Hang on.'

She wanted to shout, 'No, I can't hang on. He has to be on his way even as I speak!' but she breathed heavily into the phone, hearing the tremor in her breath as she let it out. Down the line she could hear various shuffles and clonks and distant voices chatting. Even laughing. She gritted her teeth.

Another arrow of pain shot over her eyebrows and she winced. This was beyond the call of duty. And it was all his fault. What's more, she just couldn't wait to tell him so.

She waited. More scuffles in the background. It sounded as if they were having a tea party. Had he forgotten he'd left her on the end of the phone, mugged and furious? This was all far too much. Finally she heard the receiver being lifted again and a male voice speak.

'Hello?'

'Now listen, you.' She attempted to pull herself out of the sofa's gullet. It was trying hard to swallow her whole tonight. 'I don't want any bloody excuses. Get into your car and get round here.'

'Miss Norton? Jaz is on his way. I've rung him at home. He's not on duty tonight, but he should be with you very shortly.'

'Oh.'

Her breathing steadied. He wasn't on duty. Why not? Well, she supposed he couldn't be there twenty-four hours a day after all, but that's where she'd imagined him when he wasn't lurking around the house. At a desk somewhere, drinking coffee out of a plastic cup, by the phone just in case she rang with an emergency. How dare he go home?

But he was coming anyway. Quite right too.

'Thank you.'

She hung up and as soon as she had, felt nervous again. She got up and drifted around the sitting room, rubbing at her arms. Very soon the others would be back from the pub. As long as they didn't hang around for a late drink. Or go on somewhere to drink coffee with Giles and Paul. But they wouldn't do that. Faith was with them, and if she wasn't in bed by eleven she gained a glassy look in her eyes. They'd be back any minute. She heard a sudden clawing at the kitchen door, growing into a frenzied scrambling. She jumped back clutching her chest. Simon let out a long, low howl.

'Oh my God! Simon, you poor devil!'

She rushed to the door and opened it for him. Since they'd bought him a big basket and filled it with blankets he preferred to sleep in there, even if they fell all over themselves offering him the sofa. It was a relief, soft furnishings wise, but now she wanted him with her, wherever she went. He bounced all over her in a flurry of saliva, paws and whimpers. She grabbed him in her arms tightly and held him like a baby. She'd been so panicked when she got in, her ears crashing with her frenzied pulse, she hadn't even remembered he was there. It still took some getting used to, having a dog in the house, when you were accustomed to living on your own. And especially on occasions when you'd been savaged by drug dealers ferreting through dustbins.

She collapsed on the sofa again and Simon stared up at her contentedly while she rubbed his belly. As long as they didn't come back.

But they'd found whatever it was they'd come for, she decided, taking a few long, calming breaths, the back of her head where she'd been clouted starting to ache naggingly. And she hadn't seen them. There was no way she could do a description. Or an identity parade. So they had no reason to come back and finish her off. And if they were going to shoot her, or pummel her to a pulp, the best time to do it would have been while she was unconscious. The fact that they hadn't was slightly comforting. So, she must have disturbed them, coming back like that. Maybe they'd even seen her, Miranda and Faith go out earlier.

She gasped at the thought. Maybe the dealers had been watching their every move from the house, waiting for a time when they'd all be out. And then Ella had ruined the plan, coming back early from the pub – and now she remembered that she'd run the last few yards full pelt. It must have been pretty terrifying for them to have a lanky woman speeding towards them with ragged breath when they had their hands in the bin. Perhaps they thought *she* was going to attack *them*? She almost felt sorry for them. What a shock that must have been. No wonder they'd panicked.

She soothed Simon as if he was the one who was startled and he groaned at her in contentment. Poor little darling. He had no perception of the wicked ways of humans. It was so much more simple, being a dog. Dogs never got together in the park and said, 'Christ, this is boring. Let's go and get stoned.' It wasn't as if Simon would ever sit by the phone wondering if it was all on or off. He'd know. His choice of mate would either let him, or she wouldn't, and that would be the end of it.

But then she'd be stuck with the puppies, and not just a couple of them probably. A whole brood, without his support. And he'd be off, up the park again with the boys, sniffing around the bushes for the latest bit of totty, not a care in the world for his poor, suffering last conquest with teats down to her paws and exhaustion from caring for her young all by herself. Her frown became a scowl as his contentment grew and he closed his eyes and stuck his willy out.

'You can put that away. You're selfish, all of you. Not a principle between you.'

He moaned in agreement.

She glanced at her watch. She chewed on her lip, her head throbbing, one eye on the curtains at the front window as if she'd miss something if she didn't keep her eyes pointed that way, and waited.

Miranda and Giles had disappeared. Miranda had gone to get a round and Giles had offered to help her, which Faith thought was silly. She could have done it in two trips, or she could have waited at the small back bar where they were and yelled for Kevin's attention. But they'd both vanished, leaving Faith to stand awkwardly with her darts in her hand, concentrating on the chalked numbers on the board and wondering why it was that everyone could add up, but nobody could take away. She'd got so fed up with Miranda cooing over the subtractions that she'd started calling out the scores for her to write down. In the last game, Miranda wasn't even bothering to try, just glancing at Faith for the score.

Paul was taking another sip of his drink now and fingering his belt. She knew he didn't know what to say to her. She knew he felt as uncomfortable as she did that they'd been left alone together in the bar. And nobody was playing pool, so it was very quiet apart from the hum of conversation and the distant beat of Robbie Williams coming from the main part of the pub. Her brain raced, trying to come up with ideas. She could grab her handbag and go to the toilet. That would kill a few minutes. In fact she could wait in there until Miranda and Giles got back. Then they'd all be chatting when she resurfaced and she could just answer the questions she was asked, or laugh if somebody said something funny. And Giles was funny, she had to admit. Paul was too, in a quieter sort of way. Even Miranda had missed some of his muttered asides, but Faith hadn't, and they'd made her smile. She heard Paul clear his throat. This was excruciating. She spotted her bag on a chair and made a move towards it.

'I'll just go—'

'Have you ever been to Herefordshire?' he asked her. She glanced at him. His head was on one side as if he'd been watching her.

'Er, no. I went to London a while ago, with the school.'

'Ah. Schools don't tend to arrange trips to Herefordshire. Not many landmarks by comparison, I suppose.'

'Yes.' She picked up her bag and hooked it over her shoulder.

'It's very beautiful. It's nothing like Oxfordshire. Plenty of huge spaces, a low population, lots of cows, fields and trees, not many people. Or cinemas. I found it a bit difficult to adjust to at first. But I like it now. It gives you plenty of time to think. The pace of life is different there. Just coming here feels like an adrenaline rush. You can imagine how I feel about going to London.'

'Oh.' No, she couldn't really, but it probably didn't matter.

'It's chaos. I hadn't realised it until I moved so far away. Now I feel ruffled just getting to the outskirts. As if I want to turn tail and run back to the country again.'

'You do?' She blinked at him. He was too – well, sorted out really for her to imagine him being daunted by London. Only shy people felt that, she was sure. She'd hated her trip to London. They'd gone on the underground, and she'd been white-faced with claustrophobia, her palms breaking out into a sweat. She'd been in too much of a panic to enjoy it. Even thinking about it made her panic. But perhaps one day, if she went with somebody who felt the same, she might like it. It was just an idle thought.

'Hmmn.' He swilled the dregs of his beer around in his glass thoughtfully. 'My family's in Hampshire. Near the New Forest. My father used to run a farm when I was a boy, but they went bankrupt.'

'What sort of farm?' She'd asked him a question. It was probably a stupid one. She held her breath.

'Pigs.'

'Really?' She could see him with pigs, just as she could see him trudging over a muddy field in Herefordshire. It just looked right.

'I hated it. I got too attached to the piglets. Gave them all names. Spent my childhood out in the barn playing with them, then they'd suddenly all disappear.' He pulled a rueful face. Faith's stomach contracted with sympathy.

'Oh how awful!' she breathed.

'It was.' He nodded. He wasn't taking the mickey out of her either. He meant it. 'I can't tell you how relieved I was when the business folded.'

'I would have been too,' she told him from the heart. He nodded at her.

'So I decided that instead of farming animals, I'd mend them instead. And I became a vet.' He laughed. 'And I mend them for other people who farm them. Doesn't make a great deal of sense, does it?'

'Oh it does,' she exclaimed, forgetting for a moment that she was clutching her bag to her waist and intending to flee to the Ladies. 'You're easing their suffering and making decisions in their interest. You're not thinking of them as business units and just counting their worth. You're doing something so worthwhile. I think it's a wonderful thing. The most noble thing you could do.'

He looked at her seriously with his dark eyes for a moment, then he laughed again.

'I wouldn't go that far. You know you can train to be a vet at almost any age, don't you?'

She stared at him.

'What I mean is, at our college there were plenty of older students. People in their twenties and thirties who'd decided to train properly, who hadn't thought of it before for various reasons.'

She continued to stare at him.

'Why don't you do that?'

She was utterly dumbstruck.

'It's just that I was talking to Giles about you. He said you've got three science "A" levels at top grades, but you've never used them.'

Her body was suffused with shock.

'H-how would he know that? I mean, he can't . . .' she trailed away.

'Don't know.' Paul shrugged pleasantly. 'I guess you must have put it on an application form or a CV at some point when you applied for the job. Or maybe Suzanne mentioned it to him. I can't remember what he said.'

'S-Suzanne doesn't know. I mean.' She swallowed. Her throat was tight.

'Seems such a waste of a capable brain. I mean, you've got the passion for the work, you've got experience and according to Giles it's almost like having another vet working with him. He was telling me that Suzanne had said you're the only person she's met in her life who never needs to be told anything twice. You just remember it, bang, like that. Next scenario, you're in with an idea. That's quite unique.'

'I—' Her face was burning with embarrassment. How could they have all sat round and discussed her like this? What were they thinking of? Why would they do it?

'I've embarrassed you,' he said. He smiled at her kindly and she felt tears welling in her eyes. Oh God, don't cry. Not now, in front of him. This was ridiculous. She swallowed the lump down her throat again. Why was he being so nice to her? Was it a set-up? Was that why Giles and Miranda were away for so long? Were they all going to laugh about it when they came back? Bewilderment engulfed her.

'I – I don't know what to say.' She sniffed and it turned into a gulp.

'I'm sorry, Faith. I really am. When something's

obvious to me I tend to go jumping in. When you were flinging the numbers around when we were playing I realised how right Giles was. You're incredibly bright. It just seemed clear to me that you should go and train.'

'T-train,' she echoed. She was being so stupid, repeating his words, stuttering, gulping, blushing. But he was a nice-looking man with such gentle eyes and a lovely figure. A real man with muscles and a shape, not a thin, small man like her father. It was overwhelming. How could she know what to do?

'Tell you what. I could send you some numbers and addresses and you could make enquiries. Would that be helpful?'

'But—' This was all going too fast. Did he really mean that he thought that she should train to be a vet? Herself? But how? And where? And how could she pay for it? And what if she wasn't good enough? And what about her room in Ella's house? She couldn't take it all in.

'Look.' He touched her arm. She stared down at his hand on her sleeve. It had calluses around the knuckles and strong, firm fingers. Heat rushed through her stomach, leaving her legs feeling as if they had no strength. It was an alien sensation. It was frightening. 'I'm on leave so I'm staying up with Giles for a few days. How about we go for a drink on our own one night and we can chat about it properly? We can have dinner somewhere in Oxford if you like. You know the town. You could recommend somewhere. Perhaps somewhere you've always fancied but never got round to going to. On me. I've just been paid.'

She gaped at him in horror. She was intelligent? She should be a vet? And he wanted to take her out on her own for a drink followed by dinner?

The tears burst through the flimsy defence and cascaded down her face. She turned and fled from the bar, crashing out of the swing door and knocking Miranda flying.

'Flipping heck, Faith. What's up?' She staggered back with beer slopping from the glasses in her hands.

'Just – just shut up!' Faith flung at her. 'And that goes for you too, Giles.'

Ella heard a car pull up and sat with her head pulsing with pain while she waited for the doorbell to ring. When it did she placed Simon artistically on the marshmallow cushions of the sofa where he flopped sleepily, and stood up and rubbed her hands on her thighs.

'Right, Mr Jaz-min-bin-zing. This is it.'

She took a deep breath, strode out to the hall and flung the door open wide. Jaz looked up at her from under his eyebrows. He looked cagey. And so he should, she thought with satisfaction. This wasn't the first time she'd felt impelled to have a good row with him, and this one was going to be a good 'un.

'Come in,' she instructed, allowing him to walk past her into the sitting room and throwing the door back in the hole. She followed him into the room and slammed that door too for good measure. Simon stuck an ear in the air and went back to sleep.

'Are you all right?' he said, his hands on his hips.

'Of course I am!' she exclaimed. 'I've just been

attacked on the doorstep of my own house. I've got concussion and I'm no longer safe in anything I do. Everything's going swimmingly. And how are you?'

'All right, look, let's take this a step at a time.' He put out his hands to her in a gesture.

'No, let's not!' she stormed, pacing up and down past him to make the point that she was very, very angry. A blast of pain shot over her skull again and she blinked it away. 'I never felt comfortable about getting involved with this but I was trying to help. It's earned me a strange man creeping about in my bedroom, comments about me going for a shower in my underwear, and now I've been bludgeoned half to death on my front path. I've got a camera in my room which means I have to sneak around on my hands and knees when the light's on because I can't close the curtains fully at night, and now I'm probably going to be lynched whenever I leave the house. It has to stop. And I want you to find whoever who did this and – and make sure they aren't going to do it again.'

She stopped pacing as an attack of dizziness assailed her. She blinked again and it went away. Perhaps the blow had been more forceful than she realised.

'I think you should sit down.' He indicated the chair for her. 'And you should let somebody look at your head. We'll deal with all of this in the right order, but first you'd better be sure you're not really concussed.'

'Course I'm concussed!' she claimed victoriously, the room spinning slightly then stopping again. 'It felt like a bloody baseball bat. I'm not just going to have a little graze, am I?'

'Please, Ella.' He moved towards her purposefully. 'Let me look at the wound. You may need stitches.'

She closed her eyes as her mouth went dry and her head gave an almighty throb. She felt as if she was coming round from an anaesthetic. It was very weird. Perhaps this really was concussion. She'd never had it before. It was like seasickness with a drunken brain and crunchy teeth thrown in. She'd had a drink in the pub and a swig from the wine bottle in the fridge to calm her nerves too. That hadn't helped. She swayed and found herself propped up against him.

'Have a look, please,' she murmured. 'It doesn't half hurt.'

She felt his fingers on the nape of her neck, moving under her hair. They were warm against her skin. From the depths of her anaesthesia she realised that it was an extremely pleasant sensation. She bowed her head against his chest and allowed him to probe her head, parting her hair and touching her scalp gently.

'Does that hurt?' he said into her ear.

'Hmmn. It's nice. Don't stop.'

She felt him stiffen and take a step away from her. She opened her eyes blearily and smiled at him. 'I was enjoying that. Am I concussed then?'

He gave her a very odd look. He seemed remarkably handsome tonight. His blue-black hair, usually sleek and smooth, was a bit ruffled. It was like crow feathers blown into disarray by the breeze. His skin seemed as smooth as a dark gold silk, his eyes charcoal black. Why hadn't she noticed how beautiful his face was? Somebody should point it out to him. Perhaps he didn't know.

'You are extraordinarily good looking,' she told him, swaying violently forwards in time to be caught in his arms.

'Ella,' he said practically. 'I really think you need to get down to the JR.'

'Men don't usually try to hospitalise me when I pay them a compliment. You're a bit strange.'

She felt his breath against her cheek as he let out a soft laugh and tried to prop her upright again.

'That bump on your head's nasty. There's not much blood but it's swelling already. You need an X-ray.'

'No I don't. I need to tell you where to stick your bloody camera.'

'You can do that,' he said, 'after you've had your X-ray. Come on.'

He was propelling her towards the door now, picking up her bag from where she'd left it and throwing her jacket over his arm. He was well trained. He knew a woman didn't go anywhere without her handbag. He'd make his fiancée a lovely husband. Even if he was a bit arrogant. Some women hated that, but Ella didn't mind. She quite liked it. She could be a bit arrogant herself. They'd make a good couple, actually.

She twisted round to have a better look at him as he marched her to the front door. He had four faces, going round in circles. She stretched her eyes but there were still four of them.

'Does your fiancée know what a good catch she's got?' she asked him factually.

'You're definitely concussed,' he said with more

urgency. 'Let's get on our way. I'm worried about you.'

'No.' She stopped on the doormat. 'Not until you tell me about your fiancée. Does she appreciate you? That's what I want to know.'

He let out a short breath and gave her a pained look. At least, that's what it looked like, but although he had only one face again it was very blurred.

'I hardly know my fiancée. We've met three times. But yes, I think she appreciates me, as I appreciate her. Now can we go?'

'Hang on!' Ella caught his arm. 'So you don't love her then?'

He clapped his hand to his forehead in despair. 'Oh dear God, Ella. What's all this about?'

'Well, you've met me three times. More, in fact, and you don't love me. So how can you love her?'

'Look, Miss Norton—'

'Don't call me "Miss Norton",' she complained indignantly.

'Ella, there are things about my culture you'll probably never understand. My forthcoming marriage is one of them. I've met Sasha, I like her very much, we have a lot in common. There's no reason why it shouldn't work. That's all I'm prepared to say about it. Now I have a serious job to do here and right from the start you've been making it very difficult.'

'I have?' She gave him a sloppy smile and fell against him.

'Yes,' he said tightly, pushing her in front of him and getting her to the front door. 'So if you don't mind I'm going to get you up to Casualty, make sure

196

that you're well, and sort the rest of this situation out. I'm not here in a personal capacity.'

'No,' she agreed. 'Neither am I.' She nodded at him emphatically. 'But if you were, would you like it?'

'I beg your pardon?' There could be no doubting the despair on his features now as he fiddled with the front door latch.

'I mean, if you weren't Indian and if you weren't going to marry Sasha and if you could make your own mind up, would you like being here in a personal capacity?'

'I have made my own mind up about Sasha,' he growled at her. She stiffened. The door went in and out of focus again and she stumbled towards it.

'Sorry,' she muttered. 'I must sound so ignorant. I don't know what's come over me.'

'I do,' he said, shoving one of his arms under hers and forcing her to grip hold of it tightly. 'And you're going to want to crawl under a stone when you're in your right mind again. Come on. Let's get you to the car.'

Chapter Twelve

It was only once she was in the seat of his car that Ella realised how low the carriage was. This obviously wasn't the vehicle he used for work. Or maybe he did. It was definitely a sporty model of some sort, but she was too fuddled to absorb any details other than a mahogany dashboard, a whiff of leather, and the fact that the seat was very firm and cupped her body. He'd helped her into her seat belt, which seemed to wind right around her and clip into a catch in the tiny back seat. Once she was secured, they shot off into the night.

It was odd being driven around by a policeman. She wondered how the partners of police officers felt while they were bombing around doing mundane domestic things in the car. The weekly shop up at Sainsbury's. Or down to Do-It-All for a new toilet roll holder. Or off to see Auntie Maisie in Kidderminster. There was something amazingly comforting about it. If someone leapt out at the traffic lights and tried to bop you through your window, he'd just pull out his badge and wave it at them. That'd chuck a bucket of water over the odd blaze of road rage. And if you were in a hurry, surely he'd just put a flashy light on top of the car and whiz through all the red lights?

But she wondered too if Jaz was capable of going anywhere without being a policeman, whether he was on duty or not. How would he react down the chip shop if a scuffle broke out? Would he be muscling his way up the queue shouting, 'Now everybody calm down and tell me how this started'? What did he say if he got a short measure on his pint down at the pub? Ask for a top-up, or threaten to report the landlord to Weights and Measures? And would dating a policeman put you forever on your guard? What if you were driving? You'd go every-where at twenty miles an hour just in case he gave you a point on your licence. What if someone lent you a CD to record? Would he stand there like the Jolly Green Giant in your living room as you scribbled the tracks down on the tape inset and boom, 'Home taping is illegal, and it's killing the music industry'?

But he'd said he'd joined the police because he wanted to be a Wild West hero, and cowboys were never that pedantic. They were more into sweeping gestures. She could picture him in his cowboy hat and fringed leather jacket on his day off, swaggering down Oxford High Street with one hand on his holster, catching babies as they fell out of prams and plopping them back with a nod of the head and a 'My pleasure, Ma'am.' What exactly did he do with his time off? Watch endless episodes of *Mahabharat* on video, or go down the pub to watch the footie?

She shot him a glance. He was very quiet beside her, and she was feeling more subdued as well. She had a horrible feeling she'd offended him with the way she'd behaved in the cottage. It was all very hazy. Her head was buzzing and it was difficult to think clearly about anything. And it was odd that they'd just jumped in the car and sped away from the house. Shouldn't he have been asking her a thousand questions about her assault or dusting for finger-prints?

'I – Jaz, shouldn't you be checking out the bin? They might have left something.'

'Not yet.' He clicked his tongue as if he was thinking it over as they wound through the lanes. 'The minute we show an official interest out there, the scam's over. I could call in and get a couple of the guys to come over and check it out now, but that'd be an end to it. Do you see?'

'Oh.' Her skull tingled again and she flinched. 'So they're going to get away with it? What about my concussion?'

'It's assault. Possibly ABH. It'll all be dealt with in good time, don't worry, Ella.'

'But . . . how?'

She tried to turn round to look at him properly but she was bound very tightly to the seat. He glanced at her. He didn't look annoyed. That was good. Perhaps he'd forget that she'd fallen all over him just now.

'The camera. Remember? That should tell us quite a lot.'

'Ah.' She thought about it in a refreshing moment of clarity before the fog rolled over her again. 'Ah yes. It'll be on tape. So it will. Clever you.'

'Do you still want to tell me where to stick my camera?' He allowed himself a soft chuckle.

'Of course,' she said logically. 'If the camera hadn't been put in, they'd never have attacked me in the first place. It's all because of you guys.'

'Not necessarily. They were working from outside

your house anyway. This could have happened regardless of whether we were there or not. And it's even less likely that they'd have continued if they knew we were on to them. It's actually very helpful to us. With any luck we'll have something interesting to look at.'

'I'm sure it'll be fascinating,' she guffawed at him, not sure how offended to be. 'You can show the tape at your Christmas party.'

'You know what I mean. I'm sorry you've been hurt, you know that. It's a relief it's not more serious. But it could just be the catalyst we need to act.'

Ella blinked at the vanishing white lines on the tarmac ahead as they slalomed their way round a series of roundabouts and pushed on to the ring road. She played his words through her head. Suddenly, something struck her.

'Wh-what do you mean, they were working from outside our house? You mean, before you put the camera in?'

He didn't know that. She forced her brain to work. No, he definitely didn't know that. The only time she, Miranda and Faith were aware of any activity had been when Faith had found the foil packet of drugs and she'd gone and stuffed them in a hedge. She'd never told Jaz about it. They were implicated in hiding them and Faith had said that concealing evidence was incredibly serious. She'd never had the courage to mention it to him, even in an 'oh weren't we silly' sort of way.

'Are you telling me you weren't aware of it?' he asked her quietly, skilfully swinging the car out into the overtaking lane. She massaged her forehead, her eyes throbbing. Now wasn't the best time to be quizzed on anything. Perhaps he knew that. Perhaps he was an expert in getting information out of people when they weren't in their right mind. She gave him a sidelong glance. His eyes were firmly on the road ahead.

'Of – of course we weren't. We'd have told you.' She swallowed.

'Would you? When none of you in the house are strangers to drugs yourselves?' he continued in the same seductive tone. Ella swallowed even harder.

'I don't know what you're talking about, Jaz.'

'I'm not an idiot, Ella. Think what you like of me, but don't take me for a fool.'

'I – I don't.'

She fell silent, muted by confusion. What on earth should she say to him? Her thoughts were far too muddled to give her any answers.

'How long have you known Miranda?' he asked as they slid into Headington and he turned the car from the main road towards the John Radcliffe hospital.

'Miranda? Only a couple of months now.'

'And Faith?'

'The same. I told you, we came together to share the house. I'd never met them before that.'

'You don't really know them at all then, do you?'

'Well, er. Sort of.'

'And you could probably say that they don't really know you either?'

She twisted round to him as they veered off towards the hospital and slid up the sloped drive.

'What are you saying? I don't understand any of this.'

202

'Let's leave it there for now.'

He slowed down to roam the car park until he found a space and swung the car into it.

'Hang on, Jaz, or should I call you detective inspector seeing as you're interrogating me now?' She put a hand out to his arm to stop him as he was already unlatching his seat belt and reaching for the door handle. 'You can't say all these cryptic things and then just leap away. I don't know what you're getting at. What's going on?'

'You tell me, Ella,' he said.

She stared at him as he turned back and gave her a long, even look. It wasn't exactly unfriendly. His eyes were quizzical in the weak beam of the overhead light. Her skull was still throbbing but the dizziness was leaving now. His face suddenly seemed very clear. They sat perfectly still, their eyes searching each other's for information.

'Jaz, you can't, surely you can't suspect me of anything. I'm the one who's just been mugged, for heaven's sake. I can't make you out at all.'

He put a finger up to her cheek. It was such a shock that she jumped, but it was over in a flash, his fingertip merely tracing a soft line down her skin, then disappearing again. She blinked, wondering if she'd imagined it.

'And I can't make you out either,' he said, before easing himself out of the car, shutting his door and waiting on the tarmac for her to do the same.

'Faith!'

Faith jumped and her grip tightened on the door. She'd been in the Ladies so long she was sure by now the others must have assumed she'd left. She'd been fiddling about, wiping her eyes, taking deep breaths, muttering reassurances to herself, her mind whirling round and round in circles. Only after that reaffirming process had she plucked up the courage to pull the toggles tight around her tracksuit hood, grab her bag, and ready herself to leg it out of the toilet, make a dash out of the pub and down the lane towards the cottage. Miranda could follow in her own good time, if she was going to follow at all. The way she and Giles were flirting with each other – and given Miranda's track record in the time Faith had known her – she expected that she and Giles would disappear off together for a good bonk. That seemed to be the way she worked.

She'd made it out of the Ladies, across the public bar and was just heaving the swing door open when she heard her name called right behind her. She turned round to see Paul with a hand outstretched towards her. He caught hold of her sleeve. The material ballooned out, making her arm look huge.

She stopped and looked down at his hand for the second time that night. She glanced up at his face as he showed no sign of letting go.

'I'm sorry,' he said, and dropped his arm. 'I just don't want you to rush off yet. Please.'

She brushed her top back into shape.

'I – I'm just going home. I don't feel too well.'

'Well, will you let me walk you back?'

She cleared her throat, the bubble of confusion welling there again. She couldn't answer, so she cleared her throat again.

'I can walk back to Giles's from your house,' he

continued. 'Miranda said you only live up the lane. Giles and I walked down here tonight anyway as we were going to have a couple of pints, so it's no trouble. It's not far out of my way either.'

'But he'll – won't he wonder where you are?' She frowned at herself. That was like saying that he could walk her home as long as Giles did know where Paul was. That wasn't exactly what she'd meant.

'It's fine, I said I was coming looking for you, and I've been lurking in the bar for fifteen minutes already waiting for you.' He grinned at her suddenly. Her stomach curled in that odd way again. 'The barman told me where you were. Not very discreet, I know, but I did ask him.'

'I – I wasn't hiding,' Faith lied quickly, her cheeks growing hot all over again.

'No, I know. Just taking a moment on your own. I do that all the time.'

'Do you?' she asked with dry lips.

'Yeah, all the time.' He laughed. 'But not in the Gents. You can get some funny looks if you go in there to meditate.'

'Well, I'm going now,' she said decisively, hitching her bag on to her shoulder. 'And you'll probably want another drink before you leave.'

'Not really,' he shrugged. 'I've had enough. I'm not a big drinker really. I'm ready to walk with you now.'

'Oh well—' She stopped short as she saw Mike with Tracey Fellingham, one of the girls who'd been in her year at school, laughing their way towards the door. Her skin grew cold and she shuffled to one side to let them pass.

'Hi, Faith!' Mike stopped to give her a slow smile. 'How's Randy Miranda?'

She ignored him, pretending to be interested in finding her keys in her bag instead.

'Never thought you'd be sharing a house with the new village bike. You want to ask her for a few tips.'

'Who's this?' Paul took a step forwards and made the pleasant enquiry of Faith. She shot him a startled look. Perhaps he could see she was uncomfortable. She hoped to God he wasn't going to mistake Mike for a friend and start chatting to him.

'Hi, mate, the name's Mike.' Mike nodded at Faith as if she was out of hearing. 'You picked the wrong one. Randy goes like a train. Faith goes more like a veggie van.'

Tracey snorted, pulling at Mike's sleeve. 'C'mon, let's get out of here. I can smell turnips.'

'I think,' Paul said slowly, taking a step towards Mike, gripping his arm and bending it behind his back so that he was fixed into position like a statue, 'that you're about to apologise.'

Faith's eyes nearly fell from her head. There was no doubt that Paul had Mike in some sort of hold that he couldn't escape from, and judging from the sudden look of fear in Mike's eyes, it must have been hurting him. He gave a jagged laugh.

'Hey, hang on, mate, I'm only kidding about.'

'Fuck you!' Tracey squealed and flapped at Paul's arm. But he was strong – Faith hadn't realised just how strong. He ignored Tracey's flailing, his eyes boring into Mike's with a hostility that had Faith gaping with shock.

'I said, apologise.'

'I'm sorry, Faith,' Mike stumbled. 'You can take a joke, you always could. You're a great girl. You've got it all wrong, mate, we were at school together. She knows we're only larking about.'

'If I ever hear you make derogatory comments about Faith or Miranda again, I'll break your arm. Got that?'

'For God's sake, let's get out of here!' Tracey yanked at Mike as Derek the landlord peered over at the door from the bar with his usual twisted expression and appeared to be showing an interest. 'I don't want to be banned from another flippin' pub.'

As suddenly as he'd gripped Mike's arm, Paul released it. Mike clasped his shoulder, his face crumpled, and headed for the door. He turned as he was about to push through it to yell, 'You're a fucking loony, mate. You two should be a perfect match!'

The door swung behind them as they disappeared.

Faith hadn't realised that her nails were biting into her handbag strap. She hadn't moved a muscle throughout the entire encounter. She was still staring at Paul in utter fascination, not knowing whether to be horrified, jubilant, or just relieved. The shock of somebody wanting to break Mike's arm on her behalf was too great for her to take in. She would have loved to have done it herself, but she just wasn't strong enough. But Paul had grabbed him, twisted his arm, and made him apologise to her. It was stunning. Nothing like it had ever happened to her before.

'You okay?' Paul asked effortlessly, zipping up his leather jacket and smiling.

'I—'

'They should be on their way now, but we can give it a couple more minutes if you want.'

'Er, no. They go the other way home, and Mike usually drives. He's got a Toyota jeep. He likes to drive it round the village so that people think he's adventurous.'

Paul smiled ruefully.

'Jerk, eh?'

'Yes.' Faith expelled a long, overdue breath. It was relief she felt, she could identify it now. And not only that, but it was tinged with jubilation after all. She wasn't horrified at all.

'C'mon then, if you're ready.'

'I am.'

They left the pub in time to hear the jeep's tyres squeal up the road in the direction of the estate and see the tail lights disappear into the night. They walked slowly across the car park together. As they joined the lane and began to walk away from the bustle of late night drinkers making their way home, Faith glanced up at the stars. Orion's belt was dazzling. The sky seemed to be jewelled with stars tonight, like tiny diamonds floating on a black velvet sea. She surprised herself with the idea. Usually they were just stars, and the sky was just the sky, tinged with orange on the horizon from the lights of Oxford. She took another steady breath, savouring the taste of the autumnal air. The breeze was squalling tonight, exciting the drying leaves on the trees and tossing orange and yellow around them.

'Thank you, Paul,' she managed at last. She'd been wanting to say it but didn't know how, and then it just came out.

'At your service, Ma'am,' Paul said with a laugh in his voice. 'I used to do judo when I was a kid. Didn't think I could remember any of the holds, but there you go. Mind you, I've never had occasion to use them in recent years. Nice to know it still comes in handy.'

'Judo,' Faith mused aloud. 'I should have done judo. I never thought about it.'

'I only did it because some of the guys at school were picking on me. I was quite short then. I suddenly put a spurt on when I was about sixteen, and they stopped it then. Then my shoulders filled out, and they started actively avoiding me. It was quite funny.' They walked on along the line of sycamores and he added, 'At least, it's funny in retrospect.'

'W-why did they pick on you?' she asked, casting him a curious glance.

'Why not? They've got to pick on someone. I was the shortest. That's about it. No logic to it. You don't realise it until you're older, but there wasn't anything personal in it. I even see one of them for a beer now. He's a decent bloke. He was a prick when he was younger, but he grew out of it.'

'You're so kind.' Faith shook her head, deep in thought. 'I could never feel like that. I hate them. All of them.'

'Ah,' Paul said, slowing his pace a little. Faith slowed with him. Any minute they would turn the corner in the lane that led to the long patch of straight where the cottage was. She didn't want the walk to be over just yet. And she didn't want to get him home and have to ask him in. Ella would be there. She'd take over the conversation. She didn't mean to do it, but she was sociable and friendly and she just would. 'I suppose it would depend on how they picked on you,' Paul finished.

'Yes.' Faith gave an involuntary shudder. 'It was pretty nasty.'

'Hmmn.'

They slowed even more until they were almost shuffling along. The wind ripped at the trees around them, but Faith hardly noticed.

'Look, Faith, I don't suppose you're hungry, are you?'

'Hungry?' She stopped and looked at him. She could be hungry. If she thought about it, she could be very hungry.

'It's just that I noticed there was a small Chinese place in the centre of the village. I don't suppose you'd fancy going there and getting a quick bite?'

'Oh.' Chinese? Late at night? It was something she did with the girls from work sometimes, if they were all going out. It was something she could do with Paul. That would mean they could talk for a bit longer. 'But it's right back the way we came, then on into the centre. Don't you mind walking back?'

'Not at all,' he countered. 'You're not cold, are you?'

'No. This thing's very warm.' She played with her toggles to demonstrate and felt silly, so left them flapping instead.

'And it's such a clear night, I fancy being out under the stars for a bit longer.' He laughed again. Faith had never known a man who laughed so much, and at himself mostly. She liked that. She gazed upwards again. Had the stars ever been as sharply defined as tonight? And a new moon was lazing its way over the dome of the sky. It was lovely being out in it. Suddenly, she had no doubt at all.

'Let's go to the Peking Palace then,' she said.

'I wonder where Paul's got to,' Miranda said idly, willing him to be away for as long as possible.

'Hmmn,' Giles gazed over at the bar again.

They'd abandoned darts once Miranda's partner had fled and seemingly was not returning. One minute Miranda had been cheerfully buying another round and surprising herself with the realisation that Faith was quite a laugh in a group as long as she was doing something she was good at, the next Faith had burst through the door and nearly knocked her flying. She still had a beer stain on her top where she'd been splashed. They'd gone into the back bar and asked Paul why she could be so upset, but his face was equally plastered with confusion. After a moment's thought, he'd declared that he would find her and walk her home if she'd shot off that way, and then he'd vanished. Miranda hadn't offered to go after her. There was very little point. If she was having one of her cyclical strops, she'd only lay into Miranda too, and if she made one more comment about drinking, smoking, having sex or dying hair, Miranda was going to have to cause her physical damage. And she'd been getting on with Paul in a Faith sort of way, so it seemed appropriate enough.

So left alone, Miranda and Giles had slipped into the low chairs at one of the tables and while Miranda was doing her best to make the most of her opportunity by plying Giles with flirty questions, he was giving her straight answers and every so often dropping away into his private thoughts. He wasn't even noticing when she was leaning forward to touch his arm playfully, giving him an eyeful of cleavage, or when she tossed her hair to allow the loose glossy curls to bounce around her neck. It was actually getting a bit frustrating. Especially as she was starting to suspect that he was missing Suzanne.

'I wonder if Faith's all right,' Giles said, scratching his head.

'She'll be fine. Don't worry about her.'

'I wouldn't want her to walk home on her own.'

Miranda stiffened. Why was Faith deserving of all this compassion? Most of the men she flirted with didn't give a stuff whether she ever walked home on her own or not. She was independent, and they picked up the signals. They assumed, therefore, that there was nothing they could do for her at all. Just like Ella. She'd slipped away without floods of tears and tantrums, and nobody seemed to think she'd come to any harm. What was it with men? It was as if you had to wave a banner saying, 'It's all right to be concerned about me at this juncture', just to mark out the difference for them between being patronising and being considerate. Her thoughts spilled out into words, but she kept them playful.

'So if I run out of the room in floods of tears, will you be worried about me walking home on my own too?' Perhaps there was a little too much edge to her voice, because for the first time since they'd been alone together he seemed to focus on her, giving her a very direct look.

'I don't like walking home on my own, Miranda. It's got nothing to do with floods of tears. You came up here on your own, though, and some people don't give it a second thought. I wouldn't know which you'd prefer, but I'd offer, of course. If you declined the offer, I'd believe you knew your own mind.'

She was temporarily stumped. She took another sip of her wine while she concentrated. Better to seize the moment.

'Would you be good enough to walk me home then?' she asked with a disarming smile.

'Of course.' He smiled back, his eyes warm, and she felt a wave of relief. She thought she'd lost him for a moment there, but he was still with her.

'And perhaps you'd like to pop in for a coffee when we get there?' She gave him her most devilish look. It usually worked. And she really did want to bag this one. He was worth a thousand of most of the men she encountered. Not only was he gorgeously handsome, he genuinely didn't seem to be aware of it. Or if he was, he didn't use it as an ego massage like so many other good-looking men she'd known. He was a truly nice bloke. He was funny, bright and kind with it. She ran the adjectives through her head as she drowned in his chestnut eyes. Yes, he really was a catch, and the more she thought about it, the more she wanted to be the one to catch him, Suzanne or no Suzanne. She maintained the devilish look for as long as she could, but he was giving her a very blank stare back.

'I've got Paul staying with me,' he replied at last.

'Ah yes, Paul. But he's gone off somewhere with Faith, I assume, since it's nearly half an hour since we last clapped eyes on him. Hasn't he got a key?'

'Well, yes, I gave him a spare set seeing as he's been coming and going from the house while I've been working.'

'Well, there you are then!' She patted her knees decisively and curled a suggestive smile in his direction. 'He's disappeared so he won't mind at all if you disappear for a bit too, will he?'

'Miranda.' Giles laid his hands flat on the table and leant forwards, his eyes thoughtful. 'Can I ask you a question?'

'Of course,' she gurgled back, allowing her chest to jut out a little further. 'Ask me anything you like. What is it you want to know?'

'I'd like to know why you never give a serious answer to anything.'

Her eyelashes fluttered. That wasn't quite what she'd expected.

'I do sometimes,' she smouldered, deciding quickly that smouldering was the best option here. 'It depends what I'm asked.'

'So will you give me a serious answer if I ask you a serious question?'

'I'll try.' She flashed him a smile and took a deeper sip of her drink. While she was at it, she lit a cigarette and inhaled on that too. This was becoming a bit disconcerting. 'But that means you've asked me two questions, you know.'

'Okay. So tell me what it is you want from a man?'

'What do women want?' She laughed lightly. 'A man with a six-inch tongue who can breathe through his ears. It'd be an added bonus if he'd turn into a tub of chocolate ice cream at three in the morning, but you can't have everything.'

She fixed her grin in place but he was waiting, with a serious face, for her to answer him properly. She sucked on her cigarette quickly and flicked it towards the ashtray in agitation.

'I can't answer for all women. It depends. Someone like Faith doesn't want a man at all. Ella wants men who don't interfere with her life. And someone like, say . . .' She scrunched up her nose in thought. 'Suzanne, for example. Now she probably just wants someone to share the bills with who'll take turns walking the dog.' Had she made Suzanne sound dumpy enough? She should try harder. 'She'd probably want someone who'd be happy to sleep in single beds by the time you were forty and play ludo with the grandchildren. I imagine,' she finished sweetly.

'There you go.' Giles sat back in his chair, gesturing towards her. 'You've done it again. I didn't ask about women, I asked about you.'

'Me?' Miranda chuckled, nearly choking on a large gulp of her wine. Now she was starting to want to run out of the room. Maybe she had a small insight into Faith's psychology after all. But Faith wasn't proud. Where she just went for it, tears, snorts and all, Miranda would sit still and face it. 'What do you want to know about me?'

'What you want in a man,' he repeated patiently.

Oh Christ, she thought, he wasn't going to let it drop. And he wasn't flirting with her, his eyes weren't playful enough for her to keep fobbing him off. She took a sharp breath, stretched her full lips into another smile and waved a hand dismissively.

'I've been married, Giles. Ask me another.'

'No, I want you to answer this one.'

'I just said, I've been married,' she echoed herself slowly. 'It doesn't make you feel very optimistic about the romantic world.'

'Is your marriage over?'

She widened her eyes at him. That was one she hadn't heard for years. But it gave her a jolt. Of course, she'd thought of the marriage as being over for a very long time. They both had. That was why they hadn't bothered to do anything about it legally. Until now.

'Of course.'

'Has your ex-husband remarried?'

She drew on her cigarette again, alternating between puffs and sips of wine. She really didn't want to sit and confront these questions right now. Giles couldn't know that his timing was particularly awful. But she could only find a straight answer to give him.

'He – as it happens he – Lance, that's his name. He's American. A pilot. A bit corny, I know, air hostess and pilot. But there you are, we got hitched, it didn't work, we were both away from each other a lot, and well, there you go.' She drained her glass and swallowed. 'He's getting married again. So now we have to sign the papers and yes, it will all be over. Properly.'

'You must feel very sad about it.'

She cleared her throat noisily and shook back her hair.

'Not really. It has to happen. Whatever we had is long dead and buried. Any contact we've had since then has been purely –' she hesitated slightly, 'businesslike.'

'Yes, I guessed that, but it must be difficult to have to sign a piece of paper to say your marriage failed.'

Failed. The word had been bolting through her head ever since Lance had unexpectedly announced his impending betrothal. That's what he had said. They'd both failed to make it work. But now he'd met someone else and started again. He was going to find happiness, so he could put his failure behind him. She, on the other hand—

'So,' Giles interrupted her thoughts. He maintained his gaze on her. 'What is it you want from a man?'

She looked up at him suddenly, her eyes shining with unshed tears. He'd cracked her veneer, somehow, and now she could only tell him what was in her heart.

'I want to be loved for who I am, Giles,' she whispered in a tight voice. 'That's all.'

There was a silence. She cleared her throat again, stubbed out her cigarette and pulled on her jacket. So much for her grand seduction. She had to get away. She'd revealed far, far too much. Giles pushed back his chair and stood up with her.

'Miranda?' he asked, touching her arm as she was about to march away ahead of him.

'Yes?'

'You interest me and I want to get to know you properly, not just dive into something impulsive and physical. Would you like to share a coffee or a meal somewhere? I'd like to talk to you. And then I'll make sure you get home safely.'

'Not tonight Giles,' she said, and turned away.

Chapter Thirteen

To Ella's horror, it was the perky Irish nurse weaving her way around Casualty who spotted her first. The bright overhead lighting was dazzling but it was impossible to mistake the diminutive figure making a beeline for her.

'You again! What have you done to yourself this time? Not been at the do-it-yourself, have you?'

'Not this time,' Ella tried to smile but it was difficult not knowing what medical procedure she was about to endure. 'I – I banged my head.'

'You're an accident going somewhere to happen, aren't you?' She was treated to a wide-eyed grimace. 'Have you reported in to the desk?'

'Yes.'

'Right you are.' The nurse paused to assess Jaz, standing silently next to Ella with one hand on her elbow. She wasn't quite sure why he'd put it there. She wasn't about to pass out, but she couldn't think of any reason to tell him to remove it. At least he was showing genuine concern, and that was gratifying. The nurse rolled her eyes at Ella with a cheeky smile.

'This your boyfriend, is it now?'

'Er, oh no. He's – er.' She groped for words. He's a copper? He's the surveillance guy? He's engaged to someone else?

'I'm her boyfriend,' Jaz declared, causing Ella to

jump round and stare at him. He was even smiling suggestively back at the nurse. 'You can tell she's concussed, can't you?'

'Nice!' The nurse stuck her tongue in her cheek and nodded at Ella. 'Well, you're in good hands. We'll see to you as soon as we can. It's lovely and quiet tonight so far, so we won't keep you waiting too long. You just take a seat.'

'Thanks.'

She bustled away and Jaz guided Ella to a plastic chair. At least he didn't pick the same spot she'd sat in before. She'd hate to think of it as her regular seat. As soon as they'd both sat down she turned to him.

'Why on earth did you say you were my boy-friend?'

'Simpler that way.'

'Simple? There's nothing simple about having strange men going around pretending to be your other half.'

'Think about it. I've turned up at your house at odd times, even late tonight. It's probably as well if people do think we're romantically attached. Just for the moment.'

She stared at him in astonishment then burst out laughing. She clapped her hand over her mouth.

'I'm sorry, it's just so stupid. What's this nurse got to do with anything? She's a nurse, for God's sake, not a drug smuggler.'

He gave her a straight look.

'It's a small world round here. What else do you suggest we might have said?'

It was true, she couldn't think of an alternative.

'You could have said you were my brother, or

something.' She bit her lip to stop herself laughing again. This time he smiled at her with good humour.

'You've got an Asian brother?'

'Well, you know what I mean. One of us could have been adopted.'

'And how long did you want to stand there explaining that one?'

'All right, fair enough. For now.'

She settled into her chair and tried as hard as she could to relax. For the moment she couldn't think about all the questions he'd asked her in the car. They were too confusing, and she couldn't work out what he might have been angling for. It was nice instead to sit fairly peacefully side by side. After a short silence she turned to him again.

'Jaz, I'm sorry for saying what I did about your engagement. I can't remember exactly what it was, but I know it was crass.'

He assessed her quietly for a moment.

'I know you didn't mean any offence. Forget it.'

'It's hard to comprehend, that's all. It's difficult to understand an arranged marriage when you've never known anybody who's met that way. It's your way of doing things, and I'm sorry if I was rude.'

To her utter astonishment he let out a long sigh, leant forward and rested his elbows on his knees to study the shiny tiles of the floor. He seemed fascinated by a blob of dried chewing gum.

'I'm not really sure what is our way of doing things any more.'

'Really?' she asked, amazed by his attack of intro-spection.

'It used to be very straightforward. It was all sorted

out by the families. There were checks done on the sort of family each side was marrying into. There'd be visits back to India, long discussions with every distant cousin you could name. It was very, very thorough. By the time you met, it'd be pretty much decided. You'd have to like each other, of course. You'd be able to back out but you'd need a pretty sound reason. And largely, it worked.'

She bit her lip and held her breath. She didn't want him to stop. He pushed a hand through his hair and continued, his eyes still fixed on the chewing gum.

'It's a bit more confusing now. Some families still go the traditional route, but it's more common for the man and woman to meet several times, decide they like each other and make a move from there. Now the checks into the families aren't as thorough, more of it rests on the opinions of the two people concerned.'

'That's – that's good, isn't it?'

He expelled a long breath. She wasn't convinced he was conscious of who he was talking to. He almost seemed to be thinking out loud.

'I'm not sure. You don't know someone well enough to be in love, but the families haven't done their homework. You could be falling between two stools.'

She was biting her lip so hard now it hurt.

'Is – did – I mean—'

'It's difficult when you've been born and brought up in this country. In this culture. You have more in common with your mates from school or from work than you might have with your family back home. You make different judgements. Sasha's been brought up here too. She understands all that. Her family come from Madras. She's there now looking at wedding clothes.' He took in another audible breath and let it out. 'My family were originally from the Punjab. It's another part of India altogether. As different in many ways as another country. But Sasha and I are both British. It's our common ground.' He laughed to himself softly as if he was enjoying a private joke. 'Our families weren't too happy about it. As far as they were concerned, I might as well have chosen to marry a Martian. But they said it could have been worse.'

He sat back in his chair, crossing one long leg loosely over the other. She gazed ahead, peering sideways at him from time to time. She didn't want to put him off by seeming too interested.

'One of my uncles married an English woman,' he said simply.

She was too intrigued by that comment not to turn round and stare at him again.

'Really?'

'Yes.'

'And—'

'They're still married. It was tough though, back then. They moved house three times because of abuse.'

Ella was aghast. She'd heard of such things, but they were extreme cases, surely? And why had he told her about it? She studied his profile, his full lips, a shadow of stubble around his chin, the firm line of his nose. Then suddenly he turned his head and stared back at her.

'How are you feeling now? Still dizzy?'

'Erm—'

'Right then, trouble.' The Irish nurse appeared from nowhere still wearing the same grin. 'Let's see what you've done to yourself. Would you like your boyfriend to come with you?'

'Oh, no, there's no need for that.'

'No, she's a big tough girl,' Jaz said, relaxing into his chair and giving Ella a broad wink. She gave him an indignant stare in return. Then she was led away in a deeper state of confusion than she'd been in before, although she wouldn't have thought that was humanly possible.

'He's a dish,' the nurse announced, leading Ella to a cubicle guarded by pulled curtains and plonking her down in a chair. 'Where did you meet him?'

'At, um. At the laund—' She stopped herself. At the launderette? Oh come on. Besides, there wasn't one anywhere near her. 'At the pub.' Ella cringed. She'd have liked to have suggested she chose her boyfriends in a slightly more discerning manner than picking them up down the pub, but it'd have to do.

'Lucky you. Reminds me of a younger version of that Imran Khan fella. He married an English girl too, didn't he? Jemima whatshername. Mind you, she was loaded.'

'Yes.' But she was white, and he married her, nonetheless. Ella mused over the thought while the nurse furrowed her fingers through her hair and found the offending bump. She gave it a sharp prod.

'Ow!'

'Yes, that hurts, doesn't it. Any dizziness, sickness, disturbed vision?'

'Yes, all of that. It was about an hour ago, though. I don't feel too bad now.'

'Hmmn. And what's he like in bed then?'

'I'm sorry?' Ella was so surprised by the question she giggled.

'Your fella. Any good?'

Ella smothered a belly-laugh. If only Jaz could hear this.

'Fabulous,' she allowed her voice to sound dreamy. 'Very well endowed. Extremely well endowed, in fact. Quite took my breath away the first time. And he has the most incredible stamina. He can keep going all night.'

'Oh, you are a lucky thing. Mine's got a weeny one and he falls asleep and snores afterwards. It's nice while it lasts, though.' Ella snorted. This was getting more surreal by the second. 'And he's black. It's not true what they say.'

'Who's black?' Ella twisted round to look at the nurse and got a painful stab in the bump with a swab of disinfectant. 'OW!'

'Sorry. My boyfriend. We always laugh and say we're made for each other. You know what they say. The blacks and the Irish.'

'Oh.' Ella sat still for a while and let that thought wash over her too. You never knew about people, and who they were with and what they did when they weren't talking to you. You just made assumptions and formed conclusions, and they could be completely wrong. She wanted to smile, but she wasn't sure why.

'How on earth did you manage to bang your head right back here?' the nurse tutted at her. 'Fall over, did you?'

'Er, yes. Fell back against—' Against a baseball

bat? She'd have to think again. 'Something really hard. I think it was the coat hook.'

'Ooh, you've been lucky then. I'll get the doctor to check you out and they might want to do a scan just to be sure, but if you're not dizzy any more you're probably going to be fine.'

'Okay, thanks.'

'And those little cuts on your face have vanished. Just don't go causing yourself any more injuries, now.'

'I'll try not to.'

She waited patiently and eventually a young doctor appeared looking tired. She probably wasn't the most urgent case of the evening. He poked and prodded her bump and asked her the same questions, to which she gave the same answers.

'I think for now we can leave it there, but if you get any more symptoms you should come straight back here. Okay?'

'Fine.' Ella stood up with relief. 'Can I go now?'

He'd already wandered off looking distracted. Ella took the opportunity to smooth her hands over her jumper and ruffle her hair into shape again. When she left the cubicle and made her way back to the waiting room, Jaz was standing to one side near a wall, talking into a mobile phone. She waited, watching him with his back to her. He was very broad across the shoulders. She hadn't realised it, but as he was slightly bent over, talking into the phone, the material of his jacket was pulled tight. Her eyes wandered over the rest of his form. He was in black denims again. It seemed to be his personal uniform. They were a good fit, showing off a very firm rump and long, solid legs. She picked her jacket up from the chair and slipped it on. What would it be like, to actually be his girlfriend? Sometimes she'd been able to tell how she might feel by watching a man when he didn't know she was there and was off his guard. Hooking her bag on to her shoulder, she realised that the idea gave her a sharp pang of regret inside. She wasn't going to find out, was she? So she should abandon the idea now.

He flipped the case to his phone shut, tucked it into the inside of his jacket, and turned around to find her there. He smiled at her, and she smiled back. Then, as if they both remembered that they were here on business, they straightened their faces. He strolled over to her and spoke in a low voice as several people wandered over to their side of the waiting room to find seats.

'What's the verdict?'

She was tempted to reply, 'You're a dish, apparently,' but she controlled herself.

'I'm fine. May be a mild concussion but they don't want to do any scans or anything. So I'm free to go.'

He nodded. 'Fine. Let's get back to the car then.'

They bumped into the Irish nurse on the way out and she gave Ella a broad wink.

'Sleep well. That's if you get any sleep.'

Ella laughed lightly. In the car park, Jaz gave her a sideways look.

'What did she mean by that?'

'I told her I always have a strong coffee before bed. She reckoned it wasn't a very good idea.'

She thought he might laugh, but he seemed pre-occupied. He opened the door for her and she was settled in the car before she realised that nobody had ever done that for her before, then when he'd fastened his seat belt he paused with his keys in his hand.

'I've got a slight problem. It's the call I just had. I have to drop in at home and send something in by fax. Do you mind if we do a slight detour on the way back?'

'Oh, no. Of course I don't mind.'

He nodded and flicked the keys. The engine purred in response and he drove away from the hospital smoothly. She couldn't really say she did mind. And she was curious to know where he lived. Was the flat smothered with black leather and chrome spikes about to emerge as reality? But then, there was no way he was going to ask her in. And he was supposed to be off duty. Did this sort of thing always happen? Perhaps this was what going out with a policeman was really like. Perhaps there'd be plenty of time to record CDs illegally while he was running around bringing peace and harmony to the suburbs of Oxford.

And there was also the fact that she wasn't in a rush to go home and be alone again. Although Miranda and Faith would no doubt be back by now, they'd probably be in bed, and she was still unsettled by the whole experience. She was far from sleep. Another thought had crossed her mind now that her skull had stopped buzzing. Should she have left a note for Miranda and Faith warning them not to hang around outside in the dark? Was it something they'd do anyway? Would telling them what had happened just worry them without their being able to do anything about it? If Jaz was right, and they really were going to act soon, whatever 'acting' meant, it could all be over in no time, and she could tell them later. Although Miranda would probably handle it well, Faith would be terrified. And who could blame her? Ella was more uncomfortable about the whole thing now than she liked to admit.

The car nosed down into Cowley. She'd been wondering where he'd be based and she found out as he pulled into a leafy side street lined with terraced houses, many of which had been smartened up. It wasn't the bachelor flat she'd pictured, from the outside anyway. She'd marked him down for the town centre or Jericho, where modern flats were springing up. He paused as he reached for the door handle. He looked at her as if he was undecided about what to say.

'Would you like to come in and wait?'

She was surprised, yet again. She'd been expecting him to run in and run out again. But then, it was late, and she guessed it wouldn't be very gallant of him to leave her sitting like an abandoned *A to Z* in the front seat. But he looked a bit awkward. A trip to his home hadn't exactly been on the agenda as part of the evening's entertainment.

'No, it's fine, I'll just wait here.'

'Don't be noble, Ella. I'm sorry I've got to do this now, but you can't sit out here.'

'It's – no. It's okay. You go ahead.'

'Look, I've got to find what I'm looking for, get it sent, and to be honest I fancy a coffee. I was in bed when they phoned me earlier, and I rushed straight out. Surely you'd like one too?'

'You're asking me in for a coffee?' she teased with an attack of flippancy. This was all a bit strange. How was the best way to handle it? He laughed under his breath.

'Put it this way. I've seen intimate details of the inside of your house, so we'll be quits.'

'Ah, but you've been in my bedroom,' she quipped, and swallowed. That shouldn't really have been voiced aloud. He hesitated, watching her for a moment, then levered himself out of the car.

'Come on.'

The house was immaculately decorated. Along the cream walls of the hall were hung a series of prints. She recognised them as Hogarth's *The Rake's Progress* and arched an eyebrow while keeping her lips firmly jammed together. He led her through an archway into a long living room running from the front to the back of the house. It looked bigger on the inside. He flicked a switch and two low lamps and a tall standard lamp at the back of the room glimmered with light. The walls were plain white. That much was stark and minimalist, but nothing else about the room was. A silky rug daubed with exotic colours was smoothed over a pale carpet, two sofas draped with white linen throws stood opposite each other, dotted with bright silk cushions in scarlet and peacock blue. But her attention was grabbed immediately by an imposing silk hanging which covered the chimney breast and dominated the room. It was an interwoven design of birds of paradise in sumptuous colours. She gazed at it, absorbing the vibrancy. She scanned the rest of the room, finding an incongruously black and solid wide-screen television on a stand with a video lodged under it. It rose above a sea of video cassettes, some with the cases open. She squinted and realised that they were mostly about football – Manchester United, to be specific.

Jaz waved a hand at one of the sofas and disappeared through a door into what she assumed must be the kitchen.

'Grab a seat. I'll put some coffee on.'

'Oh. Thank you.'

She crept around the silky rug, peering down at it. It was exquisite. Surely something that beautiful wasn't meant to be trodden on? She sank carefully on to the edge of the sofa against the wall, worried that her buttocks might leave a dent in the pristine surface of the drape. She'd thought she was neat, but he was amazing. Did he do all this himself, or did he have someone in to straighten it up for him? She pondered as she heard him clink around in the kitchen, straining her neck to try to see through the door, but he'd left it only partially ajar. She could see some grey kitchen units that had a sort of a marble effect, but that was all. Perhaps he kept his chrome spike out there?

She tried to relax a little, leaning back and prodding one of the blue silk cushions. It was so soft. She ran her fingertips over the material and gazed around again. If he did have someone in to tidy up, they'd obviously been warned away from the video collection. She bit her lip. He seemed to be happily preoccupied in the kitchen. She stood up and tiptoed over to the video, sinking down to her knees to have a quick rummage through his collection. You could tell a lot about somebody by the videos they owned. It was like scanning a stack of CDs for clues, only much more revealing.

She buried a smile as she crawled under the television and poked around the videos at the back. These would be the ones he hid from visitors. It was a bit like keeping Tolstoy in the living room bookcase while you sneaked Jilly Cooper upstairs and kept it by the bed. What would be his equivalent? She squeezed herself forwards and reached for a pile stacked against the wall. She almost laughed to see *Shane* there. And *High Noon* and a series of classic John Wayne movies. So when he said he wanted to be a Wild West hero, he'd been deadly serious. It was quite endearing. When she'd been younger she'd wanted to be Stevie Nicks when she grew up, and had played Fleetwood Mac's *Rumours* endlessly in the hope that she would transform from a lanky, olive-skinned brunette into a dizzy blonde siren through hours of exposure. She still had the tape in the stack in her bedroom, and sometimes she still played it. Did he still sit down and watch his Westerns, in the same way some people listened to motivational tapes in the car? 'I *will* right all wrongs. I *will*.'

She tried to stifle a giggle but it came out as a snort.

'Do you take sugar?'

'Aaagh!'

She thrust herself upwards and clonked her head sharply on the bottom of the television. Pain shot though her bump and electrified her teeth. She slumped face down on top of his video collection.

Great. So he'd kindly asked her into his home, gone off to make them both coffee and she'd been discovered on all fours with her bottom in the air, nosing through his possessions. She decided to answer his question first. She couldn't bear to twist round and see the expression on his face.

'One please.'

'Fine.'

She heard him go back into the kitchen. That was odd. No comment about the fact that she was lying on top of all his videos. She slowly crawled around in a circle. He reappeared in the doorway before she had a chance to get to her feet. She looked up at him from the floor. Well, at least this time she was facing him.

'Milk?' he enquired down to her politely.

'Just a dash, please.'

He vanished again. Painstakingly, she got up and inched her way back to the sofa. She perched on the edge again as if nothing had happened. Perhaps if she sat here looking like the ideal guest he'd come back into the room next time and think he'd imagined it.

He returned with two earthenware mugs.

'It's decaff. I hope you don't mind. Bit late for rocket fuel.'

'That looks lovely. Thanks.'

She peeped up at him but he only gave her a mildly curious look and handed her the coffee.

'Just make yourself at home. I've got to go upstairs and sort things out.'

'Upstairs?'

'I've got an office up there. When you've finished

exploring the kitchen I'll give you a guided tour if you like.'

She bit the insides of her cheeks and gave him an appealing look.

'I'm concussed, remember. I'm not myself.'

He merely raised an eyebrow at her. Darn it, she was going to have to apologise to him again. As long as it didn't become a habit.

'Look, I'm sorry, Jaz. I'm not a nosy person.' He looked unconvinced. 'I – that copy of *Shane* you've got. Is it the same one you've had since you were a kid?' She quailed inside. 'I was only curious about what you watch in your spare time.'

'That copy of *Rumours* you've got,' he replied evenly. 'Is that the same one you've had since you were a kid?' She gaped at him and he smiled. 'I was only curious about what you listen to in your spare time. I won't be long.'

He sauntered out under the archway leading to the hall. She stared after him as his footsteps disappeared up the stairs.

Chapter Fourteen

'And that's exactly how it happened.' Ella sank back against the silk cushions again. She didn't even have to try to be relaxed now. After two more cups of coffee and several accounts of her ill-fated jog home from the pub she felt much more at ease. Talking about the assault had unburdened her of the tension she felt about it, her bump had ceased to throb, and Jaz, his legs casually crossed on the sofa facing her, had been teasing information out of her in a way that she hadn't found stressful at all. She had to admire him for it. Perhaps he'd done weeks of training. But it showed that he could be sensitive as well as scary, whenever the particular mood took him. And perhaps that was why he was an inspector. He seemed quite young to have the responsibility. Now she was feeling wonderfully sleepy. If only she didn't have to think about going home, she could doze in the comforting cocoon of Jaz's house.

A peaceful lull in conversation fell between them. She supposed that at some point very soon he'd be taking her home. For the moment she was content to flop and let him make a move in his own time.

'What does your boyfriend think of your new career?' he asked her in the same gentle voice. She opened her eyes a little wider at him. This was a change in trajectory.

'My boyfriend?'

'Am I prying?'

She scratched her forehead and tried to think.

'Why would you think I'd got a boyfriend?' She ran her mind back to their various encounters and suddenly froze in embarrassment. His first visit to the cottage. She'd been hungover after only a few hours' sleep and had shown them all into her bedroom where the evidence of her attempted seduction of Matt was there for all to peruse. She flushed violently. 'Oh God!'

He chuckled.

'I'm sorry if that brings back disturbing memories.'

'Oh no, it's just—' She gathered herself quickly, propping herself up a little straighter. 'No, Matt's not my boyfriend.'

She shuddered at her explanation. What was he, then? Just somebody she'd spent the night with? That sounded awful.

'Well, not exactly.' She tried to put a brave face on it, but his eyes probed hers from across the room. She gave up and flopped again. 'He's married. I'm not particularly proud of that, but there you go.'

She might have added 'not that it's any of your business', but there was something strange in the way she and Jaz were relating to each other. Perhaps it was because they were only brought together through his work. It was almost like telling intimate details of your life to a stranger in the secure knowledge that you'd never clap eyes on them again. Once his work was finished he'd vanish as suddenly as he'd appeared. He only touched on her life in a professional capacity. He was just like a hairdresser.

He wasn't exactly asking her where she was going on holiday this year, but it was the same sort of thing.

'Tricky,' Jaz said obliquely.

'Yes.' She paused to take a sip of her coffee. 'I'd say it was very tricky, but it's less tricky now. It seems to have fizzled out.'

'You known him long?'

'No.' She shook her head and gazed up at the ceiling. 'I don't really know him at all. I just felt that we had things in common and it might work out. It sounds appalling, but I hadn't given his wife too much thought. But it seems to have brought them back together. I assume that, anyway. He hasn't shown much interest in the last couple of weeks.'

'Local, is he?'

'Hmmn. Yes.' She took a deep breath. Now she was going to look like a dizzy schoolgirl, but she might as well go the whole hog. 'He's my course tutor. And no, before you say anything, it's not a silly crush.'

'I wasn't thinking that. You're an adult and so's he. I guess it's more like meeting somebody at work.'

'Yes.' She thought about it and rambled on. 'It's just like that. In fact, everybody I've ever been out with has been somebody I've met at work.'

Jaz paused to drink some of his coffee before answering her.

'Really?'

'Yes. I suppose that's odd. Or is it? I don't know. I've never really thought about it like that before. I've met people socially, but something's always held me back. I just don't think there'd be enough shared direction.'

236

He shrugged.

'It depends what attracts you to people, I suppose.'

'Well, how could you get on with somebody who didn't understand what you'd been doing all day at work?'

He laughed suddenly and she looked at him in surprise.

'Depends what you mean by "get on". Have you ever been drawn to anybody completely different from yourself?'

She stopped musing and peered over her mug at him.

'I— Why?'

'It's just that you make it sound as if you're looking for a business partner.'

She sat up straight and gripped her mug. For a moment she wondered exactly what she'd burbled to him in their past encounters, since he sounded as if he knew all about the warning voice in the back of her mind. The one her father had put there. She found herself echoing his advice aloud.

'It's more important to work together than to play together, isn't it?'

'What do you think?'

'Crikey, I assumed you had all the answers.'

'Don't be defensive.' He put his mug down on the beautiful rug. She stared at it. What if he knocked it over? He didn't seem worried by that possibility. But he was far too poised to do anything so daft. He could probably ride round it three times on a motorbike without so much as causing a ripple. 'I'm thinking out loud really. It's just that it's not very often I have a chance to talk to a woman properly about these things. Most of my colleagues are men.'

She blinked at him, travelling further down the road of unexpected corners.

'I—'

'I'm sorry, Ella. It's probably inappropriate. I'm invading your space far too much at the moment. I really wanted to ask you about the married man you're seeing.'

'Eh?' She was utterly confused.

'Do you know if he's told his wife about you?'

'If you don't want to invade my space, why on earth are you asking that?'

'Because you were attacked this evening, and I'm trying to ascertain whether you have any enemies.'

She held on to her mug and allowed her spirits to shrivel into flatness like a deflating lilo. Just for a moment there she had been seduced into thinking he was interested in her personal life. She was telling herself that his curiosity was genuinely provoked by her wit and charm. But now it was clear. He was just doing his job, and for an instant he'd allowed himself to be sidetracked while he considered his own relationship. Business partners. That was what *his* impending marriage was about. It had nothing to do with her at all.

'Have you met his wife?' he continued with ease.

'No,' she said shortly, unwilling to be manipulated into baring her soul. 'But she's an artist and she's more likely to poison me with turps than creep up on me in the middle of the night and clout me round the head. And in any case, he hasn't told her about us. There'd be no reason to. He's obviously not going to leave her.'

Jaz nodded calmly, apparently unfazed by the sharpening of her tone.

'Did you ask him to?'

She stiffened.

'Of course not. I'm not clingy. I've never asked a married man to leave his wife.'

'Never?' he repeated quietly.

'No, never,' she defended. And as she calmed herself with a long breath, she realised what he'd meant, and what she'd said. She felt her cheeks growing warm again. 'Fine. So Matt's not the first, but no, none of their wives have sufficient grudges against me to seek me out in the depths of Oxfordshire and lunge at me with a baseball bat. They're in the past and forgotten.'

A brief silence fell between them again. She gazed at the rug, the wall, the standard lamp, anything but meet his eye. For some reason she felt humiliated by her accidental admission. She'd never allowed herself to feel that. She couldn't take the blame in situations where two consenting adults were involved. And yet, she wanted to crawl right back under his television and hide at the back there, somewhere behind the stack of John Wayne videos. Finally Jaz ended her squirm of embarrassment by speaking again in a low voice.

'I'd like to ask you a question now, but it would be a personal one. I'm really not sure if I should.'

'If it's whether I've ever suffered from a guilty conscience or not, then the answer's yes, of course I've had pangs. I haven't planned to have affairs, they've just happened. I think that's all I want to say about it.'

He leant back into his own heap of silk cushions just as she was thinking of edging her way out of hers and getting ready to leave. He didn't seem in a hurry. It had to be very late by now. Perhaps the intimacy of the early hours of the morning, the time when anybody was least on their guard, was pervading her senses, but she wasn't ready to bolt out of the door and face the night either. She sat back again.

'It's only happened three times.'

He pulled a thoughtful face. There was an ironic look in his eyes and she tutted.

'All right, three times is too many. That's what you're thinking. But I had no idea at all that the first guy was married. He managed to hide that small fact from me for a good while. By the time I found out we were already comfortable with each other. I was horrified, don't think I wasn't, but somehow it carried on anyway. Most people wouldn't understand that, but I was only twenty-two, in my first proper job. I had to work at it all hours to prove I was as good as the men around me. I didn't have space for true love. I needed to stay focused on what I was doing, and I'd grown to like him. It was difficult to throw him out of my life just like that. Perhaps I was naive and stupid, but that's the way it happened.'

He nodded slowly.

'I – the other two were a similar pattern. Except I probably knew in advance they were attached.'

He nodded again.

'I didn't want to break up any relationships. As far as I'm aware I never have done.' She gave a short sigh. 'That sounds insincere, but it's true. I – I don't know how to explain this, but when these situations happened I sort of went along with them. It was simpler to see people I couldn't get involved with. If anything, I was always the loser. I seemed to be the person who showed them what they really wanted out of life, and that was always the woman they were married to.'

She bit her lip. She'd never really sat and voiced her thoughts like this and they were coming out haphazardly.

'I've never meant to hurt anybody,' she finished quietly.

'I understand,' Jaz said.

'I don't think you do.' She gave him a rueful smile.

'You don't think I could understand?' He seemed alert suddenly. 'When I've lived my adult life knowing that whoever I meet by chance is unlikely to be approved of by my family? That I have to bide my time, build up my career, and then form an attachment that's considered appropriate for somebody like me? I know what it's like to hold people at a distance. I understand detachment. Don't think that you're so different from me, Ella, because you're not. What surprises me is how incredibly similar we are.'

She met his eyes, her emotions stirring. He stood up suddenly and pulled his car keys from the pocket of his denims. He seemed agitated.

'If you're ready, I'll drop you off at your house.'

She stood up too, not knowing what to say. He patted his shirt and turned a full circle as if he was gathering his thoughts.

'I don't want to alarm your housemates, so I'll come back tomorrow and deal with the camera. For now I'll just make sure you're back safely and we'll leave it at that. That's what we'll do.'

'Oh, okay.'

'Bugger it.' He looked down. He'd knocked his half-full mug of coffee over the rug. A pool of beige liquid oozed over the sheen of the surface. 'Oh bugger!'

He raced off to the kitchen and returned unravelling a mile of kitchen roll.

'It's all right. I've got a tissue somewhere.'

She grabbed her bag, retrieved a pack of tissues, produced one and threw herself down on her hands and knees, mopping up as much liquid as she could. At the same time he landed on the floor and smothered the rug in acres of dimpled paper.

'Oh sod it,' he exclaimed, padding it all down. 'I've never done that before.'

'It's late,' she soothed, ineffectively prodding with her soggy brown tissue. 'We're both tired. It's no wonder you weren't concentrating.'

He started to laugh. She stopped her dabbing and glanced up at him. They were face to face, crawling around the rug. She smothered a snort of laughter. It was his rug after all, and it wasn't really her place to snigger at its demise. But it was funny.

'It's all your fault.' He shook his head at her.

'No, it's not. I was miles away from the mug.'

'Yes, it is,' he insisted.

'No, it's—'

She was muted by the look in his eyes. It was her fault, because she'd upset his concentration. Just as he habitually upset hers.

'Come here.'

His hand snaked around her neck, pulling her to him. He hesitated momentarily, drawing her up to her knees while he knelt next to her, pushing his hands into her hair, raking her face with his gaze.

'I want to kiss you.' His hands were trembling on her. She could feel it. And her body trembled in reply.

'I want you to kiss me,' she whispered.

'I've never done an unprofessional thing in my life. This would be the first.'

'I believe you,' she murmured. His lips were only inches from hers and she couldn't take her eyes off them. They were full and warm, and she desperately wanted him to kiss her.

His lips brushed hers and she shuddered. He held her more tightly.

'I know that I can't do this,' he muttered, kissing her again. He feathered the soft touch of his lips over hers, around her mouth, on her cheeks, and returned to place his lips more fully on hers. She felt the heat of his tongue against hers.

'I've never been in love in my life,' he said huskily, teasing the corners of her mouth with his tongue.

'Neither have I.' Tears swelled in her eyes but she kept them closed. The heat of his mouth, the force of his hands around her head, her neck, her body, pulling her against him was overwhelming.

'I'm not going to start now,' he groaned into her ear.

'And neither am I.'

'But I want you so much it's starting to hurt.'

'I want you too,' she breathed back at him. Her cheek was against his, her lips, her body, every part of her craved to be crushed against him. He pulled away from her and she felt an icy gap between them. For a despairing moment she thought he was going to deny them the experience they were craving, but his eyes burned into hers as he gently pulled her to her feet.

'Not here, Ella. Come with me.'

Dizzy with the sudden flame of passion that had erupted between them, she allowed him to lead her from the room. Her hand in his was almost more arousing than his lips on hers. His palm was hot and soft, but strong and firm as it enclosed hers and led her through the hall and up the stairs.

'I must be mad,' he said, pushing open a door leading off from the landing and tugging her in after him.

'Then we're both mad,' Ella smiled.

He kicked the door closed behind him and they were engulfed in darkness. The feel of his skin against hers and the urgency of their touching enveloped her. Somehow they tangoed across the floor and she found herself cushioned on a duvet.

'I want to see you. Hang on.'

She blinked into the soft light as he flicked the switch on a bedside lamp. She watched mesmerised as he unbuttoned his shirt and his denims and they fell to the floor. His boxer shorts were intact, but there was no hiding the reaction within.

'Good grief!' She let out an inappropriate giggle.

'This is no laughing matter.'

He crashed on to the bed next to her and wound an arm around her, kissing her softly at first, and then more demandingly.

244

'You're so beautiful. So unique. So – cross,' he murmured into the corner of her mouth.

'And you're an arrogant git,' she replied as he slid her jumper over her head. It was only stuck over her head for a second, and he took the time to unfasten her bra.

'I really shouldn't be doing this.' He smoothed his palm over her breasts and her nipples jumped into action. She shivered as he put his lips around them in turn.

'Absolutely not. And neither should I. Perhaps we should get dressed and you should take me home,' she stuttered at him as her jeans left her body in one swift movement.

'Or maybe I'll do that later.'

He returned to her, and this time the boxers had vanished. As had her underwear, although she hadn't been aware of it. He lay next to her, his body warm against hers. She wriggled against him, heat sweeping through her legs and stomach. She was aching for him to crush her completely now. All she craved was to take possession of him, and for him to take possession of her. It was an urgency beyond her experience.

'I just—' she uttered incoherently. 'I want – just—'

He crushed her in response, shocking her with the impact of his body inside hers. All abstract thoughts dissolved as he began to move over her. There was only this moment, this experience, with no past, present or future involved. And as she felt the tremor build to a shock wave in her limbs and the answering reply in his, she knew that it had happened at last: she had abandoned planning and logic, brushed aside the sensibilities that she was usually so driven by. She had allowed herself to do something devoid of reason, and it had unwittingly mushroomed from a surreal chance encounter into an experience that was overwhelming.

Being with Jaz wasn't like anything she'd known before. It was possible that she wouldn't know anything like it ever again. With that flash of understanding came a depth of emotion that slayed her with its intensity. There was a bubble of joy in her heart to know that she could feel this, but with it came panic. She'd controlled every situation she'd ever been in until Jaz probed her mouth with soft kisses, his breathing slowing against her lips. She should be feeling satisfied, content, comfortable, but bewilderment speared her thoughts.

Insecurity grabbed at her and held her fast, just as Jaz's touch lightened on her as if now he could let her go. She kissed him back, her throat constricted with her unvoiced questions. Inside she cried out to ask him to whisper his raw thoughts to her now, just as they'd whispered to each other in the heat of the moment. But now he was quiet, dropping kisses on her face, her forehead, her neck, her shoulders. It wasn't enough. There was a horrible, diving feeling in the pit of her stomach. She needed him to say something. She had to know that it was as profound for him as it had been for her, however strangely it had come about.

'You're incredible,' he murmured.

'So are you,' she said softly.

'Thank you for letting me get close to you,' he

breathed into the nape of her neck. 'I've been wanting to make love to you since I first laid eyes on you.'

She wound her arms around his back and held him to her in reply. She couldn't say that she had wanted him since she first saw him. It had grown on her. With an alarming intensity. And now she'd overtaken him. She closed her eyes in the soft yellow light of the room and let out a long, slow breath.

She'd never been in love before, and she wasn't going to start now. But she'd never thought that being in love could suddenly jump out of the sky and land on her like a Monty Python foot. She would deal with it. She dealt with everything else with a cool, calm head, and she'd deal with this. Jaz would have no reason to know that he'd made such an impact on her.

'So, what are you going to do about the rug, then?' she asked him, swallowing back the bulb of emotion rising in her throat and injecting a laugh into her voice.

He paused as he was rubbing his lips against her skin and lay to one side of her, coiling an arm around her waist.

'I'd rather not think about it right now.' He pulled her to him and brushed a kiss against her cheek. 'If it's all right with you, I'd just like to enjoy this moment.'

'Fine.'

'I thought I had a practical head, but you're straight back in there, aren't you?' he said softly.

'Hmmn, yes. Forever practical, me.'

She tensed but then melted against him as he

pulled her close. She snuggled her back up against his stomach and he draped one long leg over hers. She realised that he still had his socks on. In any other situation she'd have been horrified, but they were nice socks.

'Is it all right with you if you stay the night? It's just that I'd like you to.'

'Yes I will.' She gave him her hand as he was reaching for it. He squeezed it tightly.

'Good.'

'I snore like a chainsaw,' she ventured.

'That's okay. So do I.'

'Tomorrow morning we're going to be horrified about this.'

'No doubt.'

His breathing deepened. She prepared herself for a long night, her thoughts churning backwards and forwards. His breathing became rhythmic. Any time now it would turn into rapturous snoring. If only her brain would shut down her exhausted body would follow suit. Her eyelids drooped. She pulled his hand up to her lips and kissed his fingertips.

'You fool,' she exhaled to herself, dissolving into sleep.

Chapter Fifteen

'Oh my God. What have I done?' Ella chanted to herself as she held on tightly to the hedge strimmer. 'Oh my God, my God, my God.'

Matt's face was grey. She'd read about faces looking grey but she'd never seen one that actually could be described that way. His usual tanned vigour had drained away, his eyes were dull, and his cheeks were shallow. Even his hair looked depressed.

He'd captured her arm as they trotted in a group out of the tutorial hut and across the practice lawn to an obligingly overgrown hedge to study the art of hedge cutting. As the others had gone ahead, he'd pulled her back and bored his eyes into hers urgently.

'I told Lorna about us.'

'You what?' She'd smothered her shriek so that it came out more like a squeak.

'She's leaving me. I've done it now, Ella.'

She'd stared at him open-mouthed. After several aghast moments she wanted to say, 'Okay, let's go back and take that again. We leave the hut, you grab my arm, and you say, "Thanks, Ella, my marriage is rejuvenated."' But he was there, in front of her, looking broken and desperate.

He'd blinked at her, and strolled on towards the group, adopting his tutorial aspect with as much gusto as he could probably muster under the circumstances, but devoid of his usual humour. The others had noticed it. When Pierre asked a question in broken English, Matt snapped, 'Speak up, I can't understand what you're saying.' When Valerie declared that she always got someone in to do hedges and didn't see how she'd be able to wield a strimmer with her weak arms, he'd muttered, 'Fine, go and polish your nails instead then.' And when John had come out with his usual robust remarks, including, 'What's the point of all this bollocks then?' Matt retorted, 'Shut up and you might actually learn something.'

The result was that they were a very subdued group of horticulturists, nodding obediently as Matt pointed to the various knobs and buttons on the strimmer, and watching with restrained breath and clenched teeth as he yanked on the pull-start string over and over in an attempt to fire up the strimmer's engine. When he stopped, red faced and sweating, to yell, 'Fuck it!' into the air, they all shrank back and stared at him in nervous awe.

They'd been forced to take it in turns to hack away at a stretch of hedge. Each was given about a yard's width to trim, and seeing as the hedge was nearing seven foot tall, it stretched the muscles of even the burliest of them. Ella watched distractedly as Pierre, slim, elegant and more used to manipulating small handfuls of herbs than gigantic lumps of machinery, staggered around with plastic goggles and huge ear-phones on, waving the jagged edges of the strimmer above his head. He looked like a serial-killing Mighty Mouse. John, strong but as ever expressing the desire to be somewhere else, was the most successful, flipping the strimmer around as if it was a washing-up brush and finishing with a wonderfully straight edge to his piece of work.

Then it was Ella's turn, and Matt had gone through the procedure again with tight lips, refusing to help when the pull-start didn't start, standing back with folded arms and a vacant expression as if his body had turned up at the college and somehow left his mind still brushing its teeth in the bathroom that morning.

And as Ella was poking at the waxy leaves with the strimmer and succeeding in making a series of cavernous holes punctuated with tufty sprigs, she realised not only that a career in freelance hedge strimming was not going to be an option for her, but that something profoundly dreadful had happened.

'Oh God,' she whispered, lunging again at the twigs and disappearing up to her armpits in hedge. She pulled herself out and tried again. She didn't dare look round. With the earphones on and the grating whine of the strimmer deafening everyone else, she was in her own world. Her arms were killing her. The strimmer weighed a ton, but she couldn't do what she'd do under other circumstances, which would be to switch it off, crack a joke with the others, pull a rueful face and claim that she'd try anything once.

Why, in the name of everything that was sacred, or even everything that wasn't, had Matt gone and told his wife that they'd spent the night together? What on earth had he been thinking? This had never, ever happened before.

The men she'd become involved with had been sophisticated, polished liars. She had to admit that, although it didn't say a lot for her taste in men. They'd approached the situation like professionals. They were masters of discretion and double standards. Even when on one or two occasions they'd got carried away and declared that their marriages were teetering on the edge of ruin, she hadn't believed them, and she'd always been proved right. Not one of them would have gone home and said, 'Guess where I was last night, honey?' The thought of it made her nauseous. How would it feel to have your husband say that to you? The man you trusted, whom you'd built a home and a life with, the man who could be the father of your children?

She hacked away at the hedge, destroying evidence of foliage wherever she found it. How could he do that to Lorna? What on earth would she have said to him in return? What did you say in a situation like that?

She ground her teeth together forcefully, striding down the face of the hedge and strimming everything within reach. Her arms were ready to fall off, but she gripped the handle tightly, crossing her eyes with concentration behind her goggles.

'Oh God!'

So, she'd wondered how she and Matt would be as a couple. She'd hoped at some point that his marriage would disappear. A nice, clean disappearance. Like he'd written 'I'm married' in pencil, and they'd taken an eraser to it and rubbed it out, leaving no evidence that it had ever been there. She'd thought that if he'd been single, as she'd been single when they met, and mutual attraction was obvious, they probably would have gone out together, maybe even formed a good relationship. He could have been a consultant to her nursery, leaping in to give her all the advice she needed. If it was a success, she could have made him a partner. He still could have taken time out for teaching and helped her run the nursery at weekends. He would have known all about composts and soils and the right time for taking cuttings without her having to refer to her copious notes and piles of reference books. They would have laughed together at the end of an exhausting day. That would have been good. But now he had devastated Lorna, the artist whom she had never met, and that was bad.

And what made the shock even greater was that Matt had been the last thing on her mind when she'd turned up, half an hour late, at the college that morning. Less than twelve hours ago she'd been wrapped in Jaz's arms.

He'd taken her home in the morning. They'd both been pensive in the car and said very little, but it had been comfortable. He'd even dropped a kiss on her lips as she'd got out, vaguely saying something about coming back later to check things out at the cottage, but she hadn't been concentrating on that. Her whole body had been throbbing and wonderfully weary from too much passion and too little sleep. She'd smiled at him, and he'd smiled back. A warm, wide, content smile. She was still carting it around in the front of her mind like a photograph. Miranda and Faith had already left for work so she'd cast herself around, got ready, and bolted off to college. The very last thing she expected was for Matt to choose this day of all days to announce that Lorna was leaving him.

'Oh God!' She urged the strimmer on, stumbling into thin air as she reached the point where the hedge ended. She staggered back, twisted the lever to switch off the engine, pulled up her goggles, wrested off her earphones and stared at her effort in amazement. She'd decimated five yards of hedge, leaving a pitted stubble behind. It didn't look so much like a strimmed hedge as a row of dead stems with a few twigs sticking out. The grass was heaped high with leaves.

She felt the strimmer being gently prised out of her hands. John gave her a curious smile.

'You got a bit carried away there, duck. Didn't you hear us yelling at you?'

'Blimey, no I didn't. Sorry about that.'

'Not much left for me to strim then, is there?' Emma complained with her hands on her hips. Ella turned round sheepishly to look at Matt. He was chewing his lip and gazing abstractedly at two teen-aged students from another course who were having a spitting contest in the yard during their tea break.

'Matt?' she almost whispered at him. The class shuffled about and waited for a response. He turned round slowly.

'Hmmn?'

'I've – I've finished.'

'Good, good. Well, it's pretty much time to go over to the greenhouse now. Eric's there to do more work with your cuttings. So off you go.'

'I haven't had a strim!' Emma protested. 'You've got to assess me for the practical.'

'Oh right. Fine. Well, we'll do it again another time. Go on then. Greenhouse.'

One by one they moved away, Emma giving Ella a deeply resentful stare before stomping away in her steel-capped wellies. Ella hung back. Pierre tapped her arm and said in a low voice, 'I sink he's had a row with 'is wife, no?'

'Oh, who knows?' Ella gave a strangled laugh and pretended to be caught up in her earphones. 'You go ahead, Pierre, I'll see you over there.'

When the others had vanished around the side of the barn towards the greenhouse, she finally pulled her earphones off and stood still, waiting for Matt to speak to her again. They were alone, only the guttural sound of the spitting contest invading the silence. He looked at her, then seemed to focus on her properly. He took a long breath and let it out in a series of shudders.

'What the hell am I going to do, Ella?'

She approached him and touched his arm lightly.

'I'm so sorry, Matt. I had no idea you were going to do this. I did say it wasn't a very good idea, didn't I?'

'But I had to sort it out somehow. I couldn't like you and her at the same time. That sounds so juvenile.' He snorted at himself. 'I thought at least if I told her it would be a catalyst. I couldn't stand the tension of nothing happening. I wasn't free to see you, and I wasn't free to enjoy my marriage, not in the way I have done over the past eight years.'

'Eight years?' Ella gulped back at him.

'Eight years of happiness. Down the pan.'

She was gradually feeling smaller and smaller. It was as if Matt was taking a strimmer to her, clipping away all the growth, all the fresh, green optimist bits, lopping stuff off the top too, and leaving her like a little woody stick in front of him.

'I – I don't know what to say. Nothing like this has ever happened to me before.' That much was true. She'd been so sure that it never would, either. He looked at her sadly. She'd never seen such sorrow in a man's eyes. Any moment now she was going to pick up the hedge strimmer and do the decent thing and go for her wrists. The perky Irish nurse wouldn't be able to mend that with plasters.

'It was my fault,' he said quietly. 'Don't blame yourself. I wanted it to happen. I took the opportunity when she was away that weekend, and I made it happen. I even thought that you and I could make a go of it. In some sort of dream world, perhaps.'

'One where Lorna didn't figure in the picture,' she finished for him.

'But now I don't know. I even thought that if telling her made her leave, and if I was on my own, I might have a clearer head. Part of me willed her to storm off. But all I keep doing is wandering around the house, thinking of all the things we have together. The photographs, the memories, the holidays, the laughter, the mutual friends.'

This was becoming unbearable. Ella decided with a leaden heart that death by hedge strimmer was far too good for her. She should just throw herself at the hedge and hang there, impaled on all the spiky twigs she'd left, as an example to any other student who might turn up at the college and decide that Matt was a bit of all right.

'I went into her studio last night. I just sat in there

with a bottle of Scotch and absorbed everything about her. The smells, the easel, the paintings stacked against the wall. Her successes and failures. I've shared them all.'

No, hanging to death on the hedge was too kind. She should be removed when she was still alive and beaten mercilessly by the rest of the class with lifting irons.

'She was crying when she left. She kissed me, said she was sorry for attacking me, and went off to her sister's. I don't even know if she's coming back.'

And then pelted with raw manure and stoned to near death with plant pots.

'I've lost the woman I love. Perhaps the only woman I will ever love. She was everything to me, and I risked it. I'll never forgive myself.'

And finally left in a greenhouse with the doors locked to dry to death.

'And we were just about to start a family. She thought the time was right.'

'Hang on,' Ella said. 'Did you say she attacked you?'

Matt nodded miserably. 'I don't blame her. Sometimes words aren't enough to express what you feel.'

Ella frowned. It sounded like a catch phrase from a flower delivery service. What about a service for wronged wives? Say it with baseball bats, sometimes words aren't enough to express what you feel?

'Matt, how did she attack you?'

'Oh, she just went for me with the palette. It probably wasn't a good time to tell her, when she was actually working. But I was sitting there on the window ledge watching her paint, as I do just to relax sometimes, and it all came out.'

'Did it – I mean, did she do you any actual damage?'

He gave her an odd look.

'Nothing that would be visible, but it doubled me up at the time.'

'Oh! She got you in the—'

'Yes. Which is the obvious place to go for from her point of view, if you think about it.'

Ella nodded sympathetically. The next bit was going to be delicate.

'Look, it may sound like an odd question but does she – has she – is she very sporty?'

He screwed his face up at her with lack of comprehension.

'What?'

'I just wondered if she'd own anything like . . . well, like a baseball bat, for example?'

He gave her a long, pained look, and finally expelled an impatient, 'No. Why?'

'I'm sorry.' She grabbed his arm again and squeezed it tight. 'I really am sorry. It was just a thought. I – it's because I just don't know what to say to you, Matt. I'm horrified by what's happened. I hadn't thought of the consequences either, and if we could go back and undo it, we both would. But we can't. And we're going to have to find a way to put it right.'

With a tidal wave of relief, she realised that Ella the problem solver had come to her rescue. There was going to be no need for suicide after all. She nodded at him vigorously.

'Yes, that's what we'll do. We'll get it all in perspective, she'll understand and forgive you and your marriage will come back together, even stronger and happier than it was before. This isn't the end of things, far from it. Nothing's ever so badly broken that you can't fix it, I learnt that much in my job. A cup is either half-full, or half-empty, and this one's definitely half-full. Believe me. We'll get Lorna back.'

He was studying her lips as if he was having trouble following her.

'We?' he repeated.

'Well, yes. I was a part of this and I'm not going to hide from the responsibility. If there's anything at all I can do, then I'll do it.'

He was still staring at her in confusion.

'I really will,' she reassured him.

'Ella,' he said with a patience that she was sure he didn't feel. 'If you go within a hundred yards of Lorna she's going to lay you out with a right hook. I don't advise it.'

'Well, if she knew who I was, maybe she would,' she reasoned.

'No, Ella, trust me. She knows who you are. She wanted every detail from me. Once I'd told her, she wanted to know who, where, when and how.'

'Where?' Ella echoed faintly.

He nodded wearily.

'You can't blame her. In her position I'd probably have done the same.'

Ella stopped in at Do-It-All on the way home. She couldn't think of anything to do that would be therapeutic, but a quick coast around the warehouse seemed the best of her options. She still had a pair of matching craters in her living room wall where she'd tried to bang in the curtain ties, so she grabbed a trolley, slid around the floor with it as it insisted on transporting her around the store sideways, and collared an assistant.

'Are you looking for anything in particular?' he asked her with a pitying glance which she decided could not be a psychic reflection on her state of mind and must be on account of the two bumps on her chest which declared to him that she was female and alone in a world created for the amusement of men.

'Have you got a sticky hook?' she asked.

'I've got a sticky knob,' he parried. She stared at him stonily and he dropped his grin. 'I'll show you where they are.'

She picked up a blind for the kitchen door while she was at it. It was the right shade of green and would look restful. Restful would be very good under the circumstances. She flitted around bedroom fittings apologising every time she crashed into somebody's legs. The trolley was obviously being driven by poltergeists, and she was only nominally in charge of it. And as she zig-zagged back to the exit it struck her that a full-length mirror was a good idea too. If they stuck it on the landing, they'd all benefit. It was the same height as her but she grappled with it and managed to slide it on to her trolley. Then she headed for the checkout.

She waited at the back of a queue of six people as the other four checkouts were closed. There were rows of paints stacked to one side of her. The blue was nice. It would look wonderful in Faith's bedroom, with the curtains she'd hung in there. She wandered off to examine the pots more carefully and heard a shriek of pain.

'Look what you're friggin' doing!'

She leapt back in time to find an irate father clasping a wailing child. It appeared the poltergeists had decided that this was a good moment to decapitate him and the trolley had surged forwards. Well, his head was actually still on his body, but the child was obviously going to create the biggest scene possible.

'I'm so sorry.' She dumped the blue paint on top of her purchases anyway.

'Bloody women,' the father muttered, piling handfuls of mysterious metal objects into his carrier bag. 'Shouldn't be allowed in here.'

'Disgusting really,' she agreed, not having the energy to argue.

'Christ!' He gave her one more disdainful look over his shoulder as he strode into the back of an assistant hovering near the door, his child rebounding into a stand of half-price hand towels and screeching with renewed vigour. 'You should watch who you let in here,' he instructed the assistant who was rubbing his shoulder painfully. 'Some people are just flippin' dangerous.'

She skidded her trolley around the car park for what seemed like several hours until by chance she found herself beside her car. She slid the things she'd bought inside. The mirror was a bit longer than she'd thought, but she managed to rest it between the back ledge and the headrest of the front seat. As long as she didn't have to stop suddenly, it would be fine.

'Good day?' Faith smiled.

Ella stopped dead in the kitchen as Simon cavorted around her shins and begged to be petted. She dropped to her haunches and obliged, overcome with yet more confusion. Faith had smiled. Faith had asked her if she'd had a good day. Faith was wearing make-up. Faith was chopping onions, and there wasn't a can of spaghetti hoops or a Crunchie wrapper in sight. And now, Faith was whistling. Okay, she was whistling 'Telephone Line', but she was whistling. It was as if she was happy.

'Er, no. Appalling day. What about you?'

'Great.' Faith began to hum instead. Ella concentrated on giving Simon sloppy kisses until she noticed something.

'Oh my God! Simon's not in plaster any more!' Even in her state of aggravation, she was overjoyed that Simon's leg was mended, and could see that that was why he was bouncing around with more excitement than she'd ever seen, and why Faith was happy. 'That's terrific news. Isn't it, Simey? Isn't it. Yes, isn't it?'

'Oh, right. Yes, it came off today. We can take him for longer walks now, bit by bit. The garden's great, but he'll need more of a romp than that as he gets better. I'll do a rota and we can take it in turns. Mind you, it was funny.' Faith stopped to giggle.

Ella stared. Faith had giggled.

'I was out the back playing with him and Doris appeared in her nightie. I mean, that bit wasn't funny, but she actually talked to me. She said if we didn't want him, she'd have him. I said, yes we do want him, and she said that was all right, because she'd always loved dogs and could understand how you couldn't just hand them over to someone else once you'd got attached to them, but it was funny she actually spoke, wasn't it? I thought I'd do a bolognese for us tonight. Janet gave me the recipe. That okay with you?'

Ella was stunned. Had Miranda encountered Faith this evening? What did she think?

'Er, yeah, great. Is Miranda back yet?'

'In the bath. She just went straight up there when she got in. Didn't even speak to me. One of those days, I reckon.' Faith started to sing 'Sweet Talkin' Woman' under her breath.

'Right. Erm.' Ella cuddled Simon while she tried to arrange her thoughts. Ella the problem solver. Everything in its turn. And first things first.

'Any messages for me on the answerphone?'

'No. No calls.'

'Oh. Was – was Jaz here today?'

'Jaz?'

'You know, the surveillance guy. I thought he might have been here today. I thought maybe you might have seen him here if you came home at lunchtime.'

'Ah, him!' Faith expelled thoughtfully and Ella perked up. 'No.' Faith shook her head. 'I came back to get Si but there was nobody here.'

'And no notes or anything?'

'No, no notes.' Faith plopped the onions into the oil. They fizzled violently.

'I think maybe you need to turn that down a little bit. A lower heat is good.'

'Oh, okay.' Faith obligingly flicked the knob on the cooker. She didn't so much as pout. Ella chewed her lip as Simon yanked on the lace of her DMs and growled appealingly.

'And no visitors at all? Nobody came to the door while I wasn't here?'

'What, like who?' Faith stabbed at a clove of garlic with the tip of the carving knife and wiggled it around.

'Well, like artistic looking women.'

Faith shook her head as if she'd thought about it carefully.

'Nope.'

'Okay. Just one more thing then.'

'Shoot,' Faith said, springing across the floor to grab a green pepper from the unit. But there was time to be bemused by Faith's personality transplant later. There were some things that just couldn't wait.

'You know this area, don't you? And local workmen, and things like that?'

'Sort of. Why, what's up?'

'You don't know anybody reliable who does windscreen replacement, do you?'

Chapter Sixteen

'You're a twit, you really are.' Faith picked up the bottle of wine from the coffee table and splashed another measure into her glass. She grabbed a handful of Hoola-Hoops from the bowl and returned to the sofa with them, descending with such a thump that Ella had visions of herself flying off the other end like a see-saw act in the circus, turning a somersault and landing elegantly on her feet somewhere near Edinburgh. But Faith was right, she was a twit, for more reasons than Faith could possibly know. However, on this occasion Faith was referring to the windscreen.

'Don't rub it in, okay?' Ella sucked up a mouthful of white wine.

'If you'd told me we could have borrowed the van. Mum wouldn't have minded. She'd probably have driven us there and back too.'

'I didn't plan it. And if that guy hadn't suddenly pulled out on me it would have been fine.'

'Just as well it happened in the village then. You'd have been stuffed if it'd happened on the ring road.'

'Well, maybe.' Ella felt ruffled. It was a calculated risk which hadn't paid off, but she didn't like Faith constantly making her feel like a helpless female. She'd been out there, with the blokes, doing blokey things that Faith couldn't even imagine. 'What do people normally do when a full-length mirror goes through their windscreen? I'd have coped.'

'Yeah, well.' Faith guffawed and Ella took another deep drag of wine. She contemplated the current situation. There were several things that were predictable about it, and more than a few things that were odd. Predictably, Faith had known who to call to get round to fix the windscreen, and thankfully that had been done without trauma. Ella had been suitably grateful for her input and more than a little relieved that she hadn't just bounced out of the front door declaring, 'I'll fix it. You just need the right sort of glass.' Nobody need ever know that it had happened, apart from the fact that her windscreen was now clean and shiny and not spattered with bird droppings. It was solved. Practical problems like that could be solved.

But oddly, Faith was in a good mood and calling her a twit instead of loping about quietly and waiting to see what happened next. And even more oddly, Faith was talking all the way through *EastEnders*.

'Anyway,' Ella continued, trying to relax into the bosom of the sofa and trying not to think about Matt phoning, or Jaz phoning, or even Lorna phoning. 'The blind's pretty and we probably didn't need another mirror anyway. We've got the one I painted.'

Faith shrugged. 'The blind's too small for the kitchen door but maybe we could cut it down and put it in the bathroom. I'll put the mirror up in the hall if that's really how you want it to look.'

Ella bit back a sigh. 'But I picked up a lovely colour of paint.'

'Yes, it's nice. I like it. Where are you going to put it?'

'I thought your bedroom. It goes with your curtains.'

'Oh right.' Faith fell silent and crunched on her Hoola-Hoops. Ella studied Albert Square absent-mindedly. Faith didn't seem too keen on the idea. And it was her bedroom after all. Perhaps she'd been a little presumptuous. She took another sip of wine.

No, she hadn't just been presumptuous. She'd been incredibly, arrogantly presumptuous. Why on earth hadn't she chosen a moment when Faith was with her to choose a colour to paint her bedroom? How would she have felt if Faith had suddenly arrived home with a brown candlewick bedspread and said, 'Here you are, Ella, I've bought this for your room.' And it was worse than that, it was emotional blackmail because she'd paid for it out of her own pocket, and it was *her* house. And what made it all even worse was that when she thought back, she was still suffused with guilt for the way she and Miranda had ignored Faith in the pub when they were going to play darts with Giles and Paul. And she hadn't told anybody that she'd been assaulted outside the house, something that Jaz had seconded when she'd asked him for advice, but which left Faith and Miranda ignorant of the dangers they might face every time they took a bin bag out the front. Nobody had asked her where she'd been last night. They'd just assumed she'd had an early night as planned and got up late. But she'd just wrecked one person's marriage and trampled all over the purity of another's engagement. And although that was nothing to do with Faith, it seemed to her, curled up on the sofa next to Faith, that Faith was an extraordinarily good person and she was a horrifically bad one.

She lunged at the wine bottle, filled herself up and crept back to the sofa, sneaking Faith a repentant glance.

'I'm really sorry, Faith.'

Faith turned to her with a mouth full of Hoola-Hoops. 'What for?' she asked in a muffled voice.

'For buying paint for your room without asking you.'

'Oh.' Faith swallowed her mouthful. 'Well, it's funny because I liked the wallpaper in there at first, but now I think painting it's quite a good idea. It's up to you really.'

'You do?' Ella cheered up. Perhaps she wasn't so horrifically bad after all. An accidental favour would ease the chaffing of the hair shirt she was wearing.

'Hmmn. Yes. But not that one, though.'

'Oh.' Ella was crestfallen again. 'What colour would you like then? Just say, and I'll buy it. We can go down there and you can choose it yourself. Black, red, silver, I don't mind. Whatever you fancy.'

'No, the colour's fine,' Faith explained with a confused look. 'But I assumed you just meant the skirting boards. You've bought wood paint.'

'Oh,' Ella said in a tiny voice, shrinking into the sofa again. 'But I bought sticky hooks. They'll cover up the holes and we can drape the curtains.' The need for approval was becoming desperate. She peered at Faith in hope.

'Yes, they'll work as a botch job. At least it won't look so awful. They may not take the weight of the curtains, though. They might peel off, but it'd do for now.'

'Thank you.' She clutched Faith's arm in relief. Faith seemed surprised. 'You've got no idea how many things I've got wrong. I've got things wrong for ages, but I really knew about it today. And even if the sticky hooks aren't right, at least they'll do for a botch job, and that's a bloody sight better than anything else that's happened to me.'

Faith blinked at her. Even with her glasses on she seemed to be stunningly attractive, competent, intelligent and successful. Ella's insecurities doubled in on her. If only somebody would pick up the phone and tell her that she was really a nice person but had made some dreadful mistakes, she could feel better about it all. She darted a glance at the phone again and willed it to ring. When was Jaz coming back? What was he thinking? What was Matt doing tonight? Had Lorna come back, or was he on his own, sitting in her studio, picking up the palette she'd whacked him in the groin with and fondling it tearfully? Why couldn't he ring her to say they'd had a happy reunion? Why couldn't Jaz ring and say it had been a phenomenal experience and that he'd face his family and risk seeing her?

Or at least Jaz could ring and say she hadn't ruined his life?

'Where's Miranda?' Faith asked, playing with the remote control. Ella realised that *EastEnders* had finished.

'Still in the bath? Surely not.' Ella crawled off the sofa, into the hall and yelled up the stairs. 'Miranda!

There's wine down here. I would have thought you could smell it.'

'Coming down,' Miranda called back after a moment's pause.

'There.' Ella returned to the sofa and grabbed the only free spot seeing as Simon had now decided that he'd take the middle cushion. They heard Miranda's footsteps and she appeared a few seconds later.

'There you are.' Ella pointed at the bottle and the empty glass. 'All yours. And fill yourself with snacks. Faith's still brewing the bolognese.'

'Okay. Thank you.'

Ella glanced round at the softness of Miranda's voice. It was then she noticed that she had wet hair and no make-up, her eyes were red, her face was pale, she was clutching an envelope and she was draped in her blue kimono. It looked three sizes too big as she crept over to the coffee table and filled herself a glass.

'Budge up,' Miranda arrived at the sofa. They both shifted obligingly further towards the arms and Miranda dumped herself on top of Simon, who wriggled out of the way and finally collapsed happily across their laps. All three of them on the sofa, side by side. That was a first. But then, Ella wasn't herself. It didn't seem that Miranda was herself either. And Faith certainly wasn't herself.

'That bolognese smells lovely, Faith. I could probably eat in a bit. I'd like a drink first, though.' Both Ella and Faith swivelled to stare, and their eyes met as Miranda fixed her attention on the television. 'How many bottles have we got? And isn't there anything funny on?'

'What have you got there?' Ella indicated the envelope.

'Oh this? It's just my decree nisi.' She pulled the papers out of the envelope and handed them to Ella.

'But I thought you were divorced?'

'Noo,' Miranda slurped her wine. 'I wasn't quite, but I will be very shortly. First time I've seen it on paper.'

'But it's all – I mean, it's over, isn't it?'

'Yes.' Miranda drained her glass in one. 'That's not the point. It's still awful.'

'Oh, I'm sorry.' Ella linked an arm through hers. It was a bit of a rash gesture, but Miranda put her head on Ella's shoulder affectionately.

'Thanks. I need to hear that.'

'And I'm sorry too.' Ella was astonished to see Faith wind her arm through Miranda's from the other end of the sofa. Miranda looked at her, gulped, and swung her head over to rest on her shoulder instead.

'Thank you, Faith. You have no idea how much that means to me.'

'There, there.' Faith patted Miranda's hand. 'You'll get it right one day. You'll see.'

Simon stretched out his paws and broke wind loudly.

'And thank you, Simon.' Miranda caressed his head affectionately. 'I appreciate the gesture.'

They sank back into the cushions. This was what it was all about, Ella decided, feeling warmed and emotional. Three women, sharing a sofa, all so different that you'd never put them together in your wildest dreams, but united they were strong. This was what she'd missed in her years in the banking world, surrounded by masculine ideals and masculine values. This was all about femininity. It was sisterhood. Men became abstract patterns in a moment like this, like a series of Picasso canvases in an exhibition that you could stroll around and leave behind when you went home.

Miranda turned to Faith.

'Did Giles mention me today?'

'Let me think.' Faith squashed her lips together. 'Actually, yes he did, now you mention it. He said he was going to ring you, and that I could tell you that if I wanted to. Sorry, I forgot.'

'Did he?' Miranda sat up straighter. 'Really?'

'Yes, honest.'

'What, tonight?'

'I don't know. Maybe. He didn't say.'

'Did he say anything else?'

Faith scratched her neck. 'Not really. He asked how I'd got on with Paul, but that was about it.'

Miranda nodded and sat back again. Ella peered round her.

'And how did you get on with Paul?'

'We went for a Chinese,' Faith said casually, sipping some more wine. 'And I'm seeing him at the weekend.'

'You've got a date, you mean?' Ella quizzed in amazement.

'Well, no.' Faith went bright red, as if acting cool had all become too much for her blood vessels. 'It's just a friendly thing, but it's nice anyway.'

'Great!' Miranda slapped her on the knee.

'Thanks, Miranda.' Faith went puce with pleasure.

'Yes, it means Giles will be free. He's going to ring to ask me if I want to do something.'

'You're not going to sit here and wait for the phone to ring all night, are you? I can't cope with both of you mooning over it. You two are far too weak.' Faith bent over her knees and delivered severe looks along the sofa. 'We could watch a video instead.'

'I'm not mooning,' Ella defended.

'Well, you are actually. You asked me if that surveillance guy had rung as if you really wanted him to. We all know you fancy him. And Miranda wants Giles to ring. I say, if the phone does ring, we don't answer it. That way we'll have a nice evening.'

Ella cleared her throat tensely. Miranda stiffened beside her.

'We'd have to just find out who it was, but we could cut it short.'

'No.' Faith shook her head. 'If you want dinner tonight, you don't answer the phone if it rings.'

'It's not so bad really,' Miranda glanced at Ella. 'We've got the answerphone. We can hear who it is.'

'Nope.'

Faith stood up, leaving them falling over each other as the sofa dynamic abruptly changed, tugged the phone out of the socket and waved it at them. Miranda gasped. Ella suppressed a moan. Faith disappeared with the phone. They heard the key turn in the back door and frowned at each other. After a few moments Faith returned, flush faced.

'There you go. No distractions. You can have the phone back tomorrow. So what's it to be then? *Star Wars* or *Bugsy Malone*?'

Miranda was the first to find her voice.

273

'I'm quite hungry actually. If we're not allowed to talk to anybody, you could at least let us eat.'

'Yes, I'm ravenous now, Faith,' Ella agreed. 'Do you want to stick the spaghetti on?'

'Oh, okay. And do you think I should take the mince out of the freezer now?'

On Saturday evening, Ella found herself alone.

Faith had indeed gone out with Paul. He'd arrived to pick her up in a taxi and she'd thrown herself out of the door in a blur of blue denim, yelling a goodbye before Ella or Miranda had a chance to comment on her sudden love of Levis. There was a whiff of perfume lingering in the hall after her, and Miranda had sniffed it knowledgeably.

'Charlie Girl,' she'd announced with raised eyebrows. 'She's been to Superdrug. Still, you've got to start somewhere.'

Shortly afterwards Miranda had disappeared upstairs and returned in a silky top and khaki trousers with neat brown leather ankle boots that looked amazingly sexy. Ella surmised that it wasn't all for her benefit.

'Are you going out too?'

'Didn't I mention it? I'm going to the Sheldonian. They're doing Dvorak and something else, I can't remember what.'

'I didn't think you were into classical music?'

'Well, it's never too late to start a new hobby, is it? Anyway, it was Giles's idea, and seeing as it's about ten years since anybody asked me out on a proper date I felt it would be churlish to refuse.'

Ella sat up straight on the sofa and wiggled Simon's ears with her fingers in agitation.

'Giles asked you out? You mean, properly?'

'Yes, Ella,' Miranda explained patiently. 'Properly. In the way a gentleman would, in fact. And what's more, I'll be coming home before I turn into a pumpkin. He's made that clear, not overtly but just in the way he said things. And do you know what, I rather like it.'

Ella nodded in something of a daze.

'Well, yes. Good on you, then. He's lovely.'

'Yes.' Miranda looked pensive as she pulled her jacket around her shoulders. 'I think perhaps I've got a bit sick of snacks. I fancy a long, leisurely main meal now. But I'm going to do it in the right order. You know, starter, main course, dessert, coffee, mints, port, cigar.'

'I see. Don't you normally do that?'

'Yes, but normally all in the space of about six hours. I think I want to take my time now.'

'Good idea,' Ella had said faintly as Miranda had thrown a wave in her direction and disappeared out of the door. Ella heard her car engine firing up outside. So she was driving herself into Oxford, and that meant she wouldn't be drinking and was probably serious about coming home the same night. She pulled Simon's ears thoughtfully and he peered up at her adoringly.

'So much for Saturday night then,' she pouted down at him.

She flicked the remote control and gazed at the television. It had been a thoroughly awful week, all in all. Jaz still hadn't contacted her. Matt now seemed to be avoiding her completely apart from the occasional loud sigh that had the entire class gazing at him in soulful sympathy. She'd only managed to catch him on his own once and had stuttered out, 'Has Lorna – I mean—' to which he'd replied with a tense, 'No,' and dashed away back to the tutorial hut.

She was really something of a leper, she told herself to make it hurt even more. And now that the cottage was quiet and lifeless with only the burble of the television for company, she found herself darting glances towards the front garden and allowing herself to ponder on the dastardly activity down the road at number eleven. It was what had thrown CID into her path, and, to be precise, DI Jasbinder Singh. So, Jaz had evidently decided that one night of uncontrollable passion was going to be the entirety of their relationship and of course, she couldn't blame him. The guilt he must feel would be tremendous. And if an arranged marriage had always been on the cards for him, she guessed he must have become accustomed to reimposing control on himself swiftly and firmly, should he ever lose it. It wasn't as if he'd been vague about his situation. She knew exactly what it was, and the fact that he hadn't tried to gloss over it or toss her any false promises was in its own strange way fairly honourable.

But he still had to finish his job at the cottage, and she was utterly in the dark as to how that was going to happen. It should, at least, mean that she would see him again. And now she yearned to see him again.

She let out a long, loud sigh and stared at the phone. She shared a house with two verbose, stroppy women, but they'd deserted her and she was lonely. After a moment's consideration she picked up the receiver and dialled.

'Hi, Mum?'

Her mother's voice was enthusiastic in reply. She snuggled into the sofa feeling warmed, wondering why she hadn't got to grips with herself and rung home before.

'Darling! How's the good life?'

'Not so good, actually.'

She paused. She never burbled to her mother. It wasn't the sort of relationship they had.

'I'll get your father,' her mother said, as she always did. 'He's locked away in his study doing something on the internet, but he'll be furious if he misses you.'

Ella was about to let her go, but a realisation hit her like a thunderbolt. She didn't want to talk to her father. She'd thought she did, but that wasn't it. It was her mother she needed answers from. And now that she realised it, she couldn't let the opportunity pass. They had to have this conversation now.

'No, Mum,' Ella stopped her as she could hear she was about to bustle away. 'I'd like to talk to you, actually.'

'You would?' She sounded astonished. There was a stunned silence from both mother and daughter in reaction to Ella's declaration. She waved Simon's ears in concentration. Usually she'd talk to her father at great length about her work, her life, her ambitions, and he'd report it all back to her mother in his own good time, but she hadn't realised quite how blatant it was until she'd heard that tone in her mother's voice. 'What would you like to talk about?'

'Well, about – about men, in fact.'

'Men?' There was another silence, then her mother laughed under her breath. 'That's a first. I thought you had it all covered.'

'No, Mum, don't be prickly. I don't, and it's all gone horribly wrong.'

'All right.' It was clear her mother was settling down, probably in the armchair in the living room next to the phone. She'd gaze out of the French windows to the patio, but what would the expression on her face be? Especially when Ella said what was on her mind? Ella drew her eyebrows together in a frown of concentration. What was she doing? She had no idea what she was going to say next. When it came out she was amazed.

'I – look Mum, did Dad ever have an affair?'

The silence that followed was deafening. Ella bit her lip, held her breath and closed her eyes, pulling on Simon's ears in anguish. He let out a squeak and she released them quickly. That had come out heinously. She should never have asked it. She wriggled around on the sofa, wincing while she waited for her mother's reaction.

'Wait a minute,' her mother said firmly. Ella's emotions swirled around her stomach as she heard her leaving the armchair, her heels on the polished woodblock floor, and a door closing. Oh God, surely she hadn't gone to get her father? Had she shocked her so much that she'd rushed away upset? She slumped in despair.

'That's better,' her mother's voice returned, louder and more resonant. 'I don't want him to overhear us.' There was another awkward pause. Ella held her breath. 'Yes, Ella, he's had several affairs. Why are you asking me that now?'

Ella screwed her eyelids together as tears rose and dribbled down her face. She brushed them away in agitation and answered in a choked voice.

'Because I knew it anyway. I just needed you to confirm it.'

'They haven't come between us,' her mother continued calmly, although Ella heard her stop to clear her throat loudly. 'The first was a jolt, but I realised after a while that our marriage wasn't threatened by it. It never has been.'

'Why?' Ella blurted, her voice breaking. 'Why did he do it? Why did you accept it? Why are you so controlled about it?'

She heard her mother take a deep breath and let it out slowly.

'Because, darling, it was the way we worked together.'

'Worked?' Ella cried back. 'You're both obsessed with that word. What about fun, and happiness, and love? Weren't you ever in love?'

'Oh yes,' she replied evenly. 'I was very deeply in love with your father once. And I fell in love all over again some time later.'

'And what happened to that feeling? How could it become so calculated, so cold?'

She heard her mother take another long breath.

'After we were married, your father became very preoccupied. With work mainly, and then when you came along, with you. Our marriage became more – workmanlike. I did what was expected and I never let him down, but he lost interest in me in many ways. Then later somebody came along who did show interest in me. That's when I fell in love again.'

'What?' Ella rubbed at her wet cheeks with the back of her hand. 'What do you mean?'

'Do you remember James Briggs?' Ella blinked. He was a colleague of her father's and a longtime family friend.

'Yes?'

'We were in love, for a long time. We probably still are. But now they're in Norfolk and he and Elizabeth are settled, and the time for doing anything about it has long passed. But yes, we were in love for about fifteen years.'

'Oh my God!' Ella spluttered.

'But I don't think your father has ever truly been in love. It doesn't mean I don't care for him very much. We respect each other, Ella. We don't argue, we share plenty of interests and we're content.'

'But—'

'You have to understand that a woman of my class and generation was brought up to be a support to a husband. It's very difficult to break that mould. I would never embarrass him or cause a scandal. Nobody knew how I felt, I made quite sure of that.'

'Oh.' Ella faded into silence. She wanted to cry, whimper, shout and stare mournfully into space all at the same time.

'But it doesn't mean your life will ever be that way. You're free and you're young. One day you'll meet somebody who you will fall in love with and it will be wonderful. I've said as much to you before. You won't need anybody to tell you when it happens, you'll feel it.'

'Yes, I know,' she said in a tiny voice.

'And my guess is that it's happened to you now, which is why you've talked to me like this for the first time in your life.'

Ella gulped in a lungful of air.

'I don't know what to do. He's engaged, Mum. There's no hope of anything ever coming of it. I don't even know how it happened. It was so quick. One minute he was practically a stranger, the next thing I knew, he'd barged into my thoughts and completely taken them over. And it makes no sense because I hardly know him either, I've just got this over-powering feeling that it would be wonderful if we were together. All I know is that I've never wanted somebody around me so much. Why did it have to happen now, with somebody I can't have?'

'Oh you silly girl,' her mother scolded, but there was a soft edge to her voice.

'I've made so many mistakes, Mum,' Ella snuffled through her tears. 'I've been so bad, I've hurt people and I've got it all wrong. I can't make the same mistake again, I just can't.'

'Making the same mistake again wouldn't be a good idea,' her mother agreed. 'But don't be afraid of making a different one.'

After she had cried all over the phone, thanked her mother with a surge of love for being so wonderful, declined the opportunity to speak to her father and promised to go home and visit them soon, Ella rang off, mopped her face with a tissue and settled back on the sofa with Simon again. She let out a long, tired moo like a sleepy calf. The situation was still insoluble, but she could face it with a braver spirit now. It had happened to her at last, and it meant that maybe, just maybe it could happen again. One day. Perhaps she'd have to wait until she was fifty. Or ninety. But she would wait, and she wouldn't settle for anything less, or upset anyone else's stability in the process. She wasn't hard-nosed and practical at all, it was just a lie she had been living for twenty-nine years, and it was going to stop right away. It made everybody too unhappy. It made *her* too unhappy. It was time for a change.

There was a sharp rap at the front door.

She stopped mooing immediately and glanced around. Who was that? On a Saturday night? A pulse of apprehension threaded its way through her veins. Not the Pete Postlethwaites? Had they seen Miranda and Faith leap off? Were they just checking to see if the cottage was empty before they – did what? She swallowed back her nerves and stood up, smoothing her hands over her jeans. She couldn't hide inside. If it was anybody looking for trouble, at least they'd see there was somebody in and be put off. And there was a chain on the door.

She linked the chain across carefully, twisted the handle and very slowly pulled the door open. She peered through the gap.

It was a woman. She turned round as she saw the door being opened and looked at Ella with an enquiring face. Her hair was long, black and frizzy, her face small and shaped like a pear-drop, and she had huge, blue, haunting eyes. She looked amazingly tired.

'Excuse me, are—' The woman cleared her throat

nervously, her small fingers interlacing themselves. 'I'm so sorry to bother you, but I was wondering if Ella lived here?'

Ella stared back at her, goose pimples pricking at her skin. Then without a word she closed the door, unlinked the chain and opened it wide. She stepped back into the hall.

'I think you'd better come in, Lorna.'

Chapter Seventeen

'You're not how I imagined you at all,' Lorna said, perching delicately on the edge of the armchair and holding her coffee mug to her chest.

'You're exactly as I imagined you,' Ella returned in a pale voice.

Lorna had been so subdued when she'd entered the cottage that Ella had taken the time to compose herself by making coffee for them both. If anything, Lorna had seemed bewildered to find that this was in fact Ella's house, that Ella was in, and that they'd discovered themselves in the same room together. It was as if it was something she'd pictured vaguely, but didn't know how to handle having the elusive vision turned into reality.

'I thought you must be blonde, buxom and tanned, like something out of *Baywatch*,' Lorna said. 'And I thought you'd be full of laughter and fun, not serious like I am. And I didn't think you'd look as tired and upset as me.' Lorna swallowed and winced, her eyes huge, but never leaving Ella's face. 'Every model I've seen in a magazine since then, every beautiful woman on an advert on the television turned into you. I thought you must feel so triumphant. But you look as if you've been crying for a week as well.'

'I don't know what to say. I'm so very, very sorry.'

'But you are beautiful, just not in the way I'd

imagined you. In a more real way. Perhaps that's even worse, I don't know. But you look very strong. You must be very strong.'

'Oh no, I'm not. No.' Ella stagnated as she wanted to say more.

Lorna chewed visibly on her lips, her eyes growing even bigger.

'Are you in love with Matt?'

Ella shook her head slowly but firmly. 'Not at all. But I don't expect that to make you feel any better.'

'I see. Can you – I mean, would you tell me what happened? If it doesn't impose on you too much.'

She might as well have been clouting Ella round the head with a baseball bat, but Ella knew that this was more painful. The quiet concentration of the small woman in front of her was something that she would never, ever forget. She tried, hesitantly, to explain it all. She didn't leave much out. She could imagine now, as she'd never even attempted to imagine before, Lorna's need to know the details. At the end of her explanation there was a long pause as Lorna sipped her coffee.

'Thank you for being honest.'

'It was never an affair or anything close to one, just that one stupid night on my birthday when you were away. I'm just so, so sorry,' Ella repeated, rubbing at her tired face. She probably looked as if she'd taken a pumice stone to it by the time she sat back again but she didn't care.

'No, don't be.' Lorna set down her mug as if she felt a little stronger. 'I understand it now. Matt's so stupid, he's unable to explain things in a way a woman needs to hear them. That's why I came here. I didn't mean to startle you. I hope I didn't.'

'Yes, you did,' Ella countered. 'But it doesn't matter.'

'We've drifted apart a lot in this last year. I knew Matt desperately wanted children, but I wasn't quite ready. It created a lot of tension between us. I've been burying myself in my work. Do you know how many weekends I've been away for this year, leaving him on his own?' Ella shook her head. 'Well, no matter really, but far too many. I'm not happy about this at all. Don't get me wrong. After this occasion I never want to see you or speak to you again.'

Her eyes had gained fire and Ella absorbed it. Then Lorna relaxed again.

'I've never been unfaithful to Matt. Not ever, even though I've had plenty of opportunities. It was horrifying that he'd done it to me. The fact I've been away a lot is no excuse. No excuse at all. I'm not blaming myself, and I don't see why I should. Matt and I have a contract and a promise to love through thick and thin. If we hadn't meant it, we'd never have gone through the charade of a wedding ceremony. And he was the one who wanted a wedding. I sincerely believed that he was a unique man. The sort that can dedicate himself to one woman, no matter what. The fact that things got rough was no reason for him to wander away like an alley cat. It still makes me feel ill.'

'But he couldn't – I mean.' Ella contorted her face. 'It was obvious his mind was miles away, Lorna. I don't think Matt could be unfaithful to you, even though he played with the idea. He loves you far too much.'

'Well,' Lorna looked down at her hands and Ella felt unclamped from the grip of those enormous eyes. 'Obviously I don't want to hear that from you, but I think it is true. Your version and his are the same. It's something at least to know that there wasn't – wasn't completion between you.'

'I understand,' Ella whispered.

'No, you can't understand. You're single, you've got no attachments. That's what he told me. And I hope some day somebody does this to you, just so that you know how it feels. That's all. I don't wish any more evil on you than that.'

Ella crouched into the back of the sofa. It was what she deserved and she must sit and take it. There was no other option.

'I—'

There was a loud banging at her front door. At first Ella was too locked up in the scene that was being played out to acknowledge it, but it came again. Her heart sank with despair.

'Let me just get that, Lorna. But please don't rush away.'

'I won't.'

She stopped in the hall to compose herself. With a scarlet face, scarlet eyes and a mess of straggly dark brown knots for hair there was very little point, but she heaved in a breath and opened the door, not bothering with the chain. She gaped at the figure standing on her doorstep.

'Can I come in? I'm in hell.'

It was Matt. She continued to gape at him.

'Please, Ella. She hasn't phoned, even though I've left a hundred messages at her sister's. Nobody's speaking to me. Her mother just slammed the phone down, and her brother called me a slimy bastard and slammed the phone down too. I've got nobody left to talk to.'

'I – Matt, I've got a visitor here,' Ella stammered.

'Oh.' Matt raked his hand through his hair. It looked like a Brillo pad. 'Then can I just wait upstairs or something? No, upstairs isn't good. I don't want to go upstairs. The garden. I can go through and wait in the garden until they've gone, can't I? I can't be on my own any more. I'm going to go mad.'

'You – you can't get into the garden without going through the house,' Ella voiced, latching on to the only piece of sense she could. 'And my visitor's in the living room. So you can't do that.'

'I'll wait in my car, then. I can go and sit there until they've gone.'

'No,' Ella shook her head. When Lorna left she'd see him out there. Christ, what would she think? That Ella was an abject liar and that Matt was coming round to see her for an intimate evening? But where was Lorna's car? Hadn't he seen it outside?

'Then I'll just hover on a cloud over the house then,' Matt ejected in agitation. 'Come on, Ella. Help me out here. I need to hear a woman's point of view. You've got to tell me what to do.'

'Doesn't Lorna drive?'

'What? No, she never has done. Why the hell do you want to know that right now?'

'Hello, Matt.'

Ella jumped round to see Lorna behind her. She was leaning around the living room door, looking straight at Matt. He let out a shout of shock, clutched at his chest, and then barged past Ella and crammed himself into the tiny hall beside her.

'Where have you been?' He grabbed her shoulders. 'I've been going crazy, absolutely crazy. I didn't know if you were alive, dead, or anything. I've been so desperate to talk to you. I've tried everything. I've never been so miserable in my life.'

'Good,' Lorna replied.

Ella tried to nudge the front door shut. Somebody was walking past the front gate and had stopped to stare in at them. She flicked a reassuring smile at them, then realised with amazement that it was Doris. She'd never seen Doris wandering about at the front of the house. And she was in her nightie and slippers heading down the lane as if it was completely normal.

'Oh blimey.'

'Don't say you've gone for ever. Please let us talk. Please, Lorna. I love you so much, so very, very much.' Matt burst into tears.

'You're a complete tosser,' Lorna responded coldly.

'Doris!'

Ella hoofed it out of the door and down the front path as Doris waved and shuffled away towards the village.

'Yo! Doris! Come back here!' She swung back to the house. Matt was casting a bewildered look over his shoulder at her. 'Go inside, Matt. Help yourselves to whatever you want and make yourselves comfortable in the living room. I've just got to—'

Doris was gaining speed. She'd passed the next-door garden and was motoring on towards number eleven.

'Doris!' she called with more force.

Doris waved a hand without looking round, her nightie catching the breeze and flapping round her shins. Then, as Ella watched aghast, she turned at the gate of number eleven, carefully undid the latch, and purposefully made her way up the path towards the front door.

'No!' Ella yelled in horror, putting her hands up to her face. 'Doris! You can't go there!'

For a moment Ella was frozen with panic. Her legs wouldn't move, but she knew she had to go in that direction, very quickly, and stop Doris from doing whatever it was she was planning to do next. Then mercifully she was released and she began to run down the lane. She swerved at the gate of number eleven, grabbed the gatepost and swung around to face the path. She raced up it in time to grab Doris's shoulders just as her pale finger was jaggedly raising itself to ring the bell.

'No!' she urged hoarsely into Doris's ear. 'Come back with me, now. You don't want to do that.'

'I don't?' Doris looked over her shoulder with weak grey eyes. She seemed very confused.

'No.' Ella shook her head vigorously. 'You really don't. I'll make you a cup of tea at home. Let's get you back inside now.'

'But I don't even know who you are!' Doris stated.

'Look, I'm really sorry,' Ella managed breathlessly. 'I'm Ella. We should have asked you round. We should have gone shopping for you and made sure you were all right and all sorts of things. We can put that right now. From now on we're all going to look after you, I promise. But you've got to come away from this house. You can't ring the bell.'

'But I have to!' Doris asserted, trying to shake Ella's hands from her body. 'I have to give them the money. If I don't, they'll starve. They wouldn't manage without my help. They told me so.'

'Oh God!' Ella breathed, her face paling. The realisation of what was going on took hold of her finger by finger until it had her in a firm grip. 'Oh double God. Let's get out of here. You come with me.'

'But they need my money,' Doris protested as Ella yanked her away from the front door.

'No they don't,' Ella hissed into her ear.

'Yes they do!' Doris insisted, her face indignant. 'And who do you think you are, anyway? Adolf Hitler? Get your hands off me!'

'No, I won't. It's for your own good!' Ella propelled Doris in a circle and somehow managed to point her in the direction of the gate again. Doris wriggled away and headed back to the front door. Ella lunged after her again and clasped her arms around her waist. She carried her halfway back down the path before she received an agonising heel of a slipper in the shins. She put her down and winced.

'Bloody hell, Doris. I'm trying to help you.'

She glanced across the road as she was heaving herself up, ready to spin round and rush back to reclaim Doris once more.

She stopped, paralysed in her tracks.

The car parked on the grassy verge on the other side of the lane was a sleek, sporty model that hit her memory as one she knew. There was somebody sitting in it, looking as if they were reading a map. But she knew the car and the profile immediately her senses had finished bouncing up and down the path like a power ball and returned to admit that they belonged to her. It was Jaz's car, and Jaz was sitting in it.

She peered into the driver's window. Jaz glanced up and stared ahead along the lane leading away from the village, then seemed to gaze idly over his shoulder at her. She opened her eyes wide, contorted her face and mouthed 'help'. Surely he'd seen her? That was stupid, of course he'd seen her. What was she supposed to do now, for heaven's sake? And what was he doing?

He leant over his shoulder to adjust his seat belt. For a split second his eyes met hers. She bored him out with a desperate stare. His hand flicked over his shoulder, seemed to miss the catch on the seat belt and wave towards the windscreen.

She pulled an even more desperate face at him, but he didn't look at her again. What was he thinking of, trying to put his seat belt on like that? Where was he going? He couldn't go anywhere. Not now.

Then he flapped his hand three more times, and she realised with a flash of understanding that he was gesticulating to her. He was waving her away, back down the lane, back the way she'd come.

'Oh right! Why the bloody hell didn't you say so!' she mumbled and clamped her mouth shut again. Jaz appeared to have gone back to reading his map. Behind her she heard the muted chime of a doorbell. She gulped.

'There!' Doris said into the air. 'You may think you're Mussolini, but you're not. I can do what I want.'

'Right,' Ella called in the most cheerful voice she could find. 'Just my mistake, Doris. I'm sorry about that. You just looked a bit cold and I thought a cup of tea might warm you up.'

She fingered her way through the latch on the gate and out into the lane again, waving heartily.

'Bye then. If you ever need anything, you just give us a shout.'

'Get stuffed!' Doris called back fiercely.

'That's fine. Bye.'

She fixed a waxy smile and side-stepped her way back down the lane. She waddled inch by inch like a duck all the way back to her own front gate, and saw from an angle that the front door to number eleven had opened. She stopped.

Whatever Jaz had been indicating to her that she should do, she had to see what happened next. Doris was so vulnerable in her slippers and nightie. What if he had a purely professional outlook on this? What if Doris was somehow disposable in the pursuit of the real objective? What if she was a tiny little plastic pawn in a great big game that the poor old woman could have no comprehension of? Could she trust Jaz to do the right thing at the right time? Why should she trust him? He had a job to do, first and foremost, and if Doris got herself into trouble wouldn't that just be unfortunate? Wouldn't Jaz be surveying things on a bigger scale? Doris's ultimate sacrifice would be the gain of maybe dozens of others. That was how he would see it. But she could hear Doris croaking something, and see an arm extending out of the door of number eleven and tugging her inside by her lacy nylon lapels.

'No!' Ella found a torrent of indignation inside herself that could no longer be reasoned away. She swung round and started to stride back up the lane again.

'Sweetheart!'

She was grabbed firmly and held in an iron grip. A hot mouth descended on her neck.

'What the hell—?'

'My love.'

She was pivoted around on her heels and a mouth crushed hers. At the same time the arms encircling her waist hardened like concrete, raised her several inches in the air and started dragging her little by little back towards her house. She stared into Jaz's open black eyes. He fixed her with an equally adamant stare in return.

'Oh baby, how I've missed you.' He smothered her mouth in kisses while dragging her with trailing boots along the road and to her front path. 'God, I don't know how I've lasted since we saw each other. You're dynamite. An earthquake. A tigress.'

'You bet I'm a bloody tigress,' she shot back at him, trying to struggle out of his clench as he propelled her up the path to her front door.

'Hmmn, don't I know it,' he declared loudly, planting another kiss over her mouth.

'You bastard,' she issued in a low voice through her teeth. 'You're going to sacrifice an old lady just like that. You've got no principles at all. I'd got you completely wrong. You're just out for yourself and a result you can report back. You're not a Wild West hero, you're just a coward sending somebody else over the top instead of you. You're Horace bloody Wimp, that's what you are.'

'Oh yes,' he muttered huskily. 'I love it when you talk seventies rock music. Inside, now!'

'Don't you ever think you can order me about. You bloody well can't. I can't believe I let you touch me. You're disgusting.'

'You wanted me to touch you,' he issued out of the corner of his mouth.

'At the time. But I was concussed and confused. I can see what you are now.'

'You weren't concussed at all. That was just an excuse to get me into bed, and you bloody well know it.'

'Sod off. I didn't know what you were capable of then.'

'But it was amazing, incredible. I've never known anything like it,' he whispered at her, then declared loudly, 'You're in love with me. Admit it.'

'No I bloody am not!' she yelled into his face.

She threw herself from side to side, but his grip only tightened on her. Her temper fired like a blow torch.

'Get inside the house, Ella,' he instructed in a barked whisper.

'Don't you dare tell me what to do!'

'I dare. I can handle you. You really hate it, but I can.'

'No you fucking well can't!'

She wrenched herself furiously out of his arms just as they reached the threshold of her house.

'You're my woman!' he growled at her noisily. 'And I want you now. Get inside and up the stairs.'

'Get this, you arrogant shit!'

She swung at him with her fist. She had never done anything like it in her life before, but a tornado took control of her actions and made it happen. Her knuckles made contact with his nose, and there was a sickening crunch. He buckled in front of her, leaning over his knees and coughing painfully, both of his hands slapped over his face.

She stood on the doorstep in complete horror. Everything seemed to stand still. Very slowly she put her hand to her mouth and looked down at him. A few droplets of blood hit the pale concrete of the path. He snorted and shook his head, blinking blearily into the air, then clasped his hands on his knees and stared at the ground again.

'Oh!' she breathed.

He sniffed, pulled himself upright, and staggered towards her. For a moment she thought he was going to crash into her, but he put his hands on her shoulders and pressured her backwards through the front door and into her hall. She allowed herself to be directed, the fight leaving her as she saw the pain he was in. He purposefully shoved her back against the hall wall so that he could get hold of the door, and kicked it shut behind them. The hall was small and quiet, with no sounds coming from anywhere else, and she suddenly felt very visible and very responsible.

She waited in silence, her hand fastened over her mouth. In slow motion he extracted a walkie-talkie from the inside of his jacket pocket, leaning back against the front door for support. He gave several sharp blinks in the direction of the stairs as if he was looking right through her, and stuck his thumb on a button.

'Roy?' he groaned.

'Here,' A voice crackled back.

He let go a long breath, pulled himself upright and spoke again.

'Go. Go now. Take me out of the equation at the front. I think my nose is broken. Give me two minutes and I'll go over the back.'

'Your nose is broken? You all right, gov?'

'Save it. Go now. Subject is inside.'

'Roger that.'

He held on to the walkie-talkie and raised his eyes fleetingly to Ella's.

'You're just a waggon load of bloody trouble. And don't flatter yourself into thinking I mean that as a compliment.'

She nodded in agreement with him. She still couldn't believe what she'd done. The hand she'd hit him with was sore and throbbing excruciatingly. But it must have been worse for him. The last thing he would have been expecting was for her to punch him in the face when all he was trying to do was get her inside the house so that she didn't mess up his operation. She wanted to fall all over him in remorse, but he was already heading through the living room door. She put out a hand instinctively.

'Oh hang on!'

He twisted round, his nose red, his eyes watering.

'What is it?' he snapped. And well might he snap, she reasoned.

'It's just that Matt and his wife are in there. Matt? You remember? The married man I—'

She quailed. She didn't simply quail, she died. This, she could only assume, was what happened to actors.

'Right,' Jaz stated. 'I really don't give a damn. May I carry on now?'

'Yes.'

And with a burst of movement, he was out of her sight.

She stood utterly still in the gloom of the hall, wishing that she hadn't lost her temper with Jaz. That she'd never set eyes on Jaz. That she'd never set eyes on Matt. That she'd never thought that coming to the country was a good idea. That she'd never left banking. That she'd never gone into a career in banking in the first place. That she'd never been brought up to believe that banking was the right thing for her to do. That she'd never, ever been born.

A series of sharp barks followed by aggressive growling cut through her penitence. She rubbed her knuckles and listened.

'Oh no.'

She shot through the living room. There was no sign whatsoever of Matt and Lorna. Where on earth had they gone? She screeched to a halt, scanned the room and was completely baffled. Not upstairs for a passionate reunion, surely? God, no, not in the house where Matt had been unfaithful. So what was going on? The growling came again, more fiercely.

'Simon!' she called, pushing through to the kitchen. Jaz was there, with one hand on the back door handle, the corner of his trouser leg firmly caught in Simon's teeth.

'Oy you!' She threw herself on the dog and wrapped her hand around his jaw, levering it open until he let go. She wagged a finger at him. 'Bad boy!'

The moment Jaz was released he was out of the back door. There wasn't even time on this occasion to throw abject apologies at him. She could almost see the skid marks that his shoes had left on the lino. She could definitely see a tiny droplet of blood that must have come from the nose she had punched. She slid herself out of the back door and into the back garden, shoving Simon back as she pulled it shut after her.

'Another time,' she whispered at him. 'This isn't a game.'

Then she turned and crept around the shed.

She located Matt and Lorna. They must have walked out of the house and into the garden for a private moment together. They were at the end of the lawn opposite each other, his hand holding hers. But their heads were turned towards one of the fences adjoining Ella's garden. Ella could just see Jaz's legs disappearing as he vaulted over it.

'Save Doris!' she bellowed in a final, desperate plea.

'Fuck off,' she heard back.

She just had time to inch further up the garden in an effort to catch a glimpse across the fences of what might be going on, when a crashing sound to one side of her had her spinning around, and another man in plain clothes vaulted into her garden from Doris's, sprinted across the narrow strip of her lawn, and vaulted over the next fence.

Matt and Lorna gaped in amazement. She might have tried to say something to explain things, but another loud creak of the fence had another, younger man leaping into her garden, taking two strides across the lawn and also bounding athletically over the next fence.

She looked back towards Doris's garden again. There had to be another one coming. It was like the Royal Tournament. If she'd known they were going to do this she could have put the sofa out there in the middle of the lawn and they could have bounced off it and somersaulted through the air without touching the grass at all.

She shook away the image. This really wasn't funny. Matt and Lorna seemed dumbstruck. Things went very quiet for a moment as all three of them stared over the garden fence in the direction of number eleven.

Then the fragile peace was shattered by the sound of breaking glass, several deafening crashes and what sounded like the wood of a door splintering. There were several shouts. She thought she heard Jaz's voice yelling, 'Freeze!' She raised her eyebrows. So he did say it sometimes. There was loud scuffling.

'Crikey.' She winced as she heard another thump and a shout of pain. What should she do? Help? Duck? Put the kettle on? She chewed savagely on her lip, cowering each time there was a crash and a shout. Whoever was in there, they weren't going to come peacefully, that was for sure. As long as Doris was safe. And as long as Jaz was all right. But she was sure he must be. He had lots of other guys backing him up.

It went quiet for several minutes.

Now was the right time to pull a rueful face at Matt and Lorna who had both gone very pale, beckon them into the house, and offer them a coffee and a Garibaldi before they headed off. Or at least the chance to be together a little longer, in the living room perhaps, away from the distant thuds. And she should just try to gabble an explanation at them. She managed to catch Lorna's attention with a subdued wave of her hand.

'I was wondering if you both wanted a coffee?' she called down the garden politely. Lorna stared back at her blankly. Matt turned round in confusion.

'Ella, what–?'

They were silenced by a loud crack coming from the wooden fence as a huge man levered himself over it, splitting one of the flimsy planks. With cropped hair and an unshaven jaw, he looked like Desperate Dan. He might as well have had 'CID' tattooed on his forehead. A voice shouted into the air from the garden of number eleven.

'Get inside, Ella! He's dangerous!'

Well, he would be, she supposed fleetingly, backing away down the side of the shed towards the back door anyway. She blinked at the imposing figure as he stopped on her lawn, swung round in agitation to see Matt and Lorna in each other's arms, then swung back to spot Ella retreating in the direction of her house.

'You!' he bellowed, striding towards her. Ella gulped. He wasn't very friendly. Had he seen Jaz's nose? Was this the guy he'd spoken to on the walkie-talkie, come to give her a good dressing down for punching his boss? A chill galloped over her flesh. He was far, far more menacing than that. And then her brain clicked and she realised in horror that this man had nothing to do with CID at all.

'Inside the house!' He pushed her towards the back door. She stared back at him like a transfixed rabbit in a headlamp, shuffling backwards until she found the door handle behind her back. She twisted it and carefully stepped back into the kitchen. Simon took the opportunity to escape joyfully through the door and bounded off into the garden.

In one shocking movement, the man lurched across the kitchen and yanked the bread knife from her set of Kitchen Devils. She smothered a whimper of panic as he brandished it at her, his hand shaking.

'I'm not going to argue with you,' Ella whispered into the red, sweating face. She didn't know anything about this sort of situation, but she knew it wasn't wise to argue with a man who had a bread knife. That was only sensible.

The back door slammed behind them. She could hear noises of frenzied activity outside the house. The CID guys were there. They knew she was in here, with him. Any moment now they'd crash in and rescue her. She just had to stay alive until then. Her captor swept feverish glances around the kitchen and pushed her through into the living room. From the front of the house she heard the roaring of car engines and the screeching of tyres, followed by running footsteps.

'They know you're here,' she breathed to him soulfully.

His eyes jittered from the front to the back of the

house. He was evidently in a state of panic. Panic was not good. Especially when the person panicking had a weapon trembling between his fingers and pointed at her belly button. The phone rang shrilly from the coffee table. She twitched in shock. He stared at it, perspiration gathering on his upper lip.

'That's them,' he stated. 'Get it.'

She licked her dry lips. Then it struck her. She was a hostage. A real life hostage, and he was holding her. That was what this was all about. Shakily, she edged her way to the phone and very slowly lifted the receiver into the air.

'Hello?' she whispered.

'Darling, it's me again.' It was her mother. 'I was thinking, would you like to come round for Sunday lunch tomorrow?'

Her captor flicked his head at her demandingly. 'Tell them to do what I say,' he growled at her. She delicately placed her hand over the mouthpiece, gathered her courage and whispered back to him.

'It's my mother. She wants to know if I can come to Sunday lunch tomorrow. Do you think I'll be free by then?'

'Fucking comedian!' He grabbed the phone from her and barked into it. 'I want to speak to the boss. Get him on the phone right now!'

There was a pause. Ella waited with her fists curled into tense balls. After a moment he wiped his forehead with his sleeve and barked again.

'Right. You. You think you're so fucking clever, don't you?' Ella cringed painfully. She could distantly hear her father's bemused voice utter a monosyllable. 'Well you're not. You are completely fucking stupid, you fucking pig!' There was another pause. She could hear her father going into one of his long speeches. Her captor pulled a face. 'Who the hell is this? Who the fuck is Donald Norton?'

'It's my dad,' Ella said as softly as possible.

He slammed the phone down and fixed her with a hostile glare.

'Try anything like that again, and you'll regret it.'

She gulped. He prodded the tip of the knife towards her body again. 'Now shut up! We're going upstairs.'

Chapter Eighteen

Ella's legs quivered as she got to the landing. The camera was still in her bedroom. He would see it. He'd know she'd been cooperating with the police. He'd stab her on the spot. She headed for Miranda's door as he nudged her forwards.

'Is there a phone in here?' he demanded as they crossed the threshold.

'No,' she mouthed. 'No phones upstairs at all.'

From downstairs she could hear her phone ringing off the hook. Her father would be calling back to find out why he'd been called a fucking pig. She'd have to explain it all to him another time. They stood in Miranda's bedroom for a moment. He took in his surroundings, a frown flitting across his brow at the sight of the piles of bottles, magazines, clothes and shoes, then he strode to the window and lifted an edge of the net curtain to peer down into the garden. From the lawn Ella could hear Simon growling ferociously, and an ejection of, 'Get off me you little bastard!'

'Have you got a mobile?' He stared at her again. His body language was gaining in agitation by the second. Her legs were getting weaker and weaker with every drop of sweat that rolled down his face.

'No. I'm sorry.'

He sniffed heartily.

'I should keep mine with me all the time.' He twitched the net again and looked through the gap. 'Who's the Paki?'

She cleared her throat.

'The what?'

He sneered at her over his shoulder. 'The Paki, out there. Anyone you know?'

She shook her head firmly, and corrected indignantly, 'And he's of Indian origin actually, not Pakistani.'

'Amazing.' He looked at her more studiously. 'And yet you don't know him. He was the geezer snogging you out the front, wasn't he? I know what's going on. I've seen his car out there before. He's your boyfriend, isn't he?'

Her eyes widened into radial tyres. She shook her head again, more faintly. Her captor smiled unpleasantly and nodded to himself.

'Uh-huh. I get it. You're screwing a pig.'

She bit her lip guiltily. Her father was a pig, the man she'd slept with was a pig. It was all more than a little insulting. Perhaps he'd move on to her friends, cousins and godparents next. What angle should she take? Admit or deny it? He certainly didn't seem very complimentary about the fact that she might be screwing a pig.

'I've never seen him before today,' she stuttered unconvincingly.

'Oh yes you have.' He grinned nastily, took a sudden step towards her and grabbed her arm. He propelled her to the window and yanked the net curtain aside, pushing her face up against the glass so that her nose and mouth were squashed against it.

Then he unlatched the side window and yelled out of it.

'Oy! Paki! Get your men out of here, or I'll nobble your bird.'

It wasn't a very elegant way to be displayed, Ella felt through her fear as she slid her eyes downwards and saw Jaz in the garden walking forwards slowly with his arms in the air. Matt and Lorna were nowhere to be seen. Neither was Simon, but she could hear disgruntled barking and shuffling coming from inside the shed.

'Listen, mate, the place is surrounded.' Jaz's voice was as calm as a pond. 'You've got no chance. Let me come in and talk to you and we can sort something out without anyone getting hurt.'

Ella held her breath. She couldn't do much else as her lips were pressed like rubber suckers against the glass. Her captor cleared his throat nervously.

'No! Back off.'

'Be reasonable, Mark. If you do anything stupid you're going to be inside for a very long time. Let the girl go and let's talk. No point making it worse. She hasn't done anything wrong. Don't take it out on her.'

'Thank you,' Ella beeped.

'I want to talk to someone English!' he insisted, giving Ella a small shake for no reason she could fathom. Then he muttered under his breath. 'Fucking Pakis. They're always so reasonable.'

'This one's not that reasonable,' she squeezed out of the corner of her mouth.

'Let the girl go, Mark,' Jaz continued. He was now standing directly under the window. She peeped down at him. Not a hair out of place, not a dribble of sweat on his body despite all the leaping about. Apart from the bloody nose, he could have been advertising a deodorant.

There was a crash in the room behind her. Ella jumped and squealed. As the grip on her arm suddenly slackened, she wriggled away and dashed into the corner of the room, squashing herself into it. Three men barged across the floor. One delivered a karate chop to her assailant's arm. The bread knife clattered to the floor. The other two wrestled him to the ground and sat on him.

Ella stood like a statue with her arms wrapped around her body. They were being very rough with him, yanking his arms behind his back, thrusting handcuffs on him, and heaving him up again. She winced.

'He wasn't going to hurt me. He was just startled,' she found herself saying in his defence.

One of the men gave her a cold, blue stare.

'You wanna bet on that?'

'Thanks,' the handcuffed man uttered gruffly in her direction. She even thought the look he gave her was penitent. 'I'm sorry I called your father a pig.'

'It's okay,' she said, wondering if she was in shock as the words tripped out. 'Somebody had to call him a pig, and it's probably just as well it wasn't me.'

'Mark Vincent Heath, a record as long as my bloody arm including GBH, ABH and armed robbery,' the blue-eyed policeman told Ella scathingly. 'I wouldn't have put my pocket money on you getting out of this without a broken nail. Come on, you low-life. You're well and truly nicked.'

Two of the men shoved him out of the room in front of them, and she heard the thunder of all their footsteps descending the stairs. Her breathing began to steady again. It was over. A tremor of relief rippled through her legs. The younger man had hung back. She recognised him as one of the athletes who had vaulted over her fence.

'You all right?' he asked sympathetically.

She nodded and bit her lip. It started to wobble. Tears sprang from nowhere and filled her eyes.

'Come on,' he said softly, approaching her and extending an arm. 'Let's get you downstairs, make you a nice, hot cup of tea and calm you down. This has all been a horrible shock for you.'

She put her arms out to him, and he embraced her in a short hug.

'There, there,' he soothed her.

'Oh you're so nice,' she whispered at him. 'That was all so frightening.'

'I know. And you've been incredibly brave.'

'Okay, Dave, I'll take it from here.' She heard Jaz's voice in the room and opened her eyes blearily. He was pushing both of his hands through his hair and eyeing her intently.

'Right, gov.' Dave paused at the door. 'You want to get that snozzer seen to. Still bleeding, is it?'

Jaz didn't answer. The young man cleared his throat self-consciously and disappeared. She felt cold without those strong arms around her, and now her knees had begun to shake like a pair of metronomes. She clasped her arms around herself to stop them shaking too.

'Are you all right, Ella?' he asked in a low voice.

'I'm – yes. No, I'm not. I was terrified but I had to tell myself I wasn't. I'll be fine. Just give me a minute.'

He nodded. Her muscles tensed violently and she jumped suddenly. He crossed the room and put his arms around her to hold her still.

'I – I'm fine,' she managed through chattering teeth. 'Is Doris all right? Did you save her?'

'Of course Doris is all right,' he gently chided her. She snuggled closer to him as her legs jittered under her, and he tightened his arms around her. 'Doris was a plant.'

'A p-p-p . . .' She squashed her lips together and tried again. 'A plant? What sort of plant?' She was too shaken up to picture anything other than a begonia. What was he talking about?

'Shhh,' he comforted her, smoothing her hair. 'I'll explain much later. We need to wrap you up warm and give you some hot tea.'

'A p-plant as in a police accomplice?' she said in a shaky voice as he left her to sort through the pile of clothes on Miranda's floor, came up with a floppy knitted jumper and carefully rolled it over her head, feeding her arms down the sleeves. 'But D-Doris is d-dotty.'

'Don't say that to Dave. She's his granny. Doris was setting them up for us, but you couldn't have known that. She's very big down at the Am Dram Society. Got quite a talent for it. Brought the house down with her Lady Bracknell last Christmas.'

'B-bugger me!' She stared at him in amazement as he took her hand and led her slowly from the room. Another strange man arrived at the top of the stairs with what looked like an enormous briefcase with a

310

stiff plastic bag in the other hand. Hazily, Ella realised he must be something to do with forensics.

'Kitchen knife. In there, under the window,' Jaz nodded towards the bedroom door.

'Right you are.'

'Doris told me to get stuffed,' Ella rambled as Jaz painstakingly took her down the stairs step by step while her knees banged together like cymbals.

'Quite mild, considering. She was a switchboard operator for years down at Oxford nick before she retired. She's no wallflower. She was only trying to stop you getting involved. Don't take it personally. She's actually a great person, if you take the time to get to know her.'

'Oh. Yes. We haven't got to know her at all. We should have done. She might have needed us. I think we've all been a bit s-selfish really.' Ella stumbled down another step, clutching his shoulder for support. 'And I p-punched you. I'm really sorry.' He stopped and gave her a long, dry look. She shivered back at him. His nose was still red and throbbing. She wanted to stroke it, but thought better of it.

'Well, I told you to fuck off. Neither of us have been very polite, have we?'

'N-no, that's true.'

They reached the hall. Jaz picked a duffle jacket from their bundle of coats and wrapped it around her shoulders. The front door was open and from the lane she could hear the fizz of police radios. There seemed to be a lot of activity out there. It was mercifully quiet inside the house though, and the living room was empty. The sofa looked amazingly inviting. She wanted to sink into it now and never have to get out of it again. Her body gave another sudden, all over judder. Jaz took hold of her and placed her on the sofa. Her legs swung up and flapped down again. She huddled into the jacket.

'Don't move,' he ordered. 'There's an ambulance on its way.'

'I don't need an ambulance. I'm not ill.'

'You're in shock, Ella.' He leaned over her and touched her forehead softly with his fingertips. 'And stop arguing with me. I know best.'

'But – Lorna and Matt? Are they all right? Where are they?'

'They were bundled over into Doris's garden. They were quite safe. You've got absolutely nothing to worry about there.'

'I didn't really break your nose, did I? It's still very red,' she whispered at him soulfully.

'No chance. I was just trying to make you feel awful. It's sore, but it'll be fine.'

'Okay.' He stayed there for a moment, studying her face. She gazed back at him, too fuddled to look away. 'Well, at least you've got them now. That's a b-bloody relief. Which one of them attacked me outside? W-was it Mark?'

He pursed his lips and stroked her cheek. His eyes seemed regretful.

'You were attacked by a woman, Ella,' he told her under his breath.

'A w-what?'

'Now be quiet, and if you're really good and do what I say, I'll even let that evil little hound of yours out of the shed. He's already had one of my ties, and he's after my trousers now.' She stared after him as he headed for the kitchen. He turned back and gave her a quirky smile, his nose glowing pink. 'I don't know what you've been saying to him, but he seems to hate me almost as much as you do.'

The benched seat in the Sheldonian was so thin that Miranda was having trouble staying on it. The tiers were staggered very steeply this far up in the auditorium. She couldn't cross her legs without kneeing the person on the bench down in front of her in the neck, and she couldn't lean back without getting the knees of the person behind her in the back. Every so often she felt herself slide by the seat of her trousers towards the orchestra arranged in a neat circle below them, and gripped on to the small step in front of her with her toes and pushed herself back again. And she was getting vertigo.

Beside her, Giles seemed to be having similar problems. His legs were very long, and he'd ended up with one either side of the perm of the petite woman in front. If he coughed and brought them together, she would be deafened for life. Miranda was keeping her concentration with absolute propriety, though. She'd been brought up to be well behaved at functions however anarchic she felt internally and she wasn't going to let the creeping urge to giggle take control of her. That was the plan. And she was fine until the visiting orchestra had completed their selection of Dvorak and launched into the last section of the programme with a rendition of Gershwin's *Rhapsody in Blue*.

The pianist entered the room to eager applause, bowed, and seated herself. She then attacked the keys as if she was wearing boxing gloves. Even the conductor, a short, swarthy looking man with prominent buttocks and the obligatory mop of black curly hair, cast her horrified looks while he swung away with his baton.

Miranda held her breath. This was very possibly going to get worse as the work built up to a crescendo. She gripped her cheeks firmly with her molars and fixed her eyes ahead. So far, the orchestra had performed beautifully but it seemed as if they'd all been infected with the notion that it was going horribly wrong. As the keys crashed discordantly, the clarinets squeaked and the percussion lost its timing. Wooden seats began to creak and shift around her as the audience wriggled with embarrassment.

Miranda looked down at her lap for sustenance, squashed her fingers together and tried to think of something sad. Her divorce. Faith's taste in perfume. Chris de Burgh. Then she felt Giles twitch beside her and made the fatal mistake of glancing at him.

He glanced back. His cheeks were sucked in as if he'd been rinsing with Dettol. She clamped her teeth together. Oh no, this was no good. Not in such a place. She cast her eyes up to the elegant domed ceiling and concentrated. The conductor was trying so very hard to keep the orchestra together now as they sped from movement to movement. He was snapping his fingers along with his frenzied baton flicks. He deserved support. Her shoulders began to shake.

It wasn't funny, she urged herself. Giles snorted beside her and cleared his throat noisily. She put a hand over her mouth, opened it wide and noiselessly

314

expelled the laughter into her palm. If anything, the auditorium had become even more silent since the performance had taken a nose-dive. It made the need to giggle more hysterical. And she hadn't had the giggles like this since she'd sat her maths 'O' level. Her stomach began to ache agonisingly. She reached down for her handbag so that she could hide her face, clonking her forehead on the back of the head of the man in front. He swung round to give her a red-faced stare, then swung back again. Leaning forward was a bad gravitational move. The silky finish on her trousers ensured she swept off the polished bench smoothly and dived bodily ahead. She let out a high-pitched cry as Giles grabbed her arm firmly and held on to her. He yanked her back into her seat as a dozen heads now turned and gave them both angry looks.

She shrank into her place, vibrating with unreleased tension as Giles heaved beside her and let out an occasional involuntary squeak. She prayed with her eyes squashed shut and tears rolling down her face for the last movement to finish. As the performance ground to an abrupt halt there was a stunned pause from the crowd, followed by a hearty attempt at applause. She joined in vigorously, cheering to expel the long breath she'd been holding in. After the individual performers had received their plaudits, Giles leant towards her.

'Let's get out of here.'

They fell into the King's Arms, gasping and holding each other's arms. Thank God the place was stacked full of drinkers and the chatter was loud. She gripped Giles at the bar and let the bellows of laughter out.

'Oh my God, I'm so sorry. I didn't mean to embarrass you. I was enjoying it so much until the end.'

'Don't worry about it.' His chestnut eyes glinted back. 'I was only trying to impress you anyway. I feel as if I've spent four hours sitting on a tightrope. It was probably a really bad idea.'

'Why were you trying to impress me, you stupid bugger?'

'Because you're classy, and you deserve it. Why else?'

'Thank you.' She wiped a finger across the corner of her eyes and giggled again. 'But I thought you must be really into classical music to ask me to a concert.'

'I thought you might be. That's why I got the tickets. You've been all over the world. You're experienced and sophisticated. I honestly don't know why on earth somebody like you would find me interesting, so I did what I thought you'd expect.'

She gave a more exhausted laugh to get it out of her system, then smiled at him. He'd started to look pensive.

'Why wouldn't I be interested in you?'

'Because I'm younger than you, less worldly than you, and less cynical than you.'

'And you think I'd want to be with someone older, more worldly, and more cynical than me?'

'Maybe.' He shrugged.

'But I could easily think you wanted to be with someone who was nothing like me. Somebody far more simple to handle.' She paused as they were pushed together by the drinkers thronging around them. 'Like Suzanne, perhaps,' she finished.

'Suzanne?' He seemed confused.

'Yes,' she said airily, as if she really hadn't given it much thought.

'God, no.' He still seemed surprised by the thought. 'She's great company, made me feel really welcome at the practice and I like her a lot, but I don't feel anything else towards her. And she doesn't for me either. She's got the hots for someone else. Her mind's elsewhere, you could say.' He gave her a suggestive look.

'Crikey, who? Anybody I'd know?'

'Can't say.' He grinned. 'That'd be breaking a confidence.'

'Oh, come on!' Miranda urged him.

'Nope.' He shook his head. 'If you can get it out of her, fair enough, but I don't want to be accused of meddling.'

'Right.' She allowed this information to seep pleasantly into her system. The night was still relatively young, and unless he was rushing off they had time to get to know each other a little better. And he was free. Genuinely free. It was really starting to look like a situation that had potential. And she had her room in Ella's house. Giles had only just arrived in the village and wasn't about to up and leave, so there was no reason why there wouldn't be time to explore what they might have stumbled across in each other. She hoped, anyway. He glanced towards the bar.

'Let's have a drink. What'll it be?'

'No.' She put her hand on his arm decisively. 'This is my shout. You got us one in the interval.'

'If you insist. Just a half for me then.'

'Fine.'

As she leant on the bar and called her order she realised she was talking to a familiar face. She did a double-take. Of course, it was Andrea, the vision of loveliness who had broken Kevin's heart by leaving the Plough and coming to work here instead. They exchanged a few snatched pleasantries as the pub was busy and Andrea was rushed with shouted orders.

'There you go. Nice to see you again.' Andrea handed Miranda her change and was called away immediately to the far end of the bar. Miranda felt the push of bodies behind her trying to fill the space she should be leaving. She obligingly edged away from the bar.

She found Giles propped up against a wall to the side of the room. She was about to tell him about seeing Andrea, but he already had a sentence prepared.

'If you're hungry, I thought we could go and eat after this. It's a shame you wanted to drive in really because we both could have left our cars at home and got a taxi in and back, but if you want to eat anyway we could.'

'That'd be lovely,' she agreed. 'But I'm not sorry that I decided to drive. I wanted to keep a clear head tonight.'

'Oh.' He looked understanding. 'Things to do tomorrow?'

'No.' She shook her head. 'Nothing at all. I have to plan what to say when I ring the agency I work for and tell them I don't want another long flying assignment for the foreseeable future, but other than that, zilch.'

'You don't want to go abroad? I thought you had a terminal case of wanderlust.'

'Oh I do, and I'll go abroad again before long, but it won't be the same.'

He looked at her curiously, brushing a strand of blond hair from his forehead.

'What do you mean?'

'Do you really want to know what I mean?' she asked, edging a little closer to him as his eyes were probing hers with an intimacy which she was beginning to feel blossoming inside herself too.

'Yes, Miranda.' He touched her hand with his. 'I really do want to know. I have a vested interest in wanting to know how you feel.'

She was warmed. The caution was still there, layering itself over her heart like a series of skins which would have to be peeled away one by one before she might really be able to feel trust towards somebody, but the warmth was telling her that this was the right place, the right time, and the right person with whom to take a chance.

'I've been running away. Running all over the place. I never stopped running. At the moment I don't want to do that. I want to – to stand still, just for a little while, and see what happens.'

His thumb caressed her palm softly. The crash of noise around them was meaningless. They were alone in the crowded pub.

'I'm glad.'

'I've been living out of my hand luggage all of my life.' She swallowed away the bitterness and pointed her thoughts ahead, to the future instead. 'I just want to know what it feels like not to do that. It's an experiment, really. It's partly why I came to live up here. And I like it. I think it's one experiment I've had a go at that was worth doing.'

'Like insisting on us both driving ourselves out this evening when we were both headed in the same direction? Was that an experiment too?'

'Of a sort.' She smiled at him.

'I understand. But next week, would you like to get a taxi up to Summertown, be treated to a never-ending Greek meal at a fabulous restaurant I know, get plastered on retsina and ouzo and get a taxi back?'

The enthusiastic hope in his eyes buckled her stomach. She knew he wasn't angling for an opportunity at seduction. It was only a natural, unforced, uncalculated gesture on his part. Her guard had been up for a very long time, and she'd be pleased with herself for allowing it to drop, not completely maybe, but a little at least. There was no reason to wrestle with herself when Giles was presenting ideas as if they were so simple.

'Sounds good. In fact, that sounds very good.'

He drained his drink and she finished hers. He put out his arm.

'So let's go strolling and see what we can find to eat in Oxford at this time of night. I don't know the city very well.'

'Neither do I yet,' she admitted as they piled out of the pub, crossed the road, and headed up Broad Street.

'You don't?' he teased her. 'I thought you knew the world like the back of your hand? I'm already preparing myself for your long stories about your trips to Greece. I was expecting you to amuse me for hours on end with your anecdotes.'

'I've never been to Greece, as it happens.'

'Really?' He laughed.

'Really. Pretty much everywhere else, but my flights have never taken me there. I've seen very little of the Mediterranean countries.'

'Not even Cyprus?'

'Nope.'

'Or Crete?'

'No, not there either.'

'You've missed out,' he admonished her. 'I could always show you around Crete, if you like. My parents had a thing about it. What I don't know about Knossos isn't worth talking about. I went on a guided tour every year for five years. And a funny thing happened to me in a hotel in Rethymnon. I walked into a door. I was thirteen at the time and very, very sunburnt.'

'I think you've just given me the punchline.'

'Oh no. I haven't got on to the bit about the jellyfish yet.'

She squeezed his arm as she laughed into the air. How had she forgotten how easy it all was? Her adult life had been spent around air crews, expatriates and glamorous people in the public eye to whom travelling was as tedious as waiting for a bus. Even the man she'd married had been so entrenched in the routine of his life that he'd long since abandoned the prospect of getting a thrill out of doing it. He'd turned to other things for a thrill instead. She herself had lost sight of what it was all about. It wasn't about a job, or a way of life. It was about excitement and discovery, just like everything else should be. And if she really could find the strength in herself to stand still for long enough, she'd know what it was like to feel the joy of being on the move again, not because she had nowhere else to go, or was running away from something, but because she could be running towards it.

'Oh, but I've bored you already,' he said in fake disappointment. 'And you're just waiting for me to shut up so that you can regale me with your after-dinner story about the time the Jordanian royal family fed you with oysters and let you share their jacuzzi.'

She gave him a private glance. She wanted to know about the jellyfish. It was much more fun.

'Where did the jellyfish get you?'

'I'm not sure I want to tell you that yet. But I can assure you it's healed up and is now perfectly functional.'

Chapter Nineteen

'I'm really glad we decided to come here.' Faith gazed around the small interior of the Akash Tandoori. It was starting to fill up, but it was a friendly buzz of activity.

They'd gone for a drink in St Clements to start with, but the pub had been noisy and they hadn't really been able to hear each other. After about half an hour, Paul had suggested they go and eat now and take their time over a meal instead of tangoing around the Oxford pubs, and Faith had been relieved. There were so many things she wanted to ask him now, so many thoughts that had crossed her mind, and he was such an easy person to talk to. She didn't feel silly for anything she said, and he always replied as if she was an interesting person to be with.

She was glad she'd had him to walk with her up the Cowley Road. She'd known Oxford all her life, but the scramble of students and townies out for a Saturday night was always something she'd found a bit overwhelming. She knew it was somewhere Debbie often came to drink with a gang of her girlfriends, and they'd do the rounds of the pubs before heading off into town for one of the clubs. Debbie talked a lot about the regulars she met up with in a list of pubs they all circuited at the weekend. Everyone seemed to be sleeping with someone, or avoiding someone. Most of the time they seemed to be avoiding the person they were sleeping with. And if they were on the same shift on a Friday, or at the Saturday morning surgery, when Debbie twittered on about who she hoped would be there, and what she'd wear this time to make sure she caught the attention of whoever it was she'd got off with the previous week, it had struck Faith as more than a little neurotic. She'd felt nothing but relief that Debbie had never tried to include her in that scene.

But strolling casually up the road to the restaurant which she'd heard around the surgery was the best one in Oxford if you liked good Indian food, with Paul close by her side, ignoring the groups of high-spirited women as they clattered past but concentrating on what she was saying, she felt quite comfortable. She felt as if she had a right to be there. Nobody was going to tell her that she was out of place.

They were early enough to get a good table in an alcove and she'd shuffled herself along the benched seat with Paul doing the same opposite her. And she felt very hungry now after a lager in the pub, so when Paul suggested they go for the whole shebang and have starters as well, she turned her attention to the menu very happily. They'd exhausted the waiter with questions about the entire range on offer before they'd ordered. Now they could both sit back and relax.

'Good choice, Faith.' Paul nodded approvingly as the pickle tray arrived with a basket of poppadoms. Unselfconsciously he banged his hand on them so that they broke into smaller pieces, took one and nibbled on it. She took a piece too and crunched on it.

She'd thought much earlier in the day that once they were out they might feel a bit awkward together. After all, when they'd gone for a late meal in the week it had been an impulsive decision, they hadn't had time to plan any conversation, and it had all happened naturally. But she didn't feel awkward with him at all. She levered a selection of pickles and sauces on to her side plate, dipped her poppadom into them and took another bite.

'So, I don't suppose you managed to find anything out for me, did you?' she asked him with a smile. This was the question that had been dancing across her lips all evening.

'Quite a lot. You're very lucky that I've been at a loose end these last couple of days.'

He entered into a long explanation of the calls he'd made, the contacts he'd talked to, and the information he'd discovered for her. She flushed with gratitude, while coming back at him with all the concerns she had. He answered them easily. He had an answer for every potential problem she could think of.

'So, I've got a list of phone numbers for you,' he concluded, reaching into his jacket and producing a piece of paper and handing it to her. She smoothed it out on the tablecloth and surveyed it thoughtfully, stopping every so often to take another bit of poppadom. 'It's all there. You need to ring each of them up, ask for a prospectus and have a good look at it. Then it's up to you to decide which place would be the best for you to apply to. I can't see any problem with you getting a grant. You've never had one before, but I put the number there for you so that you can ring and talk to the council about it.'

'Oh,' she breathed.

She stared at the neat, biro capitals of the notes he'd made, her heart swelling with appreciation.

'Thank you, Paul. I really didn't think you'd have time to do this.'

'I've had lots of time. Giles and I have used each other's places as a base plenty of times in the past, so he wasn't exactly expecting me to meet him for lunch every day. I've caught up with old friends, been down to see my folks and still had time to make some phone calls for you, would you believe.'

He gave her a wry smile.

'But I'm really grateful to you. It's more than anyone's done for me. And I'd never, ever have thought of this if it hadn't been for you.'

'Well, you've got to do the work now, and I don't just mean researching the universities. Somebody I talked to thought you might have to do some sort of study now, just to prove that you're not out of the habit, and even if it's just a question of knocking off another "A" level to prove your point, you've still got to face the prospect of years of hard grind to get where you want to be.'

'Yes.' She nodded at him, absorbing the thoughts. 'I see what it's going to involve. I'm going to have to think about it really carefully.'

'Good idea. There were moments I thought I couldn't hack it, but it was well worth it. I couldn't see myself doing anything else. Convincing an interview panel that you're capable of doing it is only the first hurdle.' Then he dipped his poppadom into the mango chutney and gave her a warm smile. 'But having said that, it's a hurdle that many people fall at. I don't think you will.'

'Thank you,' she stuttered, blushing again. 'I hope you're right. I'm not sure you are, though.'

'You'll find out,' he replied. 'It's one thing to fail at something even though you've given it your best. There's no shame in that. But I've got no respect for anybody who doesn't try.' He gave her a mock-severe look. She bit her lip and smiled shyly back at him.

'Thank you.'

'And stop thanking me.'

'Okay. Sorry.' She gathered the paper and folded it carefully, tucking it into her handbag. 'But thank you so much for this. I can't tell you what it means to me.'

'Uh-uh.' He wagged a finger admonishingly. 'You said "thank you" again.'

'I can't help it. It's just that – I don't know how you knew. How could you have sensed that it was the right thing to say, when you said it?'

'It was obviously the wrong thing to say at the time,' he widened his eyes at her teasingly. 'You ran out of the room, remember.'

'Oh, yes,' she mumbled. 'But that was just the shock. It was a wonderful thing to say to me. It made me feel – as if you'd noticed things that nobody else saw.'

'But that's not entirely true, because Suzanne and Giles both thought the same, but they thought it in an abstract way. When I met you in the pub, I knew you could actually do it.'

'But – how could you be so sure?' She pulled her

327

napkin from the table and teased the corners into knots with her fingers.

'Let's just say that what was holding you back became fairly clear to me. Bullies can destroy your self-belief if you let them. The secret is not to let them.' His eyes softened towards her. 'But we went through all that at the Chinese the other night. I'm sure you don't want to go through it again.'

'No.' She shook her head firmly, drawing herself up in her seat and squaring her shoulders. 'I don't. I'd never told anybody the truth about the whole thing, and I'm glad I told you when I did, but that's an end to it now. I'm not going to worry about Mike, or any of that gang ever again. He's had enough of my energy and he doesn't deserve any more.'

'That's the spirit.'

He reached for her hand across the table and she gave it to him. He squeezed it firmly. He'd helped her more than he could ever know. For the moment, she was voicing the words and trying to find the courage to really feel it inside herself, but she knew that this was the start. She'd cowered and mumbled for far too long, and he'd shown her that she didn't have to do it anymore. And maybe soon she'd get away from the village, from the town and from the thick fog of memories which had stanched the flow of life in her. And then just maybe, at some point in the future, she'd emerge into bright sunlight. It was an image that she could now carry with her, however difficult the journey might be.

As they fell into easy conversation and savoured the dishes that arrived, she mused about how her life was changing. She had moved into Ella's house, and come across Ella and Miranda. That was something she'd never have expected. And day by day, she'd felt less embarrassed to be there, and more needed by them both. They didn't have a practical head between them, and while she'd seen that from the very beginning, the time had come for them both to stop struggling and recognise it. That was gratifying. She had a sneaking feeling that Ella actually admired her in some way now. And Miranda had seemed so threatening at first, so caustic and cavalier towards her that it had hurt. But now Miranda just seemed like somebody who tried to scare people away from her because she didn't want them to get too close. That was something Faith understood. And it was amazing that she would have anything in common with Miranda, but there was that element which before very long had taken the sting out of the jibes and turned them into a game.

Yes, it was odd how it had worked out. And without Ella and Miranda to go out with, and without seeing the way they lived, she'd never have started to think about a life for herself away from her home ground, from her mother's strength and her father's unquestioned devotion. She'd never have had a new haircut, and gone out looking for new clothes, and for the first time in her life, bought herself a bottle of perfume. And she'd never have got to know Paul.

Her fortunes had changed, and she'd felt it creepingly from the moment Giles had bought her the roses. Now she had his best friend sitting opposite her, enjoying a meal and a long conversation with her for the second time in the space of a week. He wasn't somebody who would be around to support her through the decisions she had to take next, but she was used to pursuing her objectives on her own, and the fact that he'd shown this burst of friendship towards her had given her courage. No doubt once they'd shared this, they'd stay in touch in some way. If she had questions to ask him, or even moments of panic, he wouldn't mind if she bothered him with them. And even better, the situation wasn't obfuscated by complicated emotions; it was a rare moment to be treasured between two people who had found in each other the potential to be good friends.

She gave Paul a wobbly smile as a trolley containing their meal squeaked up to the table. The waiter whisked one of the plates into the air, grinned, and began polishing it with a starched white tea towel.

'Paul, I want to thank you,' she said.

'Uh-uh.' He stuck a warning finger out at her.

'No, really. I'll say it now for the last time. I – I've been so happy to meet you. I hope that we might be friends after this, even after you go back to Hereford tomorrow night.'

'Oh yes,' he smiled at her, nodding his thanks at the waiter as he delivered an immaculately shined plate in front of him. 'No doubt about it, Faith. We will stay friends. And now that I've done something for you, maybe you can do a small favour for me?'

'Mum!' Ella gaped at her mother standing on the doorstep, shaking away a policewoman who was trying to reason with her.

'There is no reason to lay your hands on me, young woman, this is my daughter!'

'I'm sorry, you didn't explain that.'

'Do I have to show you the family tree?'

The policewoman muttered an apology, gave Ella a sympathetic glance and turned around again to stand on the path. Ella looked around the outside scene. It seemed the fronts of the houses had been cordoned off with a long strip of tape that ran along the front path, blocking the gates. Two police cars were still in the lane, and there were people coming and going from number eleven, and from Doris's house. A tall, bristling figure with long, thin legs stepped over the tape as if it were a crack in the pavement and strode up the path. He looked very angry.

'Dad!'

'What the hell is all this about, Ella? Where's the arrogant bastard who swore at me down the phone?' And as if he'd suddenly realised that he was in the middle of a crime scene, he added, 'And what have the police got to do with any of this?'

'Look, I think you'd better come in.'

She stood back to let them both enter the hall and reached round them to shut the door again in an attempt to establish a bit of privacy. They huddled together in the tiny hall. With Ella the shortest of the three of them at five foot nine, her mother an inch taller, and her father at six foot four, it was as ludicrous as them all trying to cram into a phone box. She took a bracing breath, closed her eyes briefly, and pushed open the door to the living room.

'You'd better go through.'

They spilled into the room, Ella following. Her father strode across the room immediately, as he had a habit of striding everywhere. Her mother followed, casting a critical eye around the furnishings, apparently sizing up somewhere well dusted to sit. Ella closed the door behind her and leant back against it, waiting for them to notice Jaz.

He'd made several phone calls since the ambulance had been and she was grateful he'd chosen to stay with her personally for a while, rather than leave her with one of the uniformed police that she didn't know. The paramedics had assured themselves that she was well, wrapped her up in layers of jumpers and gone again at her insistence that she couldn't face another trip to Casualty. She'd been able to picture the conversation with the perky Irish nurse. 'What's happened to you this time?' 'Oh, it's nothing really, it's just that I was taken hostage.' Perhaps at that point she'd be offered a season ticket and a loyalty card for the League of Friends. Oh no, no, no. She couldn't cope with that.

She felt much warmer now, had stopped shaking, and apart from feeling subdued, was well over her initial wobbliness. It had been nice of Jaz to anticipate that she might be clinically in shock, but thankfully there'd been no real sign of that. Simon had been more ruffled than she was after his brief captivity inside the shed, but once she'd made a huge fuss of him he'd decided it was much more fun in the garden mauling the rat-thing that jingled, so she'd let him out there to bound around. Jaz had expressed relief. He'd insisted on making her another hot cup of tea and she'd let him take control of the kitchen. He'd just been saying that he needed to leave any moment and was trying to persuade her to sit with one of the policewomen after he'd gone when she'd heard the insistent knocking at the front door.

Now she could hear the kettle boiling and clicking from the kitchen while her father swung round with his hands on his hips, a mixture of indignation and confusion plastered over his face.

'So where is the swine now, Ella?' he fired at her. She wasn't daunted. She knew her father too well. Anger arrived for him when he was thrown by a situation. It was the terror of not being in control. She knew he was blustering, and she couldn't help feeling sorry for him.

'Look, it was just—'

'Ah. The kettle's just boiled. Am I making tea for three, then?'

Both her parents swivelled to stare at the Asian man with the top button undone on his shirt, his tie loosened, and his hair a mop of jet-black silky strands, leaning in Ella's kitchen doorway as if it was his second home.

'I'm sorry, I should introduce myself. My name's Jasbinder, but just call me Jaz.'

He stepped forward and offered his hand to her mother. She extended hers limply in a daze, and he shook it. He did the same to her father, who only stared back at him in bewilderment. Her father's eyes seemed to be darting from Jaz's red, swollen nose and back to his hand again. Then he turned back to Ella instead with a frown.

'Ella?'

Jaz held the hand out a little longer, then allowed it to drop to his side.

'Dad, this is Jaz. Jaz, meet my parents,' she said. She bit her lip.

'Is this . . .' her mother began in a faint voice, then stood up straighter. 'Ella, is this – is this the gentleman we referred to earlier?'

Ella flushed. Her mother was obviously in shock over the situation herself, otherwise she wouldn't have come out with anything so peculiar, and so publicly too.

'Mum!' she protested in a muted voice.

'It is, isn't it!' her mother confirmed, sizing up Ella's expression and body language in one glance.

'Are you the man who called me a fucking pig?' her father suddenly demanded with a raised voice, bringing himself up to his full height and meshing his eyebrows in a way Ella had seen him do only when he was trying very hard to be imposing.

Ella cringed. She hadn't had a chance to tell Jaz exactly what had happened when the phone had rung and she'd been forced to answer it. She certainly hadn't mentioned the insults. It must have seemed a very strange question coming out of the blue like that.

Jaz looked thoughtful for a moment, then amusement flickered across his face.

'No, sir, I've certainly never said that to you.'

Her father seemed further confused by the response. Ella put out her hands in an appeal.

'No, that's it, you see, Dad, because the man who grabbed the phone off me when you rang thought he was speaking to Jaz. That's why he called you a fucking pig. He didn't mean you at all.'

Her father's face contorted in bafflement.

'But how on earth could he confuse *me* with *him*?'

Seeing the two of them in the same room, her father angular, white-faced and strained, Jaz sturdily built, brown-skinned and relaxed, it did seem a bizarre idea.

'It's because I'm used to being called a pig. It's how I get referred to,' Jaz explained without edge. 'I'm pretty immune to it now.'

'So you are a habitual philanderer, are you?' her mother shot at him, with a burst of protectiveness Ella thought, trying to be generous.

'Philanderer?' Now Jaz looked confused.

'This isn't the first bit on the side you've had while you've been engaged? Is that it? Well, Ella, you're best out of this one.'

'No, Mum—'

'You want to be involved with somebody everyone thinks of as a pig? Then you're on a hiding to nothing. I've taught you more self-esteem than that.'

'No, no—'

'So who was it who called me a fucking pig?' her father almost shouted, his face flashing red and white with frustration.

'That was the drug dealer.'

She'd managed it at last. They were both stunned into silence. She took a long, slow breath and put a hand to her forehead.

'So can we please start again? Both of you, sit down.'

'What drug dealer?' her father ejected.

'Sit down!' she commanded forcefully. They both obliged, her father slipping into an armchair and crossing his legs, her mother attempting to perch on the edge of the sofa, but falling back into it as the cushions dissolved under her.

'Now, Jaz, please go ahead with the tea. I think we all need a cup, if you've still got time.'

'No problem. And you should sit down too. You look tired,' he said as if it was a private comment to her across the room. She nodded and sank into the beanbag, trying to retain an authoritative presence from the floor. Her mother looked at her with sudden concern.

'Oh, you poor dear. Are you all right? We were so worried about you. It's the only reason we jumped in the car and came over here. What's been happening?'

She composed herself, gave them both even looks, and began.

'Jaz is with the police. That's why he's used to being called a pig. It's nothing to do with his personal habits, I just want to clear that up.'

Jaz popped his head around the door with a carton of milk in his hand.

'Thank you,' he said, and disappeared again. At another time when she was less exhausted, she'd have thought it was comical.

'So, he's been here over the last few weeks to conduct a surveillance operation on a house down the road where they've been dealing. Drug dealing. That's why he's here now.'

Both her parents nodded. They seemed too engrossed to interrupt now.

'And today they busted into the house and got them.'

'Oh that's good,' her mother whispered, and clenched her hands in her lap again.

'But things went a bit wrong, and one of the guys got into my garden and grabbed me, and brought me in here for a bit. Then they broke in and arrested him and took him away. That's about it really. It's all over now.'

There was a further stunned silence.

'You were taken hostage?' her mother mouthed.

'Not exactly. Well, sort of, but only very briefly. And you just happened to ring as we were passing the phone and he made me pick it up, and then he thought it must be the police making contact, so he bellowed at you. He didn't know it was you at all, really he didn't.' And she added with a special look of apology for her father, 'And when they cuffed him to take him away, he said he was sorry he'd called my father a pig.'

'Did he really?' Her father sounded astonished.

'Oh yes, Dad. I wouldn't make that up. I was surprised too, but that's exactly what he said.'

Her father stiffened in his armchair, then gave a formal nod.

'I wouldn't doubt anything my own daughter told me. I know you too well for that. Very proper of him. I'll say no more about it.'

'Right,' Ella breathed. 'So no harm done all round. I'll be fine, Doris is safe and you're not offended any more.'

'Doris?'

'My next-door neighbour. And she's as right as

rain. She thought the whole thing was quite a wheeze, apparently. So the only real casualty is Jaz.'

'Ah yes,' her father declared, leaning forward as Jaz arrived in the room with a tray full of mugs and laid it down on the coffee table. 'You've got a bit of a war wound there. Cop one from the villain, did you?'

Jaz handed the mugs around and indicated the sugar bowl on the tray. Ella was amazed he'd found it in her kitchen cupboards, but he did seem to have his domestic skills perfected. If he'd been setting out to impress her parents, he'd have managed it with that small detail, but of course, he wasn't. He handed a mug to her father with an expression of polite enquiry.

'I beg your pardon?'

'Your nose. Awful mess they've made of it. I expect it's a hazard of the job, isn't it?'

'Oh this?' He smiled and stood up straight. 'It's nothing.'

'Well, do take a seat yourself. I expect you're going to join us for a cup of tea seeing as you've made it, aren't you?' her father said gruffly.

Ella looked up in surprise. Her father seemed to be making something of an effort. More than that, there was a strange male bonding ritual going on. And Jaz slipped her a slow wink when neither of her parents were looking which declared that he wasn't going to let on she was the one who'd actually thumped him.

'I can stay for a very short while, but I must get back to the station. We've got a lot of work to do now.'

'Of course,' her father agreed heartily. 'I wouldn't stand in the way of a man's work. Very important job

338

you do. We don't value our police service enough in this country. I think it's a damned shame. You go out there, day after day, night after night, putting your-selves at risk so that we lazy bounders can sleep peacefully in our beds. I've got nothing but admiration for you. I hold out my hand to you.'

He meant it metaphorically, apparently. He nodded emphatically and took a sip of his tea. Ella buried a smile, seeing as it was Jaz who'd held out his hand to her father earlier and her father had ignored it.

'That's all very well if you don't put innocent people at risk,' her mother piped up suddenly from the sofa, scrambling to sit upright in the squashy mass of cushions. 'Our daughter was held hostage by a drug dealer, Donald, don't you realise that? So what went so terribly wrong with your operation, Jasburder, if you could let this happen?'

'They've got to do their job!' her father asserted.

'Mum, it's all right.' Ella tried to sit up too. 'He was the one who kept talking to the man who was holding me. He distracted him while the others burst in. I think it was his calmness that got the situation solved so quickly. It certainly wasn't his fault.'

'Then whose fault was it, darling?' She puffed her chest out. 'You might have been killed. He must have been a madman. Where were the police then, when you desperately needed them to keep you safe? I find this utterly shocking, I have to tell you.'

'No really, Mum, it wasn't like that.'

'You're quite right, Mrs Norton,' Jaz said firmly. He was still standing in the middle of the room, and he looked completely sombre. 'There will be questions asked about this, and we'll have to explain it. There was a sequence of unexpected events that happened very quickly, but I can assure you I'm as relieved as anybody that nothing more serious happened here.'

Her mother looked partially gratified but then seemed to think better of it and fixed Jaz with a challenging stare.

'Well, it's just not good enough, and I don't expect it to happen again. She's my daughter and she's very precious.'

'I understand.'

'Well, I hope you do.'

'It's not going to happen again, is it?' her father said, splaying out a hand to his wife in exasperation. 'It's all over now. They've captured the villains and stopped them pushing drugs. We've got every reason to be proud of our daughter for taking a role in this. Most people are too lily-livered to get involved. But not our Ella. Not my daughter. The world is a safer place tonight because of her.'

'Oh Dad!' Ella groaned and put her hands over her face. 'Don't go overboard.'

'It's true! I'll write to the *Telegraph* and say as much. If only more people were prepared to have a go, the streets would be cleaner for decent people to walk them.'

Ella peeped through her fingers. Jaz did no more than raise an eyebrow cryptically at her. Then he gathered himself together.

'Well, if you'll excuse me, I'm afraid I must go now.'

Her spirits sank. She put her hands in her lap and

looked up at him from her beanbag. She knew he had to go. But she was hoping for delay upon delay on him leaving.

'Of course you must go.' Her father struggled to get himself to his feet again. He put a hand on the arm of the chair and stumbled slightly as he tried to stand upright. It struck her in that moment that he was getting older. And not just older, but old. She scrambled to her feet too and moved towards him to help, but he was standing as straight as a pole again, his face pulled into dignity.

'It's a pleasure to meet you, Jasbinder.' And, oddly, he was the one who'd remembered Jaz's name when her mother had stumbled over it. He extended his hand in a sweeping gesture, and Jaz took it. They shook hands vigorously. 'Yes, I take my hat off to you. And I'm grateful to you for protecting Ella from the worst outcome of this situation. I know you must have handled it well. I'm a good judge of character, and I know integrity when I see it. You're a good man.'

'Thank you, sir.' Jaz seemed genuinely surprised.

'You'd better see Jasbinger to the door then, Ella,' her mother contributed. She'd tried to struggle out of the sofa but the cushions were sucking her back. She stuck out a hand to him instead, looking at him intently. 'Perhaps we'll see you again.'

'A pleasure to meet you, Mrs Norton,' he replied non-committally. He took her hand and gave it a polite shake.

Ella showed Jaz into the hall, pulling the door discreetly shut behind them. She hesitated with her fingers on the latch of the front door.

341

'Jaz – is it really all over now?'

He put his hands into his trouser pockets and looked at her thoughtfully.

'Well, Ella, we're going to need some witness statements from you. And there's unfinished business here.'

She nodded, absorbing his words, trying to work out the implications of them.

'Unfinished business?' she voiced, trying not to show the flicker of hope she felt.

'You'll see.' He suddenly dropped a kiss on her cheek. 'You've been a champion. We could never have done it without you. There's a WPC outside – Helen – I'll have a word with her before I leave, so even if your parents go there's no reason for you to be alone. And someone will be in touch very soon to tie up the loose ends. You sure you're going to be all right?'

She hesitated. There was nothing in his words about the two of them. But, she scolded herself harshly, she'd known that there wouldn't be. He had his life, she had hers. Briefly, their fates had been intertwined.

'You'd better get back to work,' she said, opening the door for him to prove that she felt no pain in relinquishing him.

'Yep. And you take care,' he said, and left the house.

Chapter Twenty

'What a fine fellow!' her father was telling her mother as Ella crept back into the room. 'Got his priorities straight. That's refreshing in a young man. Honour and courage, that's what it's all about. Try telling that to football fans. They wouldn't know what you meant.'

Ella sank back into her beanbag, too tired now to do anything else.

'He is a football fan,' she contributed. 'He's got about a hundred Man U videos at his house.'

'Manchester United? Well, that's different, isn't it?' her father blustered, unwilling to be distracted from his generalisation by the facts. 'It's not like supporting Arsenal, or Millwall.' He thought about it again. 'Or Liverpool.'

'Maybe not,' she appeased. She knew what her father was like when he thought he had a point.

'How do you know that, then?' he asked Ella as if it had suddenly struck him as important. 'You wouldn't have talked about football with him, would you? You can't stand the game.'

'No, I – actually I went to his house once. I saw them. That's all.'

Her mother cleared her throat and struggled into an upright position on the sofa.

'Is there anything we can do for you, darling, now

that we're here? Make you some hot soup, or a sandwich?'

'No, I'm fine.' She smiled at her mother. She still looked shocked. As she would, Ella reasoned. If it was her parents who'd been held hostage, she'd probably be on her second bottle of brandy and have taken up smoking by now. It wasn't the sort of thing that happened to any of them usually. 'The ambulance came and checked me out. To be honest it all feels like a dream sequence now. All of it.' Including her fleeting encounters with Jaz.

'Why did you go to his house?' her father quizzed her. It was one of those situations where he just had to get a grasp of the facts, otherwise he would feel unequipped. She knew it of old. He could turn into Michael Mansfield when the mood took him. He couldn't help it. He never meant to hurt anybody's feelings. He just had to know why. It was as if he'd taken an engine apart to clean it, was putting it all back together again and suddenly found he had two spare bolts left in his hand.

'Be quiet, Donald.' Her mother won her battle with the sofa cushions, stood up and gave her husband a warning look. She turned to Ella. 'I'm going into the kitchen to make you something to eat. You can have it later when you feel like it. Why don't you come and show me where everything is, darling?'

'Okay.' Ella pulled herself to her feet.

'What? Why do I have to be quiet? Did you go to his house, Ella? Why would you do that?'

'Oh, use your sodding imagination for once, why don't you!' her mother scolded him as he sat bewildered in his chair. 'Dear,' she added firmly.

'What – you mean?' He blinked at his wife and daughter as they wandered in the direction of the kitchen. 'Ella? You and that Indian fellow? Are you courting?'

'People don't court any more,' her mother told him factually. 'They do impulsive things and they see what happens.'

Her father was finding this all very difficult to get an angle on.

'You mean you and the Indian have been doing impulsive things? Together?'

'Oh Dad, please don't worry about it.' Ella gave him a tired look.

'With an Indian?' He blinked at her again as she stopped in the doorway.

'Yes, Dad, with an Indian. Although he's British.'

'Well, yes, but you know what I mean.' His eyelids were twitching at her with lack of comprehension.

Ella waited now as her mother had gone ahead of her and had started rummaging in the fridge noisily. It was clear she was trying to help Ella with an excuse to get out of the room so that they could have a few private words together, but she wanted to deal with this first.

'But – not as a boyfriend, Ella,' he said. 'That's a bit odd.'

'A moment ago he was a fine fellow and he had a name. Now he's an Indian.'

'He is a fine fellow. That's obvious. He's doing his bit for society.'

'So?' she prompted.

'So . . .' her father fell into thought. 'It's a different culture, Ella. You'll come a cropper. His family won't like this one bit, oh no. They don't like this sort of thing at all.'

'That's not going to arise,' she said under her breath.

'Good grief.' Her father was talking to himself now. 'I'd have to turn up to the wedding in a turban. The babies wouldn't look like me at all. They'd be brown. There's never been a brown Norton to this day. I'd have granddaughters in saris. My own daughter will be running around barefoot with a pierced nose. My house will be full of the sound of jingling bangles. I'll have to learn to like curry.' This last thought seemed to pull his face into horror. He looked up at Ella like a lost soul. 'I hate curry. It plays havoc with my intestines.'

'Dad,' Ella said patiently. 'Nobody said you have to start eating curry just because I had a one-night-stand with a man who happens to be of Indian origin.'

'But I'd have to show willing!' he asserted. She realised with a sinking heart that he really believed everything he was saying. 'It's what the father of the bride has to do. I'll have to learn Hindi so that I can speak to them all.'

Ella sighed. 'It would be Punjabi, actually, but believe it or not they speak English. Just like Jaz does.'

'Have you met them then?'

She leant on the door for support. Of course she was only making assumptions about all of his relatives and it wasn't going to have any bearing on the future, but she was getting riled. It was becoming a point of principle.

'And what if I did have a relationship with Jaz? What if it did become serious? Are you telling me you'd be as hysterical as this about it?'

'I'm not hysterical, Ella.' He looked stunned. 'You've never spoken to me like this before. What are you thinking? You're my daughter, and I want the best for you.'

'And what if Jaz *was* the best for me?'

He looked increasingly distressed.

'What would I talk to his father about?'

'I don't know. The weather? Cricket? New Labour? What do you talk to anyone else's father about?'

'But I don't follow Indian politics. I only ever had a mild interest so that I could assess the financial market. It wasn't my field. What does his father do? Does he have a shop?'

Ella closed her eyes in despair.

'I can't discuss this with you any more.'

'But I don't understand what's happened to you!' he declared in agitation. 'One minute you had a blinding career in the city, were mixing with all the right sorts for you to take up with, you had it all at your feet. The next minute you're playing with pot plants and messing around with an Indian. I don't understand what's going on! You'll be off joining one of those cults next. That'll be it. You'll sit up a mountain on mind-enhancing drugs and chant all day.'

'Don't be so bloody silly.'

'I've lost you,' he said to her sadly. 'I don't know where you've gone. I don't know who you are any more.'

'That's because you always thought I was a little

347

mirror image of you.' She raised her voice. 'And I wasn't. You've got to realise that you've got to get to know me, not again, but for the first time. If you can do that, maybe we'll be friends again.'

He looked startled, his face paling.

'Of course we're friends. We've always been friends. You've been my best friend, you must know that!'

Ella stood quietly, listening to her mother chopping away maniacally at a lettuce in the kitchen, letting them talk, as she'd always done, only the frequency and force of the chopping betraying her emotions. She thought of the times she'd been ushered into her father's study. She thought of the pride she'd felt to be the chosen one. She thought of their precious, exclusive hours spent on their own, like two boys in a boys-only club. She thought of her mother, lonely and excluded, although she never showed it, finding sustenance instead in the affection shown by a man who was not her husband. She felt a surge of righteous anger.

'Well, maybe if your own wife had been your best friend we'd all have ended up a lot happier!' she bit at him. The chopping ceased abruptly in the kitchen. It was as if her mother had her knife poised in the air.

'What?'

'You know what I mean. You should have shared it all with Mum, not me. Then you two might have shown me something about happiness. I might have learned about love, instead of the cold, clinical view of marriage you passed on to me.'

'Ella!' her father was leaning so far back in the

348

armchair that she thought it was going to flip over. It was as if he was recoiling from her blast.

'You could have taken *her* into your arms and led her into your study and shut *me* out. That's what any normal husband would have done. But you didn't. You made me Daddy's girl, and you turned my head inside out. And I lost my mother in the process, because in the end she gave up and let us get on with it. But I've found her now. You've never found her. You could have done, you could have looked to see what she was doing, and thinking, and feeling, but you couldn't be bothered. You could find her now if you could be arsed.' She heaved a breath. 'Now I'm going into the kitchen and I'm going to spend some quality time with my own mother. She's the only person in the world who can help me now.'

He opened his mouth and shut it again. She watched him flap for a moment, her anger mingling with pity for him.

'Ella, I can help you. Just come to me with any of your problems, and I can help. I've always been there for you.'

Her anger started to creep away. She looked at him with more kindness.

'I know you have, in your own way. But right now I need to be alone with my mum. Do you understand?'

His face was contorted.

'I – I think I can. I can try.'

'Fine.'

'But – Ella. Tell me one thing.' His hands gripped the arms of the chair. 'Your mother knew about this, didn't she? About you and Jasbinder? She knew before we even arrived here this evening. How did she know?'

'Because I told her, Dad,' she said gently.

'But, when? You haven't been to the house, have you?'

'I rang, and Mum picked up the phone, and we had a long talk about all sorts of things.'

'But when? I didn't even know that you rang!' he said desperately. 'She didn't tell me. Why didn't you want to speak to me?'

'Because, Dad,' Ella stopped to give him a rueful smile, 'it was a girl thing.'

'A girl thing? What on earth is that?'

'Let's just say it's a recent discovery for me, and I've found out that it's pretty good fun.'

'But—'

Ella was hauled into the kitchen by her mother, who stuck her head round the door at her husband.

'Now do stop blathering, Donald, please. Ella and I are going to do some – some girlie thingies. You just sit there quietly and I'll bring you a sandwich.'

She shut the door on him. There was silence from the living room. Ella chewed on her lip, feeling the sudden urge to laugh. Her mother arched an eyebrow at her. She still had the chopping knife in her hand. The lettuce on the draining board had been utterly decimated.

'You are a surprising girl,' her mother said in a low voice as they both peered back at the door as if they had a vision of her father crawling towards it and pressing his ear to it.

'Well, you're a pretty surprising mum.' Ella smiled at her.

'We're not going to get much said with him sitting there like a stiff in the other room, but perhaps we could meet up on our own at some point. A Saturday in Oxford Street, perhaps. You could be my sartorial advisor, and I'll treat you to some lunch in return. Do you fancy going shopping together? We've never done that before.'

'That would be lovely,' Ella said with feeling, touching her mother's arm tentatively.

'Oh, come here.'

She was enfolded in her mother's arms, keeping an eye out for the chopping knife which was waving around next to her ears. Then her mother released her and brushed herself down sensibly.

'I always hoped you and I would find each other. I thought we would, one day. I never stopped hoping.' Her voice became strangled. 'And I was so happy when you wanted to speak to me about your life. So very happy.'

'And I was so relieved to do it. Maybe you and Dad will find each other too. You never know.' Her mother pulled a disbelieving face. 'No really, Mum. He's in shock at the moment. It's been a lot for him to take in, but he'll go away and think about it. He always does that.'

'You've given him a lot to think about, that's true.' She returned to the draining board, slapping two slices of brown bread on a plate and pouring the shreds of lettuce over them. 'The prospect of an Indian son-in-law. That brought out the Alf Garnett in him, didn't it? It was always there, just hiding under theoretical ideas that didn't touch his life. But you've really made him think.'

351

'Well, it was nothing but theoretical,' Ella said whimsically, watching her mother deftly putting together the most unappetising sandwich in the world.

'I wouldn't be too sure.'

'No, it's over now,' Ella told her in a quiet voice. She had to accept the facts, and it was better if people around her did too.

'I saw the way he looked at you. I already know how you feel about him, but I watched him very carefully. He's in love with you too, and he's just as annoyed about it as you are.'

Ella let out a short laugh.

'Annoyed?'

'Oh yes. Very annoyed. It's messing up his plans. He's a man with integrity, your father was right on that count, and he's made commitments. He doesn't want to let anybody down. The thought of betraying his family's trust, his fiancée's expectations, and tarnishing his reputation with a decision that would receive no support from the people close to him is something that is almost too dreadful for him to contemplate. And above all, he's got no idea at all how the future would be if he took a chance on you. He's aware that you hardly know each other, and that it could be a big gamble. He could fall flat on his face, with everybody around him saying, "I told you so". But at the same time, for some reason that he can't fathom, he's fascinated by you, and he knows that he's in love. He knows that he has to get married soon, and he's not in love with the woman who is supposed to be becoming his wife. That's enough to make any man annoyed.'

352

Ella stared at her mother open-mouthed as she crossed the kitchen and tugged at a cupboard door.

'Do you have any salad cream?'

'Mum!' she spluttered at her. 'You've been watching too many soaps.'

'No, darling.' She abandoned her search for salad cream, pulled out a jar of mustard instead and examined the label. 'What is this? French?'

'Er, no. English. It's very hot.'

'Jolly good.'

She delved a knife into it and smeared it generously over the lettuce.

'It's just that I'm better at analysing other people's relationships than I am at sorting out my own,' she said. 'Rather like you are, in fact. I think it might be a girl thing.'

Ella slept peacefully that night for the first time in ages. She rolled herself up in her duvet, relaxed and comforted. The camera had gone – they'd removed all the technical equipment from the house while they were clearing up the operation – and number eleven had been sorted out for good. Next door, Doris was probably snoring contentedly too. As she rubbed her cheek against her cool cotton pillow and listened to the occasional hoot of an owl from the fields across the road, she sleepily ran the evening's events through her head.

The villain hadn't looked like Pete Postlethwaite at all, in reality. More like Barbie's Ken, but with more sweat. Had he really taken part in an armed robbery? She snuggled into her bedding for safety. When her parents had gone, her father's eyes still watering from the effects of his mustard sandwich, she'd decided to sit and have a cup of tea with Helen, the WPC, after all. It had been nice to talk to a young woman about it all. She could drop the bravado and talk honestly about how stupid it had been to wander around in the dark and get herself mugged. Helen had talked about victim support, and counselling, and self-defence classes. Ella wasn't sure she'd need to follow them up, but it was nice that somebody had thought she'd want to know. Perhaps she would keep a few phone numbers to hand, in case she became twitchy in the future.

She'd also tried artfully to pump Helen for information about Jaz. She'd found out that he'd been transferred to their branch from London a couple of years before. The women at the station liked him, she said, because he wasn't full of shit like a lot of the guys in CID. Ella had absently made a comment about him being quite presentable, and Helen had only given her an assenting smile in return. Apparently he'd been voted the sexiest bum in the station by the women at the last Christmas party. But she didn't get far in wheedling for information about past girlfriends. Her vague comments about office romances only met with an amicable shrug and the response that he seemed very private about his social life. And then Helen turned her attention back to victim support, and Ella's mind was concentrated again.

It was over, and for the moment she was happy that it was, even if it meant that Jaz had disappeared for the time being. If her mother was right and he was as intrigued by her as she was by him, he'd be back.

And if not, then she'd respect him for doing his duty and giving it his best. She was too utterly exhausted to be anything other than philosophical about it tonight.

She'd left notes everywhere downstairs to catch Miranda and Faith's attention. She was far too drained to stay up and wait for them, or to go into any sort of rational explanation if they wanted to know all the details when they got in. And if they both drifted in on pink clouds of romance, she didn't want to bring them back down to earth with tales of muggings and breadknife waving, and she couldn't share in the pink clouds of romance either. That could all be dealt with tomorrow morning. She'd given them both strict instructions not to leave the house tomorrow until she'd got up and talked to them. She could explain everything in gory detail and they could just be relieved that they weren't a part of it.

So when she stirred at the faint thud of the door going twice downstairs, and bubbles of conversation between the two of them coming up through the floor that seemed to go on well into the early hours of the morning, she just smiled faintly to herself, glad that they were communicating, and allowed herself to be dragged away into blissful oblivion again.

Ella was the first to get up in the morning. She fed Simon and banged and crashed the kettle and mugs downstairs to see if it would get the other two to stir, but to no avail. She gave up, and took Simon out for a walk to the newsagent to pick up the Sunday papers.

It was all very peaceful outside. The tape had gone from along the path, and apart from tyre marks in the muddy verge, there was no sign that the police had even been there. Doris's house was still, number eleven was dark and had an empty feel to it, but that was probably because she knew it was empty. The fields were damp and dewy, a soft mist rising from the grass, and the trees were a mottled blend of gold and green. She inhaled deeply, Simon panting happily and pulling on the lead, his healed leg flexing and hopping as well as the other three. Now this was what it was all supposed to be like, she thought. Long walks in the country air, the smell of autumn on her clothes, the prospect of muddy fingernails from a day's horticulturing. Everything was going to fall into place now, just as she'd imagined it.

Matt and Lorna would make it all up. They must do now. And Lorna had seen that Ella was no sort of threat to her any more. With any luck, Matt would resume his cheery repartee on Monday morning, motivating them all with his hand claps and grins, flinging garden implements around with hearty enthusiasm. And she'd be sure to keep him at a very safe distance from now on, only talking to him about matters to do with the course. It was time she knuckled down and did it properly. She had plans to make, and her future direction to consider. After all, she'd be thirty next year. She'd like to feel she knew what she was doing by then.

She loosely wrapped Simon's lead around a lamppost, rubbed his nose and pushed her way into the newsagent's. There were several people gathered at the till, chatting animatedly with the shopkeeper.

'It was a fight, I reckon,' a man in a thin jacket was saying. 'Shot through the village with all the bleedin' sirens blaring like maniacs, they did. Nearly bloody knocked me over. Idiots.'

'They kill more people from speeding then any of us ever do,' a companion agreed. 'Typical. You don't see 'em when you want one, then suddenly the whole bloody lot appear.'

She bought her paper quietly, not meeting any eyes. It was odd to be in this position. Normally she might have stood and listened, and even agreed with a group moan about the police, but she felt absurdly protective.

'Hang on, you live up at them cottages, don't you?' the shopkeeper asked her suddenly. 'What was going on up there last night?'

She held her paper to her chest and shook her head vaguely.

'Oh, I don't really know.'

'You was out, was you?'

'Er . . .' She shook her head again noncommittally. She received three probing looks in return.

'Well anyhow,' the shopkeeper went on, leaning over his counter. 'I put the papers on to it this morning. They'll find out what was going on. The Old Bill never tell you anything.'

Ella groaned inwardly. Not the press. Oh please, no, not when everything was getting back to normal again.

'I reckon it was drugs,' the man in the jacket said, changing his mind and peering at Ella. She shrugged, looking vacant. His small eyes brightened. 'Yes, that's it. Spreading like a disease it is. I blame the immigrants.'

Ella looked at the three heads nodding sagely and bit her lip.

'Well, thanks for the paper. See you again!'

'Right.' The shopkeeper looked away without interest. As she got to the door she heard the man in the jacket whisper a little too loudly, 'Bloody nobs. Never talk to us lot about anything. I bet she knows exactly what happened.'

'Nobs are the worst. Look at the aristocracy. Snorting coke and shooting up. Too much money and no bleedin' brains, that's what I say.'

She yanked on the door, found Simon and walked away from the shop quickly. As she reached the long stretch of path bordered to one side by the sycamores and the open fields beyond, she breathed deeply again. Okay, so she could pretend she hadn't heard any of that. A minute ago she'd been at peace. It was elusive, but she'd grab that feeling back again. She tried to think peaceful thoughts.

There was the Miranda and Faith dynamic to be happy about. She'd been right all along, she told herself reassuringly. So there'd been a minor blip. Quite an extended minor blip. Perhaps she'd been naive in expecting Miranda to get excited about sticky hooks and curtain rails, but Faith seemed to have enjoyed it and ultimately they were getting along swimmingly. God knew what time they'd stopped talking downstairs and come up to bed, but they'd obviously been engrossed in each other's company. If she hadn't been so knackered she'd have slipped downstairs herself and joined in. It was another girl thing that she was exploring, and it was working at last. Two female friends that might last her for a while to come and – who knew – perhaps even beyond them staying at the cottage. But nothing would change for a while yet, and now they all understood each other it was great. They could get back to the DIY, a few soaps, Friday nights with Channel 4 and a bottle of wine, and giving Faith advice about defrosting food before it was due to be served up. A bit of calm and continuity was just what they all needed. She could even cope with ELO better now. She began to hum 'Mr Blue Sky' as the clouds momentarily parted above her and the gold leaves on the trees seemed to sparkle.

She bounced back into the cottage with Simon and he immediately headed for his food again.

'Anybody up?' she yelled as loudly as possible.

'In here,' she heard Faith's voice from the living room. She went in and found her on the sofa with a cup of tea and a Crunchie.

'Hiya!' Ella grinned, delighted to see her. Faith looked up blearily and waved a hand.

'Hi.'

'You'll never guess what happened to me yesterday!' Ella threw herself in the armchair. 'Is Miranda up? I should tell you both at the same time to save me repeating it.'

'You've just missed her. She took a case and jumped in her car. Shot off in a hurry.'

Ella sat still, her excitement fading. How could she tell the story of her great adventure without Miranda here? And anyhow, what was she doing buggering off with a case when she'd given her strict instructions to stay in until she'd talked to her?

'Where on earth's she gone?'

'Dunno. Said something about a job that had suddenly come up. Short notice thing.'

'Oh balls!' Ella slumped into her chair. 'It must have been bloody short notice. I've only been gone about twenty minutes.'

'I think it was. Some flight thingy. You know what she does better than I do.'

Ella let out a deflated breath.

'Oh well. I suppose I'm going to have to wait to tell her all about it until she comes back. Wasn't she even curious to know? I left you enough cryptic notes.'

'Yeah. Something about the police having it all under control and not to move a muscle until you said we could.' Faith took a bite of Crunchie. In her blue fleecy pyjamas and devoid of harsh-rimmed specs she looked very young. At least Faith hadn't shot off and left her straining to tell her story. At least she was still sitting there, all rapt attention. Faith picked up the remote and flicked on the television.

'Oh, what's on?'

'*Hollyoaks* omnibus.' Then as if she'd realised Ella was there, she blinked at her. 'You don't mind, do you? I missed most of it in the week.'

'Well—'

'Actually, I've got something to tell you as well,' Faith said, and suddenly smiled.

'You have?' Ella wriggled forward in the chair. 'About last night? Not about you and Paul?'

'Paul? Oh, I see what you mean. No, not in that way. He's a really nice bloke. I like him a lot, but it's nothing like that. No, I talked to Miranda about it for hours when we both got in. She was really helpful too. She said I should go for it.'

'Go for what?' Ella widened her eyes.

'I'm going to train to be a vet. A proper vet, not a veterinary nurse. Paul suggested it first of all, but apparently Giles and Suzanne thought I could do it too. And Miranda said I'd be stupid to fester here in this dump all my life.'

'Oh.' Ella was just starting to like living in the village, but she could see Miranda's point. Then what Faith was telling her started to sink in. 'You mean, go to university and do all those years, and qualify?'

'That's what it'll take.' Faith nodded emphatically.

'Crikey!' Ella slumped back in the chair again. That wasn't part of the plan. Not part of hers, anyway. 'But, that doesn't mean you'll leave here, does it?'

'Oh yes,' Faith nodded again happily. 'I mean, not immediately, but as soon as I can. Miranda said I should get out right away. But I've got to work it all out and apply, and all that. You'd help me with that, wouldn't you? You went to university.'

Ella was quiet for a moment as she absorbed it all, then she came back with a warm smile.

'Yes, of course I'll help. I think it's a brilliant idea. I think the procedure's changed a bit since I went, but we'll work it out together.' She watched Faith thoughtfully for a moment. She was flopped on the sofa, eating a Crunchie, her eyes on a soap as Ella had seen her many times before, but her entire body language had changed. She looked happy, even in mid-chew. Perhaps Ella needn't feel horribly guilty any more about the way she and Miranda had ignored her needs when she first arrived. Perhaps they'd both been good for her after all.

And perhaps Faith had been good for them. She'd reminded Ella that independence wasn't about striding around London in a power suit, or sleeping with somebody just because you felt like it. It was Faith herself, way back, who'd been horrified that Matt, a married man, was the object of Ella's attentions. She'd thought then that Faith was naive and judgemental, but in fact she was more in charge of herself than Ella ever had been. She knew all about the right sort of drills, and glass, and nails, and looked after herself in a way that Ella never had. Yes, she decided, regarding Faith with a burst of affection, Faith was the most independent of the three of them. That was something she hadn't expected.

'So, d'you want to hear all about my exciting adventure?' Ella teased.

'Oh, go on then.'

'Well,' Ella sat forward and began.

Little by little, Faith's attention was drawn from the television screen and directed at her instead. Her eyebrows crept up, her lips parting with surprise, her cheeks becoming flushed. Ella had just got to the bit where the drug dealer had called her father names down the phone, and Faith was sucking in her cheeks in an effort not to laugh, when there was a sharp rap on the door.

Ella stopped her tale abruptly. She squashed her feet into the chair under her.

'Oh God, I really hope that's not a reporter. I can't talk about this. I don't even know what I'm allowed to say.'

'Don't say anything to reporters, ever,' Faith advised knowledgeably. 'They did a thing on the cycling proficiency test at my primary school when we all passed, and they misquoted me horribly.'

'You get it,' Ella instructed. 'You don't know anything really, so they can't get anything out of you.'

'Let's have a look.'

Faith stood up and wandered over to the curtain at the front window. She edged herself into the corner of the room, picked up the hem and peered out.

'Oh.'

'What?'

'It's that bloke you fancy.'

'What bloke—' Ella was on her feet in a second, swinging through the door and racing into the hall. She yanked the door open in excitement just as Jaz was reaching for the knocker again. He stumbled forward and raised his eyebrows at her.

'Hi!' she gushed, leaping backwards to allow him in. He stepped in obligingly. He was in blue denims today. That was a change. And his nose looked almost normal, which was a big relief. She peeked a glimpse at his rear as he followed her pointing finger and headed through into the living room. Yes, she could easily see why he was voted sexiest bum in the station.

'Tea?' She tiptoed through after him.

'Er, no thanks. Hello, Faith.' Faith nodded from the corner of the room, her fingers still holding the edge of the net curtain.

'Hello.'

'I'm here on business, I'm afraid.' He met Ella's eyes. He looked very, very serious. She squashed her high spirits and tried to look serious too. But she'd seen him again. Clapped eyes on him, less than twenty-four hours from when she'd last clapped eyes on him. That was very gratifying.

'Is Miranda here?' he asked.

'No, you've missed her, I'm afraid.' Ella shook her head. 'Did you want to talk to all three of us?'

'Bugger it. When did she leave?'

'Er, about an hour ago, I think. Faith knows.' Faith nodded her agreement. 'Why?'

'Did she say where she was going?' Jaz demanded of Faith in a firm but low tone.

'Well, yes. Off on another job. She packed a case and took the car,' Faith breathed. Her eyes were wide and black. Ella studied her in confusion, looked back to Jaz and the dark intensity of his eyes, and her pulse began to crash like a street thumper.

'Jaz,' she whispered at him. 'What is it?'

'Heathrow,' he said aloud. 'I should have known.' He immediately turned on his heel and began to stride back to the door.

'Wait, Jaz!' Ella grabbed his arm. 'What's this all about? What's Miranda got to do with it?'

'Plenty,' he told her bleakly. 'She's not only involved, she's a key bloody witness. You two stay here. If she makes contact with you, call this number immediately.'

He shoved a card in her hand. Then he burst back out of the house as suddenly as he'd arrived, grabbing a mobile phone and calling into it as he broke into a run.

'Jaz!' To Ella's shock it was Faith who bustled up beside her and leant out of the door. He screeched to a halt, stuck his mobile under his chin as he pulled open the door of his car, and jerked his head in acknowledgement.

'I think—' Faith swallowed. 'I think she's gone to America.'

'Terminal three,' he said aloud. 'Thanks.'

And with a slam of the car door, a roar of the engine and a squeal of tyres, he was gone, leaving Faith and Ella standing like dressmakers' dummies on the doorstep.

Chapter Twenty-one

Miranda walked away briskly from the check-in desk, tucking her boarding pass into her passport and slipping it back into her handbag. She glanced at her watch. Plenty of time, although on this occasion she didn't relish having plenty of time. She reached for her sunglasses again and rested them casually on her nose, glancing around terminal three. She had time for a coffee, a cigarette and a leisurely look at the paper. It would be better to do that airside. The terminal was quiet this morning. Not many autumn travellers, and not that many business passengers on a Sunday, although she could identify a few groups of well-pressed suits who would be making their way to New York ready for Monday meetings.

She always found it strange being a passenger. She aligned herself mentally with the uniformed crews, manning the desks, providing the smiles, doing all the tedious, painstaking work which had to be done to make sure it all ran smoothly. A couple of stewardesses passed her as she hovered at Immigration ready to go through. She flicked them both a smile. They looked cool, aloof, polished. She put her shoulders back and stood up straight. It was a while since she'd worn the uniform of a major airline, but she could still do the walk. She gave terminal three a last glance, and walked elegantly to the immigration desk, producing her passport pleasantly. He glanced at the outside and waved her through.

The flow of passengers was thin through security and she scooped her bag from the conveyor belt and on to her shoulder, and flopped her jacket over her arm. She headed over the smooth carpet, past the duty free and stopped to buy an *Independent*. Then she found a quiet table where she could drink a strong coffee, gaze over the headlines and smoke.

Her head was thick this morning. It was Faith's idea to attack Ella's bottle of Tia Maria last night, and somehow between the two of them they'd almost finished it. Ironically really, since she'd returned home after her evening with Giles practically stone cold sober. Her eyes wandered over the front page unseeingly and she lit a cigarette, took a sip of her coffee, and sat forward to lean on her elbows, staring into space.

Lance. She wished she'd never set eyes on him, ever. He was the one who'd got her into this. Just the final, crushing insult that he'd choose this time, when he was leaning on her to make her do things she didn't want to do, to send the divorce papers. There wasn't anything personal in it, just a cool judgement that she was in so deep it was pointless her trying to get out now.

She didn't really know why she'd allowed herself to be sucked into it in the first place. Excitement, initially. The rebel in her, the girl who'd been expelled from Benenden for smoking pot, had emerged again, covertly thrilled at the prospect of living a secret life and thwarting those in authority who had the arrogance to assume they knew her.

She'd do the prim and proper stewardess act, secretly laughing to herself. And she'd been in love with Lance. So in love that it had hurt. It had been a shock to discover that the blue-eyed, raven-haired pilot from New Jersey who all the women drooled over was not quite as clean-cut and respectable as he'd seemed. But after her shock came a strange tingle of anticipation. If it was as if something they shared would join them together in an irrevocable bond of complicity. And who was there to advise her otherwise? Who had ever been there to show her the difference between people drawn together by love, or by practical need?

And then the stakes had risen. When, thanks to Lance pulling strings for her, she was headhunted for private work, her record unblemished, her character flawless since her 'understandable' teenage rebellion, she was utterly flattered. She got to meet anybody from rock stars to key political figures on the world stage. But her marriage started to crumble. She started to spend more time in England. It was then that Lance turned on the heat.

He needed a contact he trusted, somebody who would supply on his behalf to the people they both encountered on the exclusive flights. The private clients, as he called them, who needed discretion when they visited Britain. She'd met them, mingled with them, was invited to the parties. She was the only one who could cope while he looked after things his end, he said.

She took a slow drag on her cigarette, held in her breath to calm herself, and expelled it very slowly.

The bastard. He'd known how much she wanted to

put it behind her. As her responsibilities grew, and the trust in her confidentiality became unquestioned, her queasiness became unbearable. She'd even tried to physically change her surroundings. It had been her way of freeing herself from her past habits, from routines which made it too easy not to move on. Ella's cottage, the temporary office work in the town, the local pub, Faith and her damp personality that had proved itself to be something solid to hold on to, embracing that had all been part of making a new life.

The corners of her mouth drooped sadly as she sipped her coffee again. It had been a bizarre conversation that the two of them had had last night. Faith had suddenly launched into a story. It was brought on by some mention of Mike. Yes, she remembered now. Faith had told her how glad she was that Miranda hadn't pursued anything with Mike. Miranda had laughed. She knew herself that she never would have done. It was gratuitous, some way of punishing herself to have pointless flings with even more pointless men, but she hadn't explained that to Faith. And Faith had suddenly decided to tell her why she hated Mike, and Oliver, and someone called Tracey, and a couple of others whose names she couldn't remember, but Mike had been the ringleader. Miranda had actually been shocked.

The story was a bit confused – not in the way Faith had told it, but in the way Miranda remembered it with a hangover. It turned out she'd been bullied and reviled at school then one day it had come to a head when she'd done well in some exam and they'd followed her home. They'd taunted and oppressed

369

her and sent her on her way without her shirt, leaving her to sneak in the back door at home and up the stairs in her skirt and bra. Mike had led the assault.

Miranda took another swig of her coffee and sucked on her cigarette. The calming process wasn't working as it usually did. Her agitation was growing. She shouldn't think about that waster Mike, the cowardly bully who she'd had a one-night-stand with, who had tried to blot out Faith's hope, her confidence, her life. And she really shouldn't think about her knowledge of the drug ring in the village. How the dealers up the road passed to Mike, who passed on out of the village. He thought he was a wily shark in a small pond, but he was a tadpole in something that was very, very big. He had no idea what was at stake, or that Miranda, who he now probably thought of as just the loose woman sharing with sad old Faith, could know anything about it.

And what had really turned her stomach was the knowledge that she had something in common with Mike. That she'd also been buying from the dealers at number eleven, enough cocaine to sell on to the clients Lance kept her in touch with while they stayed over in England for gigs, meetings, holidays, filming. Whatever the excuse, good old Miranda was supposed to keep them topped up on Lance's behalf. They were old and ugly enough to make their own decisions, she'd always reasoned, whereas Mike hadn't got a clue who he was selling on to. He did it because it earned him extra cash, and it made him feel important. For Miranda it had never been about money. She got a small cut, yes, but it had been about

Lance and her love for him and, if she was completely honest, the cheap thrill of doing something risky.

When she had moved out of London and told Lance she definitely wanted out, he had refused to let her escape. He needed her, and he was prepared to threaten her to keep her. Trapped, she'd had to oblige. It wasn't difficult to find somewhere local to buy from. The Oxford area was bursting at the seams with dealers. She told him it was a last-ditch favour, but her heart had been quailing. It seemed as if it would never end.

And then Jaz had turned up at the cottage and set up his surveillance equipment. She'd arranged to meet Patrick, Lance's sidekick, and tried to explain.

Lance's instructions came back. The best bluff was a double bluff. With her track record of security clearance, and given the innocent household she was living in, she should cooperate with the police at every stage. Any other form of behaviour from her would strike the police immediately as suspicious, and Lance didn't want a trail leading back to him. She should stay put. And finally Lance had promised her that if she did this for him, he'd find a way out of it for her.

She picked up her cup again, gripping the tiny arch of the handle with white fingers. The cup trembled in her grip and she set it down again quickly, clearing her throat, stubbing out her cigarette. She crossed her legs, looked around and lit another.

Then she had met Giles. The first person ever to look at her with interest. Real interest, not in her looks, her flippancy, the fact she was an easy prospect because she'd be moving on and out of the way before anything nasty and complicated like emotion was involved, but because he liked her and wanted to get to know her. With him she'd been able to pretend that nothing else was happening. She could talk to him about travel, different cultures, the excitement of exploration. And she'd known that if she could only squeeze through these next few weeks, maintain the bluff, lie to Giles, Ella, Faith, the police, anybody who moved around her, she might just be free of it. Really free, just as the divorce papers officially declared her impending freedom. And then she could try to put it all behind her.

Early this morning she'd got the call on her mobile to move. Something had gone wrong and she had to get out fast. There was a ticket waiting for her at Heathrow. She had to get down there, dump the car and meet Lance in New York. If it was a false alarm she could return at some point, but not until the heat was off. Better though, he'd advised, to think of it as an extended trip away that could become a permanent one. She could explain that back to the people she shared with, and they'd think of it as completely normal. They knew her work was unpredictable, and that she'd lived an unpredictable life. They hardly knew her anyway. They'd have no interest in where she really might be.

The smoke was biting at the back of her throat. She squashed her cigarette and thought about moving. It was still early for the flight. She readjusted her sunglasses and fixed her attention on the newspaper again. As she ran her eyes over and over the first line of the leading article, Faith's face flashed into her mind. There hadn't been a hint of tears, of weakness, of self-pity. She'd told Miranda that it was a secret she'd kept to herself until she'd told Paul about it a few nights ago, and had decided to tell Miranda too. She'd suddenly felt enough trust in Miranda to do that – and even Ella didn't know. She was released by being honest about it, she said, at long last. She'd been held to ransom by people who were worth nothing. They were scum, and she'd only come to realise just how much better she was than them, and really start to believe it, since she'd moved into Ella's house. It had changed her life, she said. Now she was moving on and at last trying to fulfil the potential she thought she had inside her. She had self-belief for the first time in her life, and she was going to act on it.

'Good on you, girl,' Miranda whispered in a choked voice.

She looked at her watch again and tried to focus. It was time to head for the departure gate. Maybe at some point in the future she'd be able to make contact with Faith again and find out if she made it as a vet. Perhaps she'd find out that Ella was a successful businesswoman with a chain of garden centres. Perhaps she could contact Giles and . . . No, not Giles. He'd never forgive her for disappearing. And by the time this had blown over and she was safe, he'd have moved on himself. So, she'd left a stack of things in that broken down old cottage. Clothes, shoes, make-up, perfume. She wouldn't see them again, but then what was new? And even Simon the limping dog had captured her heart. Genuine friends, a chaotic room she could call her own, a family dog. It was a taste of the life she could lead after she'd sorted this out with Lance once and for all, and got herself out of it.

Her gate was called over the speakers, and she readied herself. She folded her newspaper, tucked her cigarettes into her bag and settled it on her shoulder. She hesitated in her seat and smiled into space, oblivious to the figures lounging on seats waiting for a gate to be announced, or the latecomers bustling their way through. So Paul had the hots for Suzanne, and she for him, and neither of them had any idea that their feelings were returned? That had been a fun moment to cherish with Faith. That was something she'd like to have seen develop – Faith attempting to play Cupid. She'd probably go in like a shovel although she'd have every intention of being subtle. And Miranda could even think fondly of ELO now. She'd never be able to hear another ELO song in her life without thinking of Faith. Simon, Suzanne and Paul's potential romance, and ELO were all parochial concerns in the big picture, but she knew she was going to miss them. Maybe soon she could embrace such things properly. She'd attempted to this time, but she'd had a hand tied behind her back all along. Next time, when she was free, she would live her life without fear of a hold that somebody else had over her. She would look forward to it.

Her flight was called again over the speakers.

'Calling America,' she whispered under her breath. She stood up and sauntered towards the long, airy corridor that would take her to her gate.

Ella and Faith sat opposite each other, sipping tea.

'I don't understand any of this,' Ella said tensely. 'I

came here for a simple life. I don't know what's gone wrong.'

'It's a bummer,' Faith agreed quietly.

'I like Miranda!' Ella complained, sticking out her arm in protest. 'I know she's a bit prickly, but I don't mind that. She makes me laugh. And she's a nice person underneath all the veneer. They've made a big mistake here. I don't see how she could possibly be involved.'

'Probably another police bungle,' Faith peered over the rim of her mug. 'I mean, I know you like Jaz and all that, and I can see why actually, but he's probably got it wrong. They do get it wrong, you know. Lots of times.'

'Yes.' Ella nodded. She wasn't sure whether to defend Miranda or Jaz. She liked both of them, very much. One of them had to be acting like a git in this situation, and she wasn't sure which scenario would be worse. 'Although he seems to have got most things right so far.'

'He did let that crazy bloke escape over the fences and hold you at knife-point in here.'

'Yes, but that was probably my fault,' Ella reasoned. 'I went out there and tried to carry Doris away just when they needed her to go in and hand over some money.'

'Okay.'

'And if Jaz hadn't been so reasonable when he was talking to him through the window, that dealer might have panicked and stabbed me, or something awful. And it was all down to Jaz that the guys crept in and grabbed him while he wasn't looking.'

'I can see that,' Faith complied.

'And he was great with my parents. He made tea for all of us.'

'I believe you.' Faith nodded vigorously.

'So, he's not a git. That's all I'm saying. Even though he's got this wrong.'

Ella fell into thought again. How on earth could they think this of Miranda? It would be so stupid of her to buy drugs from a house that was being watched. She was anything but stupid. It was just impossible. And look how friendly she'd been with the police when they'd arrived to announce that they wanted to use the cottage for surveillance. It was Ella herself who'd been daunted by the prospect. Miranda had been completely comfortable with the idea. Not a sign of nerves or apprehension. She thought back to the day Jaz had arrived with the young PC, the day after her birthday, when they'd thrown the household into chaos. Miranda had been on the sofa, her eyes draped with cucumbers. She'd merely stood up and made them all at home. That wasn't the reaction of somebody who was involved in drugs. Absolutely not. Unless she was a hard-nosed criminal with great acting skills, and Miranda was neither of those things. She couldn't be. Look at the way she'd treated Faith. She was honest to a fault. Painfully so. She was tactless, yes. Cruel at times, yes. Perhaps a little cavalier with other people's feelings, that would be fair. But a liar? No. No way.

'She was great to me last night,' Faith said whimsically, playing with her glasses in her lap and putting them back on again. 'We had a long talk about all sorts of things. I decided I really liked her a lot. That sounds strange, but I did. I told her some things that were very private about myself, and she was great.'

'Really?' Ella grabbed Simon as he pogoed past and plonked him on her lap. He lunged at her hand with his teeth, hopeful of a play-fight, but she rubbed him into submission. She needed the therapy.

'I'll probably tell you about it another time,' Faith continued. 'But it was her reaction that was interesting. It was as if she was really moved. I mean, not out of sympathy but as if it was something that had happened to her too. I didn't really understand it. But it was the way she looked at me that was odd.'

'Was it?' Ella was all attention. Somebody had to make sense out of this, and Faith was the last person who'd talked to Miranda properly.

'It was like . . .' Faith peered into space. Ella watched her avidly. 'Well, it was like empathy. You know, it's different from sympathy. When somebody says, "Oh you poor thing" that's not the same as the look in someone's eyes when they say, "I know". And maybe they don't even say it, maybe it's just their expression that tells you that, but they're two totally different things.'

Ella crouched over Simon.

'So – what are you saying?'

'God knows.' Faith shrugged. 'Just that I know the difference and it was as if she knew exactly how I felt. But Miranda can't have been bullied. She's too pretty.'

'So?'

'Well, I don't know. She was quite pissed. She drank a lot of your Tia Maria very quickly. I hardly had any, but she kept topping us both up. And this morning the bottle was nearly empty, so I reckon she was pretty out of it.'

Ella sat back again. Another red herring. Anybody could look sincere when they were that plastered.

'So she's only off on another job, and she'd already said that she'd probably have one in the States soon, and she disappeared at short notice before, so it's no big deal. They've obviously got it wrong.'

'Oh no, that's not why I said I thought she'd gone to America. It's the way she was talking about it last night.'

'About the States?' Ella frowned and grabbed Simon's ears again. He complained a bit, but she guessed it was something he was probably learning to expect in her moments of concentration.

'Yes.' Faith flopped back on the sofa and stared at the ceiling. 'Let me think. We were talking about laying ghosts and she said that when she did that herself she'd have to go back to America to do it. I was saying that all my ghosts are here, and that was when she said I should get away.' Faith nodded to herself. 'Yes, that was it. And she said it was funny because she'd have to go back there to sort hers out.'

'Well, that's it then!' Ella slapped her lap in triumph. Simon jumped and she pulled him back again muttering words of apology.

'What's it?'

'It isn't complicated at all. It's really simple. The conversation you two had last night prompted her to leap on a plane, go back to Lance and talk it all out with him. She was upset about the way he approached the divorce, she feels distanced, and she's gone out there for completion. Then she'll be able to move on. I can understand that. It makes total sense.'

Faith guffawed suddenly, her body giving a small wobble under her blue pyjamas as she lay draped over the sofa with the ceiling in view.

'No, there's more to it than that.'

'Well, how do you bloody well know that, Faith?' Ella carefully put Simon on the cushion of the armchair as she stood up, feeling the need for a good pace. 'This is all very woolly. Poor old Miranda's on a plane jetting off to America to try to sort things out with her ex-husband, and everybody's being so suspicious. It's only because you've watched too many episodes of *The Bill*. There's nothing weird about it at all.'

'Look, Ella, I like her too.' Faith sat up straight and adjusted the lapels of her pyjamas. 'I don't want to think that she's involved any more than you do, it's just that the more I think about it, the more I think she was doing a runner this morning.'

'And why would you think that when it's her job to jump on planes and fly off at short notice?' Ella asked elaborately.

'Because she looked so upset when she left. I mean, if that had been a short-notice job, like she's done before, why would she look upset? She's never looked upset when she's left before. She's just hopped off and come back again. And why would she give me a hug and ask me to take care? And why would she say that I could have the half-empty bottle of Coco that she'd left on her dressing table because it would smell less like cat's piss than anything else I'd got? And tell me to say goodbye to you? And why would she seem so unhappy that she hadn't been able to say goodbye to Simon? And she told me as she walked out of the door that if Giles asked after her, I should say she'd be in touch. Not that she'd be in touch when she got back, but just that she'd be in touch.' Faith shook her head with foreboding. 'I'm sorry, Ella, but when I put it all together I think the police are right. They can't have come here like that looking for her in a panic without some sort of information. They know something that we don't. Maybe she's not on her way to America, I might have got that wrong, but she's on her way somewhere. And I don't think we are ever going to see her again.'

Ella stopped pacing. She stood still and looked at Faith. Then she gazed around her cottage, at the sticky hooks she'd put up that were peeling off the wall with the weight of the curtains, and the naked bulb above their heads where her uplighter had fallen off. She thought of the exploding shower screen, the mirror that had crashed through her windscreen, the mess she'd made of buying the right sort of paint. Faith didn't assert her opinion very often, but every time she had done, she'd been right.

'What if you're right, Faith?' She took a harrowed breath, the fight leaving her. 'What if Miranda has got herself involved?'

'I think I am right.' Faith clasped her hands over her pyjamaed knees confidently. 'I really do.'

'So, she can't have meant it. She's not a loser. And we've both agreed that she's a soft person underneath all the bluff. She cut your hair for you, and it still looks lovely. And she's got a kind heart. It can't be her fault.' Faith nodded. They both bit their lips and looked at each other unhappily.

'She might have got into it and not realised what it meant,' Faith said, her eyes clearing. 'She can't leave now. Giles is perfect for her. He's a really nice bloke. I thought he was a conceited prat, but he isn't. He couldn't have a friend like Paul if he was a prat. I think she's just very muddled up.'

'Yes.' Ella nodded emphatically. 'And what's more, I was the one who took that packet of drugs out into the lanes and dumped them in a hedge.'

'Yes, you did.'

'And you knew all about it. You told me that ignorance of the law was no defence.'

'Yes.' Faith's eyes were flashing now. 'We're guilty too.'

'We're guilty as sin. She's not alone in this. Somebody's got to her, somehow, but she doesn't have to be alone in it.'

'No.' Faith stood up. 'It's horrible being alone with a secret. She shouldn't have to go through it.'

'And she needs a bit of support.'

'Yes.'

They stood in the middle of the room listening to Simon snoring as they stared at each other. Ella chewed on her lip in anguish. Faith fiddled with the buttons on her pyjama top. Time passed.

'What can we do about it?' Faith said faintly, the fire fading from her demeanour.

'The card!' Ella dived on the phone, squinted at the card Jaz had left, and pressed out the mobile number. She sprawled against the thick arm of the sofa and closed her eyes. 'Come on,' she urged. Then she pulled herself upright.

'Jaz?' She heard the crackle of his voice in reply. She powered on. 'I just think you should know that I took some drugs from our dustbin and hid them in a hedge. And Faith knew all about it.' She screwed up her face to listen to the response. It was breaking up. She raised her voice. 'So we're both implicated. We didn't know what we were doing, but that doesn't count, so you should consider us involved too. We'll expect you to come and get us when you're ready.'

She pulled the phone away from her ear as it buzzed at her aggressively. She carefully placed it back against her ear.

'Can you hear me? Miranda's not a bad person. You should know right now that we're both going to be character witnesses. We think that if somebody's led her astray then it's not her fault.' The phone hissed and she shook it. 'Can you hear anything I'm saying?' The hissing stopped and was replaced with an insistent whine instead. It was obvious that they'd been cut off.

'Anything?' Faith quizzed, all attention.

'Nope.' Ella put the phone back on the hook despondently. 'I don't think he heard a word of that. For the moment, she's on her own.'

The phone by her elbow shrilled. Ella jumped. Faith jumped.

'That's him, he's called me back.' Ella grabbed at the receiver.

'Ella?' A tearful female voice came down the line.

'Miranda?' Ella shot to her feet, the phone wedged to her ear.

'It's Lorna. I just wanted to say I'm so sorry for attacking you. You took me by surprise, but it was a terrible thing to do. You won't let them prosecute me for it, will you?'

Once she had fixed the departure gate in her sights, found herself a seat close to the last-minute checks by the airline crew and unwrapped her paper again, Miranda tried to settle herself. It was only a question of waiting for the last call now. One thing she had learnt in all her years of flying was that there was no hurry to get anywhere. The more you rushed, the more you held yourself – and everyone else – up. Flying was as natural to her now as walking across the room, and she'd never understood those who saw it as a race.

She peered over her sunglasses with pity at two businessmen, red-faced and wheezing as they sprinted down the corridor which divided the rows of departure gates, ground to a halt, then hurled themselves through the gap in the glass compartments towards the British Airways steward who was calmly ripping off sections of boarding passes as the passengers fed themselves through. Maybe she'd been doing it too long, or maybe she just wasn't in the right frame of mind today, but it didn't seem all that funny. She looked back at her newspaper, unfolding and refolding it.

She laid it on her lap and pointed her eyes in the general direction of the newsprint while she reasoned it all through again.

This was her last act on Lance's behalf. He wouldn't take advantage of her again. She flapped the paper against her knees, annoyed that she kept reading the same article, and still she hadn't absorbed a single word of it. There were several prominent columns about somebody who had died who'd been a great philanthropist. She began to read it properly. Numerous works for charity, selfless deeds, no thoughts for fame and fortune, a life dedicated to the rehabilitation of the lost. She flicked her eyes over the photograph. A wrinkled, smiling face with weak but kind eyes.

She slammed the paper back on her knees and blinked up at the perforated dots of the high ceiling tiles. She didn't need this, not right now. She had to maintain her composure, get on the sodding plane, and wing her way to New York. That was how it always was. Somebody pulled a string, and a long line of people twitched. And she couldn't do anything about her yearnings for the dog, or Giles, or Ella, or Faith, or any of them without implicating so many people that her life simply wouldn't be worth living any more. Turning tail just didn't equate with a happy life. Or even, perhaps, a life.

She pressed her lips together and stared down at the newspaper again. The face on the front page looked back at her. She threw the newspaper to one side. The title glared at her. *Independent*. She slammed her hands against the seats, earning herself an arch look from a silver-haired man in tweeds at the end of her row. She glared at him, then, possessed with frustration, stuck her tongue out at him. He looked away quickly.

'Yes, that is rebellious,' she muttered, standing up. 'Quite the anarchist, I am.'

She gathered her jacket on her arm, hitched the strap of her handbag on to her shoulder, gave a short glance out of the high windows at the gaping view of the runways and the slim carriage of the British Airways plane that would take her to freedom. Then she turned on the expensive leather of her heels and walked steadily towards the crew at the desk. With most of the passengers now on board and the rows of textured seats arranged around the gate nearly empty, they met her with bright smiles and welcoming eyes.

'May we see your boarding pass, please?'

'Independent,' Miranda said.

The glass-blue eyes of the young man fixed themselves on her pleasantly.

'I beg your pardon, madam?'

Miranda cleared her throat.

'Independent,' she repeated. 'It's what I'm going to be. I'd like you to contact the police, please.'

The blue eyes were now alive with the possibility of a crisis. Miranda knew. She'd been through the training, and it didn't matter which airline you were attached to. They knew a hazard when they saw one, and the blue-eyed man and the tanned stewardess who was his accomplice in the halving of boarding cards were alert to the situation as quickly as she would have expected. So much for paper ripping and dishing out dinners. She mentally applauded them both.

'Is there a problem, madam?'

'Oh yes,' Miranda said steadily. 'There is somebody the police would very much like to question booked on to this flight. They may already be on their way. Although if they are,' she peered around vaguely, 'I have no idea what's holding them up.'

'All right, madam, perhaps you'd like to step aside with me just while we clear the remaining passengers for departure.' His colleague calmly dealt with the last few passengers arriving as the young man motioned her to one side, his eyes watchful of her. 'And would you have a particular description of this person to give us?'

She smiled at him indulgently.

'It's me, you dope. I'm giving myself up. Call the cops and let's get this over with.'

He nodded at her very slowly and motioned into the distance with a slight gesture of his hand. At the same time he responded to a call at the desk.

'Excuse me just one moment.'

'I expect that's about me,' Miranda told him. He picked up the phone and listened, never letting his eyes drop from her. She turned away and faced the direction of the corridor. Perhaps somebody was on their way already? Ah yes. Now she could see two men in the distance racing down the carpet alongside the slow passenger conveyor belt. People gliding along with their hand luggage were turning to look with curiosity. The two men jostled past travellers strolling to other gates, weaving around the obstacles, their jackets flapping. Plain clothes, not uniform. That confirmed it then, they already knew, although by now it was only academic to her.

'No hurry,' she murmured. She waited calmly as the men got closer, swung into the small lounge surrounding the gate, and slowed to a purposeful stride. One of them, the one with a hefty beer gut straining through his shirt, reached inside his jacket. The other man, darker and slimmer, put out a hand to stop him.

'No need for that,' she heard him instruct.

She tapped her boarding card against her hand, counting down the last few seconds as they approached her. They stopped in front of her. The more heavily built man was pink-faced from their run. He could be Interpol. One of them probably was, and it wasn't the good-looking one, sweeping back the black shaggy hair of his fringe and fixing her with an exasperated stare.

'Hello, Jaz.' She nudged her sunglasses down her nose to peer out at him. 'What kept you?'

'Miranda.' He stopped to put his hands on his hips and gather his breath. 'What the fuck are you playing at?'

'Not playing any more.' She handed him her ticket, boarding card and passport. 'I want witness protection and I want to land some control freaks in the shit.'

Chapter Twenty-two

The weeks that ensued left Ella in a daze. If she'd thought the events of her life had become dream-like prior to Miranda's arrest, it was nothing compared to the series of hallucinations that followed.

Miranda had been detained in custody and refused bail. This had stunned both Ella and Faith, who had protested to everybody they thought might be influential that it was ludicrous to suggest that she posed any threat to anybody, but the fact remained that she was not allowed home. Ella had a blazing argument with Jaz about it -- one of several that arose in those weeks when she was frequently thrown into his company again -- but despite her righteous anger he remained unmoved, only giving her monosyllabic answers in response to her lists of questions. She despaired of him. How could it be possible to have such powerful feelings for such an obdurate, insensitive git? But she hid her secret emotions and buried them further and further from his sight. Only once he touched her hand and said, 'Trust me,' and she shook him away. She didn't know who to trust any more.

Ella and Faith both managed to visit Miranda, and found her pale and wistful. She alarmed them with her vagueness after the acid-sharp wit they were accustomed to. They couldn't get any sensible explanations out of her. Ella had grabbed her hand and promised her that her room would be kept for her, exactly the way it was, so that she could come back to them when she was let out. And Faith had burst into tears and promised that she'd talk to Giles about it too and try to make him understand. Then Miranda herself had become misty-eyed and thanked them both in an uncharacteristic burble for being such wonderful friends, and promised that she'd treat them both to a holiday if she was ever given her passport back, and if not, they could go without her.

On the way home from that trip Faith came out with such a depressing list of horrors that she'd heard occurred in women's prisons, that Ella decided that concerted action must be taken. She'd phoned, written to and met with everybody she could think of that might be able to pull some strings, but the fact remained that it was down to Miranda's own lawyer to put the pressure on, and she – a powerful looking woman from Birmingham with no taste for small talk – was very cryptic, assuring Ella that their character references would be called upon and extremely valid, but that otherwise Miranda was best off where she was for the time being. Their best hope, it seemed, was that she might eventually have her sentence reduced for good behaviour. And the lawyer was as enigmatic as Jaz himself in her assertion that it was inevitable that she would go down due to the evidence stacked against her and that they should just trust those in charge of the situation to deal with it appropriately.

So, thwarted on almost every count, Ella found

relief in one outlet of power open to her. Having been invited to the police station on several occasions now, to complete statements, to give witness accounts and to finally tie up the loose ends, she found it was becoming a place where she was almost treated as a friend. They saw her as cooperative and reasonable. So when she was shown a segment of the tape taken on the day she was attacked outside her house, in a gloomy room with a WPC to one side of her and Jaz to the other, flicking the remote and pausing the tape to demonstrate to her without a doubt that it was Lorna, Matt's wife, who'd been hovering on her path with a letter in her hand, apparently wavering between putting it through the letterbox and knocking on the door when Ella had appeared out of nowhere and received a firm bash on the head with an empty wine bottle that had been pulled from the bin, Ella found her chance to act.

'I don't want to press charges,' she'd said quietly, her eyes burning with the outrage in Lorna's reaction. It was poetic justice that she'd been clouted with a wine bottle, seeing how drunk she'd been the night she'd slept with Matt. 'You've got enough to deal with, and there's no need to waste any police time with this. It's a private matter.'

'Are you sure?' Jaz had raised his eyebrows at her. 'It's assault, whichever way you look at it. We recognise her and so do you. I expect even her husband knows now. You're not going to be upsetting any apple carts.'

Ella had shaken her head adamantly and stood up. 'Nope. She won't do it again.'

'But she wasn't hitting out at a stranger. It was an

act of revenge. You have no idea if she'll continue a vendetta against you if you don't act. You don't know what she's capable of.'

'Yes I do. It's over.'

As the WPC switched on the lights with a shrug at Jaz, Ella had made her way to the door and looked back at him.

'It's amazing what people will do in a moment of passion. It doesn't mean they have any intention of acting on it again.'

And, leaving him staring after her, she'd whisked herself away before she could blurt out any more double-edged profundities at him. As time inched on, his wedding would be imminent. He wasn't discussing it with her at all any more, and oblique signals were all she could content herself with as a form of resolution.

They had a further passionate row, about a week later, when she was making a last attempt to persuade him to view herself and Faith as accomplices for hiding the packet of drugs they'd found. The less they could do to help Miranda, the more they wanted to share at least a tiny portion of the guilt with her. It wasn't so much the three musketeers as the three racketeers, Faith had announced in a burst of inspiration, but the spirit was just the same. He'd driven her out to the same spot, they'd climbed over the gate together and she'd tramped along the hedgerow and uncovered the sellotaped plastic bag, still there. She'd yanked it out from under the now yellowing strands of bracken and stuck it under his nose.

'There! What do you say to that, then?'

'I say you've been daft, but it'll be overlooked as a panic reaction, which is all that it was.' And taking it from her, he'd gazed around the dome of the field and commented idly that it was a beautiful spot and he could understand why she'd often stopped there.

'How on earth do you know that?'

'I've seen your car parked over in the lay-by before when I've driven past.' And as she'd gaped at him, he added, 'I'm a copper, remember? We notice things like that. Sometimes you'd be sitting in it, just staring out at the sunset. Other times you'd be leaning on the gate, as if you were trying to blend in with it all. And with your hair colour, it worked. Quite a sight, you with that raggedy brown mop of yours, and the hedgerows thick with autumn. Each time I came to your house I half expected you to appear draped in leaves and berries, like some sort of pagan goddess.'

'You mean – you're telling me that you'd seen me before that day? It wasn't the first time?'

'Oh yes,' he'd replied, suddenly sounding vague. 'I'd wondered who you were. I was stunned when it was the autumn nymph herself who appeared that morning in her skimpy dressing gown.'

Her memories of that first morning he'd arrived at her cottage and scared her to death had become muddled with the bizarre, casual compliments he'd seemed to be throwing her way, and then she'd brought herself up short, remembering his wedding, her pride, and above all, Miranda's lonely plight, and squared her shoulders at him.

'And there's something *you* should know about that morning as well. Something you don't know already.'

'Oh yes, what's that?'

'There was a roach in the ashtray. We'd smoked a joint the night before. All of us,' she'd lied, knowing that the smell of it had made her feel sick and Faith had gone to bed in disgust, but it wasn't the point. 'So what are you going to do about that?'

He'd laughed softly at her.

'I told you before, I'm not stupid. I saw it the moment I sat down. We had more important things on our mind, and we weren't going to pull you up on that unless it became relevant. You were due a slap on the wrists, but I know it had nothing to do with you. You're not a pot smoker.'

'Oh yes I am,' she'd burned at him. How the hell did he know what she was and wasn't? It was taking his arrogance too far.

'Oh no you're not,' he'd replied in a pantomime voice. 'We can repeat that exchange a few times for effect if you like, but you're not going to convince me.' He'd looked at her pensively, the golden light of the evening sky tingeing his teak skin, and making him look more exotic, more exquisite than ever before. She'd steeled herself.

'Right, let's go then,' she'd snapped.

'Ella? I appreciate what you're trying to do for Miranda. It says a lot about you. You're an amazing woman. Fiercely loyal and up to your eyes in integrity however hard you're trying to punish yourself, but I'm not going to arrest you, whatever you do.'

'Whatever I do?' she'd fumed back. 'I wouldn't count on it, buster.'

He'd held on to her arm as she'd been about to

stomp away across the dry, uneven curls of mud left by the plough.

'Please believe me. Miranda's in good hands. There are things I'd like to tell you but I can't.'

The wind whipped around them both, sending her hair flying around her face, and he'd put out a hand and pulled a soft strand gently from her lip.

'You just don't know when somebody's trying to protect you. That's all I can say. Don't do anything silly. Leave it in our hands.'

She'd stared at him, bubbling over with frustration and confusion yet again, then pulled her arm away from his hold.

'Let's get away from here. I'm cold.' And she'd pounded away to the gate, leaving him to follow slowly behind her.

So more weeks passed, the autumn gusts heralded winter blasts and the nights began to draw in with serious intent. Ella and Faith consoled themselves with any success stories they could latch on to.

Lorna was back with Matt. Matt had taken the route of ignoring Ella for all purposes other than those to do with the course, but that was exactly as she had expected. She received one brief note from Lorna that arrived through the post in a plain envelope addressed in an artistically looped hand. It said simply, 'Thank you.' She folded it, moved by the unexpected gesture, and tucked it in a drawer upstairs to keep. She had been right to forgive Lorna her eruption of despairing rage, and Lorna appreciated it. In a way, they were quits. Whether Matt did or didn't know about the incident between them and its outcome was not for her to gauge. It was over, and their life was their own and private again. Gradually, the colour was returning to his cheeks, although the boisterous humour that they'd all known in him hadn't yet recovered its strength. It would, she hoped, in time, when her course finished and she was well out of his territory. She would stay at the cottage, but if she wanted to pursue any further training, she'd find somewhere else to do it.

Suzanne, it materialised, had been in love with Giles's friend Paul since she'd first met him at a ball they'd all gone to over a year ago, and the feelings were reciprocated. That had stunned Ella, not so much because she knew anything of either of their histories, but because she'd been so sure that something gentle and romantic was developing between Paul and Faith. She'd passed Faith's dismissals off as bravado, but she'd been wrong. And Faith, in her own elephantine way, had apparently broached the subject with Suzanne in between appointments when they'd been sorting through supplies in one of the consulting rooms by saying, 'You know Paul fancies you, don't you?'

And, so Faith reported, that had been it. Suzanne had blushed red with delight, confirmed the feelings she had for him, and then it was only up to Faith to ring him from home on a cold, rainy and windswept evening while she and Ella curled up on the sofa together clutching hot coffee, with Simon, damp from a long, windy walk, snuggling between them.

'Paul?' Faith had smiled while Ella gave her a broad wink of encouragement. 'Bull's-eye. Send her some flowers or something. You're in there.'

And then a host of flowers had arrived at *their* door one Saturday morning, leaving them both scrambling around in anticipation for the label.

'For you, Faith,' Ella had confirmed, scanning the envelope. Faith had pulled out the card.

'Paul. He's such a lovely man. And I've done something to make him really happy. That's great.'

Her success added a shine to her eyes and a flush to her cheeks in the days that followed. Then Faith bounced in from work one night in the week and crashed open all the doors downstairs looking for Ella.

'Ella?'

'Up here.'

'Where are you?'

'In the bathroom,' Ella had yelled from the bath where she was soaking off a day's mud. She'd been playing with her small plastic whale, the one that sucked in water and then squirted into the air, and musing about life, mud and the unexpected. The bathroom door had been flung wide and Faith had burst in, throwing herself at the toilet seat and plonking herself down on it, her face glowing with excitement.

Ella had slid upwards in the bath, covered any pink bits sticking out with bubbles to save any embarrassment, and gaped at her.

'What is it?'

'Mike.' Faith's voice was low and trembling. He's been nicked.'

'You what?' Ella had thrown the plastic whale into the water with a soft 'plop' and concentrated.

'I heard it on the grapevine at work. He's been

taken in. He's been dealing. Drugs. They've got him.'

'Oh my God!' Ella felt the colour drain from her cheeks.

'Yes.' Faith's eyes were alive. 'And he'll go down for it. Bastard. I'm so happy. I've never been as happy as this.'

'Wow!' Ella's mouth was wide open as her thoughts raced ahead of her. 'But, hang on. Miranda! Miranda and Mike. Do you think there's a connection there?'

'I'll tell you what I bloody think,' Faith had stumbled back, her face burning. 'I've had all day to think about it, and the walk home too. I think I've got it, at last. I think we've been really thick.'

There'd be no novelty in that, given their past record, Ella decided.

'Why?' she mouthed.

'Miranda knows all about Mike, and what happened to me. She knows about the gang, how he egged them on. Everything I told you, every detail, she knew it all. And you know I told you how she looked, so sad, so sympathetic. I think there's a big connection. But we've had it all the wrong way round. Think about it.'

Ella thought about it. The bubbles popped around her and the whale bobbed up and down, but she wasn't getting very far.

'Help me out. You're the brains in this house.'

'All that cryptic stuff from Jaz, and the lawyer, and Miranda going limp on us when we went to see her and not answering our letters.'

'Yes?'

'And that business of protecting us from stuff we'd

better not know. And her not getting bail, and every bugger out there ignoring what we said. And now this.' Faith nodded, her breathing shaky.

'Er – yes?'

'She's shopped him. She's bloody well shopped him.'

'You mean,' Ella said in a hushed voice, 'she's taking him down with her?' It was a phrase she'd heard in films, and it appeared to be what Faith was leading to. It seemed as good a moment as any to say it.

'No.' Faith shook her head. 'She'll go down, yes, but it'll be a sham. To protect her, don't you see? They'll never know that the information came from her. The police knew a heck of a lot anyway to get on to her. All she might have done is confirmed what the Old Bill already knew, perhaps added a name or two. But that's it. That's what's going on, and why it never made sense. It does now. It's the only way it all fits together. She'll be on trial with the others, and she'll go down as if she's as guilty as the rest. But they'll do something, I don't know what – let her out quickly, or move her somewhere else. Yes, that'll be it. She'll be transferred as far as everyone knows, but she'll actually be released. I saw it in a film once. They do it sometimes. You just wait and see.'

'Blimey,' Ella breathed.

'But with Mike,' Faith raced on, 'I just know it's personal. I don't know how I'm so sure, but I am. She's done this for me, Ella.' Her eyes brimmed with tears and they fell, one by one, in long trails down her hot cheeks. 'The other stuff may be for herself, to start again with a fresh slate, but this bit, the Mike bit. She's done that for me.'

Ella fell silent, her body rigid with the certainty of what Faith was saying. Of course it all made sense, and it changed everything. Miranda was a key witness and she was cooperating. She grabbed the whale, filled it with water and squeezed a fine jet at her shampoo bottle while her brain throbbed with ideas.

'So – so Jaz would know all about it.'

'Of course he would!' Faith stuck out her hands. Her bag slipped off her shoulder and she yanked it back on. She was still in her raincoat, the shoulders spattered from the rain outside. 'Jaz picked her up at the airport. He orchestrated the whole thing. And he needs her to make his case stick. He'd have been the first to know.'

'So – so he's not being as much of a git as I thought?'

'Correct,' Faith said patiently. 'Yet again, he's proved that he's not as much of a git as you thought.'

'But – but Giles doesn't know.'

'He mustn't know.' Faith shook her head sombrely. 'If we're right, and I'm sure we are, we've got to keep this idea to ourselves. Absolutely secret. Otherwise she won't be safe.'

'No, you're right. I won't breathe a word to a soul.'

'You can't, for her sake. And Giles just won't talk about her to me or to anyone. I've told him she's not a criminal at heart and that someone's led her astray, but he won't be drawn into discussing it. He's gone silent and miserable at work. I think he's still in shock.'

'Poor Giles.'

'Yep. I feel so sorry for him. He's quite a traditional sort of guy. He was stunned rigid by this.'

'He must have been.' Ella almost snorted at the understatement, squirting water at the taps. 'He didn't know her very well. Not like we did. Although I wonder how well we did actually know her.'

'We knew her, better than anyone.' Faith sat up assertively, her eyes flashing. 'She's not a coward, and she's not the type who'd be a grass. There's a reason she's done this, and I'm not absolutely sure what it is, but it's more likely to be revenge than fear. She's not scared of anyone. Pissed off by one or two people, but not scared.'

'Lance,' Ella whispered, the name coming to her in a sudden tangential thought.

'Lance,' Faith repeated confidently.

They both sat quietly, watching mesmerically as the whale shot water up the tiles and it dripped down. The steamy air swirled around them, misting up Faith's glasses. She rubbed at them so that she could see again.

'What an incredible woman she is,' she said eventually.

'I'll say.'

'I wish I could do something for her in return.'

'Yes,' Ella mused, swirling the water around thoughtfully. 'Actually, I think you can.'

'What?'

'Well, you can't give any hint of Miranda helping the police to Giles, but what you can do is work on him, in your own way, until he gives up and decides to go and see her. You know he's dying to. He's just confused with it all. He thinks she's a villain, but she isn't really, and when he sees her again, that'll be it. He'll believe in her.'

'You reckon?' Faith's face was dogged with uncertainty.

'I do. It may take time, but I think he's just what she needs. See what you can do. But none of this direct "my friend fancies you" approach. You've got to be very, very subtle about it. Work on him, day by day, week by week, and wear him down. He'll go and see her eventually.'

The following morning, Giles was at the surgery early. Faith was arranging the appointments book on the desk and preparing herself for the early calls when he floated in, looked at her unseeingly with tired eyes, and wandered around reception in circles before leaving the room again.

She thought about it. The phone began to ring, but she jumped up from her chair and raced out after him. She caught him as he was drifting down the stairs to the basement.

'Oh, Giles!'

'Hmmn?' He turned round and gazed back up the stairs at her.

She noticed the dark rings around his eyes, the mess of his hair and his drawn cheeks. Who was he kidding? He was mad for her, and it was about time somebody smacked some sense into him. She took a short breath to brace herself and fixed him with an adamant glare.

'You've got to go and see Miranda,' she shouted at him.

He didn't move, not even a muscle on his face twitching. And then he blinked.

'Why are you shouting at me?'

'Because you're being such a wimp!'

'I am?'

'Yes. You've got to stop feeling so sorry for yourself and do something about it. You've got to go and see her, and soon.'

He stared back at her again, following her mouth as if he was attempting to lip-read. Then he scratched at his blond hair in agitation.

'Wh – I mean why should I? Why would she want to see me?'

'Because she's crazy about you, you bloody idiot, and she needs you.'

'She's crazy about me?'

'Yes. And I know that for a fact, so don't even think about arguing. You could be giving her moral support now, and all you can do is mope around.'

Faith snapped her mouth shut again. She waited. The phone stopped ringing in reception, and with nobody else around, it was almost silent apart from muted barks coming from downstairs. It was tense stuff. For what seemed like an age, Giles didn't move at all. Then he turned around and headed back up the stairs again. Faith stepped quickly out of the way. He pulled off his white jacket and flung it to one side.

'Right,' he chanted. 'Right. So, what I need is directions from you, and I need you to cover for me with Michael.'

Faith broke into a slow smile that became a broad ear-to-ear grin.

'I'll say you've got the runs,' she said helpfully.

He was already halfway out of the heavy front door of the surgery, and she called him back.

'Giles!'

'What?' He swung back again in agitation.

'Directions.'

'Oh yes. And what about visiting times? Will they let me in?'

'Do I have to work everything out for you, you great big Jessie? Just get there, and sort something out.'

Life was a lot more simple than Ella gave it credit for, Faith told herself with a private shake of her head as she heard Giles's car rasping out of the loosely gravelled car park with her directions scribbled down for him. She picked up the other half of the scrap paper she'd torn in half for Giles and played with it between her fingers.

She gave a long, contented sigh and settled back down on her swivel chair behind the counter. It was just a shame that she couldn't sort Ella out too. But tonight she was going to persuade Ella to come out to the Plough for a drink with her. Kevin the barman had been rather flirtatious towards her recently, and while she didn't take him seriously, it was fun. She was free to do things like that now.

A crowd of schoolchildren passing the window chattered and called into the air. She sat still and listened to the clamour, rising as they passed under the ledge and fading away into the distance as they moved on down the road. There was a time when she couldn't hear the sound of children laughing without being turned inside out with pain and anger, but as the voices died away completely she felt at peace.

With the world, and most of all, with herself. The image of Mike's red, twisted face as he yelled at her, pulling her about, cackling at her awkwardness, appeared hazily in front of her. She picked up a pen and drew a round circle on the piece of paper. She drew two piggy eyes, a big nose and a wobbly line for a contorted mouth. She put a mean little moustache on his upper lip for good measure. Then she lifted it into the air and brought it down on the spike of the scrap paper holder. It speared through the face as if he had a long, sharp nose, the crossed eyes she'd drawn looking hopelessly up into space. She heaved a breath at it.

'Gotcha,' she said, and smoothing her hands over her lap, turned her attention back to her work.

Chapter Twenty-three

It was a late November afternoon, the cold, still air settling like dew on the students as they gathered around Matt for his demonstration of the division of herbaceous plants.

Ella was trying hard to concentrate. They'd been through the theory in the classroom and now he was jamming his boot on to the fork, levering out the roots of the *heliopsis*, lifting them and shaking them around before dividing the clumps with the fork again. They watched him repeat the effort several times, then John surprisingly stepped forward, wrestled a garden fork from the pile on the lawn in front of them and presented himself as the first volunteer to try it out.

'Grabbed your interest, John?' Matt leant on the handle of his fork in surprise.

'Yeah, well. If you can't beat 'em, join 'em. And it's nearly time to go home. Quicker we get this over with the better.'

Matt glanced at his watch.

'Few more minutes to go yet. We'll each have a quick go at this, then pack up.'

As John thundered his strength into the exercise Ella was distracted by a car rolling into the grounds. She peered over. It wasn't one of the usual boneshakers driven by the students, or the minibuses that arrived at that time of night to take the students living in Oxford back towards the town. It was a sleek, bottle-green model with a low carriage and a long bonnet.

She pulled away from the group and took a step across the lawn to squint at it more closely. It swung into the yard and pulled over.

'Jaz,' she breathed.

Her pulse stuttered. It was a while since she'd seen him. As far as she knew, business was pretty much completed between them. What on earth was he doing here?

She reasoned as she stared. Was it necessarily anything to do with her? Could it be that he'd got other interests here that she knew nothing about? She watched as he climbed out of the car and gazed at his surroundings.

She had the urge to wave at him, but that would be silly. He wasn't the sort of man you could just go, 'coo-ee!' to. She saw him spot their group, then notice her. He merely nodded over at her. Then he leant back against his car as if he was waiting for someone or something. She glanced covertly at her watch. Nearly five. Very nearly five. Even if he was here doing something else, she'd miss him if he disappeared to talk to someone while they all went off to pack the tools away in the sheds. And after five she'd have no excuse to hang around.

She turned back to the others, catching her breath.

'Matt, I've just got to—'

They were all preoccupied. Matt had given them each a section of the beds to dig to hurry things up. Pierre and Valerie were struggling to unlock the entangled spokes of their forks, and Matt was bent over Emma's efforts, applauding her precision. Nobody would notice if she just slipped away.

She turned again, nibbling on her lower lip. Jaz had his back to her now and was watching the two horses in the paddock frolicking in a last-minute canter around the grass before somebody appeared to take them into the stables. Was he imagining himself riding the range with his lasso in hand? She could bet her bottom dollar he was.

She ambled innocently away from the group then sped up when she was out of sight. She took a detour around the shrubs and the backs of the sheds so that she couldn't suddenly be hailed back, and found herself on the concrete drive. She made her way towards his car. He'd wandered away now over to the paddock and was leaning on the top bar of the fence, putting out a hand to the stallion and rubbing at its nose.

'Beautiful creature.'

He seemed to be talking to the horse, or to himself, but definitely not to her. Ella hesitated. He obviously hadn't heard her approach. Then she cleared her throat noisily and carried on walking towards him. He glanced round, then stood up properly to face her.

'Hi,' she said pleasantly. 'What's a nice boy like you doing in a place like this?'

He gave her a half-smile.

'I could come here just to look at the horses. They're fantastic. I always wanted a horse. One day I might do it.'

'You need to save up a lot of pocket money for

that.' She stuck an unpractised hand over the fence and received a nervous nip on her fingers in return. 'Ouch. And they're temperamental.'

'You just have to know how to handle them.'

'And you're the expert at handling temperamental creatures, are you?' She gave him a sideways glance. 'How's your nose? Hope it's completely healed up now.'

'Even temperamental creatures can take me by surprise sometimes.'

He fondled the forehead that the horse proffered him a little longer then pulled away and put his hands in his trouser pockets. He was wearing an expensive, tailored suit. She, by comparison, was in faded jeans spattered with dried mud, a floppy roll-neck jumper and a throw-over windcheater with her hair carelessly caught up in a ponytail with strands flying all around her head. It was the first time she'd seen him dressed formally, and two thoughts occurred to her. The first was that he looked fantastic, the second was that he must be here on official business.

'So, let's stop beating about the bush, Jaz, what brings you to the college?'

'I was in court today. It finished early and I thought I'd drive back this way.'

'So what's the news on our case?' He looked confused by the question. 'You know, I wondered if it might have some bearing on Miranda or that heinous arsehole she shopped? I thought perhaps you might want to report some . . . news . . . back.'

She tailed away, sucking in her cheeks quickly. She hadn't meant it to come out quite so knowledgeably.

Not that she could have made such an indiscreet comment to anybody other than Jaz, it was just that he was so deeply involved that it was easy to say to him. She'd been of the opinion for some time now that he was reprieved of being a git.

He gave her a very blank stare. So much so, that she knew he was bluffing. It was strange that one minute she'd been cooperating with the police and the next she was expecting them to cooperate with Miranda, but it was the way it had turned out. She didn't mean to put him on the spot about what might really be happening behind the scenes, though.

'Sorry,' she said.

'An apology? It's been a while since you offered me one of those.' He laughed.

'Yes, but it came out in a funny way. It's just that I got you wrong, and I made your life hell. Well, I mean I made it hell, then there was a sort of break then I made it hell again, but I know now that I'd misunderstood you.'

He didn't answer her question at all. She didn't really expect him to, but she was impressed by the way he cut her line of conversation off. He was good at what he did, and she had to admire him for it. Miranda was in safe hands. It was what she'd been advised all along, and she knew it was true. He wouldn't succumb to as much as a flicker of his eyes if the stakes were high enough. She was starting to understand him.

'The court case had nothing to do with Miranda,' he moved on effortlessly. 'I just remembered that you usually knocked off at about this time and thought

I'd drop in and have a look at your set-up. That's all really.'

She absorbed this information quietly, studying him without knowing what to say.

'So, um. Well, this is it.' She cast out a hand and swept it around the ramshackle selection of buildings, barns, sheds, tutorial huts and fields. Everything seemed small, tumbledown and muddy as she could imagine it through his eyes.

'It's great.' He nodded as if it really was. 'I love the outdoors too. It's one of the things I loved about the force when I first joined. Getting out there, in the air, pacing about, something new every time. It changes when you get promoted. More desk work, more management responsibility, less time actually out there on the beat. I used to love the beat, you know.'

'Really?' She listened with her head on one side, trying to fathom what he was thinking. Why would he come here impulsively like this, and start sharing all this with her?

'Yep. It was the real me, though a short-lived experience. One consolation with my work now is that I actually get out still.'

'Consolation? But I thought you were married to your job!'

She bit her lip as he shot her a look at the word 'married'. She let it roll away into the cold air. He held her eyes inscrutably for a moment then looked away again.

'It's becoming more the way I like it. After a while you can imprint your personality on it a little, have some say in the way you run your team and the role you play. It's coming together.'

410

'Autonomy. That's what I'll have myself when I set up on my own,' she breathed as the horses had a final flick of their hooves around the soft turf and gathered to stand together, the neck of one leaning comfortably over the other.

'Nobody works alone,' he said, watching the horses too. 'Even creatures we think of as solitary aren't solitary at all. Nobody really is.'

'No, well.' She rubbed her cold fingers against each other and jammed them in her jacket pockets. 'That's not going to be an issue for you, is it? I'm surprised you're not off honeymooning somewhere. You never told me the exact date of your wedding, but it must be pretty damned close, if it's not happened already. So I don't count you as somebody who's solitary.'

'No, you're right.' His eyes were still fixed on the horses as if he was miles away from her. 'I'm not, and I never really have been.'

'Well.' She scanned her brain for something to say next. 'Well, I expect you just had an image of yourself galloping around on your own like a Wild West hero, didn't you? We all have dreams. It doesn't mean we can actually live them.'

He laughed into the air again. The horses stirred, looked over at them and went back to chewing quietly to themselves again.

'Do you know, I actually went and bought an ELO album all because of you?'

She screwed up her face at him.

'Me? Oh please. It's Faith who's the fanatic.'

'But you were the one who told me I wasn't a Wild West hero after all. So I went and listened to that track. And all the bloody others. Including "Horace Wimp". You really got under my skin with that.'

She stood up straight and pulled her windcheater around her body firmly. Her temper was rising, and there was little she could do to stop it. After the poker face he'd offered her time after time in their recent dealings, as if the night they'd shared had never happened, it was galling to have her brief influence on his life passed off as some kind of irritation.

'Well, I'm bloody sorry. The last thing I'd want to do is get under your skin. Just because we had the most incredible, amazing night of passion together that I've ever experienced with anybody in my entire life would be no reason for me to want to cause you even a momentary flicker of disquiet.'

She could feel her nostrils flaring and she sought to control them. She didn't want to look like the race-horse her mother had compared her to, especially not with a couple of ageing specimens in the paddock there for a quick comparison. But why had he come here? What was he doing? If it wasn't work, and it wasn't to do with Miranda, then what the hell was the purpose of it? Why should he be even vaguely interested in where she did her course, or what her surroundings were?

'It was incredible, wasn't it?' he said, examining her face.

'I just said it was, didn't I?' she burst at him.

'Why are you always so cross?' He sounded bemused. 'Even when you say the words a man's been longing to hear, you manage to fling them at him like javelins.'

'Well, now you've got that out of me and your

ego's nicely boosted, you can go back to Sasha a complete man, can't you?'

She just couldn't stop herself. It was him standing there, in that dark suit, with his soft, black hair in smooth feathers over his collar, his eyes huge and watchful, his lashes so dark and long, with the rich, brown skin she longed to touch, not just now, but over and over again. The beautiful image he presented was taunting her. It was the sort of self-congratulatory experience that a man might seek just before his wedding to another woman, but not one she was willing to be a part of.

'So you'd better get on with your life, hadn't you?' The words ripped themselves from her throat. 'And I'd better get on with mine. I've got – I've got a herbaceous border to divide.'

'Ella?'

'Shut up. I want you to be really quiet from now on, which means silence.'

She swivelled on her heel in her steel-capped wellingtons and faced where the class had been, over there in the distance somewhere, ready to march away. But everyone had gone. She could hear a faint clatter from the sheds. They'd obviously finished and decided to pack away. She pursed her lips together. There had to be somewhere good to stomp to. If this was the last time she was going to see him, she was going to make a damned fine exit. She pointed herself towards the tutorial hut, over in the other direction. It would mean stomping past him, but it was better than stomping off across the empty lawns with her lack of purpose painfully evident.

'Ella? Will you listen to me?'

413

'Goodbye, Jaz.' She took a large stride over the concrete and skidded on a smear of cow dung. She steadied herself quickly.

'Ella, just hang on, will you?'

'Goodbye. I'm off. You'd better go too.'

She headed off again at high speed, this time managing not to skid on anything at all.

'Right, that's it.'

He grabbed her around the waist. She squealed in shock. Then she found herself hoisted in the air and thrown over his shoulder. She was so stunned that for several seconds she went limp and heavy, like a sack of compost, but then she began to wave her rubber boots in the air.

'Jaz bloody Singh, if you don't put me down I'm going to kick the shit out of you in the place it will hurt the most, and then you'll have no married life to look forward to at all. I promise you that.'

He didn't answer, striding away from the paddock with her. The two horses bounced up and down in front of her eyes. For ever, it seemed, she was hauled around on his shoulder as if she weighed no more than a pillow, then she was dumped down on the ground again and she found herself on her feet with her back to his car, his arms on either side of her pinning her to the bodywork and preventing her escape. The world spun for a moment, then steadied again. His black eyes were boring into her.

'I'll scream,' she threatened.

'No, you won't.' He sounded very sure of himself. 'Now it's your turn to shut up and listen to me. This isn't work, and I'm not here in a professional capacity by any stretch of my, or even your very negative,

414

imagination. I came here to find you and talk to you, and that's what I'm bloody well going to do.'

She opened her mouth but his look silenced her. He had raised his voice to her. A lot, actually. So much so that she was vaguely aware that the shuffling group of students gathering for a cigarette while they waited for the minibus to collect them were somewhere over his shoulder, watching avidly. Any minute her class would arrive in the yard for their goodbyes before they all headed off too.

But what struck her above all was that she had riled him. It was the first time in all their encounters, however much she'd provoked him, that he'd shown his frustration. And it had come out in quite a blast. Her blood was still simmering too much to realise what it signified.

'What is it?' she demanded.

'I'm in love with you,' he stated fiercely. 'I've done everything I can bloody well think of to make the feeling go away, but I can't. It started when I first saw you mooning about by your car in that sodding lay-by with your hair all – all red and gold in the sunset. And it's just got bloody worse since then. And every time I've seen you and I've got to know you a little bit better, it's just got more and more insistent, until now it's like a bloody born again Christian knocking at my door. I just can't make it go away.'

'Try getting married,' she yelled back at him, his words bouncing off her head like paper darts. 'That'll make it bloody go away.'

'I can't get married any more!' he bellowed back.

'And why bloody not?'

'Because Sasha broke off our engagement about a

month ago. I've got nobody to bloody marry!'

She blinked back at him. She was still too furious with him for putting her over his shoulder to react with anything other than indignation.

'Good for Sasha!' she issued back, then fell silent while his eyes consumed her insistently.

She stood still, her breath coming in ragged gasps. His breathing was unsteady too, but his expression softened. One by one, his words started to find a way into her brain. She relaxed back against the car. He let first one arm drop to his side, then the other. Then he stood and looked at her with uncertainty. She felt her breath slowing. 'She did?'

He nodded.

'Why did she do that?' she lowered her voice.

'Because.' He stopped to gather himself. He stuck his hands into his trouser pockets again. 'Because she said that it's not fair on either of us, or on the families. She's met somebody in her working life she's too fond of. An Indian, as it happens. But they like each other too much to part.'

'Oh my God.'

He expelled a long breath, as if it came up from somewhere well under the muddied concrete. 'Well, not really, although that pretty much sums up my father's reaction when he first found out, but I've smoothed it over. I've assured them that I'm happier this way. There was no way I was going to let Sasha carry the can for this. She's only the first to say what we've both been privately thinking, and I've made sure that everybody knows it's mutual.'

She swallowed. She had been so busy fighting her corner that she hadn't stopped to think too carefully about his feelings over the matter. He must have had visions, and hopes and plans himself. She felt an uncomfortable twang in her solar plexus.

'Are you happier this way, Jaz?'

He gave her a crooked smile.

'Do you care?'

'Yes, actually.' Her anger had entirely faded now. She was only concerned about him and what he felt. The realisation filled her with warmth. She put out a hand very delicately and touched his arm as if it was hot and might burn her.

'I'm relieved, Ella. I didn't quite know what we were both getting ourselves into, but it felt wrong. I thought I should go ahead regardless. It seemed the only option given everyone's hopes and expectations, but thank God it's resolved. It was wonderful to talk to you about it. You're the only woman I felt I could talk to. I don't know why. I guess I knew you wouldn't judge me harshly. The way we'd done things had been too similar. The way we'd both approached life had been too alike.'

His face was so different now from the strong, professional face he had habitually shown her. His eyes were full of emotion. It was like the man she had been given a rare glimpse of when she had spent the night with him. On that occasion she had seen the soul inside the tough shell. It had been a different man, within the clothes of the outer one. She liked both, but she liked the man with the soul better. She had craved his return, and he was here again, right in front of her.

'I can't imagine how this is for you,' she ventured. 'It's beyond my experience. It would be arrogant for me to even think I know what this means and what you might be feeling.'

'Thank you,' he said. 'You have no idea how much it means to me for you to say that, but I can try to explain it. Sasha and I might have made it work, like a couple of colleagues perhaps, and maybe there would have been affection between us at times, but we'd both been allowed too much freedom to form our own attachments in the past. It's a kaleidoscope, the world we live in now. It's confusing. Dealing with it as if it can be organised and controlled just doesn't work in the way it used to. It's changed. We can't pretend it hasn't.'

She nodded slowly at him. He might have been speaking of a world she didn't know, but she could share his sentiments. They applied equally to the world she did know. And her efforts to organise her own world had been laughable in their futility.

'Night, Ella.'

She was dragged away by John's robust voice assailing her across the yard.

'Oh, night, John!'

'I put your folder in the cupboard. You'll find it there tomorrow.'

'Oh, cheers. Thanks.'

She tried to turn back to Jaz with more focus but she was distracted again.

'Goodnight, Ella,' Pierre called, tripping his way around the tinges of dung on the concrete and heading for the car park. He gave Jaz a meaningful look over his shoulder. 'We invented it, but you does it better zan us!' he laughed and went off towards his Renault.

'Béarnaise sauce, I think he means,' she muttered, then anticipating further farewells coming in her direction called, 'Night, Val, Emma, Kathy, Nev. God, it's like the Waltons.' She gazed over Jaz's shoulder at the robust figure striding purposefully back towards the administrative building. 'Matt,' she finished in a whisper.

'Let's get out of here,' Jaz said. 'This isn't the right place for us to talk.'

She rested her eyes on him again, searching for more information.

'And should we talk, do you think?'

'What do you think?'

'I think—' She stopped. It was as if her feelings had been centrifuged in this moment between them and she understood herself properly for the first time. She'd always thank him for that. She chose her words carefully.

'Jaz, I'm worried that I'm a loner, and you're not,' she told him from her heart. She hoped he would understand her, and believe her. 'But I don't want to let you go while you're here in my life. If we can enjoy knowing each other I'll be very happy. I think that's what life is. A series of experiences that bring you joy or pain, and I know that you bring me joy. I can't promise you a happy ending, but I'd like to make the most of it while I can. Does that sound too clinical?' Then self-consciously she added, 'I'm sorry. You did ask. It's how I feel.'

He lifted a finger to stroke her cheek. They held each other's eyes until she felt she was falling right into the inky wells of his irises and scuba diving her way inside him. He lowered his mouth to hers and brushed her lips gently in a kiss so soft it was like the touch of a primrose petal.

'Jaz,' she put her hands up to touch him. She so desperately needed to do it. She pulled him back to her and kissed him with all the passion she'd tried so hard not to show him. She felt him respond, gathering her into his arms and holding her tight while they locked themselves in an embrace.

'Wahey!' The chorus from the crowd waiting for the bus was accompanied by raucous cheers.

Jaz pulled away from her slowly, his eyes bleary with desire.

'We've got to get out of here,' he said urgently.

'Oh yes, please.'

'Your place or mine?'

'Yours. I don't want ELO to play any further part in this.'

'Agreed.' He kissed her again hurriedly.

'Yes,' she agreed huskily. 'And we'll talk at some point. When we can.'

It was a full year since that wild spell of physical exploration had begun.

It had been the most mind-blowing encounter of Ella's life. Now her life had changed completely and moved on.

She'd finished her course, decided not to pursue any further study but to apply her business sense to the venture she'd been itching to immerse herself in. Emma and John were in it with her, Emma providing the guts and stamina she needed to echo her own, and John pulling his weight with a renewed sense of purpose that inspired both of the women. They'd proved an unlikely, but so far very dynamic team. And they'd bought up a garden centre between them with a combination of loans and capital, and were determined to make it a success.

It was a blustery late November evening, the wind bashing at the windows, when Ella settled herself next to the phone, heaving Simon on to her lap, his hefty adult body flopping over her. It would have been nice if Faith had warned them all how big he was going to get, but it was something she relished when she wasn't complaining to Faith about it. When she got the chance, that was.

Faith was calling less frequently as her new life at university was overtaking her, just as Ella had expected. But now Ella could take Simon up to bed at night without being nagged about it, and throw an arm around him on the long nights she spent on her own. And although her sentimental guard over the two bedrooms of the friends she valued was fierce, at least she could afford to subsidise them. Faith's room was there for her whenever she wanted to drop back in, which she'd already done twice, even though she was only in her first term, and Miranda's room was still waiting, untouched, as they'd promised. It seemed that it might not be long before she came back, and even then it was likely that she'd have to move on and settle right away from the town. But she had the unquestioned devotion of Giles now, and for that Ella was happy.

'And you've got my unquestioned devotion, haven't you, babe?' She dropped a kiss on Simon's head and he snored at her deliriously. 'You know nobody will ever come between us now, don't you?'

She smiled indulgently at him, lowered the volume of the television on the remote and picked up the phone. She dialled and settled into the wide arm of the sofa, ready for a long call.

'Mum?' she quizzed as soon as the phone was picked up the other end.

'No, it's only me I'm afraid,' her father coughed back at her with good humour.

'Well, I'm glad. I haven't had a chance to talk to you for ages. I hope Mum's keeping you up with all the news?'

'Oh yes. And she's given you the update on her sunburn? It seems to be almost gone now.'

'Oh that's good.'

'Silly woman that she is,' he said warmly. 'Going out like that in the midday sun, dressed only in a skimpy bit of material. I was quite amazed. I'd warned her about the tropics but she had to find her own way.'

'I bet she looked gorgeous though, didn't she? She told me she bought a bikini specially. Can't wish for much more than a woman with a figure like hers at your age, can you?'

'Oh. Well yes. She did look very gorgeous.' Her father coughed again and Ella smiled to herself. She'd heard her mother's version of their holiday away together and what it had done for them both. She knew she wouldn't get anything like the same story out of her father.

'So anyway, are you both there?'

'Your mother's here, making us some sort of cocktail in the kitchen. Something she found in a recipe book somewhere. I'm quite looking forward to it.'

'Oh, well I'll tell you and you can tell her then.'

Ella hesitated. She rubbed at Simon's ears, then as she heard her father call her mother into the room, pulled at them instead. Simon didn't budge an inch. He was too used to her foibles by now, she guessed with a nervous smile down at his sleeping form.

'What is it, Ella? What do you have to tell us?'

She could hear the excited anticipation in her father's voice. It filled her with pleasure, but at the same time the words hovered on her tongue. She wanted to savour them. They tasted so wonderful. He'd be so happy, she knew that now. And so would her mother. And moments as special as this only came once in anybody's lifetime if they were lucky. It was a moment she'd never expected to happen in her own. But here she was, on her sofa, ringing her parents, and expecting at any minute now to hear the key in her lock and for the person she loved with all of her heart to walk in and embrace her. And later, when they'd shared the news of the day, they'd fall into bed and relish the time they had. It was what they always did, at his house or at hers, whatever their work commitments were. They found a way, and then they held each other as if it was their first night together, and as if the other person might disappear if they didn't hold on tightly enough. They were two independent creatures who together were stronger than she ever could have imagined. She was autonomous, but not the loner she'd thought herself. The realisation had filled her with joy.

And tonight, when she heard the key and he came in she knew he was going to bring her news of his declaration and she was due to give him news of hers. Once that was done, they would move forward together, but this was a time for his and his own, and her and her own.

It was as Faith had said the last time she'd been down to visit. 'If you want to live the simple life, Ella, why the heck don't you just stop imagining it's so complicated?'

Her father was now totally silent, waiting for her statement.

'Well, Dad, you know that wedding outfitter's that you hold in such high esteem?'

'Yes?' two voices chimed.

She could picture her parents side by side, about to down their cocktails, cramming the phone to their ears. She squashed the exuberance within her and tried to keep her voice even.

'You don't know if they do turbans in your size, do you?'

NOW AVAILABLE IN ARROW